Sera was trying to determine what to tackle next when her eye was caught by a UPS box that had been left by the front door. Probably the one Asher had mentioned the day they'd first met. "Might as well see what's in it," she muttered to herself.

She grabbed her pocketknife and headed for the cardboard container. For all she knew, it could be kombucha food, or maybe matching belly dancing outfits for the rest of the Back Room Babes.

But no. It was weenies.

Knife in one hand, packing tape sticking to her fingers, Sera stared into a carton of cock. There were glow-in-the-dark vibrators shaped like Japanese manga figurines. Glass wands Glenda the Good Witch would have blushed to wave. Double-duty probes that looked more like Joshua trees than something one ought to be filling one's happy crevices with. Dildos, vibrators, and strap-ons packed the box to capacity. A note taped to the invoice read, in flowing cursive, "Dearest Pauline—Hope these keep you humming! (Batteries included, of course!) Love to the Babes—Your friends at the Ecstasy Emporium." The tagline beneath the wholesaler's logo read, "Premium Pleasures. Down and Dirty Prices."

"Dildos," she muttered. "Why did it have to be dildos?"

Bliss

HILARY FIELDS

www.redhookbooks.com

This book is a work of fiction. Names, characters, places, and incidents are the product of the author's imagination or are used fictitiously. Any resemblance to actual events, locales, or persons, living or dead, is coincidental.

Redhook Orbit
Hachette Book Group
237 Park Avenue, New York, NY 10017
www.HachetteBookGroup.com

First edition: November 2013

Redhook Books is an imprint of Orbit, a division of Hachette Book Group, Inc.
The Redhook name and logo are trademarks of Hachette Book Group, Inc.

The characters and events in this book are fictitious. Any similarity to real persons, living or dead, is coincidental and not intended by the author.

10 9 8 7 6 5 4 3 2 1

RRD-C

Printed in the United States of America

PCN: 2013949269

ISBN: 9780316277389

My dearest Quinn: You are a paragon among husbickles, my partner in Playstation, bad sci-fi, and passion. Your patience, encouragement, and faith remind me daily what an incredibly lucky woman I am. From concept to completion, and a thousand drafts in between, no wife could have a more loyal cheering section. Here's to great things for us both!

Bliss

Chapter One

Neither here nor there

Albuquerque airport, present day

Pauline Wilde didn't look like a woman in mourning. Unless by widow's weeds one envisioned a lemon yellow and sky blue broomstick skirt studded with what had to be at least half a quarry's worth of turquoise and intricately worked Native American silver disks, topped with a ratty, oversized T-shirt proclaiming, in half-faded but still defiant lettering, "Orgasms Aren't Just for the Young!" Add to that a fiercely pink headscarf barely binding a wild-and-woolly extravaganza of hip-length salt-and-pepper hair and a pair of ancient gardening clogs with roses and kittens hand-stenciled on them in flaking acrylic paint, and you had the very picture of a woman *not* suffering the loss of her beloved life partner. But then, Serafina thought, that was Pauline—she didn't believe in catering to societal expectations. Never had, never would.

"Bliss! Hellooooo, Bliss! Over here, kiddo!"

Her aunt's voice was exactly as it had always been—warm, slightly fruity, like a cross between Julia Child and Jane Goodall, blended with a dash of throaty Kathleen Turner for good measure. Sera smothered a grin at the sight of her impatiently elbowing past the rest of the folks waiting for friends and loved ones at the terminal. Only Pauline ever called her by her ridiculous middle name—a name Pauline herself had gifted her, and which was now echoing through the boarding area to the amusement of the other passengers disembarking from Sera's flight.

The Albuquerque airport was surprisingly posh, Sera saw as she took her first gander around at the fabled Southwest. *Not at all what I imagined from the place where Bugs Bunny made his wrong turn.* Airy, clean, and decorated in pinkish earth tones and expensive native pottery, it was a far cry from the chaos she'd left behind at JFK just a few hours earlier. But she didn't have much time to absorb her surroundings—her aunt was treating the place like a linebacker in a championship game, barreling past all obstacles to get to her objective.

Nothing had ever stood in Pauline Wilde's way. Not for long, anyhow. Ever since Sera could remember, Pauline had been pushing boundaries, defying convention, sticking her middle finger in the face of anyone who told her she couldn't do something she wanted to do. She was a woman utterly estranged from the concepts of shame, modesty, and deference. In comparison, Sera, raised by stolidly conventional yuppie parents until she was thirteen, had always felt somewhat small and apologetic, though Pauline had done her utmost to yank her niece from beneath her towering feminist shadow and lend her some chutzpah when her own wouldn't take Sera the distance.

It hadn't worked, even when Sera had gone to live with Pauline after her parents' sudden deaths. If anything, the contrast between Sera's shy, repressed thirteen-year-old self and her ballsy aunt had made Sera shrink down even smaller, despite her deep love for the older woman. She knew Pauline would be horrified if she realized her efforts to toughen Sera up had done more to make her squirm than make her strong. She admired Pauline's ideals of striving for self-fulfillment, even as she doubted her own ability to advocate for her deepest needs and wants. She simply didn't feel she had the *right* to happiness the way Pauline so obviously did.

Shaking herself firmly, Sera reminded herself she was nearly thirty, and had been self-supporting since college. She'd faced—and conquered—some extremely tough demons, particularly in the last year. She'd seen a bit of what her inner mettle was really worth, and learned to trust her instincts more and more. Pauline's support had done a lot to set her on that path. Now it was time for Sera to do the supporting.

Her aunt's frantic call had come just yesterday.

Hortencia's gone. I need you, Baby-Bliss.

Sera's heart had sunk. Pauline and Hortencia had been inseparable for the last few years. Her aunt must be devastated. *I'm coming, Aunt Paulie,* she'd assured her aunt over the phone. *I'm on the next flight.* And she had been.

Before Sera could so much as set down her carry-on, Pauline had wrapped her arms around her niece and was squeezing for all she was worth. Instantly, Sera was swamped with that familiar Pauline smell: part musky herbal—mugwort or pot, she'd never been sure—part fairy godmother. Tears sprang into her eyes.

"Fuck, it's good to see you, Aunt Paulie."

"Ditto, kid-bean. Aren't you a sight for sore eyes, too." Pauline took her time eyeballing her niece, flipping the short, chin-length ends of Sera's new bob approvingly, putting her hands on Sera's hips and turning her this way and that. "Lookin' good, kiddo! I see all those sweets you bake aren't hurting your sweet figure any. You've still got a tush on you like a couple of hot cross buns. You didn't get that from me, that's for sure. Tuchas like a freakin' pancake, that's what I've got. A crepe even, these days. Ah, but what am I babbling about? Baby Bliss, let's get your shit and blow this taco stand. I can't wait to finally show you what heaven's all about."

Bemused, Sera trailed after her aunt down the long, wide ramp that led to the baggage claim. Had grief made her loopy? Er…loopier than usual? Because she'd expected sorrow-stricken. Wan. Shaken. All the sad emotions the joyful, fearless Pauline Wilde had never seemed susceptible to, but surely must be feeling after the death of her life partner.

At least, that had been the impression she'd given Sera when she'd called to tell her that Hortencia was suddenly gone. *I'm devastated, Bliss. Utterly wrecked,* she'd said. Could Sera please drop everything and fly to New Mexico to help her deal with her loss?

Given that Pauline was, quite simply, Sera's single favorite person, she hadn't hesitated for a second. *After all the times she's saved my bacon,* Sera thought fondly, *she'd be within her rights to ask for a kidney. Hell,* both *kidneys.* In any case, considering how little anchored her to New York these days, taking time out was no great hardship. And she'd been missing Pauline a lot lately.

"So how's your love life, kid?" Pauline asked—loudly—over her shoulder as they headed for the bag claim. Her skirt jingled in counterpoint to her strides. "You getting any?"

I didn't miss this *part,* Sera thought with a mental wince. She avoided the smirking glance of the college-aged bohunk trotting down the ramp to meet his gloriously tanned, crunchy-granola girlfriend, her arms outstretched as if to announce to all and sundry, "Now you... *you're* getting some."

"Um, I'm doing okay," she said weakly. "Not dating anyone seriously right now. Mostly trying to keep the catering business out of the red, keep myself on the straight and narrow. That kind of thing."

"That wasn't what I asked," Pauline said, huffing a little as they made it to the conveyor and started scanning the bags. "I asked if you were getting *laid.* Don't really need a boyfriend for that, though of course, it never hurts to know where your next O's coming from. One of the benefits of a steady relationship, I s'pose." Her face clouded over momentarily.

"I'm so sorry about Hortencia, Aunt Paulie," Sera jumped in, eager to change the subject, and also to comfort the woman who'd once been *her* sole solace after her parents' deaths. "It must have been quite a shock, her passing so suddenly. I had the impression she was healthy as a horse, with all that hiking and mountain climbing you two were always doing. I'm just sorry I never got to meet her. From everything you've told me, she must have been a really special lady." Sera patted Pauline on the shoulder. "How are you holding up?"

Was it her imagination, or did her aunt flush, just slightly?

Pauline made an impatient, fly-shooing gesture. "Don't get me started with the wailing and weeping just yet, kiddo. I need these eyes to see. It's a long drive to Santa Fe, and we have a lot of catching up to do. So," she finished, briskly clearing her throat and pointing at the luggage rattling around the conveyor, "I'm gonna guess yours is the one that looks like a giant pink cupcake with rainbow sprinkles on the front?"

Sera had to admit it was.

"Great, let's get that cupcake to go."

As she stepped out into the sunlight, Sera took her deep first breath of New Mexico's thin, dry air. Goose bumps rose along her arms, but somehow she didn't think the cool September breeze was to blame. She sensed a weightlessness, a sense of potential—as if destiny had taken a vacation and left her with a wide-open fate. She couldn't say how she knew, but she had a feeling her life—her very being—was about to change.

And considering the woman she'd been until recently, that might be a very good thing.

Because *that* chick had been a real fuckup.

Chapter Two

The Maidstone Club, East Hampton, New York
One year and two months ago
June
Saturday
3 p.m., give or take

The Anderson wedding was tanking.

It wasn't because the bride was a 'zilla, or the groom had cold feet. It wasn't the work of an obnoxious mother-in-law or a spiteful stepsister. No meddling ex-lovers were waiting in the wings, ready to spill salacious secrets during the best man's toast. Even the weather was idyllic, and the twelve-piece band stood ready with the perfect playlist to get the whitest of the white practicing their funky chicken. The ceremony was at this very moment going off with precisely the proper amount of hitching, the happy couple sniffling sentimentally through vows they'd written themselves as their friends and loved ones looked on, beaming beneficently.

But though they weren't yet aware of it, the whole honking show was sinking faster than the *Titanic* upon hitting a *Love Boat*–sized 'berg.

And it was all the fault of one person.

The pastry chef was drunk as a skunk.

She was also, apparently, in a meat locker.

With Lorenzo the busboy.

And very little clothing on.

Helluva time for one of my blackouts, Sera thought woozily. *Worse time to come out of one. How did I get myself into this mess?*

She remembered snagging a bottle of vodka from the service bar. She remembered drinking to her soon-to-be ex-boyfriend's ill health—more than once. More than five or six times, probably. And she remembered catching sight of the teenaged Enzo, who had been making eyes at her ever since signing on to their catering company a couple months back. She had a vague image of herself crooking a finger at the kid, like some floozy in a Mae West movie. After that, things got a little hazy. But clearly, there'd been some disrobing going on. And some hanky-panky, if the tongue currently licking her left earlobe was anything to go by. But this was no place she'd ever have chosen for a seduction, if the booze hadn't been doing the choosing for her.

Holy frozen buns, Batman, it's cold as the center of a Baked Alaska in here.

The brushed steel walls were rimed in frost. Trays of *hors d'oeuvres*, tubs of sauces, and carts of canapés practically shivered on the shelves. Her breath was coming out in puffs of eighty-proof steam, and her increasingly exposed skin was all gooseflesh. Her meat locker *compadre,* however, was quite obviously not chilling out. In fact, he was rather on fire, if his hot hands and hotter lips were any indication.

Oh, God. What if my boyfriend finds us? she thought. Horror sobered her up, and fast. The door didn't lock...and half the food for the wedding was stored in here. Any second someone from the staff was sure to walk in, if not her boyfriend himself.

Said boyfriend, however, had other priorities.

"Where are my shrimp cocktails? What the *fuck* did you clowns do with *four hundred* shrimp cocktails? And why the hell didn't anybody warn me the avocados were hard as a stone?"

The person so politely inquiring was celebrity chef and society caterer extraordinaire Blake Austin. *He* was not drunk. But boy, was he pissed.

"Who is responsible for this atrocity!" Austin wheeled around in the country club's gleaming industrial kitchen, his glare hotter than a *brûlée* torch. As executive chef of a Manhattan restaurant so sophisticated one's taste buds needed a graduate degree to properly appreciate its cuisine, as well as a frequent guest on the Food Channel's *Hot Chef!*, he inspired instant obedience in any kitchen he commanded. A dozen frozen faces were caught in his headlights, like deer in chef's whites.

The tall, reedy *chef de partie* piped up timidly, "Ah, Chef, I think you put Serafina on shrimp-and-guac duty since she was done with the cake and desserts."

"Then *where* is Serafina?" roared Austin, glaring about. "Produce Serafina Wilde before me in the next ten seconds or explain why you cannot!" He waved a filleting knife with reckless abandon to emphasize his point. "Why can none of you troglodytes accommodate this simple request?" he mused, taking his wrath down a degree from rolling boil to simmer. He shook his leonine head in disgust. "Why do I bother? I might as well ask Paula Deen to cook without Crisco as expect you twits to give me a straight answer."

"Um, Chef?" squeaked the quaking *commis* chef, raising his hand.

"Um, *yes?*" mocked Blake. "Have you found the balls to speak up, peon? Because you're clearly not wearing them."

The unfortunate *commis* gulped, wavering on his feet as though debating whether to bolt or pass out on the spot. "I . . . ah . . . I think I saw her headed for the walk-in with that new busboy Lorenzo, um . . . a few minutes ago?"

"Well, then, why have none of you worthless fart knockers seen fit to fetch her lazy arse? And no, that wasn't a rhetorical question!"

A snide, rawboned girl (who had endeared herself to no one with her attempts to seduce Austin into advancing her from her lowly position in vegetable prep) stepped forward. "Chef, she didn't exactly look like she'd appreciate an interruption, if you know what I mean." The girl crossed her arms over her chest and smirked, ignoring the glares from the crew for her disloyalty to a fellow cook. Especially when that fellow cook was Blake Austin's long-suffering girlfriend. No one liked a kitchen snitch.

Even if the snitch was right.

"Whoa, whoa, whoa, whoaaaa!"

With one Godzilla versus Tokyo collision, Sera's half-frozen derriere obliterated the fish-shaped savory sculpture it had taken the *poissonier* hours to perfect. Cold, rich puree of smoked salmon squished between her cheeks, and behind her, Sera heard a crash as an enormous platter of *hors d'oeuvres* went down. The close metal walls of the walk-in rang as if they were under artillery fire as cutlery and trays flew. But it was what loomed above her that had really gotten out of control.

Lorenzo was in the zone. And if Sera couldn't intercept him, he was about to score. Enzo groaned, mashing both of them deeper into the carnage of the carefully arranged appetizers atop the locker's small prep station and grinding for all he was worth. Hot, adolescent kisses were raining down on her neck and shoulders, her heavy cotton chef's blouse was unbuttoned halfway down her chest, and her bra was migrating south alarmingly quickly under the direction of his busy fingers.

Clearly, she'd been rather persuasive when she'd invited him in here. *Wish I had that kind of charisma when I was fully conscious,* Sera thought ruefully. "Enzo...we need to stop before someone walks in," she panted, trying to catch her breath and simultaneously capture Lorenzo's hands before they could denude her further. But Enzo's English wasn't so hot, and in any case he wasn't in much of a mind-set to hear about her change of heart just now. "*Esperar... basta, basta!*" she pleaded breathlessly, wondering if she even had the Spanish words right.

Maybe if I was a better lover, a better girlfriend, I wouldn't be in this situation to begin with, she thought with a rush of panicky regret. Sera's breath caught in a sudden sob. *Maybe Blake wouldn't have...*

But he had.

She'd stumbled on the pectorally enhanced blond hostess of the Food Channel's *Hot Chef!* going down on her boyfriend in the storage pantry of their flagship restaurant last night, and she hadn't been sober since. Last night, she'd drunk to ease her hurt. Hell, she'd drunk because drinking was her go-to pain reliever in pretty much every situation. This morning, hungover and humiliated, being forced to work with Blake—looking fresh as the proverbial daisy and smug as shit—had had her reaching for another bottle, and damn the early hour. But it didn't seem to matter how much she guzzled—the sight of that skank sporting one of Sera's own chef's caps as her head bobbed rhythmically with her oral ministrations was a bitter gall that wouldn't wash away.

Worst of all, Blake had merely shrugged when she'd confronted him later that night, humiliated and furious. "What did you expect, Serafina?" he'd said with a philosophical shrug. "Someone with your... *issues*... could never keep a man like me satisfied for long."

The last of Sera's illusions—that Blake was all bluster, a demanding perfectionist but more driven than truly cruel—died in that moment.

Hot Chef? Stone-cold bastard was more like it.

And I think... maybe I'm being a bit of a bitch myself right now—to poor Enzo if not to Blake, Sera realized, suddenly shamed. It was coming back to her now. She'd invited the eighteen-year-old Lorenzo, who had made no secret of his crush on her these past couple months, to this chilly rendezvous out of some vague notion of payback. *If Blake can make out in the kitchen right under my nose, why shouldn't I do the same? Serve the chef some of his own sauce; see how he likes it,* she'd thought with a spurt of juvenile spite. But all the time another part of her had been thinking, wishfully... *Maybe he'll be jealous; regret what he's done?*

Dumb ploy, Sera. Really, magnificently, dumb.

Enzo didn't seem to think so. Her pants, thanks to his efforts, were puddled around her ankles, and the lusty busboy had only his jockey shorts going for him at the moment. Smashed salmon paste caused Sera to slide precariously atop the marble-topped prep station, threatening to topple them both to the floor in fishy disgrace. *As if this wasn't enough of a mistake,* she thought, wincing. *Nothing says "oops" like your naked ass skidding in the salmon mousse.*

She'd met Blake over mousse, as a matter of fact, though it had been chocolate, not salmon, back then.

It was Sera's final semester at the French Culinary Institute, and she was just a credit or so shy of graduation. She was also deeply, alarmingly in debt and facing a future of pitiful pay and ungodly hours for the next several years—a purgatory known in the industry as "paying your dues."

She'd made her peace with that, though it meant putting off her dream of starting her own line of custom cakes and confections until she was more established. But in order to *get* established, she'd have to land that all-important first job.

Blake Austin had the power to offer her that. Those who worked in his kitchens...well, they could write their own tickets—if they survived the experience. It was whispered that not everyone did.

"He looks like Gabriel Byrne," her friend Mindy murmured in her ear as they held up the wall in the institute's test kitchen, making themselves inconspicuous. "With a little Colin Farrell mixed in." She said this with none of the sighing or breathlessness such an observation might be expected to engender. Rather, her tone was clinical.

Mindy was a butcher. Big, burly, with a nostril ring and short, spiky bleached blond hair, she was prone to wearing T-shirts with logos like "Meat Is Murder...Tasty, Tasty Murder" under her bloodstained aprons. She could butterfly a veal chop in seconds flat, make you a sweet Italian sausage fit to weep over, or cut you a chateaubriand that would have your guests offering you sexual favors for life. But she couldn't care less about sweets. She was only in this class to fill out her requirements. Thus, she alone among the twenty or so students assembled in front of their final projects failed to tremble at the palate of the great Blake Austin, who had deigned to drop in on this class—on the condition, it was rumored, that he got to poach the best student for his newest restaurant venture.

"Shite!" A fork ricocheted from the nearest sink. "Absolute shite. You call this a torte? My aunt Sally could shit a better torte, and she's been dead seven years! Get out of my sight."

One by one, her classmates were dismissed and humiliated. By the time it was Sera's turn to be critiqued, she was sweating, nauseated, and not at all sure she wasn't about to faint. When Austin's spoon dipped into the deceptively simple triple chocolate mousse she'd concocted, it felt like he was delving into her soul. But would he find it wanting?

"Hm," he grunted. "Hm, hm, hm." Cunning black eyes skewered Serafina, and she felt herself grow warm unexpectedly. "Is that...

cardamom I taste?" One arched brow cocked itself, as though almost too weary to complete the gesture, but was making a special exception for her.

Sera nodded, her tongue glued to the roof of her mouth. She'd added the spice to the white chocolate layer at the last second, wanting just a hint of the exotic to linger on the tongue.

"And do I detect a *soupçon* of...what, is that, orange essence...in the bittersweet?"

"Ah...yes, Chef."

There was a pause, during which Serafina died several times.

"Bloody brilliant," he proclaimed. "I don't mind telling you, when I caught sight of that mousse, I thought I might perish from sheer boredom—I mean, really, who makes chocolate mousse anymore? But you've surprised me, and that doesn't happen often. Damned if you haven't completely reinvented the dish. It's like you've perfumed the air *around* the mousse, the spice is done with such a light touch. And yet it adds ten dimensions to the taste. And the *texture.* Fuck me, but I've never had a mousse so bloody delightful. It's like getting blown by a thousand-dollar hooker, that mousse is. Makes you beg for it. You—what's your name, little bird?"

"S-S-Serafina, Chef," Sera stuttered, oblivious to both the envious glares of her classmates and Mindy's alarmed gaze.

"Sera-fucking-fina. Bloody brilliant. Well, *Serafina*"—he drew her name out like he was licking it off the spoon he still held—"they're going to be begging for you at my new restaurant. So what do you say, girl? Are you in?"

And in a quavering voice, Sera had said she was.

She'd said the same when he'd asked if she was game for a quickie.

Somehow, she hadn't said no to anything since.

She'd signed a contract to be Blake's executive pastry chef, and her life had never been the same. Her career had taken off, her name and fame spreading throughout Manhattan's culinary circles. When he'd suggested branching out into socialite weddings and celebrity events, she'd been one hundred percent on board—not so much because she liked rubbing elbows with the rich and famous but because those were the people who had the disposable income to pay for the kind of fantastically elaborate cakes and pastries she most loved to craft. With his knack for knowing what the fickle foodie community craved and her timeless confectionary brilliance, Blake had assured her, they would have the A-list beating down their door. She'd believed him, and he hadn't been wrong.

Sera wasn't quite sure she'd *loved* Blake Austin exactly. But he'd easily engulfed her whole world.

Getting to the top of the heap in New York City's exclusive culinary circles was like being the lead singer in a rock band—you had groupies of all shapes, sizes, and sexes panting after you. To her eternal shame, Serafina had been one of Blake's. She'd been flattered by his attention and extravagant praise of her talents in the beginning, dazzled by his practiced charm as he pursued and easily won her. In awe, shy and insecure, she'd written off his abrasive manner, excusing his hot temper and over-the-top insults as part of his celebrity chef schtick. *He isn't the first egotistical chef to rule a kitchen with an iron hand,* she'd told herself. *He's just striving for perfection—in his own way. It's admirable, really.*

And at first, he'd been so charming when they were alone. Whispering sweet nothings about her sweet creations in a way that was absurdly gratifying, and more than a little sexy. She'd felt like she was the only woman in the world who truly knew the real Blake Austin—brilliant, demanding, intense... and all hers. To have the attention of such a man... to be the woman he chose? What woman wouldn't be a little swept away?

By the time he'd dropped the flattery and begun belittling Sera for her very personal, private "shortcomings," telling her no other man would tolerate what he termed her "limitations," she'd been so humiliated and confused she'd actually felt grateful that he continued to "put up with her," as he put it. Desperate to please, to *measure up,* she'd put on a brave face, kept a bottle of liquid courage in her apron, and soldiered on. *At least,* she'd consoled herself, *he appreciates my professionalism in the kitchen.*

Or he *had.*

If he catches me like this, drunk in the walk-in with the busboy.... Oh, God... he'll eviscerate me! And God only knows what he'll do to Lorenzo.

I've got to stop this, Sera thought, panicked. But it was too late.

Two things happened at that moment.

Enzo made a play for her panties...

And the door swung open.

"Serafina, stop your dawdling and get back to work!" Blake roared before he was halfway through the walk-in's wide doorway. He stopped stock-still, however, when he caught sight of his girlfriend *en deshabille* and *in flagrante delicto* with his most junior busboy.

"Ahhhhhhhhhhhhhhhh!"

Sera let out a shriek that probably shattered half the country club's champagne flutes.

Lorenzo yipped like a coyote and dove for his pants, leaving Serafina exposed on the marble-topped counter among the smashed appetizers and smeared *amuse bouche.*

For a moment Blake said nothing, simply surveying the scene as the rest of his prep team gathered behind him to witness the confrontation.

Oh fuck, oh fuck, oh fuck...

With fingers made clumsy by booze, Sera reached for her bra straps and fumbled to fix her clothes. A knife of dread cut through the last of her fast-dying buzz. Her face burned bright red as she saw her fellow cooks peering avidly over their leader's shoulders to see what was going on.

One thing was immediately clear. She might have served the chef a taste of his own sauce, but it was *her* goose she'd cooked. Sera's mouth worked, but no words emerged. She was frozen, breathless, gaze riveted in terror upon her boyfriend's face.

Blake's black eyes narrowed, but his countenance remained expressionless. It was a conceit of his that he always dressed for the weddings he catered as an invited guest rather than in chef's whites, mingling with the partygoers and schmoozing before getting down to business in the kitchen. Today he was sporting an impeccable cream linen suit, silver-blue pocket square, and pale pink Ralph Lauren shirt she herself had picked out to complement his swarthy Black Irish good looks. And look good, he did—only the slight twitch around his deep-set eyes marred his appealingly louche features. By comparison, she looked like someone had dropped her off a three-story building to land—*splat!*—on a loaded banquet table.

"Well, well." He sighed as if positively smothering in ennui. "Of course it *would* be the freezer. You've always been a cold fish in the bedroom, Serafina. I suppose it only stands to reason this is where you'd go to get off."

There were gasps and titters from the cooks and caterers behind him. None of them, however, could guess how pointed Blake's barb really was. It struck Sera a devastating blow. The high color drained from her face and left her completely gray. She struggled to her feet and righted her stained garments, standing panting before the marble-topped altar of her shame.

I didn't even practice a revenge speech, Sera thought with a pang. Instead of "How's it feel, big man?" or "See how you like it!" she could do no more than gulp wordlessly now that the moment was upon them. It was that, or throw up in front of all of these people. Her head spun. *Man, I could use another drink right about now. Maybe twelve.*

Her boyfriend didn't appear concerned with her lack of explanation—or her betrayal. In fact, he seemed to have dismissed her from his mind entirely. Addressing his crew, he said, "All this will have to be thrown out. The Wagyu filet mignon. The wild Alaskan sockeye. The Petrossian caviar. Anything that has been in contact with this *filth*"—he waved demonstratively—"is unfit to be served to our guests. Oh, and Lorenzo you're fired. *¡Estás despedido! ¿Comprendes?* Now, Serafina..." He returned his attention to her with menace as rich and smooth as one of his famous terrines of *foie gras.*

"Perhaps, Serafina, once you have...composed yourself, you will care to explain to four hundred of New York's wealthiest, hardest-to-please socialites that they'll be eating Mickey D's for dinner when they return from their mimosas on the beach instead of the *six-course feast* they expect."

"I...but..." He couldn't seriously mean to trash all this food? But the others were already filing past her with garbage bags, reaching into the shelves with stoic expressions. Out went the *amuse bouche.* Out went the gravlax. The blinis and the cheese puffs and the crab-stuffed mushrooms also met their doom. Sweet heavenly biscuits, the appetizers alone represented three days' work on the part of their entire team! All because her unclothed bum had been somewhere in the vicinity? "No, Blake, wait! We can still save—"

"No excuses!" Blake snapped coldly. "You have single-handedly ruined half the comestibles in this kitchen. Fix this, Serafina, or face the consequences," he threatened, waving the filleting knife under her nose. "Now get out of my sight. I have no time for amateurs."

He thrust himself away from the refrigerator door with a shrug of his shoulders and turned to snap at his minions. "And would somebody, for the love of all that is holy, be so good as to *sanitize this fucking station* before the health inspector arrives and demands to know why there are *arse prints* on surfaces on which food is prepared!"

When nobody moved, Blake's voice rose to its usual roar. "Move!"

The kitchen crew scattered.

❧

The ladies' room door couldn't shut behind Sera fast enough. Not wanting to run into any of the catering staff—who were surely snickering into their sleeves at her misfortune right now—she'd escaped the kitchen and found a restroom down one of the country club's lavishly decorated halls. Safe at last, she darted into the stall farthest from the front, snapping it locked behind her and leaning her back against the divider. Her hands trembled as she reached in her pocket, withdrew the flask she'd secreted there. Just one more belt. To take the edge off. To calm her down. To forget the awful, hateful look on Blake's face and make this disaster somehow just a nightmare she could still wake up from. Screwing the cap back on, she stuffed a piece of gum in her mouth, chewed despite the dry Sahara her mouth had become. Wouldn't do for the Andersons to catch their pastry chef smelling like a distillery, would it?

Though how Blake expects me to explain to them why he threw out $20,000 worth of perfectly good canapés just to make a point, I don't know, she thought with a spurt of terror. He hadn't had to go that far. But Blake was given to grand gestures—the more spiteful, the better.

Yet who was more hateful in this situation? After all, hadn't she just gotten an innocent kid fired due to her shenanigans? Wasn't she the one kicking up drama and putting a woman's wedding celebration in jeopardy in the process?

Fix this, Serafina. Stop fucking around and figure out a way to salvage the situation.

Exiting the stall reluctantly, Serafina washed her shaking hands and splashed cold water on her face. She stared at her reflection in the mirror with loathing, and not just at the outward signs of her distress—the bloodshot gray eyes, wan greasy skin, and lank black hair unflatteringly caught back in a hairnet. Bad though she looked on the outside—like a candidate for A&E's *Intervention*, if she were being honest with herself—it was what was inside that truly appalled her. What would her parents have said had they been alive to see how their daughter had grown up? What would Aunt Pauline think of the darling niece she'd raised to know right from wrong? There was little trace of that bright, hopeful girl in the mirror now.

"C'mon, Sera," she said to her reflection, slapping her own cheeks to snap her back into focus. "This is no time for a come-to-Jesus moment. You've got four hundred hungry WASPs to placate—and fast."

Inhaling the deepest breath of her life, she forced herself to face the music, striding back into the country club kitchen with her spine stiff and the vodka singing a siren song through her veins. *C'mon,* it was telling her, *it isn't that bad, you're Serafina Wilde! You can fix this. You can fix anything.*

Maybe the Maidstone Club could do something—after all, they regularly hosted several hundred guests at a time during the summer season. Their deep freezers had to be packed with the fixings for your basic surf-and-turf. If she could track down the general manager, if the staff would cooperate, maybe she could still salvage something of this mess—at least, if not to save her own reputation, to keep the bride from having the kind of disastrous wedding her social set would whisper over for seasons to come. She owed Lexi Anderson that much. The girl might be a starveling size two with a five-carat ring and highlights that cost more than Sera's annual income, but she wasn't half bad for all that. To ruin her big day... *Christ on a cupcake, that's enough bad karma to keep me in crappy boyfriends for the next six lifetimes.*

At least, Sera consoled herself, the *cake* would exceed all expectations. It was her masterpiece. Her finest creation in a long line of justly celebrated and much-coveted confections. It was gorgeous. It was scrumptious. It was...

At a kid's party in Brooklyn Heights.

Serafina stared in horror at the contents of the oversized box marked, inexplicably, "Simpson Birthday," trying not to scream at the sight of the pirate-ship-shaped chocolate fudge galleon that sailed gaily on a sea of foam-flecked fondant.

No way. It wasn't possible! No amount of vodka would make Sera fuck up this bad. She knew she'd packed up and correctly labeled the right cake for this wedding. One didn't easily mistake a lovebird-themed, lemon buttercream–filled extravaganza with twelve tiers and eighty hours' worth of gum paste flowers and sugarplum birdies painstakingly appliquéd to each layer for a third-grader's dark chocolate buccaneer boat! She'd seen the Simpson cake off on its maiden voyage just this morning. So how had it drifted so far off course...

There was only one explanation. And it was wearing a cream linen suit.

And smirking at her.

Sera could feel the eyes of the kitchen crew on her. Watching her wither under Blake's bullying, as she'd done so often in the past. Watching her lose what little was left of her self-respect.

Something inside her snapped. The years of humiliation, of kowtowing to this man... groveling for his approval, apologizing for her shortcomings while excusing his. God, why had she never seen what a douchebag he really was? Why had she so easily swallowed her pride, along with her self-esteem, washing them down with alcohol when they stuck in her craw? This wasn't the woman Aunt Pauline had raised.

Enough was e-fucking-nough.

"What. Have. You. DONE!?" she roared.

She ignored the gasps from the kitchen staff. One didn't raise one's voice to Blake Austin. Ever.

Then again, one didn't cuckold him while he was in the midst of catering a wedding reception either, so this was a day for firsts.

Blake's chest puffed up. "I hope you don't mean to employ that tone with me in *my* kitchen after what *you* have done, you disgraceful little pastry pissant." His smirk turned sharklike, threatening. Sera wanted to retch. *God, how did I ever think he was charming?*

"You absolute creep," she swore. That last shot of vodka emboldened her enough to get right up in his face, though his cologne—which she'd never liked—played havoc with her roiling stomach. Sera poked a finger into Blake's solar plexus, wishing it were a knee to the groin. "First you cheat on me, then you sabotage my cake?" She stomped her foot, too furious suddenly to care how much of a scene she was creating. "You want to hurt me? Fine. But now you're hurting poor Lexi Anderson, whose only crime was paying you a fortune to make her day special. I mean, Christ, your name's on this event, too. Why? Why would you do this?"

"Did you think I would simply wait to see whether you'd get the gumption to leave on your own?" Blake sneered. "Wait to see if you'd steal my best clients and blacken my name? Hardly! I suspected you had something planned to revenge yourself for that little incident last night—though I had no idea how pathetic your efforts would be—and I had no intention of sitting around waiting for you to strike. In fact, I grew tired of you and your whining, clinging ways some time ago. Quite frankly, Serafina, you're a drag. You're also *fired.* Any half-wit with a culinary degree can make a decent *crème anglaise,* so we shan't miss you."

"What?" His words rocked her back. This job—her career—was all she had. He couldn't.... "But I... we're partners in this venture, Blake. I have a contract. You can't just fire me without cause. I could sue you!"

Austin shook back the longish black hair she'd once thought so debonair. With a shrug and a lazy smile crossing his hawkish features, he dropped the bomb on her. "Oh, I think I can make a fair case for 'cause' after today's misconduct. Fooling around in the food prep areas? Forgetting the wedding cake? Those are just the final nails in your culinary coffin, Serafina. I've been documenting quite a pattern of erratic behavior on your part over the past several weeks, much to my regret." Blake smiled down at her, enjoying his moment of power. "And if you're thinking you'll just take a position with one of my rivals, don't bother applying. The two-bit bloggers, the big reviewers... they've all been tipped off. In fact, right now, all anyone's talking about in the culinary world is my *deep* distress over your fragile mental stability and your *troubling* substance abuse. Everyone with gustatory pretensions and a soapbox will be buzzing about you, if they aren't already. Of course, I've also made it known that I was *so* concerned about your conduct in the kitchen that I'm being forced to boot you out of our catering outfit." His smirk was working overtime now. "So *my* name won't be associated with this fiasco. No, sweet pea, this one's all in *your* lap."

Serafina's defiance crumbled. The sheer malice on Blake's face was enough to steal her breath away. The booze-born courage deserted her, her confidence fleeing faster than the fleeting high the 80-proof liquor had provided. Her knees buckled and tears formed in her red-rimmed eyes. "But... I... You can't..."

She was trying to catch a breath, holding on to the edge of a counter for support, when a vision in white silk swept in.

The bride. Lexi Anderson stopped stock-still as her gaze took in the pirate ship cake, then swung to witness the gray-faced, sweaty baker practically sobbing at the feet of the handsome restaurateur who'd earlier been dazzling her party guests with *bon mots* over cocktails on the club terrace. Lexi's beautifully made up face took on a look of almost comical bewilderment.

"Hi, Chef Austin," she began hesitantly. "I just came in to check how things are going—the natives are getting a bit restless out there and wondering when they're going to get their canapés. Plus," she continued with a dimpled smile, "I couldn't wait to get a peek at Serafina's cake. I just know it'll be perfect." Vera Wang dress rustling, she crossed to the Simpson ship, taking in its three dark chocolate masts and miniature corsairs dubiously. "What's this?" she asked. "Is it a groom's cake? You didn't have to do that, though it's awfully sweet—Carl just loved *Pirates of the Caribbean*. Funny, I don't remember mentioning that to you during our consults."

Sera's heart sank, and a fresh wave of remorse washed over her, threatening to swamp more than just the buccaneer cake. Just as much as Blake's spite, it was her own poor judgment that was about to ruin this sweet lady's big day. The last of her buzz fizzled out, and she felt her stomach lurch. Sera opened her mouth, searching for some sort of explanation or apology that could begin to address the magnitude of the disaster. But Blake cut her off before she could begin. He swept an arm familiarly across Lexi's shoulders, managing to ogle her slightly more than politely even as he guided her away from the cake—and its creator.

"My dear, I'm so sorry to have to tell you this. I'm afraid Ms. Wilde is having an unfortunate..." He circled his wrist, hand waving descriptively as he lowered his voice conspiratorially. "...*breakdown.* She seems to have committed herself beyond her capacities and imperiled your nuptial feast. Indeed, I arrived just in time to witness my former protégée displaying both criminal forgetfulness and some disgraceful behavior of a rather... personal nature. Fortunately, I am here. And I assure you, as my name is Blake Austin, I shall not allow any unpleasantness to mar these festivities."

As he towed Lexi across the kitchen, Sera heard Blake telling her not to worry, he always prepared plenty of extra food when cooking for important, high-profile clients like the Andersons—food that he could personally guarantee had not been contaminated by a certain young lady's shocking misbehavior. And never fear, he happened to have a friend—yes, *that* Trump—who would loan him his pilot and have the correct cake choppered in before the band even had a chance to mangle "Celebration" and the guests began drifting off the dance floor in search of dessert.

One look at Lexi's dismayed, betrayed face made Sera realize she'd never convince the woman that Blake was responsible for the cake mix-up and that it was his high-handedness (well, except for a platter or two of *hors d'oeuvres* and one unfortunate salmon mousse) causing the other comestible snafus. Instead, he would end up looking like a hero for swooping in and saving the day, while she played the role of the fuckup who'd almost condemned the Anderson family to total social ostracism.

Helpless rage and shame inundated Sera, making her head spin and her guts churn. She barely made it to the nearest sink before she was violently ill.

At least, she thought as tears overcame her, *I didn't puke on the $30,000 wedding dress.* A dry-cleaning bill like that could ruin a person's whole day.

"Pick up, pick up, pick up." Wedged into the corner of her bathroom floor next to the tub, a half-empty fifth of vodka tucked by her side, Serafina chanted into the phone like a mantra, sending a prayer out along the long-distance line. "Please pick up. *Please* be there."

"Hel-looo!"

Sera had never heard anything as comforting as her aunt's signature trill. "Aunt Pauline?" she fairly slobbered. "It's Sera."

"Bliss! Hey, kiddo! I was just thinking of you. I was at my wheel this afternoon, throwing a *fabulously* phallic new vase, and I thought, 'This would be perfect for my niece.' Maybe in the living room, by that god-awful sofa of yours."

Serafina choked on a sob that was half laughter. "That's really sweet of you, Aunt Paulie," she said in a strangled tone. "But you don't have to go to all that trouble." *Keep it together, Sera,* she told herself woozily. Willing as her aunt had always been to give of her time and her life experience, she didn't want to burden Pauline with her troubles—she'd just needed to hear her voice.

"Nonsense, Baby-Bliss. The only trouble is packing and shipping the damn thing, and I wouldn't have to do that if you'd just come and visit like you've been promising..."

A great, raw-edged sob tore free from Sera's throat, despite her best efforts to contain it. The sleepless night, the booze, and the awful, accusing look in that poor bride's eyes...It was too much.

"I know, Auntie. I'm sorry. I'm so, so sorry. For *everything.*" For several minutes Sera was incoherent, sobbing and sniffling into the phone.

Her aunt allowed the wailing and gnashing to go on for a few more breaths before interjecting a dose of reality. "Now let's not be dramatic, kiddo. You haven't killed anyone, have you?"

Pauline's pragmatism surprised a watery laugh out of Sera. "No." *But I feel like I'm dying.*

"So what's going on, Baby-Bliss? It's not that creepy boyfriend of yours, is it? I know you asked me not to trash-talk him, but I just can't get myself to like that one. I hope it's good between you in the sack at least, because I can't think of another reason to keep such a smarmy snake around."

Not even. *If you knew just how* not *good it was, you'd have a conniption,* Sera thought. Pauline, with her vast experience in all matters intimate, would never understand—and given her life's work, would probably never *forgive* Sera either. But Sera's problems were bigger than Blake Austin. Even in her current state, halfway to oblivion with half a bottle of vodka in her, Sera was beginning to see that.

Whatever else she could lay at his door, Blake wasn't to blame for her drinking.

Sera had known there was something unusual about her relationship to booze the first time that, as a shy teenager, she'd been introduced to a corner bodega beer and she'd felt that *click.* That click that turned her from awkward social outcast to someone who could maybe tell a joke or two. Who could hang out with the cool kids (okay, the drama geeks) and not feel like she was wearing a neon sign that said "Pitiful."

Someone who could swallow the sudden, wrenching loss of her parents and bury the aching loneliness that attended it.

Only Pauline's loving guardianship had kept Sera on the straight and narrow then. College had had more than a few wince-worthy moments—scary blackouts, hangovers, and humiliations that, if she'd been honest with herself (and she hadn't), far outpaced her friends' experiments with alcohol. But it wasn't until she hit culinary school that her drinking really took off.

Still, the way her fellow students partied—and booze was the *least* of what these dudes crammed into every orifice—it had been easy for Sera to convince herself she wasn't out of control. That people with a *real* problem looked nothing like her. *Those* people landed face-first in the bouillabaisse. *Those* people hung out in service alleys waiting for guys in hoodies who wouldn't tell you their names. *Those* people sniffed a lot and talked really loud and had a wild look in their eye and could tell you stories that would curl your hair.

When Sera drank, she just felt... normal.

Until she'd *needed* to drink to feel normal.

She'd started getting scared about a year ago. The pressure of working under Blake's exacting standards and famously hot temper had had her reaching for the bottle more often than ever. Part of her had known their relationship was a disaster, but she'd been too caught up in the whirl to really take a long look at her life. It was easier to drink away her shame and hurt than to stand up for herself and walk away—from her high-flying career *and* her high-handed boyfriend.

After a few particularly hazy, horrible nights, she'd pulled back on the reins, stopped hanging out after hours with the crew. She'd gone as much as a couple months at a time without a drink, ignoring how the sight of it in her restaurant kitchen made her sweat; how the champagne flutes at the parties they catered seemed to be filled with cool, crisp elixir, begging her for a taste. How her mouth would go dry when she'd pour Kahlua over the thirsty ladyfingers in a dish of tiramisu, and how the mere sight of her boyfriend's signature sneer made visions of vodka dance before her eyes.

She'd been *trying,* damn it. But then came Blake's betrayal. And it was exactly the excuse she'd needed to let go and fuck up royally.

Sera laid her burning cheek against the cold porcelain of the tub, awash with shame.

"So is it Awful Austin?" Pauline prompted.

"Well...it *is* kind of about Blake, but..." Sera didn't know quite how to describe the nuclear meltdown that had just incinerated her life.

Pauline harrumphed. "Spill it, kid."

Where do I start? The booze was way out of control. Her career had just died a violent death. And she was so alone. Sera opened her mouth to try to explain, to justify, to deflect. What came out instead was a simple admission, born of grace.

"I think...I think I need help."

Pauline didn't chide her, question her, or tell her she was being dramatic. Instead, she said the six simple words Serafina most needed to hear.

"Help's coming, baby. Just hang on."

Chapter Three

Santa Fe, New Mexico
Right about now

"Dry and crumbly."

Serafina delivered the verdict dolefully into the cell phone cradled between her shoulder and cheek as she let the rest of the batch of red velvet cupcakes tumble like little boulders from the pan into the waiting trash bin in her aunt's capacious kitchen. She'd frosted only one; now she had enough cream cheese icing left over to… well, try again, she supposed. Once she figured out exactly what had made one of her most tried-and-true recipes fall flat.

"Aw, hon." Margaret's sympathy came through two thousand miles a little tinny, but just as warm and honest as ever. "I'm sure they're not all that bad. I mean, c'mon: When was the last time you made a dessert that wasn't mind-bogglingly delicious?"

In Sera's opinion, there was delicious, and there was *delicious*. She'd been born with olfactory bulbs that could sniff out the faintest subtleties of anything edible. (In her wine-drinking days, she'd amused people at parties by allowing herself to be blindfolded, then identifying—by smell alone—the origin of any vintage placed before her. That was, until she'd passed out after guzzling too many of her test subjects.) And if anything, her taste buds were even more discerning. When it came to chocolate, for instance, she could instantly parse the difference between a single-source

Peruvian and an Ecuadorian free-trade blend, then tell you the precise percentage of cocoa in each. Texture and flavor captivated her the way a dicey derivatives market enthralls an investment banker, and she'd known from early childhood that she was destined to work with food.

Determined not to rely solely on her innate gifts, Sera had trailed some of the best pastry chefs in New York while still in cooking school, even taking a semester in France to apprentice herself under one of the most legendary chefs in Paris. She'd worked hard to hone her baking skills, studying the alchemy that turned simple yeast, flour, salt, and water into heavenly bread. She could have written a dissertation on the effects of gluten on those lovely bubbles that characterized the crumb of her tender, crusty loaves. But it was in her confectionery creations that Sera's perfectionism truly came to the fore. She'd spent hour upon hour training herself to pipe precise lines with a pastry bag, until she could have written a perfect "Happy Birthday" on any cake with her arms behind her back. In fact, Sera was so adept at shaping lifelike sugar sculptures that the couples who'd ordered her wedding cakes had often refused to believe they could actually eat the flowers that adorned them.

Of course, all that was before booze and Blake Austin had done a double whammy on her. But she'd promised herself she wouldn't dwell on the bad old days. Instead, she focused on her sponsor's encouragement.

"Thanks, Maggie, but they really *are* pretty inedible. Don't worry, I'm not getting down on myself." Sera wouldn't dare, after all Maggie's hard work helping build up her self-esteem this past year. "It's not that I've lost my touch, it's just the altitude." She sighed, tucking a lock of chin-length black hair behind her ear. "That and the dry air. They screw up the rise and mess with the proportions of wet and dry ingredients. Not to mention, play absolute hell with my head." Sera rubbed her temples. The headache had started soon after she'd touched down at the Albuquerque airport, and had only worsened as she and Pauline made their way north to her aunt's home in the mountains of northern New Mexico. Seven thousand feet above sea level was no joke.

"I've heard altitude headaches usually go away within a week, especially if you keep hydrated," Margaret offered kindly. "And hey, they're nothing compared with your average hangover, so you're still ahead of the game, right?" She paused, then said delicately, "I know you always bake when you're flustered, or when you're trying to feel more at home. I assume that's what tonight's test cupcakes were about. So tell me: How *are* things out there, really?"

Serafina had to smile, both because Maggie had pegged her nervous baking habit so accurately, and because her introduction to "The City Different" had been a source of unexpected delight.

Heading north from the Albuquerque Sunport that afternoon, she and Pauline had driven Pauline's old Subaru shitheap along the sixty-mile stretch of Highway I-25 that led from the state's biggest city to its most enchanting.

Santa Fe.

Before they were halfway there, she'd been so dumbstruck she'd almost asked her aunt to pull over just so she could gape. The landscape was like nothing she'd ever experienced. As the miles slipped by, her eyes had grown wider and her heart had lifted with the sort of elation she'd once only associated with a night out drinking. She'd even checked the Subaru's dashboard, feeling as if she were being swept along on the strains of one of her favorite songs, but the car stereo was silent. Even her normally voluble aunt had grown quiet, though Sera suspected her silence had more to do with her recent loss than appreciating scenery she must have been intimately familiar with after years in the area. But for Sera... it was all so magically new.

There, big as life, and big *with* life, loomed the Sangre de Cristo Mountains, their rounded, wrinkled peaks stained shades of rich, variegated brown by layer upon layer of dense mineral deposits, dotted all over with neat puffs of fragrant green sagebrush. Almost like sprinkles, Serafina had thought, smiling to herself. There arched the achingly blue sky and the endless horizon. Discrete, meringue-like swirls of cloud only served to accent the vast cerulean dome—a ludicrous wealth of sky for a woman from a city whose idea of a decent view was a gap between brick walls. In her mind, Sera was already whipping up batches of sky blue buttercream, picturing herself crafting a confection that captured all the airiness, the lightness and intensity of what she was witnessing. Perhaps a lemon curd or passion fruit layer at the center, with just a hint of crisp wafer for balance...or maybe something with cinnamon, an earthier note...

She hadn't felt this inspired in ages.

Serafina had laughed aloud in tickled disbelief as swaths of flat, undeveloped high desert whizzed past the windshield, the wind restlessly sifting what grass and scrub managed to cling to the rocky terrain. Then came a momentary disappointment—a long, commercial strip of big-box stores and auto dealerships, motels and cheap eateries as they approached the outskirts of town. But as the little car eased through the congested artery that was Cerrillos Road and into historic Santa Fe proper, she'd been enchanted all over again by the low-slung, sun-baked adobe shops and residences with their rough-hewn, weathered wooden beams and the gnarled yet noble piñon trees they nestled among. Other trees Pauline identified for her as larch, willow, and cottonwood lined the riverbanks of the narrow Santa Fe River, while juniper and ponderosa pine proliferated in the drier side streets Sera glimpsed along the way. And as they neared the end of the journey, wildflowers and hardy grasses were overshadowed at last by the aspens blazing bold yellow with autumn color on the mountains above winding Artist Road, where her aunt's home stood.

"Santa Fe is every bit as beautiful as Aunt Pauline always said," Serafina told Margaret, a wistful smile in her voice. "I just wish I'd taken her up on her offer to come out here and visit sooner, while I still had a chance to meet Hortencia. Now, instead of the three of us eating green chile cheeseburgers and shopping for souvenirs like we always talked about, we'll probably be busy planning Hortencia's memorial service and tying up her affairs. I hate seeing my aunt this way—it's like she can't even focus on next steps, she's so devastated. One minute she's her old self, brash and ballsy as ever, the next she's gone all subdued. She's having a hard time even speaking of her life partner in the past tense, let alone wrapping up her estate. Whenever I bring up anything related to the issue, she just goes silent or changes the subject. Poor dear."

A lump formed in her throat, and she couldn't attribute it to the subpar cupcake. Sera took a gulp of tea from the mug that had been steaming on her aunt's colorfully tiled kitchen counter, pausing to appreciate the delicate herbal blend as well as the hand-thrown pottery mug in which it had steeped. The taste of her aunt's signature blend brought a wave of fond nostalgia. How many times had Pauline brewed her a cup of strong, fragrant tea when she'd had some teenaged angst to get off her chest? Tea and sympathy, Pauline-style, had been a ritual that always eased Sera's pain. Could she offer her aunt the same solace during this time of loss? Sera blew out a breath and continued. "I've done my best to be a comfort, but I didn't really know Hortencia—we'd only ever spoken on the phone, and she never tagged along when Pauline came back to New York to see me. Afraid of flying, I think."

"I still think it's kind of funny that your aunt ended up with a woman," Margaret said. "Didn't you tell me once that she used to be kind of a femme fatale when it came to men?" Sera could hear the gentle amusement in Margaret's voice. "They must have been quite the couple, if Hortencia convinced your aunt to start batting for the other team."

"I think they were, even though they only got together two or three years ago. From everything Aunt Paulie told me, it sounds like, after a lifetime of flitting from guy to guy, my aunt finally found happiness with the right lady. I just feel bad that I never..." Sera made a frustrated sound.

"What, that you never made it out West before this? C'mon, Sera, I think you're being a little hard on yourself." Margaret made a reproving noise that managed to be simultaneously gentle and slightly impatient. "You've had a tough road of it. Getting sober is no picnic. Most of us addicts never manage it. And *you* did it while enduring one of the most vicious smear campaigns a woman's career ever suffered through because of that dipshit ex-boyfriend of yours. Just keeping your business afloat and staying away from the sauce are enough to keep anyone busy. I think your aunt and Hortencia both knew you had too much on your plate back in New York to be taking time out for a visit. From everything you've told me, a *guilt* trip is the last thing they'd want this trip West to be."

"Now you sound like Pauline," Sera said, smiling into the phone. It was true, though. From the moment she'd left culinary school, her life had been a whirlwind of ninety-plus-hour weeks, racing to meet Blake's expectations and her own high standards, medicating herself with alcohol when it got to be too much. By the time she'd bottomed out, Sera had been in no condition to scrape herself off the bathroom floor and hie herself off to parts unknown. Instead, Pauline had dropped everything to come to Sera, gotten her into a program, and stayed long enough to make sure it stuck. In the year since then, all of Sera's nonrecovery energies had been spent on trying to salvage some semblance of a career—no easy feat with Blake Austin still actively out to ruin her. But now there was a glimmer of hope for something better...

Serafina cleared her throat, her voice strengthening a bit. "Margaret," she began cautiously, "Pauline floated a bit of a radical idea my way tonight, and I wanted to run it by you."

It had seemed more than a *bit* radical when Pauline had broached the subject over the homemade *chile rellenos* she'd prepared for their dinner. Yet Sera had liked the taste of the idea even better than the flavor of the traditional New Mexican dish. "What would you say if I told you I've been thinking of not coming back to New York for a while? Of... of... actually *staying* out here and trying something different with my life?" She spoke hesitantly, ninety percent sure her sponsor would trot out the "no major changes" mantra she'd drilled into her head so often during her first year of recovery.

There was a bit of a silence.

"I actually think it could be a great idea, hon," Margaret said at length.

"Because, quite honestly, lately, when I think of the future, I'm just really unenthused. You know how slow things have been for me. I make a decent enough living letting restaurants and cafés sell my stuff under their own labels, but my career's never really recovered from what happened, and I don't see how that's ever going to change so long as He Who We Don't Deign to Name is around to keep the rumors fresh." Sera tried to keep the bitterness from her voice as she plowed on. "Anyhow, Carrie practically runs the catering business on her own these days—or she could; she's been angling for more responsibility for a while now. And what else do I have tying me to New York? I mean, shit, my social life consists of stitch 'n' bitch parties with the crocheting circle from our AA fellowship and walking my neighbor's nine-thousand-year-old pug while *she* whoops it up salsa dancing with our superintendent. I don't have kids, houseplants, or pets of my own to worry about, and it's not as if I couldn't find someone to sublet my loft..."

Belatedly, Serafina's ears caught up with her tongue. "I'm sorry, *what* did you say?"

Margaret's laughter tickled her ear. "You're how old now, honey? Twenty-eight?"

"Twenty-nine, but I'm stopping there," Serafina joked cautiously. Had Maggie really said...

"Twenty-nine. Old enough, now that you've got your feet firmly under you, to make these kinds of big life decisions for yourself. If you want to investigate a new possibility—follow your 'Bliss,' as it were—well, that's what the whole process of getting healthy has been about."

The knot of anxiety Sera hadn't even known she'd been holding on to began to loosen in her chest. Maggie was the person she most trusted to tell her if her secret hope—a hope of a future that looked nothing like her past—was a mere pipe dream, or something worth pursuing.

"So you think it makes sense to stay out here?"

"Well, I mean, obviously you're going to need some kind of a plan, a job, and a structure to keep you on the straight and narrow. But there's no reason not to investigate the possibilities while you're already out there. What ideas have you and Pauline been tossing around so far?" Maggie inquired.

Sera set her mug down and toyed with the errant lock of hair which, ever since she'd allowed her stylist to cut it into what he'd promised was a *très chic* angled bob, never stayed tucked away for long. Twisting it between her fingers, she spoke hesitantly. "Actually, Aunt Paulie's got a whole lot of ideas for me, if I agree to stay. And I'm starting to get the feeling I'm needed here more than I knew. I think, for the first time in her life, she's feeling less than confident, not so independent as before. Hortencia's passing really seems to have shaken her, though she's still avoiding talking to me about it." Sera glanced guiltily through the doorway leading from the kitchen to the bedrooms on the other side of the house, but Pauline hadn't stirred since heading to bed awhile earlier. "She's lonely, and who can blame her, after the loss she's just had? She's offered to have me come live with her, and I'd like to support her during this tough time. It'd be nice to be able to give back a little after all she's done for me. And I think maybe it'd be okay for us both to stay here together for a while. The house is plenty big."

Boy, was it ever. Compared with Sera's tiny Tribeca loft, the house was practically palatial, if more homestead than showplace. From cobwebbed rafter to crocheted rag rug, her aunt's three-bedroom adobe fairly screamed "rustic." But the kitchen . . . ah, *that* was a cook's haven of wide countertops, airy open spaces, herb-lined windows, and pot racks clanking with heavy-bottomed copper cookware. There was even a kiva-style fireplace big enough to bake her own wood-fired pizzas, should she ever manage to get the dough to cooperate in these high-and-dry climes. Next stop, a bookshop for some books on high-altitude culinary techniques. Pauline had mentioned there was an excellent cooking supply store in the downtown area . . .

Serafina pulled herself back to the present, aware that Margaret was waiting for her to continue.

"So I'm covered for a place to stay as long as I want—or as long as I can take a daily dose of Pauline Wilde." Sera's lips turned up at the prospect. "Aunt Pauline had some great suggestions for what I could do out here, careerwise. Honestly, I think she's been plotting a life for me here for quite some time." She chuckled. "Her plans are a wee bit grandiose, but the first *practical* hurdle is going to be scoping out the shop and deciding what to do with it."

"Shop?" Maggie sounded surprised, then belatedly enlightened. "Oh, right. You mentioned your aunt leases some sort of a storefront in town. But I got the impression it was on its way out of business or something?"

"Pretty much," Sera confirmed. "I don't think they get a lot of customers, and I doubt it's providing much income for Pauline. It's just about defunct, as far as I can tell. But the lease is paid through the end of this year, which gives me a few months to decide if I want to make something of it."

"Like...open a bakery of your own?" Maggie's voice rose excitedly. "Oh, hon, if anyone could do it, it'd be you. And I know you've always dreamed..." Her sponsor was practically beaming over the phone.

Now it was Serafina's turn to be the voice of caution. "Well, I haven't seen the space yet. Pauline's really eager for me to take a look and see if it might be suitable for my needs. She tells me it's fairly roomy, but it may not be equipped—or zoned—for anything like that. And I haven't done any market research...Still." Sera choked up. "Ah, hell, Maggie. I don't know what I ever did to deserve this. It's like Pauline is handing me my wildest dreams, gift-wrapped. She's as much as said that, if I like it, the store's mine to do with as I want. Who *does* that?"

Pauline Wilde, that was who.

"What's the space used for now?" Maggie wanted to know. "I don't think you ever told me what your aunt does for a living."

Color stained Sera's normally ivory complexion. "Um, no...I didn't." There was no way to put this delicately, but damned if she wasn't going to try. "Pauline was big in the seventies' feminist movement. But, ah...she kind of took women's lib in a different direction than a lot of her contemporaries. She had a bit of a following, back in the day. Started a movement that had about fifteen minutes of fame, and she's been living off it ever since."

"A movement?" Margaret sounded curious.

"Yeah. It was called, um..." Serafina blushed harder, closed her eyes briefly, and blurted it out.

"Ourgasms." She cringed, anticipating Maggie's reaction. "It was supposed to be sort of a tie-in with *Our Bodies, Ourselves*, I think," she rushed to explain. "Pauline is very much a believer in the importance of the female orgasm, and empowering her liberated sisters to have them on demand. Her followers were called the *Pink Panters.*"

A strange yipping sound came through the phone's earpiece. After a moment, Serafina recognized it as her sponsor's wild, uncontrollable laughter. "Oh my God, I *remember* that! I think I had one of her books, or maybe it was a lecture recorded on an old eight-track tape. It was right around the time *The Joy of Sex* came out, wasn't it?"

"Yes, that's right. There were books and lectures and seminars and videos that, um, Pauline kind of...'starred' in. Like, ah, 'how-to' videos." Remembered embarrassment made Sera's voice faint, and to cover it, she busied herself rinsing the cupcake pan in the deep, chipped porcelain sink. It wouldn't do to leave crumbs and crusty pans around for her aunt to deal with when she got up in the morning, Sera told herself, running a worn linen dishrag around the pan's cups and laying it in the dish drainer to finish drying. She'd probably plop herself down on the counter and end up getting gunk all over her voluminous skirt tails, trailing crumbs for the rest of the day. It wouldn't be the first time.

"So what's the store all about?" Margaret interrupted her mental nattering. "A feminist book shop or something?"

"I'm not a hundred percent positive, but I think it might be some kind of a...*sex shop,*" Sera confided in a pained whisper.

More laughter sounded from faraway New York City, and Sera relaxed at the sound, picturing her sponsor leaning up against her own scarred kitchen counter, absently twirling the cigarette she never lit while she scratched through a junk-heaped drawer in search of a menu for some Vietnamese takeout.

Margaret was about twenty-five years Serafina's senior, and far less squeamish about all things bodily. It was one of the things that had first attracted Sera to Maggie when she'd seen her around in meetings—her no-apologies, no-prisoners self-confidence. "We used to pass those Pink Panter pamphlets around in study hall when I was a teenager and think we were *so* risqué," Maggie reminisced, still chortling. "There was one called *She Stoops to Climax* that we particularly relished. Too bad our male counterparts weren't nearly as interested in what your aunt had to teach. Ah, well."

"Ah well, indeed," Sera muttered, rolling her eyes. She was glad one of them could laugh about Aunt Pauline's proclivities. But then, *Maggie* hadn't had Pauline for a guardian while she was growing up, nor suffered all the awkwardness that had entailed.

When Pauline Wilde had first had occasion to get acquainted with her painfully shy preteen niece, her women's lib heyday had already been over for many years, though she continued to run "clinics" and write guest columns for various media outlets. Royalties from her seminal books had continued to subsidize her freewheeling lifestyle, which had taken her from Amsterdam to Bangkok, Brazil to Berlin and back, pursuing a career in cultural anthropology with a specialty in women's sexual norms. Sera vividly remembered her first encounter with her "hippie-dippy aunt," as her dad had teasingly liked to call his big sister. It had been both an awkward and an intriguing moment in her adolescence. Had she known that, less than a year later, the woman who had asked her point-blank if she'd ever examined her "love-bud" in the mirror would be her sole guardian in the wake of the senseless car accident that had claimed her parents' lives, Sera would probably have run screaming into the night.

But Pauline's generous heart had more than compensated for her total lack of filter on word and deed. Upon inheriting her thirteen-year-old niece, she'd put a screeching halt to her travels and settled down in Serafina's home city to carve out a niche as a women's studies professor at New York's New School for Social Research. And she'd done it all, Sera knew, so that she could raise the orphaned girl and give her some much-needed stability. It wasn't until Sera was safely off to culinary school that Pauline retired from teaching and followed in the footsteps of another female sexual pioneer, Georgia O'Keeffe, absconding to New Mexico.

Enmeshed in her own *mishagos,* Sera hadn't really had much idea of what Pauline's life out here looked like. Apparently, she'd made some pretty wise business decisions for an aging hippy. This three-bedroom house and the store in town weren't even the whole extent of it. Pauline's book royalties still brought in a fair chunk of change to this day—and now, it seemed, she wanted her favorite niece to take advantage of all this largesse by helping her get started with her very own bakery

Sera's embarrassment paled by comparison with her gratitude for the strong women in her life. "Anyhow," she told Margaret once her sponsor's laughter died down, "the upshot is, I seem to have a bit of a unique opportunity brewing here. It's going to take some time to see what that amounts to, and I'm actually really glad of that. I want to open myself to whatever possibilities present themselves, you know?"

"I *do* know," Margaret said approvingly, "and I think it sounds great, provided you keep your head on straight. Now listen, hon, *CSI Miami*'s about to start, and I've gotta order some dinner before they stop delivering and I'm forced to gnaw on the curtains for sustenance. But before we say good night..."

Sera grinned, knowing what was coming.

Sure enough..."Run your plans for tomorrow down for me, sweetie," Maggie prompted.

Sera rubbed her forehead once again, trying to massage away the last vestiges of headache and clear her thoughts. "Right now we're just focusing on what's right in front of us, the little stuff." Sera's lips twisted wryly. "'One day at a time,' right? Isn't that what you're always telling me? For tomorrow, Pauline's going to show me around downtown in the morning and we'll see the plaza and the most famous sights. She swears all else can wait until after I've had a taste of the City Different, which she likes to call 'Fanta Se.' Then we'll go see her shop in the afternoon. Anyhow, that's my plan. Check out her store, see what we might make of it."

"And then?" Margaret prompted.

Sera had to smile. "Then hit a meeting. Yes, boss."

"You're a winner, kiddo. Don't forget that."

Sera pressed the "end" button on her cell phone and set the device down on the Talavera tile counter next to her now-empty mug. She let out a shaky breath. She was in a strange house, in a strange city, sharing it with a woman whose major preoccupation in life was with whether or not one was sexually satisfied, and she had not a clue in the world about what tomorrow would bring. She was perched seven thousand feet up the side of a mountain, there were coyotes—real, live coyotes—howling away in the arroyo outside her window, and she was contemplating saying a great, big "fuck it" to everything she'd ever known.

And for the first time in a very long while, she *felt* like a winner.

Chapter Four

Pauline's House of Passion made itself comfortable in a spacious enclosed courtyard containing a cluster of small businesses sharing common walls around a terra-cotta-paved open space carved out of Santa Fe's upscale Palace Avenue. A decorative iron gate with fanciful Spanish-inspired scrollwork and a long, arched entranceway gave only token resistance to the outside world; the discreet signage advertising the shops within flirted coyly with foot traffic from downtown Santa Fe's main thoroughfares, as if daring shoppers to explore the hidden treasures at the end of the trail. At the apex of the gate, a rustic wooden sign announced *"Placita de Suerte y Sueños,"* and Sera's Spanish, rusty as it was, translated it as something like "Place of Luck and Dreams."

Once inside, the visitor encountered a wealth of sunlight streaming through the open center of the miniature plaza, lending the area a warm, cozy feel that could not fail to entice shoppers to stay and browse. Each of the buildings had a wooden porch, so that one had to climb up a couple steps to enter the shops nestled within, as though to protect them from flash flooding, or simply to give them a more rustic feel. A few shade trees planted in terra-cotta pots provided hints of green. At the center of the courtyard, a Spanish-tiled fountain basin had been grafted to a whimsical modernist sculpture of a Native American earth mother type, water splashing merrily from an urn upheld in her ample arms. The one-story adobe dwelling that housed Pauline's storefront was at the rear of the courtyard beyond the fountain, holding pride of place and drawing the visitor's eye.

The visitor's wide, *incredulous* eye. Sera inhaled a long breath.

Her aunt's shop was a jungle.

Or more precisely, the high desert equivalent. The storefront was overrun with a curtain of climbing vines, succulents, and cacti gone wild, their juicy, spiny petals plump and thriving across every surface. The wide, turquoise-trimmed front window was half obscured by tangled drapes of white moonflower, the fragrant, night-blooming petals now furled against the early autumn sun. Brushy yellow wildflowers competed with sweet-smelling lavender bushes to flank the front porch, while huge agave rosettes thrust their spears up from terra-cotta pots that stood like bristly sentinels on either side of the turquoise-painted wooden door. Purple passionflower twined round the weathered wood porch rails in a lover's embrace. Red cactus buds and orange Indian paintbrush added vibrant splashes of color from their homes in planters hung along the window frames. The chocolate gelato–hued adobe walls of her aunt's shop were barely visible through the profusion of foliage, and the sign painted on the front in faded purple cursive—*Pauline's House of Passion*—could scarcely be read.

The effect was intense. It was overpowering. It was beautiful—and vaguely frightening.

"What *happened* here?" Serafina asked Pauline in a shocked whisper.

"Oh dear," Pauline murmured, pushing her battered straw cowboy hat back on her head and scratching the salt-and-pepper mane underneath. "It's been awhile since I took a proper interest in the shop. Looks like the Wolf's been letting his babies have the run of the place in my absence." She tsked her tongue. "I'll have to speak to him about it."

Sera tried to find a part of that pronouncement that made sense, and failed. Then she noticed there was not just one shop affected by the floral invasion, but two. Catty-corner to Pauline's was another, somewhat smaller shop at the far right. A wooden sign hung above it, carved with silver-gilt letters.

"Lyric Jewelry," Sera read aloud, moving closer to investigate.

If possible, the jewelry store was even more overgrown with foliage than her aunt's. Sera couldn't be sure, but it looked as though the migration had begun from the smaller shop and crept inch by inch until it engulfed its neighbor like some primitive jungle.

Then, out of that jungle, stepped Indiana Jones.

Or at least, his doppelganger.

Tall. Lanky. Sandy blond, beneath a battered leather outback hat. Dressed in slouchy olive cargo pants and a waffle-knit thermal shirt that clung almost indecently to the angles and planes of his lean torso. He sported scuffed motorcycle boots and a heavy, intricately wrought silver chain about his neck. Another chain snaked from his belt around to his back pocket, probably anchoring a wallet as beat-up and worn-in as the rest of his attire.

The man brushed aside a stray vine and exited the jeweler's shop, pausing momentarily to adjust to the afternoon light. As he encountered the oddly lucent sunlight that seemed unique to Santa Fe, he squinted and tipped down his hat, but Sera had already caught a glimpse of the most astonishing green eyes beneath the battered brim. Her breath caught as the man vaulted easily over the porch rail, eschewing the two wooden steps and landing lightly on the dusty pavement beside the two women.

"Miss Pauline, so nice to see you today," said the adventurer, nodding politely to Sera's aunt and tipping his hat to them both. "We have missed you around here."

Sera's imagination couldn't have picked a more intriguing accent for Indy had she been writing his dialogue herself. It wasn't Southern, or British, or even Australian. No, it was... *Israeli?* It was very faint, but she'd lived and worked in New York long enough to recognize the distinctive lilt of the soft vowels, and the exaggerated precision of his diction.

"And who is your lovely friend?" Moss green eyes sized Serafina up from beneath the brim of that hat—a hat that should have been ridiculous, and somehow wasn't.

Lovely, my ass. Sera had the unmistakable impression that his choice of words was no more than a courtesy. There was something chilly and imponderable in that green gaze—like the opaque waters of a hidden forest pond. She knew she was no supermodel; working around so much rich food meant she would never be anything but pleasingly curvy, and her petite stature—just five feet two—had earned her the nickname "short stack" in culinary school. Still, Sera wasn't used to such casual disregard from the male sex.

She squelched a childish urge to sniff her pits, crossing her arms defensively under her breasts instead. *Well,* he's *not that good-looking either,* Sera consoled herself. *Ruggedly appealing, yes.* But closer inspection of his features revealed they were a bit too strongly stamped upon his visage to be called traditionally handsome. His nose was a little too prominent, his incisors just a teensy shade crooked. He was on the south side of his thirties, with deep laugh lines around his eyes. And those lean cheeks could use a good going over with a razor—his five o'clock shadow, she guessed, probably started around eight in the morning. Plus—*ugh*—she'd always hated guys who wore chains around their necks. Still, with eyes like that, who was complaining?

Pauline drew Sera forward, beaming fit to crack her face. "Kiddo, I'd like you to meet Asher Wolf, who owns that marvelous jewelry store next door and is single-handedly responsible for every exquisite work of art inside. He's also the author of that floral exuberance that's been...ah... decorating our shops. Not to mention, quite easy on the eyes, if you hadn't noticed." She winked outrageously at Asher, who seemed to think nothing of it, merely winking back companionably.

Oh, she'd noticed. This guy was a jewelry maker? With an Incredible Hulk–sized green thumb? And a name like Asher Wolf? She would have pegged him for a biker, maybe, or a kung fu expert—or maybe an artist's model. Ladies probably tucked panties with their phone numbers embroidered on them into his pockets as he strolled down the streets. The women he dated would be sensual, uninhibited, sophisticated. And probably stellar in bed. It should come as no surprise, Sera acknowledged painfully, that he failed to take notice of *her.*

"Asher, allow me to introduce you to someone very special," Pauline continued warmly, interrupting Sera's thoughts. "This is my niece from New York, Serafina Wilde. My very *single* niece. Everyone calls her Bliss."

"*No one* calls me Bliss," Sera mumbled uncomfortably, squirming under the Israeli's curious regard. "You're the only one, Aunt Pauline." As Sera's godmother, Pauline had had the honor of gifting her niece with that fantastical middle name. Sera had secretly always liked it, even as it made her feel vaguely embarrassed to cop to it.

The lanky artisan had the grace to pretend not to notice Sera's ungracious tone. "Your aunt has a way with words," Asher complimented in his lilting accent, filling the awkward space. "It is a true pleasure to meet you, Bliss. Any relative of Miss Pauline is a welcome addition to our little town."

Now why did she get the feeling there was not a chance in hell of getting him to stop calling her Bliss and start using her given name?

And why, further, was she having an even more unsettling fantasy upon hearing the way the word "bliss" rolled off his tongue, of that name being a promise he might collect on?

"You had a delivery a few days ago," Asher told Pauline, interrupting Sera's squirrelly thoughts with disheartening practicality. Somehow, she'd expected the guy to spout movie dialogue, not prosaic everyday stuff. "When you couldn't be reached, I put the boxes inside for you."

"Oh, dear. I'm sorry, Ash. I did mean to call you back, it's just that things rather got away from me since... since Hortencia..." Moisture gathered in Pauline's coffee brown eyes, and she crinkled them valiantly to keep tears at bay. Sera felt a pang, and reached out instinctively to rub the older woman's shoulder. There were so many reminders of her life with Hortencia, and it had to be hard on her to carry on alone. They may have found each other late in life, but there was little doubt the two women had been soul mates.

Asher's quick gaze took note of her gesture and seemed to warm a bit. Sera wasn't sure what to make of that and glanced away uncomfortably. She did *not* need to get herself enthralled by another charismatic man, damn it! Especially not one as inscrutable as Indy over here. 'Cause yeah, that had worked out *real* well for her last time.

"Thank you for taking care of that for us, Ash," Pauline resumed when her composure returned. "I always said you were a good egg, and I have *great* instincts when it comes to men."

Unlike her niece, Serafina thought.

"It was no trouble, I assure you," Asher demurred gallantly.

Even the tiny half smile he offered was enough to threaten the steadiness of Serafina's knees.

"Bliss here has been thinking of taking over the shop and turning it into a bakery," the older woman informed Asher blithely.

"Thanks for spilling the beans on that one, Aunt Paulie," Sera muttered with a wince. She wasn't at all sure she was ready to share her secret hopes with the world just yet.

Pauline just rolled her eyes at Sera's modesty. "She's a famous pastry chef back home," Pauline further confided.

Sera blushed. "Infamous, more like," she mumbled, shooting Pauline a quelling glance.

One slashing eyebrow rose beneath the hat. "Is that so?" Asher murmured.

"Oh, well, I... that is, yes, I was fairly well known in the industry at one time..." Sera muttered uncomfortably. *"Laughingstock" would have been a better way to describe it.* "As for opening a bakery, well, Pauline and I have discussed it briefly, and I'm really not sure yet, but I thought it would be worth taking a look at the space just to see... you know, whether it might be something I could try... that is, if it's suitable..."

Gawd, why am I blathering on like this?

Maybe it was how fragile this opportunity felt, how badly she wanted the chance for something new, and how afraid she was that something would come along and dash her dream before she could even fully develop it in her mind's eye. Maybe her hopes would sound foolish to him—a little girl's fantasy of being surrounded by sweets and sweetness 24/7. Then again, the guy was practically wearing a T-shirt emblazoned with the word "iconoclast." And wasn't she in a town famous for its free-spirited dreamers? If she were ever to find herself *not* judged for taking a flyer on an out-there idea, she had to hope it would be here, in the land of enchantment. But she'd get nowhere with a faint heart. Serafina took a deep breath.

"What I mean to say is, yes, I might open my own business here if the conditions are right." There, that sounded dignified, didn't it?

"Indeed?" Asher smiled politely. "I should enjoy hearing more about this venture sometime, Bliss."

Her heart fluttered. Wow, he sounded legitimately interested in her plans! Despite her determination not to let this ludicrously sexy man distract her, she couldn't help feeling flattered. Then she mentally smacked herself upside the head. *Duh, Sera.* He probably just wanted to scope out whether she was going to be competition or good for his business, given that his own shop was located right next door. "Um, right, ah... thanks, yeah, I'll be sure to let you know what I decide," Sera muttered, going crimson for no particular reason she'd care to admit.

"Now, where did I put those darn keys?" Pauline was muttering, fully engrossed in rummaging through her voluminous tapestry bag. Sera half expected her to pull a Mary Poppins and drag forth a lamppost or a midsized potted plant from that monstrous sack. "Dang it! I was so sure I swapped them from my *big* bag the other day. But maybe they're still in Hortencia's purse? Of all the stupid..."

Pauline's voice wobbled and her eyes threatened to well again.

She's going to have to talk about it sometime, Sera thought. But right now didn't seem like the moment. Pauline would share her grief when she was ready. "That's okay, Auntie," she soothed. "We can come back tomorrow."

"Not necessary," Asher said smoothly. "I have a set of keys."

Oh, right, he'd mentioned he had put their delivery inside the store, hadn't he? So he must have his own way in. But why would this man have keys to Pauline's business? Maybe people were just more neighborly around here than she was used to back in Manhattan?

Asher dragged forth the heavy silver chain from his pocket, revealing a massive array of jangling keys at the end of it. Sera noticed that, similar to the one he wore about his neck, the chain was wrought from large, intricately scrolled silver links, handsome and masculine in design, yet with an almost musical flow. Before she could inquire into why he had the means to enter, he bounded up onto the porch ahead of them and wrestled with the locks, swinging open the door to Pauline's House of Passion and gesturing with a flourish for them to precede him inside. Sera suppressed a little shudder of purely feminine awareness as she passed in front of him to enter the store, close enough to appreciate the scent of strong, healthy male—pheromones mixed with the sharper aromas of metal, oil, and wood. Tools of his trade, perhaps?

"I'll stay until you're finished looking around so I can lock up for you after," he offered, and Pauline nodded. Sera smiled her thanks, feeling as tongue tied and awkward as a high school girl.

Asher flipped on the lights for them, though it barely made a difference. There was precious little illumination to be had.

Sera forgot pheromones momentarily as she gazed around at her aunt's establishment. She didn't know what she'd been expecting, but it certainly wasn't *this.* Inside, the shop resembled nothing so much as a cozy Victorian tea parlor. Well, cozy verging on *gloomy.* Shawl-like draperies swaddled every window, and tasseled shades encased the low-wattage lamps scattered about the room. Dusty mahogany bookshelves lined the walls, half-filled with little figurines and knickknacks. Sera could barely make out the massive rafters and spacious expanse of smooth-planed pine floors that formed the framework of the shop. She could tell that the walls were whitewashed adobe, but the Southwestern flavor of the structure had been effectively smothered in kitsch and weighted down with heavy pieces of vintage-looking drawing room furniture. What was odd, however, wasn't so much the décor as the fact that she saw little evidence of the "items" her aunt had so enthusiastically promoted over the years. Where were the Kama Sutra posters and Day-Glo sex toys? Where were the strawberry-flavored edible undies and belly-dancing costumes?

"Huh," she grunted, nonplussed. "Not at all what I expected. Pauline, what exactly were you *selling* here?"

Pauline smiled wryly. "Well, not much, really." She ticked off items on her fingers. "Some self-help books—my own and others'—and some videos. I stocked incense and massage oils, too—you know, the sort of aromatherapy stuff women like to pamper themselves with. We also carried some scarves and local trinkets for the tourists—you really can't have a business in Santa Fe without 'em. Most months we didn't even make enough to cover the rent, but I just couldn't bear the thought of closing the shop. You see, my vision was of a collective or community center where women could come to be themselves, read about issues that pertained to them, have tea, and gossip. I mean, of course, there's the *back room*"—Pauline waved dismissively—"but really, Pauline's House of Passion was always about empowering women and bringing them closer together. Over the years, my store's been more like a neighborhood clubhouse than anything—a lot of the ladies coming by after hours on their way home from work to chat and catch up, bitch about their menfolk, that kind of thing. No offense, Ash."

"None taken," said their nonchalant next-door neighbor, leaning against the wall with his arms folded. "As I understand it, bitching is the sacred right of women."

Sera chose to ignore that comment and the appealingly playful tone in which it was delivered. She was remembering all the causes her aunt had fought for so passionately over the years. When Sera was a teenager, Pauline's painfully explicit discussions of women's most intimate concerns had made her squirm and long to flee. Her high school friends, *so over* the feminist movement, had teased her and made fun of Pauline's values. As she'd grown up, however, she'd learned to appreciate what her aunt was about, even if her own sexuality was—to quote Pauline—positively Puritanical.

Pauline Wilde had always believed that women's strength came from their solidarity. Her work with feminine sexuality had encouraged women to be frank and open about their needs, to explore them with each other as well as with men—and always with a spirit of adventure. She could easily see Pauline making her shop a place of warmth and intimacy for her visitors.

Too bad she couldn't see the actual shop as easily.

"Do you mind..." she asked, gesturing toward the draped-over windows.

"Go for it, kiddo. I want you to think of this place as your own now. I've had my go at it, and I'm ready to pass on the torch. Frankly, it's getting too much for me. Feel free to pillage as you like!"

Sera strode to the nearest window and stripped away what appeared to be a Spanish lace mantilla dyed in a particularly purple hue. Light flooded into a quadrant of the store, and she took a relieved breath. She'd always needed lots of light and space to feel comfortable—a condition that hadn't made living with Pauline's congenial clutter and preference for what she called "Blanche DuBois style" lighting easy while she was growing up. Sera had often teased her that her lifestyle was more Blanche Devereaux than DuBois, but Pauline had just smiled and kept the lights low.

Well, Pauline had given her the go-ahead, so go ahead she would. She gently freed the rest of the windows from their shrouds until the full space was revealed. Her breath hitched.

Wonderful.

You simply didn't get this kind of real estate back in New York. Not unless you were Jacques Torres. Sera's heart lifted as she surveyed the airy, elegantly proportioned interior. Little popcorn kernels of ideas began exploding left and right in her mind, sending corresponding zings of excitement whizzing through her system. There, where the long, low mahogany counter stood, she could install a bank of glass-fronted refrigerated display cases for her hot-ticket items. There, on the far wall, nestled built-in shelves currently holding what looked to be statues of fertility goddesses from various cultures throughout history. In her mind, the shelves began stocking themselves with brass-appointed whole-bean coffee dispensers and high-end espresso machines. Custom-printed cardboard goody boxes with gaily colored rolls of ribbon to wrap around them would lie in readiness for customers' take-out orders.

Best of all, she'd have *counter space.* The shop had a ridiculous amount of square footage. She could even divide off a third of the place for her ovens and fridges, and still not feel cramped. Her customers could stretch out and stay awhile—provided they purchased something, of course. Serafina envisioned her place becoming a hangout where people came for their morning coffee and a flaky pastry, then returned to buy a cupcake or two during the siesta hour. Tourists would line up with their cranky kids for a swift sugar infusion before trotting off to visit local museums or lay down their hard-earned cash in one of the gorgeous, one-of-a-kind boutiques that Sera herself had window-shopped this morning. Perhaps she'd even accept custom cake commissions again, eventually.

Next to the horsehair-stuffed armchairs lolling in exhausted postures around the edges of the space, she pictured vintage marble-topped side tables for customers to lay their cupcakes and confections on while they relaxed and sipped a latte. She'd have a stand for newspapers and periodicals. Maybe even offer Wi-Fi, though she wasn't sure she wanted to go that route. (The laptop-toting student/starving writer crowd didn't tend to lay down a lot of cash.) She wanted everything elegant, appealing, and absolutely delectable. Fresh flowers in bud vases would add notes of color, while the aromas of chocolate, coffee, and piping hot cake would surround her customers in a sensual web.

But hold on. Speaking of scents, something didn't smell quite right around here. Serafina was used to identifying ingredients and judging flavorings by their odors, and this one was... odd, to say the least. Vinegary. Following her nose, her attention was drawn to a large glass jar sitting on a dusty shelf. Was that... She drifted closer, afraid of what she might find. Plucking up her courage, Sera reached out with thumb and forefinger and gingerly drew aside the cheesecloth covering the top of the jar.

"Yeeeoowza! What is *that?*"

Pauline drifted forward to peer over her shoulder. "Oh, that? It's nothing to worry about. It's just Big Mama. Hello, Big Mama!" She leaned in to whisper confidingly in Sera's ear, as though to keep the contents of the jar from hearing. "Don't mind the smell, dear. She's just hungry. I'm afraid I've been neglecting her shockingly since the... well, since Hortencia..."

"Big... *Mama?*" Sera breathed, staring at the enormous brown glob floating in the jar of sickly-looking liquid. "You don't mean—"

"Yup," Pauline confirmed. "Kombucha. It's my own special culture. Go ahead and taste some if you like, but it'll be better if we feed her first."

Ugh, no thanks, Sera thought. She knew about kombucha, of course. Chefs heard about all the crazy ingestible trends out there in the world. She'd read somewhere that the mushroom-like culture that floated at the top—mostly comprised of a form of yeast—was known as a "mother," and that these mamas sometimes spawned "daughters" that brewers used to spin off their signature blends for family and friends. In theory, it sounded okay, if a bit unsanitary. But until today, she'd never actually seen the fermented home brew in person. And now that she had, she didn't think she cared to see it again. It smelled like hippie feet, and it looked like a monstrous, wet, flabby mushroom. Or a dead stingray. *Gross.*

"It was very popular with our ladies," Pauline offered. "A lot of them thought it had special *properties,* if you know what I mean." Sera blushed as the meaning became clear, but her aunt must not have noticed, because she continued in a stage whisper, "*Sexual* properties, dear."

A snort sounded from behind them. Asher was staring studiously into the middle distance, but he couldn't hide the little grin that lifted his generous lips.

"What, *you* want some?" Sera flashed, teasing the outrageously sexy Mr. Wolf before she could think better of it.

"My sexual properties are in no need of enhancement at the moment, thank you," he shot back with elaborate politeness, and the blush on Sera's cheeks bloomed into a full-body affair.

"Um, right. Moving on!" Sera wasn't about to discuss aphrodisiac beverages while a hot guy stood around making quips about his sexual prowess. Even if it was secretly kind of fun.

"What's back here—the restrooms?" Sera asked as she headed for the rear of the store. A beaded curtain with an image of Ingres's *La Grande Odalisque* hand-painted upon it hung across a discreetly placed doorway. Maybe that "back room" Pauline had mentioned so offhandedly a few minutes ago?

Pauline beamed. "Why don't you have a look?" She placed a palm on Sera's spine and steered her through the doorway, flipping on a wall switch as they parted the beads.

Sera was confronted with wall-to-wall wieners.

Rubber. Latex. Glass. Metal. In every shape, color, and size—and then some.

Damn it. I thought I was done with dildos, Sera thought, stomach sinking. The sight of sex toys brought nothing but humiliating memories for her.

Pauline moved deeper into the room ahead of Sera, turning on more lights.

It was a temple devoted to the Big O. Every tool the imagination could envision in service to this laudable objective existed in some form or other on the shelves and in the display cases in the windowless room. Images ranging from the instructional to the downright lascivious papered the walls, with geishas, Greek figurines, and Kama Sutra postures at every turn.

Sera's blush burst into flames, especially when she felt Asher's presence filling the space behind her. She wanted to back up, but was already perilously close to connecting with his sinewy frame as it was.

Yikes, did he see me ogling that… wait, what the heck is *that thing?*

"I suppose you'll want to shut it all down now," Pauline said glumly, interrupting her niece's horrified/fascinated reverie. "I know you're—forgive me, dear—but you've always been a bit of a prude in this regard."

Sera shot Pauline a look that would have quashed a more sensitive woman. But Pauline just patted her on the arm as if to say, *None of us is perfect, dear.*

Sera wanted to sink through the floor with mortification. *Just what I needed to start out my new life in Santa Fe,* she groaned inwardly, *a reputation for having a stick up my ass. Er, maybe not such a great analogy—eek,* anal-*ogy!—to think of when surrounded by butt plugs.* Her blush was physically painful now.

"Well, I… I mean, what I had in mind for the store doesn't exactly, um, dovetail with this, ah…" At a loss for a descriptive adjective, Sera gestured lamely at a series of strap-ons.

Behind her, Asher made a rumbling noise that sounded suspiciously like stifled laughter. At the sound of his merriment, Sera's spine experienced a shiver of awareness that wasn't a bit unpleasant.

"I understand, dear." Pauline sighed. "But I must tell you, the contents of this room were an invaluable resource for the women of this community. What income we did draw from the shop mainly came from sales of these pleasure enhancements. I can't tell you how many times we received thank-you notes from ladies swearing we'd revolutionized their sex lives. Saved a lot of marriages, too."

"I'm sure," Sera murmured, eyeing what looked like a nubbly pink jellyfish attached to a series of elastic straps. *Where do you put tha… oh.*

"I can personally vouch for that one, dear," said Pauline, following Serafina's scandalized gaze.

Now Sera did retreat a step or two, but the heat from her next-door neighbor brought her up short. As she peeked over her shoulder, she saw he was braced casually with one arm on either side of the door frame in a posture that showed off his physique to mouthwatering advantage. She could feel his warm, minty breath on the sensitive juncture of her neck and shoulder.

Sex toys ahead of me, boy toys behind. It was certainly not how Sera had envisioned her afternoon unfolding. She wasn't sure whether to laugh, pray for a teleport to whisk her away, or pass out from sheer sensory overload. Having spent the past year burying all thoughts of a sensual nature, devoting herself to work, recovery, and little else, Sera was unprepared for the effect the back room, and Asher's presence in it, was having on her.

With an effort, Sera turned around. Her head was barely level with Asher's neck, he was so tall. But that was fine—it meant she didn't have to look him in the eye. "Excuse me, please," she muttered, gesturing politely for him to stand aside. "I think I've got the gist of the place now. Quite a dichotomy between what you see in the main room and what's in stock in the back, that's for sure!" *God, I* must *be nervous,* she thought. *I couldn't sound more like a Victorian schoolmarm if I strapped on a bustle and started rocking the granny boot look.*

Asher was more colloquial, though perhaps his command of English was a tad questionable.

"That's Pauline's House of Passion for you. Prim and proper up front, orgasms in the rear," he commented innocently.

A voice channeling *Beavis and Butthead* giggled sophomorically in Sera's mind. *Heh-heh. He said "orgasms in the rear."* Her face flamed. *Get a grip, Serafina,* she admonished herself. *Grown women don't freak out at the sight of a few vibrators.*

Since Asher seemed to be taking his time moving out of her way, Sera ducked under his arm and squeezed by, taking a welcome breath of nonsexualized air when she reached the main space. Pauline trotted up behind her, hands on hips and a hopeful expression on her face.

"So what do you think, kid?"

"Think?" Sera was finding it rather hard to think at the moment, actually. "Well, the space is amazing," she said when she'd gathered her wits. "What we can make of it—well, I have some ideas, but I want to hear what *you* think first. I don't want to railroad you out of something you love, Aunt Paulie. I can see how much this place has meant to you, and I want to honor that. As far as I'm concerned, you should make the final decision on what happens with the shop."

Pauline's sharp brown eyes softened and her face glowed. "I raised a wonderful niece," she trilled. "Didn't I, Ash?"

Asher hopped up to sit on the mahogany counter and grinned, arms bracing his weight behind him in a way that emphasized his broad shoulders and corded arms. "Indubitably," he affirmed.

Sera shot him a suspicious glance, but there was no trace of a leer on his face, and he seemed quite sincere—even detached. Inexplicably, disappointment flared within her. Though she had no intention of becoming distracted from her dream by another charismatic male, she found herself wishing that this one *was* flirting with her. But if there was any trace of chemistry in the air, it was apparently one-sided. He was being charming—engaging even—but definitely not suggestive.

"Well, kiddo," Pauline continued, "the sad fact is, since Hortencia, I've lost a bit of my customary mojo. And I ain't getting any younger. I haven't got the energy—and let's face it, I *never* had the business savvy—to keep P-HOP going the way it should, but I'd be sorry to see my dream die out *entirely.*" A hint of deliberate mystery colored her voice, telling Sera she had something on her mind.

Her aunt might look like a Grateful Dead camp follower, but Sera was beginning to suspect the old gal hadn't lost her edge.

"Spill it, Pauline," she commanded.

"We-lllll," Pauline drawled, enjoying the moment, "your specialty is giving people pleasure, right?" She waited expectantly, like the retired professor she was.

Sera was willing to bite, despite her awareness of the interested audience observing their exchange. "I guess that's one way of putting it. My desserts are definitely made to invoke all the senses and delight the palate." She hoped she didn't sound like too much of a prima donna. Still, her confections did deserve a certain gravity. They were *that* good. Modest Serafina might be about her own attributes, but her baked goods were out of this world.

Pauline wasn't put off by Sera's hesitance. She beamed at Sera and Asher alike. "The way I see it, I've been doing the same thing, just working in a different medium. So I thought, what if your new shop included both sinful desserts *and* earthly delights?"

"You mean...cupcakes in the front, climaxes in the back?" Sera asked incredulously.

"Chocolate produces the same endorphins as sex, I've heard," Asher put in helpfully from his perch on the counter.

"Oh, is that what you've heard?" Sera shot back, a smile quirking her lips when Asher mugged an innocent expression. But only half her mind was on her new neighbor, for a wonder.

She was beginning to see the possibilities...

Considering her "shortcomings," Serafina had never had the slightest inclination to frequent a pleasure palace, let alone become the proprietor of one, be it ever so genteel. But now...Ever since her aunt's distress call, Sera had sensed she was facing another crossroads in her life—not as dramatic as her decision to get sober, certainly, but perhaps even more profound. Her life in New York was unsatisfying, to say the least. She had gotten her one-year chip just a couple months ago, and was only just beginning to see the "promises" spoken of among the recovery community come true in her own life. She'd stabilized, sure—but in a lot of ways she was still the same scared, insecure girl she'd been before she'd picked up the bottle and lost so many years to it. One of the things she had learned, watching others who had the sorts of lives she wanted for herself, was that those who were happiest were the ones who were open to life's possibilities, and who challenged themselves to accept new things, however scary they might be.

Maybe it was time to live up to her surname and do something wild. Something totally out of character. Never mind that she was hardly one to speak on the subject of orgasm aids—Pauline could take care of that aspect. Sera had absolutely no intention of letting Pauline retire, gracefully or otherwise, and she suspected Pauline herself wouldn't have it any other way. They'd be the dynamic duo of sensual gratification! And Sera would be someone who proudly owned a streak of mischief, instead of someone who buried her *joie de vivre* beneath a stifling blanket of timidity.

Yes. This is what I want.

Sera's inner certainty, absent for the last several years—hell, since she'd met Blake Austin—returned. It didn't sneak back a bit at a time; it flung open the door, tossed its hat and coat on the sofa, and announced itself "home!" in a loud, Ricky Ricardo voice. She could do this. And she could have the time of her life in the process.

"Two great tastes that taste great together, huh?" she said with a grin spreading across her face.

"Exactly, kiddo."

"But what would we call it?"

"How about Climactic Cupcakes?" Pauline offered.

"Little Death by Chocolate?" Sera countered.

They both smiled.

"Bliss," said Asher.

"Yes? You want to weigh in, Mr. Wolf?"

"I thought I just did," he corrected with a smile. "And please, no need to be so formal. Call me Asher, or Ash—I won't bite."

Said the wolf, thought Serafina.

"What I meant was, I think you should name the store after what it offers, *and* who's offering it. Call it Bliss."

There was a moment of silence.

"It's perfect!" Pauline cried. She clapped her hands with girlish glee. "Leave it to the stud to call it like it is. Good job, Gorgeous."

Asher just grinned that stupendously engaging grin, tipping his hat once more.

Sera had to admit, the name *was* perfect. But she didn't want to give Asher a big ego—his looked healthy enough as it was. "I'll think about it, you guys. We still have a lot to consider before we can be sure this will work out. Permits, zoning, financial stuff—I've got a lot of research and number crunching to do."

Sera dusted off her hands and took a last look around. She didn't want to admit it aloud just yet, but her heart was soaring. For the first time in as long as she could remember, the future looked exciting. Challenging, sure. But so, *so* promising. Eyes sparkling, she gestured for the others to precede her out of the shop and then shut off the lights after them. As the door closed behind them, she felt a sense of rightness—of certainty. She'd be back soon to honor the gift—and opportunity—Pauline was providing her with.

"I would be happy to help with the store in any way I can. Please, be welcome to visit me at any time, Bliss," Asher said as he locked up after them. "I'm always just next door."

"I'll do that," Sera promised. As she watched him retreat—no hardship there—she had a feeling she'd be making an excuse to do so at the earliest opportunity—just to be neighborly, of course. Maybe it wasn't such a great idea to fly so close to the flame with a guy that hot, but hell, a girl could look, couldn't she? *No harm pursuing a friendly acquaintance,* Sera told herself staunchly. She'd just have to keep her...limitations...in mind, and she'd be fine.

"Wow," she said to Pauline, "what's the deal with that dude?"

"What do you mean?" Pauline asked innocently.

"Well, for starters, why does he have a key to your place?"

"Oh, that." Pauline waved a hand dismissively. "Why wouldn't he have a key to his own building?"

At Sera's uncomprehending look, she continued, "Oh, didn't I mention that? Asher owns the place. If you decide to reopen the shop, he'll be your landlord, kiddo. And he's single, too, you know." She leered in that signature Pauline Wilde way—almost too cute to be obscene. "Maybe if you two start *schtupping,* he'll give us a break on the rent."

Chapter Five

It wasn't the next day, or even the next, before Sera got back to *Placita de Suerte y Sueños.* A full week passed in a haze of logistics and alarmingly grown-up concerns before she was able to visit her dream shop again.

Armed with advice from accountants, recovering from cauliflower ear after several marathon phone sessions with local officials, and newly expert in the bylaws of Santa Fe's small business association and community boards, she finally felt prepared to say with reasonable certainty that, yes, opening Bliss *might* work out. But first, she'd have to talk to her landlord.

And Sera was feeling a wee bit woozy at the prospect.

The jungle around both Pauline's shop and its neighbor had been pruned back a bit, she noticed as she arrived. But from under the slightly more manicured curtain of foliage draping Lyric Jewelry, a series of alarmingly animalistic yips, snorts, and whines was emerging.

Too bad I couldn't get my pepper spray through airport security, Sera thought with a twinge of unease. But whatever it was doing the Animal Planet impression under there, she'd have to get past it to see Asher Wolf. And she hadn't come all this way to get fainthearted now.

Leaving the package she'd brought with her balanced on the porch railing, she stepped up on the dusty boards, ducked under the canopy of leafy growth, and discovered that the source of the sounds appeared to be a... *hm, is that a doghouse?* Yes, definitely a handmade wooden doghouse, more old-school Snoopy-style than prefab pooch palace, tucked in a corner of the storefront beside a series of potted plants that were exuberantly climbing the walls and door lintel of the jewelry store.

A white, distinctly wolfish muzzle peeked out from the doghouse.

Oh, man, my landlord isn't seriously a wolf wrangler, too, is he? she wondered. She had enough mental nicknames for Indiana Jones as it was; Dances with Wolves was just one too many.

Sera was uneasy with dogs. Cats were okay by her—the more aloof, the better—but if truth be told, she'd always been more of a turtle or sea monkey person than a fuzzy animal advocate. Sera preferred a pet that could be contained in a tidy display case, look decorative, and require little to no maintenance. Taking her neighbor's wheezy pug out for its nightly walk had been about as much commitment as she'd ever wanted to offer a canine. With her baking schedule—up before dawn most days; elbow-deep in flour, butter, and sugar for most of her waking hours; and catering events all over the city—pet ownership had pretty much always been out of the question. Dogs, with their constant needs and shameless attention seeking—not to mention their droolly, treat-begging ways—had just never been her bag.

Until perhaps, just now. As Sera watched, four more muzzles joined the first in the darkened arch of the doghouse door. Four tiny, mewling, tongue-lolling, ridiculously lovable puppy muzzles.

Before she knew it, Serafina's ankle-length circle skirt (one of Pauline's, as she was getting to the end of her travel wardrobe and she'd yet to do laundry) had acquired a fringe of Siberian husky–shaped pom-poms.

Their impossibly adorable little faces were scrunched up as they did battle with her hem, growling and barking excitedly while their mother, a regal-looking purebred husky with piercing blue eyes, lounged half in, half out of her doggy domain and watched her offspring indulgently.

Was it possible to die of puppy love? Her heart was melting faster than Valrhona chocolate in a hot double boiler.

"C'mon, little doggies," Sera crooned, trying to gently free the denim edge of Pauline's skirt from the puppies' mouths while simultaneously endeavoring to keep the tired elastic at the waist from giving its last gasp. Pauline was a bit more generous around the middle than her niece, and her well-worn clothing fit Sera rather more than comfortably. As playful growls and excited yips erupted, she realized she'd just inadvertently invented a new game for the pups—"denude Serafina in public."

"C'mon... let the nice lady go," she wheedled, hoping to reason with the puppies. They looked intelligent enough for a bunch of puffballs. No dice. So she tried distraction, crouching down and pointing excitedly with one hand while clutching her waistband for dear life with the other. "Look, boys! A bird! Um, puppy chow!" But nothing could possibly be as thrilling as anchoring her hippy skirt, making sure it gave no resistance to their mini-ferocious fangs.

Serafina got stern on their asses. "Drop the denim, you Lilliputian menaces," she threatened, "and nobody'll get hurt." In response, the littlest one crawled right under her hem and began having it out with her socks, just where they met her favorite pair of slouchy ankle boots. "Ha, ha... no, stop, you little punk... ah, that tickles! Shit! No, you goobers, I'm not wearing my nice undies today, quit with the peekaboo—"

"Can I help you with something?" inquired an amused voice.

Serafina gave a yip fit to outshine her canine carbuncles. She spun on her heels, puppies swinging from her skirts like a carnival carousel, coming to a stop face-to-face with a grinning Asher Wolf.

He framed the doorway of his shop with aplomb; she had to give him that. *Sans* hat today, but sporting another clingy, beat-up pullover and cargo pants with what looked to be a full complement of jeweler's tools poking from their many pockets.

Hello, Studly.

"Oh, hi, Mr. Wolf. Ah, do these limpets belong to you, by any chance?"

"Asher, please," he reminded her, "or I'll be forced to call you Miss Wilde, and Santa Fe is far too casual a town for such formalities."

"Right." Serafina colored. Calling him by his given name felt too intimate somehow, but refusing to do so would make her look like a weirdo—or more of a prude than Pauline had already painted her to be. "Asher. Sorry. Um, I seem to have Velcroed up some puppies—are they yours?"

"Temporarily," he allowed. "Sascha over there"—he gestured to the full-grown husky—"is mine, as I am hers." At the sound of her name, Sascha got to her feet and wound her way through her gamboling offspring to Asher's side, sitting on one of his motorcycle boots and looking up at him adoringly until the jeweler gave her a fond rub across her noble forehead. Man and beast exchanged identical wolfish grins. "The pups, however, are merely passing through. Three of them have homes waiting for them, but the runt of the litter hasn't been spoken for yet—that's the little rascal who seems to have developed a fondness for your sock. In a couple of weeks, when they're fully weaned, I'll have to find a place for him, too, though I'm growing perilously fond of the fellow myself." Asher leaned his shoulder against the doorjamb and crossed one foot over the other, the picture of relaxed, self-confident male. Sascha mimicked him, flumping over on her side, crossing her paws in front of her, and cocking her head as if to say, *"Isn't my master awesome?"*

You said it, bitch, Sera thought. She could stare at that kind of goodness all day long.

To cover the sudden heat that was short-circuiting her thoughts, Sera leaned down and let her fingers have the luxury of sinking into the runt's exquisitely soft fur. He gave a funny little chirrup and began lapping at her hand with a dedication that was almost embarrassing. "May I?" she inquired, indicating that she'd like to pick up the pup. Asher nodded, and suddenly, her arms were full of squirming, barking joyousness. Face, neck, hands—every part of Sera within the pup's reach was subjected to his sloppy kisses.

"He seems to have taken quite a liking to you, Bliss," Asher remarked.

Sera started, still unaccustomed to the moniker and how frankly naughty it sounded on his lips. Her face flamed—*again*—but she hoped the husky's ministrations would hide her blushes. "I'm sure at this age, they probably greet everybody this way," she demurred.

"The other pups, yes. They'll roll over and beg for belly rubs for any passing tourist—not bad for business either, I might add." He grinned frankly. "This little fellow, however, has been very shy up to now—I've never seen him take to anyone so freely." Asher folded his arms, scrutinizing Serafina. "Dogs have excellent instincts," he said. "You must be a good... what is it Pauline says? A good egg. Yes, egg." He looked pleased with his ability to whip out an English idiom.

"Well, I, ah... that is, I try to be... um, thanks," she babbled, absurdly tickled. The puppy gave a bark of agreement, seconding the sentiment. She scratched behind the little fella's gray-tipped ear, loving the distinctive charcoal-colored face mask markings that set off his snowy coat. The pup leaned into her fingers, whining with joy. "What's his name?" she asked Asher shyly.

"He hasn't got one yet. If you'd like, you may have that honor."

And just like that, standing on a rustic, sun-dappled porch, giddy with high altitude and sage-scented desert air, Serafina had a moment of gratitude so strong that tears sprang to her eyes.

A year ago, nobody had been asking her to name their puppies. She'd been lucky if she could get through a day without having an angry sous chef lobbing a saucepan at her head. Now she was trading pleasantries on a brisk September Santa Fe day with a fascinating gentleman who had entrusted her with a piece of his dog's future. Maybe to him, this was no more than the friendly gesture it seemed. But to Sera, it meant she was finally on her way to becoming the woman she'd always hoped she'd be.

"I'd like that," she murmured when the lump in her throat finally dissipated. She buried her face in the pooch's snowy fur, laughing a little when he started chewing on her hair. "I might need some time to think of the right name, though."

"He's in no rush," Asher said, reaching out to fondle the pup's ears. Sera took note of his hands: big knuckles, long, sensitive fingers—and lots of scars and calluses. She'd seen their like on chefs before—cooks collected burns and cuts like they were auditioning for a slasher movie. She guessed jewelers faced some of the same occupational hazards. Hot metal, sharp tools.

Speaking of hot stuff...

"I came bearing gifts," she blurted out. "I hope you're not allergic to chocolate or anything."

"A fate worse than death," Asher said with real horror. "Not at all. I consider chocolate one of the major food groups."

Could he be a more perfect human being? Sera wondered. *Just, please, don't let him be one of those people who believes in alien abduction or listens to Rush Limbaugh, 'cause this could be the start of a beautiful friendship.*

"Then you're going to love this," she promised, letting her dimples show as she held up the Tupperware container she'd placed on the porch rail before the puppies glommed on to her.

Asher gallantly accepted the battered plastic tub. "What is it?" he asked, already busy peeling off the lid. "I think I smell..."

"Chocolate babka," she affirmed. "I thought, since Pauline told me you're Israeli, you might like a taste of home."

Asher inhaled appreciatively. "Actually," he said, his fingers already busy tearing off a hunk, "it's not really common back where I come from, in Tel Aviv. I'd never tasted babka until I visited my cousins in New York a few years back. But once I did"—he flashed that signature grin—"I considered moving there permanently."

She blushed, embarrassed at her cultural ignorance. But Asher didn't seem the slightest bit offended. Sera watched as he freed a fluffy, chocolate-marbled wad of the sweet bread and crammed it in his mouth. His eyes slid shut with an almost carnal bliss.

So did Sera's.

There was just about nothing that compared to watching someone enjoy the foods you made with your own two hands. Watching a gorgeous, lanky, Siberian husky–owning artisan who just happened to be your landlord enjoy your food...well, it was singularly rewarding. A heat that owed nothing to the sun-washed day suffused Serafina.

A wet, warm tongue began laving her neck.

Her eyes snapped open, and were met with the curious, mischievous tundra blue eyes of her nameless puppy friend, whose tongue lolled from his doggie grin without the slightest shame. Sera, on the other hand, ought to spend at least a week doing penance for her lascivious thoughts. Thoughts, she reminded herself, that should be nipped in the bud before she started falling under her landlord's spell...

Asher swallowed, the strong column of his neck working. Sera's gaze was drawn to the hollow at the base of his throat, olive skin just barely sprinkled with golden hair at the vee formed by his open shirt collar. "Delicious." He sighed, opening his own eyes at length.

Yeah, that was one way to put it.

Suddenly, Sera became aware of the fact that they were still standing on the porch outside Asher's store, and that she'd been monopolizing his attention for quite a while.

"You must have customers. I don't want to keep you... I just wanted to check in with you about Pauline's store, if you have a few moments. If you don't, I can come back," she rambled.

"Not at all," he said with a reassuring smile. "It's early, and the tourists don't really start bombarding us full force until lunchtime, as a rule. I find the ladies are generally in a better mood for buying jewelry after they've checked a few of our town's fine museums off their list and had a bite to eat. And it goes similarly with their gentlemen companions. So business is quiet just now. Would you like to look around my shop?" he offered, licking his thumb clean of babka crumbs and shoving away from the door.

A peek inside the wolf's den. Why not? She put the puppy down, watching as Sascha gently chivvied him and the rest of the litter back to their little doggie hideout.

Asher beckoned Sera inside after him, and she followed.

And broke into a delighted smile.

Smaller than Pauline's House of Passion, more intimate, and warmly lit, Lyric Jewelry was fairly bursting with the personality of its owner. As with its plant-laden exterior, the interior was pulsing with life and energy, but here it was expressed in a different way. Inside, the atmosphere was all about flow and grace, while the outside was more about exuberant, untamed growth. As Sera gazed about in fascination, she took in antique wooden display cases with beveled glass fronts, walls lined with gilt picture frames repurposed to hang earrings and pendants, and most intriguingly, *violins* everywhere she turned.

Hung from the ceiling, resting on display stands, pictured in old lithographs of tuxedoed or beautifully gowned musicians, the richly lacquered, mellow aged wooden instruments played dramatic counterpoint to the main focus of the shop—the exquisite silver jewelry. Sera moved forward to examine the nearest display case, forgetting the creator momentarily as she marveled at his creations. Rings, pendants, bracelets, and earrings, some polished to a high shine, others treated with a patina to achieve a smoky, tarnished effect, were placed in the cases just so—neither with military precision nor with careless abandon, but with an instinctual understanding of space and artistry to best show off their unique craftsmanship.

The pieces themselves were nearly all sterling silver, with just a few gold accents and semiprecious gemstones. Some had inlays of smoothly polished, fine-grained wood or iridescent seashell, bringing an organic, living feel to the pieces. Like the chain she'd seen around Asher's neck at their first meeting, they were substantial, imposing works of metal, but they had a flow that was anything but clumsy. Neither masculine nor feminine, overly intricate nor plainly modernistic in style, still the jewelry *sang.* Clearly, Asher had been inspired by the fluid lines and shapes of the musical instruments with which he'd surrounded himself. Sera spotted a superb ring made of patinaed silver that swirled just like the neck scroll of a violin, while a pendant displayed in one of the wall cases was elegantly reminiscent of a cello's curves without flogging the likeness too literally. There were very few items she wouldn't want to own, though the discreet price tags tucked beside the pieces told her there were few she could easily afford.

Sera turned a slow circle, taking in the welcoming golden lighting, the cozy but not claustrophobic feel, and noticed, toward the back, an area with a workbench and tools. She drifted closer. A scarred wooden jeweler's table and cabinet with multiple cubbies above it showed that Asher must do at least some of his crafting right in the shop. She could appreciate how appealing that would be to his clientele—just as her customers had once loved being able to see the face of the person who'd baked their delectable desserts and wedding cakes, those who purchased his wares would no doubt proudly show them off to their friends back home. Sera pictured it. A well-dressed, middle-aged matron would boast to her lady friends at her next dinner party: "Yes, isn't it lovely? I got it when George and I went out to Santa Fe last year. It's from the most amazing little shop. The artist was sitting *right there,* making the jewelry before our eyes! And I don't mind telling you, Helena, he was quite the handsome fellow! Don't tell my husband I said so, or he won't be feeling as generous anytime soon."

Sera smiled at her own fantasy. Then she looked over at Asher, who had braced himself behind the far counter, which held a small display stand of less expensive pieces—mostly bangle bracelets and simpler rings—for impulse buyers, plus a cash register and credit card machine. The expression on his face was...anxious? Could her uber-confident, utterly laissez-faire landlord actually be nervous about what she thought of his business? The notion warmed Serafina. As a craftswoman herself, she knew how tough it was to constantly offer up one's most beloved creations to the world—in effect, inviting strangers to critique one's life's work—and how necessary it was to receive approbation once in a while. Asher Wolf deserved it. As an artist, he was clearly wildly talented and deeply in his element. But it was good to see he had his insecurities, too. Blake certainly had had none.

"It's lovely, Asher," she said simply.

That quicksilver grin flashed across his lips again, and she could see his shoulders relax. "Thank you. Would you like to see anything in particular while you're here? Or did you just want to talk business now that you've buttered me up with that phenomenal babka?"

Sera made a rueful face to hide how much the compliment pleased her. "Much as I'd love to waste half your morning trying on each and every one of these lovely works of art, I did come here to discuss some business matters with you. But if you don't mind, I'd also like to ask a few questions. Your store is fascinating."

Sera crossed the shop diffidently to stand beside him, looking over his shoulder at some of the photos and knickknacks arranged on the far wall, where a small door led to what she assumed was a back office or storage area. The store appeared empty but for the two of them, and the intimacy of it struck Sera in a way that made the comfortable temperature inside seem to ratchet up several degrees. Still, Asher didn't seem particularly aware of any unusual vibe in the air between them, and he certainly wasn't acting on it, even if he was. Just as before, his manner was friendly, engaged, as if his internal energy was a force he focused on any and all guests as a matter of courtesy and genuine, good-hearted curiosity about people. Yet something was held in reserve, Sera sensed. This was merely the public persona of Asher Wolf, and as magnetic as it was, somehow Sera was dead certain there were wells of his soul still completely unplumbed. What, she wondered, would it be like to have one hundred percent of that charisma devoted solely to her?

Best not to ask questions when you can't handle the answers, Sera-my-girl, she admonished herself.

But Asher seemed happy to answer the questions she *did* dare to venture. "Certainly, Bliss," he invited. He busied himself stacking a bunch of the elegant, treble-clef-embossed gray jewelry boxes with his store's name on them into a neat tower on one side of the counter. "Ask away."

Where to start? There was so much about him that bore comment. "Well, I...I couldn't help noticing the foliage outside. Is gardening a hobby of yours?"

Gah, could I possibly sound more banal? Sera wanted to smack herself upside the head, Homer Simpson–style. She might as well have asked him if he liked sports or if he was a fan of coffee.

"A necessity," he replied, unaware of her chagrin. "I've always been deeply connected with growing things—a habit instilled in me by my mother, whose garden was like another child to her. Back in Israel, the climate was much like here in many ways, and our plants required similar coaxing to flourish. I suppose I started tending my storefront garden as a way to remind me of my home and my family. And then I got carried away.

"I hope it wasn't presumptuous," he continued, "but when Pauline didn't seem to mind, I allowed my garden to encroach onto her shop front. You'll probably wish to get rid of it all," he said, looking as though he was trying to be brave, "and of course, I will be happy to take care of that for you."

"No—don't," Sera found herself saying, though she *had* been wondering if the wild, overgrown look really suited a bake shop. "I mean, yes, I think we'll have to cut back a little—maybe more than a little," she amended frankly, "but I would absolutely welcome your talented hands on my property."

A gleam entered Asher's eye, and Sera realized what she'd said. Her hand flew to her mouth. "Oh! I didn't mean...that is, I just meant I'm terrible with plants, and you're clearly the opposite, and I'd love it if you'd..."

Asher's shoulders were shaking with merriment. But his eyes were kind. "I'd be happy to be your personal gardener, Bliss," he said gently. "And of course, we'll take the greenery only as far as you wish."

Now why did she feel like she was on a first date, with a boy promising not to venture past first base without permission? *Don't lose yourself in a fantasy, Sera,* she warned herself. *You've only just put yourself back together.*

"Thank you, Asher. But this is all assuming you're okay with the bakery at all, and that's why I'm here." She faced him squarely. "I came to ask, do I have your permission to run an eating establishment on your property?"

"Are you kidding?" Asher said. "After a taste of that babka, no one could refuse. The thought of having access to baked goods that tasty all day long..." He rolled his eyes rapturously. "Besides, as I said, my customers are always in a better mood to buy when their stomachs are full. If someone is wavering over a purchase, I shall simply send them over to your establishment for a sugar and caffeine infusion while they dither. You *will* have coffee, I presume?" he asked as if her refusal would break his heart.

"Abso*lute*ly," Sera promised. She wouldn't be much of a recovering alcoholic if she didn't mainline several cups of strong coffee a day.

"Then, so long as you promise not to burn down the store—and pick up the insurance costs—I can see no downside."

"Well," Sera felt compelled to warn, "I did have a lot of renovations in mind... there'd be electrical work, probably some significant demolition and remodeling..."

"We'll work out the details, Bliss," Asher said firmly. "And I am very happy you are to be my neighbor—and tenant."

"So am I," Sera said, feeling another warm glow engulf her. If she wasn't careful, she'd be falling under his spell... and that wasn't what she'd come to Santa Fe for.

She shook her head to clear it. "So what's with the violins?" she asked, changing the topic.

Asher's long, sensitive fingers stopped tidying cardboard boxes and began to stack receipts. Sera had the sense she'd made him uncomfortable, though she couldn't quite say how she knew. Perhaps it was that he'd stopped meeting her gaze; his own moss green eyes turning inward with an emotion she couldn't quite place. Sadness? Regret? "Oh, that. I'm asked that question frequently."

Sera cursed herself for being just like the tourists who must plague him with stupid questions all day long. But seriously, given the décor, it was a valid question, wasn't it?

"And..." she prompted, leaving the question hanging in the air.

Asher stopped stacking. "I used to be a luthier, back in Israel," he said.

Was it her imagination, or had his answer been just a shade curt? Reticence, or something stronger? Sera couldn't tell. She only knew she'd blundered into tricky territory.

"A luthier?"

"A violin maker," he clarified.

"Oh! Wowza. I don't think I've ever met anyone who actually makes musical instruments before." Sera was fascinated by the picture of the artisan as renaissance man—a master craftsman who could work wonders in wood as well as metal, and whose knowing touch tamed and cultivated growing things with seeming effortlessness. She'd never met anyone who could coax so much beauty from the elements of nature around him. She couldn't help pursuing the topic, though she took her cue from his behavior and trod as lightly as she could, asking the most innocuous follow-up she could think of. "Do you play as well?"

"No," he said.

And didn't elaborate.

His body posture had changed, however, his loose-limbed stance going rigid and his warmth retreating.

What did I say? Sera wondered.

Before she could attempt to find out, however, she received a shock that knocked the very question from her mind.

They weren't—and had never been—alone in the shop. Without warning, the door to the back room behind Asher snicked open, and a sylphlike woman glided forth.

Long, lustrous black hair. Impossibly smooth olive skin that looked like it had been buffed and polished with pure gold. Sloe eyes of golden brown beneath winged brows a nineteen-forties movie star would have paid a premium for. And she topped it all off with a body that said, quite frankly, "Mine's better than yours." The woman slinked up next to Asher clad in an emerald silk blouse and tight-fitting black pencil skirt more suited to a corporate boardroom than a quaint tourist-town boutique, leaning familiarly close to him and eyeing Serafina with something less than warmth.

The bottom dropped out of Sera's stomach.

Wife? Girlfriend? God, how stupid was I to assume a guy like Asher would be unattached! But hadn't Pauline said he was single? The proprietary way this chick stood shoulder-to-shoulder with Asher screamed otherwise.

The two made a striking couple, she had to give them that. Good looks galore, from their bronzed skin to their dramatically chiseled features, his old-gold hair contrasting beautifully with her inky tresses, their tall, statuesque bodies straight out of a catalog.

Unlike Sera's dinky frame, which could charitably be called hourglass, but was definitely more "give-it-a-squeeze" than "ravish-it-senseless." She crossed her arms under her breasts uncomfortably.

"Oh! Gosh! I had no idea anyone was back there," she blurted out—too loudly. "Asher, is this your wife?"

Great, Sera. Reeeeal suave. While you're at it, why don't you just ask him how many kids they've got, and whether the sex is any good? She looked down at her feet, hoping vainly for a trapdoor that might conveniently swallow her up. She must have looked a total fool, bringing this guy treats and complimenting his shop like some giddy high school girl. She could tell herself all she liked that she was just being friendly, but Sera knew there'd been more than casual goodwill in her heart when she'd come here today toting goodies. And Asher was no dummy—he had to have sensed it. *No wonder he's been so nice, but so utterly un-flirty,* she thought. *He's been humoring me.* Humiliation washed over her. With a woman like this one in his life, he wasn't straying anytime soon.

When she dragged her gaze back up to assess how her oafish question had gone over, it struck Sera that her distress was only exceeded by Asher's own, though the woman at his side had straightened proudly at the association she'd drawn. Immediately, she realized her guess had been way off. The light in Asher's eyes had dimmed, and he looked almost...sick? When he replied, after a pause that went on long enough for Sera to regret the hearty kashi-and-soymilk breakfast Pauline had urged upon her earlier, he spoke slowly, as if just remembering how after a long, solo journey. His usual vigor had deserted him, and Sera had a sinking surety she'd been the one to steal it.

"Not my wife, no." He gathered himself visibly, and when he spoke again, it was with a simulacrum of his usual energy. "Bliss, this is Guadalupe. She assists me in the shop. Lupe, I'd like you to meet our new neighbor, Serafina Wilde—she's Pauline's niece."

His assistant. Ah. Well, that made sense. Asher couldn't man the shop every minute. He would need someone to help out, possibly more than one someone. *But what* else *does she assist Asher with?* Sera couldn't help wondering as the woman squeezed in even closer to her employer. Asher didn't seem uncomfortable with it, but neither did he respond to her nearness with the kind of enthusiasm that would indicate a romantic relationship. Not that Lupe would mind if he *did* make a pass, Sera guessed. From the way the woman was eating Asher alive with her eyes, it was obvious that if he wasn't her conquest now, she'd every intention of changing that situation soon. She was pumping out fuck-me pheromones at such an alarming rate, Serafina felt embarrassed sharing the same room with the two of them.

Well. This puts the kibosh on any ideas I might have had about throwing my hat in the ring for Asher's affection, she told herself. *And hell, that's for the best. Not only could I not compete with Lupe's brand of femme fatale-ry, I had no business considering flirting with my landlord anyhow.* A man like Asher, sexy from top to toe, belonged with a woman who was his match—a woman he could have gorgeous babies with and fuck senseless night after night. Not someone who...

Sera didn't care to finish the thought. She had a sudden, powerful urge to whip up a batch of rocky road bars. Somewhere far, far away from here.

"I see the resemblance," murmured Lupe, eyeing Serafina's sagging skirt and dog-mussed hair. It took Sera a moment to realize she was talking about—and subtly insulting—both herself and her aunt. "How nice to meet you," she intoned further, holding out a limp hand for Sera to shake. No calluses or scars marred *her* perfect mitts, Sera thought uncharitably as she accepted the other woman's chilly clasp. But maybe those $100 French tips were a requirement for someone who modeled and displayed jewelry for a living. She withdrew her own unmanicured paw as quickly as was polite, hoping her palms hadn't been too revealingly damp.

"Ah... nice to meet you, too, Guadalupe." Sera drew herself up to her full five feet, two inches. "Well," she chirped far more brightly than she felt, "I've taken up too much of your time, Asher. I'll get out of your hair now. Got a lot to do if I'm going to get my shop off the ground!" She turned blindly for the door, and caught her scarf—one of Pauline's brightly colored ethnic jobs, which she'd borrowed to combat the chilly morning air—on one of the countertop earring displays. Bright bits of metal scattered like buckshot, rolling and bouncing across the floor, and she choked as the suddenly tightening fabric grabbed her by the throat. Sera's face went pink, but it wasn't from lack of oxygen. Even in a lifetime of embarrassing exits, this had to rank in the top ten.

"Oh," she cried, "I'm so sorry. Here, let me just..." She began frantically trying to untangle the sparkly threads of the scarf from the tines of the earring holder so she could gather the strewn silver items from the floor and make her escape.

Asher leaned across the counter, stilling her hands on the scarf with his own warm, strong ones. "Allow me, Bliss," he commanded softly. "I untangle jewelry for a living. Lupe, would you please help Miss Wilde with the stray earrings?" he requested. It was clearly a boss-to-employee-type request.

Guadalupe looked as if she'd just bitten down on a raw jalapeño. "Of course," she murmured through tight lips. She came around the counter on stiff legs and bent over ostentatiously at the waist to collect the loose studs that had rolled across the floor. In her pencil skirt and platform stilettos, her ass formed a perfect heart shape, but the message it was sending Serafina was anything but loving. Whatever the message to Asher, however, Sera was pleased to see he was oblivious to it, engrossed in the fine work of teasing her stubborn scarf free from the wires of the earring tree. His expressive face was intent and his sensitive fingers worked with total focus over the delicate operation of untethering Sera from his artwork. He was so close she could smell that unique Asher scent again—man, metal, fire, fresh air. She tried not to inhale too deeply of its heady aroma, resisting the impulse to reach out and touch the lock of antique gold hair that fell across his brow, just to test if it was as lustrous as it looked.

Just then he looked up, catching her staring. And winked. "Don't let her get to you, Bliss," he said quietly. "Lupe doesn't like women much." His fingers freed the last folds of fabric, making bold to reach around Serafina's suddenly sensitized neck and loosen the scarf until it fell free to puddle on the counter between them.

But do you? she wondered, obediently reaching out to take the cloth as he laid it in her palm. She tried not to clutch it like a groupie clinging to some rock star's discarded sweat rag. *And could you learn to like* me, *in particular?* It took an effort of will not to ask.

"I'm tougher than I look," was what Sera said aloud. It was suddenly very important that this man not see her as some fragile flower. "No one's 'getting to me' unless I let 'em."

"Good." Asher smiled. All awkwardness had passed, the lively charm that was his armor firmly buckled in place once more. Sera didn't know whether to be happy or regretful. "I believe it. You have what it takes to succeed," he pronounced authoritatively. "That's how I know Bliss will be a massive success."

Sera beamed. "Why, thank you." She felt like she'd just swallowed a cup of sunshine, and could barely contain it.

Lupe stalked up to the glass counter and dropped a handful of solid sterling earrings on it with a rat-a-tat like machine gun fire. "All present and accounted for," she said with a disdainful sniff, "though some of them may have suffered in the... accident." The way she sneered the word "accident," she might as well have pinned a medal for klutziness on Sera's lapel.

Sera's sunny feeling clouded over as rapidly as the ever-shifting New Mexico weather. "Oh! I'm sorry... I'll be happy to pay for any damages," she hastened to assure them both, her hand fluttering to her shoulder bag for her wallet and her cheeks flaming once again.

Asher stopped her with a hand over her own. *That's twice he's touched me today,* Sera's lizard brain noted. "Don't be silly. In fact…I would like you to have these." He reached, not for the pile of assorted earrings Lupe had gathered on the countertop, but into the display area below, where some of the finest, most obviously costly pieces were showcased. He bypassed a spectacular pendant with an infinity spiral of silver limned in pure gold and inlaid with mother-of-pearl, reaching for a deceptively simple set of small hoop earrings worked in plain silver metal, but with such beautiful balance and weight that they looked still liquid, filled with energy and harmonious grace.

He lifted the delicate earrings out of the case, laying them on his callused palm and eyeing them ruminatively. He glanced up at Serafina, then back to his creation, then nodded decisively. "Yes, I believe these were meant for you. Please accept them as our way of welcoming you to the neighborhood."

"Our" was probably a bit of a stretch for politeness' sake. If Guadalupe were in charge of the welcoming committee, Sera had a feeling those earrings would be spearing her eyelids, not her earlobes. How she worked in a jewelry shop with such a lousy attitude toward women was a mystery. But Sera was so tickled, she happily ignored Lupe's outraged glower.

"I should refuse these," she murmured, already picking the first from Asher's palm and fixing it into her lobe. "But I'm just not that virtuous. Thank you, Asher, for this extraordinary gift." She slipped the second earring into place, and felt the cold metal warm against her flesh. A glimpse into the mirror on the counter showed her what she'd already guessed. The hoops were perfect for her—they went beautifully with her short, angled haircut and made her neck look longer and more elegant. "They're gorgeous, and I will cherish them. I look forward to repaying you in cupcakes and coffee in the very near future."

"Good." Asher pushed back from the counter with a satisfied air.

Good that I'm not that virtuous, or good that I'll be serving up baked goods? Sera wondered.

"You'll be slaving over a hot stove until you're ninety to pay those off," she heard Lupe mutter.

The chime of a bell over the shop's front door drew the attention of all three, and in trooped a pair of plump, pasty women sporting sweatshirts with rhinestones and puffy animal decals, clutching bags printed with the logo of a well-known Santa Fe souvenir supplier.

"Do y'all sell those...those whaddaya call 'ems...those Cocoa Puffy statues?" one of the ladies asked loudly. Her hair was an alarming shade of magenta, and looked as if it had survived the fall of Atlanta.

"It's *Kokopelli,* Marla," her friend, who had on a sweatshirt of a neon coyote baying at the crescent moon, corrected her.

"Right, that coconutty feller. The god of snacks or whatever. Y'all carry those?"

Sera bit back a smile as she watched both Asher and Guadalupe inhale deeply, plastering identically professional smiles into place. "I'll be going now," she stage-whispered out of the side of her mouth. "Thanks again." She touched her earlobes as she turned to go.

Asher's voice called after her as Lupe swayed over to assist the tourists, contempt held rigidly in check. "By the way, Bliss. If you're looking for fixtures—ovens, cooking implements, that sort of thing—I know of a restaurant auction coming up next week. I'll leave the details with Pauline, so she can give you proper directions. Be sure to ask for Malcolm, but don't be put off if he's a bit disagreeable. His bark is worse than his bite, and he's a fair man."

"I'll do that." *Restaurant auction, eh? Good tip.* Maybe she could pick up some bargains on secondhand equipment. It was a common practice in the industry, and Sera knew that, when restaurants went out of business, selling their fixtures was often the only way for the owners to recoup painful losses. She sidled past the shoppers, who were oohing and ahhing over a display of bracelets by the front window. Sera nodded briefly at Lupe, opening the front door, then turning within its frame.

"Oh, and, Ash?" She surprised herself with the nickname, not failing to note the lovely Miss Lupe's narrowing gaze. "I've thought of the puppy's name."

"Oh?"

"Yeah. Silver. His name is Silver."

The smile Asher gave her was pure gold.

Chapter Six

Serafina blinked. In the time she'd been inside Lyric Jewelry, it appeared the courtyard had acquired a new statue. To her sun-dazzled eyes, the figure, vaguely humanoid, looked as though some strange-humored god had yanked it free from its gravitational moorings, dragging it skyward and elongating it past all reason. *I knew Santa Fe had a flourishing art scene,* she thought, *but this is a bit... sudden. I'm sure this wasn't here before.* Perhaps she was still dizzy from her encounter with Asher and his unwelcoming minion. She blinked again, and the strange new sculpture resolved itself into something she recognized.

Ah. Nothing to be alarmed about. It's just a New Age spiritualist. I better get used to them out here.

Flanking—or possibly mocking—the generous curves of the earth mother fountain, a slender young woman in wide-legged yoga pants and a fairly unnecessary sports bra was poised on one bare foot, the other magically protruding from the clasp of her two hands *behind* her head, her back leg nearly parallel to her torso. She looked to be double or perhaps triple jointed, with a fluid, taffy-like muscle structure that made her pose seem like the most natural thing in the world, despite Sera's certainty that a professional ballerina would be hard-pressed to duplicate it.

She watched as the girl unwound slowly and flowed into yet another improbable posture, and then another. Just as she was wondering if she should announce herself or simply sneak past to get back to her rental car (she had planned to hit the chamber of commerce and pick up some forms before heading back to Pauline's), the impossibly lithe young woman pressed her hands together, murmured *"Jai Bhagwan,"* added in a *"Namaste"* for good measure, then bounced on the balls of her feet as if she couldn't contain herself. She opened sparkling brown eyes and sang out, "Hey, girl! You must be Bliss. I've been dying to meet you!"

The yogini bounded over to the porch, oblivious to Sera's flummoxed expression, and stuck out her hand for Sera to shake. "I'm Aruni. Aruni Sharon Lipschitz, but I just stick with Aruni," she said, pumping Serafina's hand enthusiastically. "Please, for the love of the Buddha, don't call me by my given name, or I'll never forgive you." She dimpled, a woman clearly used to charming others right out of their ten-toed socks.

Aruni wasn't precisely pretty, Sera observed; possessed of a nose that was slightly bulbous at the tip and a chin that didn't quite overcome her otherwise adorable overbite. Her shoulder-length hair, Sera guessed, would require all sorts of abstruse products to tame its woolly curls. Still, her vitality made the overall picture one of delicious, vibrant attractiveness. As Sera watched, the woman twisted a rubber band through her massive mane and secured it atop her head in a ponytail that would have done a shih tzu proud. "I run the yoga studio across the courtyard," Aruni said helpfully.

Of course she did. Sera followed the graceful line of her arm as the woman pointed to indicate a storefront at the front of the *placita.* The wooden double doors of the studio were painted a pale pink that managed—barely—not to clash with the mellow brown adobe walls. On the generously sized plate glass front window, swirly lotus flower and *ohm* symbols were painted in a purple she supposed was very spiritual. Perhaps Aruni and Pauline had shared a bucket of Benjamin Moore, Sera thought, for P-HOP's sign, she now realized, was exactly the same shade. Sera had noticed the yoga studio in passing on previous reconnaissance missions to her new venture, but only in a "Hey, I really ought to sign up for a class one of these days...ha, ha, yeah right," sort of way.

I've got neighbors, she thought to herself with equal parts pleasure and foreboding. *And I bet out here they expect you to, like, talk to them and stuff.* Another new experience. *Hmm. Well, I could probably get used to being sociable. After all, I did say I wanted to try new things.*

"Oh, ah, yes," she murmured, fumbling for something appropriately neighborly to say. "Tantrastic, right?"

Aruni nodded happily. "That's the place!"

"It's nice to meet you, too, ah..."

"Aruni," Aruni reminded. "Like the sage." Her eyes searched Serafina's face, expecting recognition.

Right. The sage. The only sage Sera was intimately familiar with came in the fresh produce aisle, and made a great addition to turkey stuffing. *Aruni?* Could she seriously call her that out loud? Then again, with a name like Serafina Bliss Wilde, who was she to take issue with unusual monikers?

"Most people call me Serafina or Sera, not Bliss," Serafina said, hitching up Pauline's patchwork skirt and wrapping the scarf Asher had so recently touched closer about her neck. "I'm still not used to Pauline introducing me to folks the other way." *And I'm getting to like Asher being the only one, besides her, who calls me Bliss.*

"Sera, then. I'm a big believer in calling people by the names they choose. For obvious reasons." Aruni pulled a rueful face. "I'm so excited you're here, Sera," she rattled on. "Pauline stopped by and told me all about you the other day. She said you'd come to take over the store, and, I quote, 'I was to give you all aid and succor' in an effort to convince you you've made the right choice. Well," Aruni said brightly, "she didn't have to ask me twice. I'm, like, totally over the moon that you're here. Finally, some new blood in *Placita de Suerte y Sueños!* With you here, we're going to lower the average age of the merchants in this little shopping center by half, and make it twice as rockin' cool."

"We are?" Sera asked faintly.

"Mos' def, girl!" Aruni slung a muscle-banded arm across Sera's shoulders. "I'm no energy reader, but I definitely get a vibe that you and I are going to be great pals. C'mon, let's go grab a burger and seal the deal."

"Ah... a burger?" Sera hesitated.

"Well, yeah—a veggie burger for me, obviously, but I won't pass judgment if you haven't made the shift to a meatless lifestyle yet." Shrugging on a sky blue hoodie, she linked arms with Sera and urged her forward.

Sera stepped down from the porch in Aruni's wake, feeling the sun warm the otherwise chilly late-morning air. Her inner voice was telling her, "Go ahead, make a friend," while her native New Yorker was shaking its head and asking her what ulterior motives her new "pal" might have. A lifetime of scanning for subway pervs and pickpockets warned her she should be checking the other woman over for concealed weapons and/or cult propaganda. But the Santa Fe sunlight and the cool September breeze were clearing away those suspicions, making room for new possibilities.

"Um, sure, I could eat," she found herself saying.

"Great! I know the perfect place, and my assistant's minding the studio for the next couple hours—we've got a beginner's class in there practicing their *durga* breathing right now—so I can sneak away for a bit. Let's walk—it's so nice out, and it's not too far from here."

And ten minutes later, after a stroll down narrow streets lined with exquisite, screamingly expensive boutiques and galleries Sera promised herself she'd take the time to investigate soon, they were sliding into a booth at the Sunshine Diner.

"Was that who I think it was?" Sera whispered out of the corner of her mouth as they unfolded their napkins and settled in at the historic-coal-warehouse-turned-chrome-finished diner, shedding scarves and handbags on the seats beside them. Her gaze cut over to the left, over Aruni's shoulder, to the gentleman who had just paid his tab and was now ambling toward the front entrance with a peculiarly bowlegged gait. "The one who was in all the Western movies?"

Aruni did a totally unsubtle gawk over her shoulder while Sera tried not to cringe. "Yup," she affirmed. "He's in here a lot. Likes the pies, I'm told. He has a compound in the hills just outside the city limits. I heard he had it built to look just like the ranch in his most famous film. We've got a lot of aging stars buying second homes in the area, so don't be surprised if you see one or two. But you must be used to celebrity sightings, being from New York and all. The way Pauline tells it, you were practically Donald Trump's personal chef." Aruni was clearly fishing for info.

Sera considered sharing a few choice stories from her days in Blake Austin's kitchens. She'd met—and catered to—enough celebs that the mystique had mostly worn off. "I did have the occasional celebrity run-in here and there," she admitted, and decided not to elaborate. She wasn't feeling particularly nostalgic for her hometown or her old life, and wasn't sure she ever would again. "So what's good here?" she asked, steering the subject away from her origins.

Aruni buried her gamine face in her menu, studying it earnestly. Her wiry corkscrew curls wiggled joyously above the top of the oversized diner menu with a life of their own. "Well, anything with green chile is great," she advised, "but I mostly come here for the desserts."

Sera privately marveled that the woman before her, slender to the point of being two-dimensional, had ever been intimately acquainted with sweets. She glanced down at her menu, her mouth quirking involuntarily into a smile as she read. The offerings were a mix of classic diner comfort foods and New American cuisine, all with what she was beginning to recognize as a signature Santa Fe twist. "The desserts are practically the only items on the menu that *don't* have green chile in them," she observed wryly. "Guess they're trying to tell me something. Maybe I'll have to invent a green chile cupcake for my bakery."

"Oh, for sure you have to," Aruni said, as if shocked Serafina might ever have entertained a contrary idea. She slapped her menu down and focused intently on Sera, leaning forward across the table with her elbows bent and her pointy chin propped on her fists. "Have you decided on a menu for the bakery yet?"

"Oh yes." Sera smiled. "About eighteen of them. It's narrowing it down to what's doable without forgoing sleep until retirement that's the tricky part."

"Hmm." Aruni's earnest brown eyes crinkled in thought. "Well, what are you best at?"

"Everything." Serafina made this pronouncement without a trace of shame, and perhaps a *soupçon* of healthy arrogance. She slung her arms across the back of her side of the booth, gesturing broadly. "From macaroons to *pain au chocolat,* meringue to *petit four,* I pretty much rock the confectionary spectrum." Seeing Aruni's eyebrows shoot up, she smiled. "Seriously, I'm like the puff pastry whisperer. I can make a choux paste that'll float your *éclair* on a sea of mocha yumminess. My lady fingers and biscotti scoff at the need for coffee. My chocolate mousse is so rich it makes Rupert Murdoch feel poor. And my wedding cakes—well, husbands may come and go, but my cakes are timeless. I've never wanted to do anything else with my life—the truth is, I've screwed up everything else I've touched—but pastries? We just seem to understand one another. It's been that way since I was a little kid."

What Sera didn't say was that, as a painfully shy child with limited people skills, cooking had been both creative outlet and peace offering. Pleasing others with her pastries had been one way to placate them, make them like her, ensure she always had an invite to the party. Well, until alcohol had taken over the role of social lubricant...and subsequently ruined her life. But Sera wasn't thinking about that today.

"Now," she continued, "all I have to do is master the altitude adjustments, and I should be wowing the taste buds of you Fe-heads in no time—that is, if they haven't been burnt off from eating all those chile peppers."

Aruni looked a bit nonplussed by Sera's vehement speech. But then a wide grin spilled across her face. "You're going to make me fat, aren't you?"

"I might try," Sera said with a smile of her own. "But maybe if we swap baked goods for yoga lessons, we'll manage to keep it in balance."

"Rock on," Aruni said, high-fiving her across the table. "I like the way you think. And as for your menu and the need for sleep—girl, you're going to need not just your z's but plenty of time to hang out with your new gal-pals now that you're living in Santa Fe. What about doing like those ladies on TV do—the ones on the Food Channel that have the cupcake chain stores? Like, just *only* do cupcakes?"

Sera had considered it. "Well, I still want to be around when the cupcake craze dies down—not that I think people will ever get tired of cupcakes, but a store that sells nothing else may get old. Back in New York they've already moved on to donuts and even 'cronuts.' Don't ask me how to describe those," she added with a smile, "but trust me, they're delicious. Anyhow, I also want to have coffee and some savories like quiches or simple sandwiches available for people who come in throughout the day, so I can have a constant flow of customers from breakfast through teatime, you know?"

"Totally. People are always poking their noses into our *placita,* asking if there's a place they can grab a coffee and a Danish or read a newspaper and just hang out for a few minutes, instead of having to have a formal sit-down meal at some spendy tourist joint. I know *I'd* love to have a place to pop by and get some tea or a veggie wrap once in a while. Coffee doesn't fit into the yoga lifestyle, but a girl *does* get thirsty." She dimpled. "Speaking of which, are you gonna keep Big Mama around?"

"I have a feeling my aunt would go into mourning otherwise," Sera said drily.

"Not just her," Aruni said seriously. "*All* us girls. We love it, and it does wonders for our...well, you know." She gestured below the belt. "Don't worry. I'm sure you'll find a way to please your customers and yourself as well, whatever you decide to serve. And speaking of pleasing..." Grinning conspiratorially, she leaned even farther forward across the laminated wooden table and lowered her voice. "Pauline tells me you've agreed to keep the back room going. I can't tell you what that'll mean to the girls."

Hm. Her new friend seemed to be quite adamant about this "girl power" thing. "'The girls'?" Sera asked cautiously. She had the feeling she'd just been ambushed by the real reason Aruni had invited her out to lunch.

Aruni waited until the waitress had come over with their drink orders, pouring Sera a satisfyingly deep ceramic mug of black coffee and providing a decaf green tea for the yogini. "Y'all enjoy," said the woman with a wink, bumping elbows with Aruni. Her Texas accent gave her away as another nonnative in a town full of transplants from other, less eclectic places. "Give a holler when y'all are ready to order. Oh, and 'Runi-baby, I'll see you next Friday at the shindig, right?" She sashayed off, a sway in her ample hips.

"You sure will. Thanks, Janice," Aruni said to the waitress's retreating back. She turned to answer Sera's question. "Yeah," she said with exaggerated relish, practically rubbing her hands together. *"The Back Room Babes."*

Sera was getting tired of playing the straight man. "All right, lady," she said to the woman she was already slotting into her social solar system on a tight orbit, "let me have it. What's with these 'Back Room Babes,' and just how much is it going to embarrass me?"

As Aruni explained it over delicious burgers—*sans* meat but rife with green chiles—the Back Room Babes were a society of local women who had come together over the past few years under Pauline Wilde's auspices, mainly in the evenings after work and kids were squared away, to gab, commiserate, empower, and educate themselves. Drawn by the titillating sexual aids—er, "pleasure enhancements"—offered at P-HOP, but unwilling to be seen shopping during regular hours, women had begun trickling in around closing time, begging Pauline for just "one quick peek" while no one else was around to see them browse. Pauline, fired up with outrage over the shame her fellow *femmes* felt exploring their natural needs, had arranged special "viewing hours" and began offering talks, videos, and even workshops for the women. Though Pauline hadn't been crazy about the group calling themselves "babes"—a feminist to the core, she wasn't keen on infantilizing women—she'd bowed gracefully to the alliteration and rah-rah spirit of the thing. Also out of deference to their sensibilities, she'd kept the lights nice and dim, served nachos, margaritas, and lots of Big Mama kombucha, and before she knew it, she had a regular group meeting twice monthly to catch up, shoot the shit, and do their damnedest to spice up their love lives.

"I got lured over to the back room for the first time when I heard howls and coyote yips coming across the courtyard one night while I was locking up the studio," Aruni said. "I was a bit leery, because quite honestly it sounded like someone was throwing a *Twilight* convention in there with all the werewolf noises, but I had just moved out here from Chicago and I didn't know many people. Plus," she said with an edge to her voice, "the *farkackte schmuck* I had come out here following had just dumped me on my ass. And this after he begged me to drop a thriving practice in Bucktown and come out to the desert so we could meld our chakras and have babies and *ohm* our way happily ever after into the sunset. That *shmendrik*." She shook her head in remembered disgust, quivering curls adding dimension to her indignation. "So anyway," Aruni concluded, touching a little charm on a string around her wrist and visibly shaking off her bitterness, "I went over to investigate what all those loony women were up to, and before I knew it, I was one of them."

Had Sera not been born and raised in New York City, she might have had trouble following, but since she had, she mentally translated the Yiddish in her new friend's description of her ex-boyfriend easily enough. Roughly: "Bastard of Blake-like Proportions." Aruni's general aura of good-natured Zen had fallen away for a moment there, and Sera had seen a bit of the tough yet wounded Chicago girl she was clearly trying to leave behind. It had the effect of endearing the yogini to her more than if Aruni had taken the breakup with enlightened good grace. She felt a twinge of outrage at any man who would ask a woman to uproot her whole life like that, only to leave her high and dry. At least it sounded like Aruni's ex had mercifully exited the picture. For Serafina, Blake Austin was like the cat from *Pet Sematary*—he just kept coming back, stinkier and more psycho every time. Even a year later, he was still doing his damnedest to ruin her name. It was one of the reasons getting out of New York City had seemed so appealing.

But she didn't want to spend a single second of her new life dwelling on old regrets. She'd much rather focus on the possibilities of the present.

"Wow. Sounds like the group's really meant a lot to you."

"Oh, totally." Aruni nodded emphatically. "I couldn't imagine my life now without the girls and our little get-togethers. And pretty soon, you'll feel the same. Not that you've got much choice in the matter." She laughed. "As the owner of the former P-HOP/soon-to-be-Bliss, you're pretty much already inducted into the club." Aruni chucked her on the arm in a congratulatory way. "Pauline's going to want to pass the torch on to you sooner or later. She's not getting any younger, and I know she sees you as the carrier of her legacy. You'll be running the whole show in no time. But don't worry," she continued bracingly, perhaps sensing a bit of Sera's hesitance. "You're gonna love the Back Room Babes, and the women are all going to love you, too. I can't say enough about what it's done for me to be a part of our little federation. Socially, spiritually, and especially sexually. It's a real source of *transformational opportunities,* you know? And isn't that what life's all about?"

A few weeks ago, Sera might have looked askance at that. But it occurred to her that, cloaked in New Age-ry as it sounded, "transformational opportunities" were *exactly* what she was after—what she was, in fact, betting her future on. "Well, ah, yes, I guess it is..."

"Anyhow, our next get-together is right around the corner," Aruni continued blithely. "You'll be there, right?"

"Isn't it a bit soon for the Back Room Babes to be meeting again?" Sera asked, surprised.

"Soon?" Aruni said, a mystified expression crossing her mobile features.

"For Pauline—after losing Hortencia, I mean."

Aruni clicked her tongue, expression clearing with understanding. "Such a senseless thing," she murmured. "They didn't have to part that way. Two stubborn personalities like that, though... it was bound to end in heartache."

Sera raised a brow inwardly. *Odd way to put it...,* she thought, but she couldn't argue Pauline's stubbornness, and from what she'd heard, Hortencia had been more than a match for her feisty aunt. What it had to do with Hortencia's passing, however, she couldn't fathom. "Er..."

"Seriously, it'll do Pauline good to get back in the swing of things," Aruni pronounced, barreling through Sera's bemusement. "And I know it would cheer her up to introduce you to our little club. So... you in?"

"I doubt I can make it," Sera hedged. "I'm going back to New York tomorrow. I have a lot of things to wrap up back East. I'll be packing and shipping not only my personal stuff but my catering and baking equipment as well. At least, what I don't leave behind for my assistant Carrie," she amended. "Then I have to deal with my apartment, and there are a lot of people I need to say good-bye to. I'll be gone all week, up until Friday," she said apologetically. "Maybe next time."

"Oh, that's okay," Aruni said brightly. "Friday means you'll be back just in time. And it's a lucky thing, too, because believe me, you don't wanna miss what's going on next week! It's Zozobra, and there's no better way to experience Santa Fe than to rock out at the big Z-fest."

"Zozo-wha?" Sera asked.

Aruni just shook her head mysteriously. "It's something you have to see to believe. I don't want to spoil the surprise. Just meet us at P-HOP—well, I guess it's Bliss now—next Friday evening and you'll find out. Oh, and bring your dancing shoes." She gave a little shoulder shimmy, as if she just couldn't wait. "Ooh, here comes Janice with dessert. Awesome." Aruni bounced in her seat, utterly enamored with the world.

Sera had the urge to lean over the booth and give her new friend a squeeze for being so cute, but she contented herself with a smile and mental promise to herself to bake the yogini something special, first chance she got. *Perhaps a matcha green tea mousse, with a white chocolate base and a marzipan yoga teacher performing warrior pose on the top...* Her mind drifted happily with sweet visions of custom confections until the reality of their dessert landed with a clink of china and the rattle of a fork before her widening eyes.

Pie.

Glorious pie.

Her nose told the tale before her taste buds even got involved. Tangy, sweet, and buttery engaged in a naughty *ménage à trois* upon her senses, first wafting to her nostrils in sinful delight, then seducing her eyes as Sera took in the airy lightness of the crisscross crust, the perfect crystallization of sugar and caramelized filling oozing through the latticework cracks. And when she *tasted* the pie...The things the flavors did to her tongue were positively unspeakable—and utterly unforgettable.

Mama, I'm home, Sera thought, and dug in with a will.

After the ludicrously nummy slices of heaven they proceeded to consume—strawberry rhubarb for Sera and cherry with crumble crust for Aruni—Sera thought perhaps she'd need not just dancing shoes but a full day at the gym to work off the unexpected midday calories. More important, she had decided that pie had to be on her bakery's menu. She rubbed her tummy and sighed.

"I forget how awesome a good old-fashioned slice of pie can be," Sera commented. "Pastry chefs in New York are always trying to one-up one another with new techniques. I've seen cooks concocting desserts with everything from liquid nitrogen to cigarette-smoked salt crystals. Half the time you can't figure out whether you're taking a bite or dismantling a fusion reactor, at some of the places I've worked. But this... This really hit the spot. The crust isn't quite as flaky as mine," she said ruminatively as she stared at the last delectable bite on her fork, "but man, that filling is just ridiculously tasty. It's not easy to get rhubarb to cooperate this nicely, the way it just practically melts under your fork. And the strawberries. *Damn,* they're good. So fresh, so tender. I wonder if I could have a word with their pastry chef..."

Aruni choked on a sip of her decaf tea. "Um, I don't think you'd want to do that."

"Really?" Sera asked, popping the last morsel in her mouth and closing her eyes to savor the taste. "Why not?"

"Well, I happen to know they get their pies from an outside vendor and he... well, he's not..."

"Not what?" Sera asked when Aruni seemed reluctant to continue.

"Not... er... nice," Aruni finished lamely. Sera could tell she was uncomfortable bad-mouthing anyone, *farkackte* ex-boyfriends notwithstanding.

"Is that right?" Sera mused, thinking of the pastry chefs she knew. Contrary to popular opinion, bakers weren't all sugar and spice. Some of them were fire and brimstone. A bit of an attitude in a fellow pastry chef wasn't going to put her off. "Well, I'd still like to meet the guy, talk shop for a couple minutes. Maybe I can get his name and number from the waitress..." She started to look around for Janice.

Aruni looked alarmed, but she didn't try to stop Sera. "I guess it can't do any harm, but don't say you haven't been warned. The guy's on a really *bad* karmic streak. But I suppose it may be your only chance to get a taste of these pies again, if what I heard from Janice is true."

Sera arched an eyebrow in question.

"Janice told me the pie whisperer is getting fired—that's one of the reasons I suggested we come here particularly, so we wouldn't miss our last chance to get 'em. Apparently, he's insulted one too many customers, and the management is sick of soothing ruffled feathers all the time. He has a bakery nearby and he caters out of it, but he keeps scaring all the customers away, and now most of the local restaurant managers are tired of his attitude, too. I heard his whole operation's shutting down. Everything's going up for auction next week."

"Huh," Sera mused. "This pie whisperer wouldn't be named Malcolm, by any chance?" she inquired.

"Yeah, how'd you know, girl?" Aruni was round-eyed. "You psychic or something?"

Sera shook her head. *Santa Fe really is just a small town at heart, I guess.* "Asher told me about a restaurant auction he thought I should check out. Said I should look for a guy named Malcolm, but not to take anything he says too personally."

"Yup, that's the one, I'm pretty sure. Malcolm the Meanie's putting it all up for sale." Aruni shrugged. Then her eyes twinkled as her train of thought switched rails. "So I guess you've met our sexy landlord, eh?"

"He's your landlord, too?" Sera didn't have to ask if they were talking about the same person.

"Asher owns our whole *placita,* pretty much. At least, the buildings are his, and he leases all the shops."

"Wow," Sera said. "He must be well off." Sexy, wildly talented, *and* wealthy. Women must hunt him down with a spear.

Aruni nodded. "I heard he was a world-class whatchamacall it, that instrument-making word... loo, lute-something, back in Israel."

"Luthier," Sera said. "I had to ask him what it meant, too."

"Well, it must be pretty lu-*crative,* because Pauline told me one time that his violins used to go for, like, fifty K a pop."

Sera smiled to herself, noting Aruni sounded a bit more hard-nosed Chicagoan than woo-woo Santa Fe head. "Wonder why he gave it up," she mused.

"I heard it had to do with his wife," Aruni said, looking suitably somber. "We think he's probably divorced, or maybe even a widower. None of us really knows the story, but we all suspect there's some terrible tragedy there."

Sera felt a pang, thinking of what Asher must have lost. Given the way he'd reacted in his shop earlier when she'd asked if Lupe was his wife, she had to agree—something awful had happened in Asher's past. "Who is 'we'?" Sera wanted to know.

"Oh, us Back Roomies. Asher comes up in conversation at our shindigs quite a lot, as you can imagine. I mean, *seriously...* " Aruni drew the word out like a veritable Valley Girl. "Who *wouldn't* have sexual fantasies about that guy? I don't care if you're happily married, gay, or stark stone dead, one smile from Asher Wolf and your libido will sit up and howl." Aruni flapped her hand as if to cool it off.

You ain't just whistling Dixie, Sera thought. But she declined to offer an opinion on the subject. She had decided she liked Aruni rather a lot, but she wasn't quite ready to start sharing girlish confidences with the other woman yet. She wasn't the type who dished about her love life with anyone.

That's because there's nothing to *dish up, other than a heaping plate of failure with a side of humiliation,* Sera's inner critic reminded her. In her mind's eye, she could hear Blake's scornful laughter, and her mouth went dry with vestigial longing for a drink. *Down, girl,* she ordered the little fiend that lurked in the dark corners of her mind, always ready to prey on moments of self-doubt. *Time to get my butt to a meeting; remind myself I'm two thousand miles and a world of recovery away from all that negativity.*

"Not that Asher pays the slightest attention to our mooning over him," Aruni went on, unaware of Sera's morose musings. "He's, like, the nicest, sweetest guy, and no way is he into guys or anything, but I've never seen him notice a woman in that way. Not even *Lupe,*" Aruni said, making the name sound as if she'd scraped it off her shoe. "And if *that* hussy can't get a rise out of him, with all her cleavage plumping and ass wiggling, I doubt the rest of us have much of a shot. Whatever it was that happened to him back in Israel, it really did a number on him." Aruni shook her curly head feelingly. "But hey, that's what a lot of us come to Santa Fe for. To ditch the past and find our second chance. Well, those of us who didn't follow our *putz* of a boyfriend out here." She laughed unself-consciously. "Oh, I never asked. What's *your* man sitch, Sera? You married? Dating? Getting over someone?"

Sera grimaced. "No, there isn't anyone special in my life, and there hasn't been for a long time. Kind of got my buns burned, if you know what I mean."

Aruni nodded sympathetically.

"Right now, I'm really more focused on getting my bakery up and running than on getting laid," Sera continued. "But please," she hastened, "don't tell that to Pauline. She'd have a spazz if she knew I wasn't keen on finding someone to hop in the sack with." Serafina flushed, lowering her voice to an agonized whisper. "You can't know what it was like, growing up with Aunt Pauline always pushing me to be more 'out there,' as if getting some would solve all my problems..."

"I hear ya, sister. I love Pauline like she was my *own* aunt, but seriously, I can't keep up with that dame. Tell you what. You keep me in sweet stuff, and I'll keep your sex life—or lack thereof—our little secret."

The two women high-fived across the Formica table. "Deal."

Chapter Seven

"I'm so glad you're not giving up on the orgasms, dear."

Serafina started, face instantly flaming. She glanced around to see if anyone had heard Pauline's overly loud comment, but the aisles of the Whole Heart supermarket were free from tittering eavesdroppers. *Could Pauline actually know?* Sera thought with a spurt of panic. Visions of what Pauline would say—and do—if she knew the truth about her niece sent tendrils of dread down Sera's spine. Then she relaxed a bit as realization dawned. Her aunt was talking about tonight's meeting of the Back Room Babes, and Sera's agreement to allow the club to continue despite the shop's changing hands.

I'm just groggy from the flight, she reassured herself. She'd only returned late last night, and the supermarket was their first stop this morning, since Sera needed some basics for the house. More than that, she'd wanted to scope out the grocery situation and get a feel for what everyday life would really be like in Santa Fe. The answer, she'd already decided, was *A-okay.* Sure, Whole Heart was wildly pretentious. Pauline liked to call it "Whole Paycheck" and mutter about how much better the place had been—how much more authentic—when it was still just a local grocery called Wild Oats. It seemed pretty authentic to Sera—at least, as authentic as earnest, sustainable supermarkets could get. It smelled like a health food shop, the dry air carrying a whiff of the musty, tangy scent that always reminded her of the inside of a vitamin bottle, commingled with the odors of homemade soaps, bulk cereals that tasted like hamster feed, and always, always, the faint hint of patchouli that emanated from no evident source. She figured it must be the echoes of generations of hippies who had settled into middle-aged complacency but couldn't quite leave behind their bohemian youth, wandering the aisles in search of enlightenment and lower cholesterol.

While you could get any kind of spelt flour, seventeen varieties of organic low-foaming shampoo, or a free-range bison steak complete with birth certificate and pictures of said buffalo frolicking on the prairie as a calf, nowhere in evidence were such simple pleasures as Oreos and Diet Coke. For that, Pauline had assured her, her needs could be amply supplied at the local Albertsons. But for the kind of yogurt Pauline preferred—goat's milk with locally gathered honey (great for vaginal balance, if Serafina knew what she meant)—and granola that would convince Sera that granola actually tasted good, nowhere but this supermarket, with its cool sea foam décor and wide, well-stocked aisles, would do. Sera had to admit, compared to the cramped, tiny-carted, uptight grocery stores she'd frequented in Manhattan, this was a pretty sweet deal, Oreos or no Oreos.

Pauline was wheeling their cart through the deli section, passing displays of farmer's cheese and sourdough bread that made Sera's empty stomach rumble longingly as she followed her aunt toward the dairy case at the back. Today Pauline had braided her rough-and-tumble hair into a long rope, just a few frizzy strands escaping to frame her lined but lively face. Her T-shirt invited readers to "Ask me how I DO IT," and Sera was grateful the accompanying diagram was covered by the gray cashmere cardigan she was sporting—a gift from Sera last Christmas that already looked like it had seen nearly as much love as its owner. Her skirt was a cheerful red broomstick affair, threaded with silver tinsel and chiming with the little Tibetan bells Pauline loved so much.

"You're still serious about keeping the back room the way it is, right, kiddo?" Pauline persisted as she scanned the yogurt selection. "I mean, I'd hate to have to tell the gals that tonight's their last get-together. Their climactic moment, if you get what I'm saying." She gave a burlesque-worthy pelvic thrust that set her skirt bells chiming.

Man, she is really attached to those rubber weenies, Sera thought. *She's, like, totally fixated. Maybe it's her way of coping with her loss?*

"Well, we'll see how it goes, I guess." Sera shrugged, dubiously eyeing a shelf of flavored soy products that promised to revolutionize her coffee experience. "I'm mainly going to be concentrating on the front of the store, to tell you the truth, and leave the back room to its own devices."

"Devices." Heh, heh.

Oh, good lord, was she going to have Beavis and Butthead chuckling moronically in her mind for the rest of her life? *No, silly,* said the little voice in her head. *Just for as long as you run a "pleasure enhancement" establishment that's chock full of instruments you can't even look at without giving yourself a case of rosacea.*

"There's so much to work out before I can open Bliss, I haven't had much of a chance to think about how we'll feature the P-HOP leftovers," Sera continued. "I still have to interview contractors after I check out those secondhand ovens Asher was telling me about at the auction today. And change over my driver's license, apply for my small business license, meet with the accountant...and I've just barely gotten things settled in New York." She sighed, overwhelmed by the scope of her to-do list, still processing the magnitude of what she'd just done in severing ties with her past. In her head, Maggie's voice chimed in. *One day at a time, Sera. Sufficient unto the day are the troubles thereof.*

"How'd that go, kid?" Pauline wanted to know. "You feelin' okay, now that you've taken the plunge and said sayonara to the Big Apple?"

Sera slung her arm across her aunt's shoulders and gave her a squeeze as they piloted the cart leisurely through the refrigerated section, feeling a wave of affection for the woman who had raised her. "I'm fine, Aunt Paulie. Excited actually. And I got a lot accomplished. I'm really looking forward to getting set up here."

It was true. Sure, she'd still have some logistics to work out back East, but she'd been lucky—her assistant Carrie had offered to take over the lease on her loft, and wanted to carry on the catering business on her own. In fact, Carrie had been quite keen to grab Sera's rent-stabilized apartment, claiming that since the majority of the baking had been done on the premises, it just made sense to move in. It might have been a little *Single White Female* for Sera if she hadn't been so comfortable with Carrie—and if she'd cared more about what she was leaving behind. Since Sera had stopped taking commissions for her signature cakes and confections, and had been subsisting on selling more standard dessert fare to local eateries, it hadn't been too much of a hardship handing over the reins.

Indeed, she'd found herself eager to box up her belongings and get out of Dodge while the getting was good. The minute she'd arrived back at her Tribeca apartment, everything from the heaping trash bags piled outside the building oozing noxious sludge to the jackhammering of the condo complex racing upward to blot out her last iota of natural light had assaulted her senses in a way they never used to. Or perhaps she'd just never realized her nerves were slowly but constantly being gnawed at by New York's frenetic pace, like rats nesting in her neural wiring. She'd immediately started looking forward to her next whiff of dry desert air. The only hard part had been saying her good-byes to Margaret and the rest of her fellowship friends. Sera wasn't too broken up over it, though—these were friends she knew she'd keep for life, and distance, while it would bring the pang of separation, could do no lasting damage to the affection they had for one another.

As for the rest, she didn't think she'd start missing life back East anytime soon.

Not when there was Santa Fe waiting for her. The spaciousness here was doing something unexpected to her consciousness. Sera could feel an opening, a widening crack in her defenses, as if her chest were expanding and warm sunlight was pouring in. After a year of slow, painful recovery, clawing her way back from the brink and getting to the point where she did a fair imitation of a human most days, it felt like she was finally ready to blossom into something more. "A bridge back to life," was what AA had promised, and Serafina Wilde was ready to start living.

Smiling, Sera realized she was happier than she'd been in a long time. Still, she found it strange that Pauline seemed nearly as chipper, especially after spending a lonely week packing up her life partner's personal items to make room for Sera's stuff. The two older women hadn't, to Sera's astonishment, actually been living together despite their three-year relationship, but Hortencia had had plenty of stuff over at Pauline's. Despite Sera's offers to be there to help and support her, Pauline had resolved to do the work alone, which Sera found odd given her desperate plea for Sera to fly out here only a week earlier. Before she'd left, she'd squeezed a promise out of a reluctant Pauline to think about what she wanted to do to commemorate her life with Hortencia. But if she'd been entertaining any such serious thoughts over the past week, it wasn't evident from either her demeanor or her conversation. Her aunt seemed nearly as jaunty and animated as she'd ever been. Sera took a deep breath. It was time to collect on that promise and make her aunt face the music.

"Um, Pauline, I don't want to press, but I have to ask. Have you given any more thought yet to how you'd like to memorialize Hortencia?"

Pauline looked chagrined. At first Sera thought it was either distress over her question or the price of the $4 yogurt she held in her hand. However, Pauline was transfixed neither by the sticker on the container nor Sera's query, but by something over Sera's shoulder.

"Yes, Pauline," an acerbic voice said. "How exactly *were* you planning to memorialize me?"

Sera spun around.

A fluffy, plump little grandmother type wearing a beige canvas fisherman's cap, sensible trousers, and a cozy crocheted vest over her Coldwater Creek blouse was leaning with her elbows braced on the bar of her shopping cart, not ten feet away. A pair of shearling-lined Merrell demi-clogs graced her tidy feet, and her hair was an appealingly short halo of white cotton candy under her hat. The only jarring element was the total lack of twinkle in Grandma's chocolate brown eyes.

"Serafina Wilde, I presume?" the woman asked when Pauline just stood there, stock-still and uncharacteristically speechless.

Sera suddenly knew who she was. Pauline's discomfited expression, her odd behavior since Sera had come out to Santa Fe, her difficulty speaking of her life partner in the past tense...

"Hortencia?" she asked incredulously. "Are you Hortencia Alvarez?" Her gaze whipped back and forth between the two older ladies.

"In the flesh, if Pauline hasn't got me dead and buried already," said Hortencia, shooting a pointed glance at Pauline.

And Pauline Wilde actually blushed. Sera could hardly credit it, having never witnessed her aunt embarrassed in the nearly three decades she'd known her, but yes, her weathered cheeks went distinctly ruddy, even as her jaw worked nervously and her eyes darted around for escape.

"Pauline..." she asked. "What's going on here? You said..."

The indomitable feminist within resurfaced. "Well, she's dead to *me,* and that's what counts." Pauline sniffed, crossing her arms under her braless breasts. She refused to look Hortencia in the eye. For that matter, she wasn't exactly meeting her niece's gaze either.

"But you said...you asked me to come out here because...," Sera sputtered. "I mean, you said you were devastated and you needed my help..."

"I *did* need your help, kiddo," Pauline muttered. "And I *was* pretty broken up after Horsey and I split up. I didn't lie—not about that part anyway."

Sera didn't know how to respond to that kind of logic. But Hortencia did.

Hortencia straightened, placing her fists on her comfortable hips. It might have been Sera's imagination, but she thought the woman's eyes had softened just a teensy bit at Pauline's confession of distress. "You, Pauline Wilde, are *una mujer loca,*" she scolded. "I can't believe you told your niece I was dead! For heaven's sake, my yarn store's just two streets up from yours. We were sure to run into each other sooner or later. What were you thinking? Just because I wouldn't marry you..." She trailed off, shaking her head and pursing her withered lips. But Sera thought there was a hint of a smile there.

Her mind reeled. Pauline, married? Her independent, free love–espousing aunt had never shown the slightest inclination to be tied down—at least in a non-S&M sense. Committing to just one person—sexually or emotionally—had never been her style, despite how she'd seemed to mellow since she'd met Hortencia. Moreover, the actual institution of marriage, she'd argued, was an antiquated tradition that no liberated woman needed in this day and age. In fact, she'd hectored Sera against its perils repeatedly over the years—not that Sera had been in any danger of being asked. Watching Pauline's expression as she tried to deflect her erstwhile lover's ire, it was obvious to Serafina that her aunt had finally encountered The One. Politics and belief systems be damned. Pauline Wilde was a woman head over heels in love.

"It wasn't 'just because' you refused my proposal—a proposal I worked on very hard, by the way," Pauline flared, tossing her yogurt into her cart with such force that Sera winced, fearing it would splatter. "That hot air balloon cost money, damn it. And do you know how fast a diamond ring travels falling—or should I say *being tossed*—from that altitude? You could have caved in somebody's head if we hadn't been hovering over the goddamn Rio Grande Gorge at the time. As it is, you probably choked a fish. But I'm not angry *that* you refused, you nitwit. It was *why* you refused. And if you can't 'fess up to it..."

"God *damn* it, Pauline," Hortencia shouted back, her own apple cheeks ripening to red, "will you stop with that nonsense about me wanting to sleep with men?!" She no longer seemed the least bit tickled. "I told you I'm done with all that, and I meant it!"

Sera was abruptly aware they were causing quite a scene in the refrigerated section. The tittering onlookers she'd earlier feared had materialized with a vengeance upon hearing the commotion, peeping out from behind cereal boxes and gawking across butcher counters. Suddenly she had the desire to be very, very far away. Above all things in this life, she wanted to stay the ever-loving hell out of her aunt's sex life.

"I'm gonna let you two duke it out," she said, backing away slowly into an aisle that advertised teas for every complaint from "feminine distress" to "involuntary astral projection." *Good thing I followed Aunt Paulie out here in the rental car, or I'd be marooned at the organic O.K. Corral.* "I'll be late for the auction if I don't get a move-on, so I'll just be going, and catch up with you back home later, okay?"

Pauline spared a nod, but didn't look away from her standoff with her beloved.

"Hortencia, it was, er, nice to meet you. I'm, ah, very glad to hear you're alive, and, um..." Sera stuttered to a halt, stymied for a socially correct exit.

"Thank you, dear," said Hortencia. Her gaze remained locked with

Pauline's. "I'll see you again soon. Tonight, in fact, since I'll be attending the Back Room Babes' get-together as usual."

"You wouldn't dare!" cried Pauline. She looked ready to swipe the contents of the dairy case clean to the floor. "The BRBs are *my* club, and I say who the members are. And you... you lying, man-loving hussy, are officially disinvited!"

"You just try and stop me from showing up, you hypocritical old harpy," Hortencia flashed back at her.

She had more to say—a lot more. But Sera had already fled to the safety of a row of esoteric canned goods, and was making a beeline for the door as the argument raged behind her.

Was I the only one Pauline lied to about this? I must have been—she'd never have gotten away with such a whopper in a town this small. Now Aruni's nonchalance at the diner made so much more sense. So did Pauline's hinky behavior this past week.

Well, hell.

Sera had a great deal to think about. The very reason she'd come out here—to comfort her grieving aunt—had just been called into question. But there was no going back now. Santa Fe, it seemed, still had a few surprises to lob her way. She'd known it was a magical place, but a full-on resurrection?

Nice one, she complimented her new home as she stepped out into the sunlight and headed for her car. *I truly did not see that coming.*

Chapter Eight

Apparently I'm destined to live in the land of grumpy people today, Sera thought as she tiptoed around the edges of the pie whisperer's going-out-of-business-sale. *So much for "enchantment," I guess.*

Still stunned at seeing Hortencia rise from the dead, she'd found her way to the little hole-in-the-wall bake shop run by Malcolm McLeod with some difficulty. (Santa Fe, she'd discovered, justly deserved its reputation as a town laid out by a drunken monk riding backward on a mule.) Tucked away at the edge of what had once been a dusty office park on Cerrillos Road, but now hosted an ersatz Chinese restaurant and a dog-grooming parlor as well as the bakery, his place was unimposing from the outside, barely deigning to advertise beyond a small sign that read "Best Pies." The windows were unwashed, as though to shield the interior from customers' too-curious gazes, and the token awning was faded and fraying. Inside, there was little charm, just a display case that doubled as a take-out counter and a cash register up front, no seats for waiting customers or even pictures on the walls. In the back, where the sale was about to start, the environment was all stainless steel business. The *atmosphere,* however, was borderline toxic.

The man of the hour was following what few customers had come to his auction about with a gimlet glare, clenching his fists with barely suppressed ire every time someone so much as peeked their snoot in a pantry or hefted a pie pan to check for dings or scratches. The guy looked positively murderous.

But it was worth enduring a little sourness. McLeod had some seriously state-of-the-art ovens. *Ah, Blodgett,* Sera thought. *You may not look flashy, but you've sure got it where it counts.* And Mr. McLeod had a *lot* of what counted—at least to Sera. His chest freezers and reach-ins were immaculate—and exactly what she needed. His convection ovens and industrial range showed the patina of use, but also the cleanliness of the well-maintained machines they were—not to mention, they were truly top of the line. His mixers were displayed next to every conceivable desirable attachment, and some Sera had rarely seen outside of a KitchenAid catalog. No dough roller, she noted. Too proud, probably, and she didn't blame him for distrusting the damn things—horror stories abounded about crush injuries and maimed cooks. Plus, they took the precision, the intuition out of baking. (Still, she'd make an exception for a nice fondant sheeter, if she ever did wedding cakes again. Back when she'd had her custom cake orders piling up by the dozen, having one of those babies had really saved her bacon.)

He had bun racks, worktables, baker's scales, dough proofers, and more—all in tip-top condition and clean to the point of making one's teeth ache. And his bakery cases—both dry display and refrigerated models—looked like they'd just rolled off the factory floor. New, they'd have run her upwards of $6,000 a pop. Used, Malcolm would be damn lucky to take in half that. Problem was, he didn't look any too eager to part with a single piece, despite the starting bid stickers on most of the bakery's fixtures, and the eviction notice glued to his front door. Indeed, the small, Santa-bellied Scotsman seemed set to slap the questing fingers of the first person who dared open an oven door for closer inspection.

Boom!

Some fool with a death wish had just sent an unwary elbow across a counter, knocking a rolling pin to the floor. Apparently, this was the ice cream on Malcolm's pie à la mode.

"Out, out, out, OUUUUUUUT!"

Except it sounded more like "Oot, oot, oot, oooooooot!"

Serafina smothered a giggle. And while the red-faced Scotsman chased the half-dozen or so other prospective buyers out of his joint, flapping his stained apron and shaking his fist, she stayed where she stood, leaning hipshot against one of his chest freezers. Swallowing chuckles, she observed the man she'd just decided was going to come work for her.

With his waist-length, white wavy hair and long handlebar mustache, he could have been Arlo Guthrie's twin. However, Serafina very much doubted Arlo would've chosen to sport Army surplus combat fatigues beneath a kitchen apron that looked like it had seen action in Da Nang. Nor would Arlo have condoned Malcolm's Rambo-style bandanna, she suspected, though the paunch was probably just *okay, maaan.*

Malcolm spotted Serafina.

"What're ye still doing here? Didn't ye hear me say 'out'?" He took a menacing step toward Sera. But Serafina Wilde was a veteran of Blake Austin's kitchens—not to mention his bed—and she wasn't afraid.

"It's not going to be much of an auction with only one bidder," she pointed out. She crossed her legs at the ankle and leaned more comfortably against the freezer.

"*One* bidder? I'll have *none* of ye! I'll rot in debtor's prison before I'll sell my beautiful ovens to a flock of philistines like ye. Now get gone, ye sodding vulture, before I call the cops." He swooped down with surprising grace for such a stout man and swept up the toppled rolling pin, examining it for damage.

Sera found the notion of debtor's prison quaint. Compared to the modern hells of bankruptcy court and predatory debt collectors, such a place might be preferable.

"Hard to part with it all, huh?"

McLeod looked up from the rolling pin, suspicion beetling his caterpillar brows. "What would ye know about it?"

"I lost everything that mattered to *me* not too long ago. I thought I'd never cook again, and it nearly killed me."

"What're ye on about, ye loon? Ye hardly look old enough to reach the back burner on the stove, let alone cook on it." If he'd scoffed any harder, he'd risk hocking up a lung.

Sera stuck out her hand, ignoring the gibe. "I'm Serafina Wilde. I'm opening a new bakery here in town, and I want what you've got. Including *you,* Mr. McLeod." She paused a beat, enjoying the way his jaw dropped. "I'd like you to come work for me."

"Are ye daft?" Malcolm couldn't have looked more offended if she'd compared his pies unfavorably with Mrs. Smith's. "Work for ye? As what? I'm no dish washer, and I ain't bussing tables at no sissified, ginned-up Starbucks—ye can forget about that right now!"

Serafina took this for the bluster it was. "It's nothing like that. What I need is an experienced opener—someone to prep the goods and set the doughs rising before the rest of the staff gets in."

"Och, aye, I ken ye now. Someone to do the *real* work, while ye get yer beauty sleep and roll in just in time to put sprinkles on a few wee cupcakes and call yerself a baker."

He was really working hard to offend her. But Sera saw past it to the scarred, *scared* man beneath. "Mr. McLeod, let me put it to you straight." She leaned forward, grabbing the rolling pin out of his hand and prodding one pointy end into his paunch. She couldn't help feeling like she was poking the Pillsbury Doughboy, though she wasn't likely to elicit any giggles here. "You're a man out of options. From what I hear, you're practically blacklisted in this town. No one will work with you; you've alienated just about every eating establishment in Santa Fe—and given how many restaurants this little city's got, that's no mean feat." She poked him again. "Your place is out of business, you probably owe thousands on the rent and the fixtures, and let's face it . . . you aren't getting any younger." Poke, poke. "You've got just one thing going for you." She plunked the pin down on the freezer's top.

"Aye, and what's that?"

"You're probably the single best pie maker on the planet."

There was a moment of silence.

McLeod's face went just a wee bit ruddy, if she wasn't mistaken, but his eyes glared pure suspicion as he sized Sera up more closely. Then he huffed, chewing his mustaches and rocking on the balls of his feet. "Tell me something I *dinna* know."

"Oh, not that there isn't room for improvement, mind you," Sera went on, biting back a smile. "We should talk about your crust. I noticed you used lard instead of shortening when I tried the pie at the Sunshine—and lord love you for it—but I think the flour was somewhat inferior. Have you tried King Arthur Fl—"

"They won't sell ta me," he grumbled, cutting her off as if her suggestion were so obvious as to be offensive. "I *know* they're the best, but after I sent them that letter about their cheap, sleazy shortcut of a pie filler, I wound up on their no-sell list. Sure, I could've found a way around it—I could've bought what I needed on the sly—but it was the *principle* of the thing."

Must have been a hell of a letter. She smiled inwardly, picturing the scandalized expression on the face of the nice customer service lady in Norwich, Vermont, upon opening Malcolm's vituperative missive. "Principle gets you in trouble a lot, doesn't it?" Sera observed.

Malcolm's expression fell somewhere between aggrieved and caught out. He crossed his arms and said nothing, but he looked less likely to shove her out the door than he had.

"What if I told you you'd never have to compromise if you came to work for me? I wouldn't tell you how to make your pies, and you'd do most of your work alone, before anyone else gets in. No human interaction, unless *you* seek it out."

"What's the catch?" Malcolm wanted to know.

Serafina became all business. "You need to know a few things, Mr. McLeod. First, I'm damn good at what I do—just like you. I don't fuck around or cut corners when it comes to pastries. I intend to bake and serve the single finest desserts this town has ever seen, and I'm not going to let anyone's ego get in the way of that. I'm no novice—I've been working in kitchens since I was eighteen, and cooked with assholes that make you look like goddamn Mother Teresa. It's going to be *my* place, *my* rules, and *my* menu. All excepting your pies. Over that, you'll keep total control—name, fame, and recipes. Got it?"

Malcolm had begun to lose his set-in scowl at her first profanity, and by the end of her spiel, he had cracked open a full-fledged, albeit rusty grin.

"Aye, I got it, lassie."

"You in?"

His hesitation was briefer than Serafina would have bet. He must be truly desperate.

"Aye, I'm in."

"Good. 'Cause I don't have time to spend all day coddling your artistic sensibilities. I've got to find a contractor and get the ball rolling. I want my grand opening to happen before I hit thirty. That is, *if* we can agree on a price for these fixtures." She waved indicatively. "I'll take the lot if you can arrange transportation—and you don't try to gouge me."

"Might be we could come to an understanding," Malcolm conceded. He pulled an order pad from the pocket of his apron, along with the stub of a pencil. He scribbled a figure on the paper, tore it off, and passed it to Sera with a flourish.

Sera examined his curiously neat schoolboy writing. As the figure registered, she paled, gulped, and snatched the pencil from him. She crossed out the number in two decisive strokes. In her own considerably messier handwriting, she scrawled a counteroffer.

His face grew apoplectic.

Hers grew pugnacious.

The pencil and paper flew back and forth several more times. In the end, Sera was left wanting a cigarette and perhaps a nice Thai massage, but they'd arrived at a figure that wouldn't bankrupt her.

She felt a wave of relief she worked hard not to show. She was running on a tight budget as it was. Her own savings were modest, and opening an eatery was probably one of the riskiest, most expensive gambles a small businesswoman could undertake. Pauline had been unbelievably generous, offering not just to pay the rent until she got on her feet, but to underwrite her initial expenses and construction costs, in return for being one of the principles of the business and a guarantee that she'd always have a job at the bakery (and get to make her own hours). Sera had known Pauline had money, but never really grasped exactly how lucrative her "Ourgasm" movement and the attendant book sales had been for her aunt. Since the seventies, Pauline had invested wisely, and she swore she could afford to take a flyer on a new venture without risking her retirement. Still, even knowing Pauline could afford the "investment," as she called it, she didn't like to gamble with her aunt's money. Any way she could minimize costs, she'd take, and gladly.

"Okay, Mr. McLeod, seems you've got a deal, provided this figure includes delivery."

He nodded. "Aye, though now ye're breakin' my back as well as my balls," he grumbled.

"The ball-breaking's a freebie," Sera said, giving Malcolm a cheeky grin as she turned to go. "I've got to be going. I have to start interviewing builders or your equipment's not going to do me much good anytime soon."

Malcolm's face took on a cunning expression. "Need a contractor, do ye?"

"Why, you know someone?"

"Know someone?" His chest puffed proudly. "Lass, I *am* someone. Licensed and bonded, and all."

"Bullshit."

"'Tis true, though ye may not credit it. I did all the work on this place m'self. Had a lot of trades in my day. Helps, when ye've had a few differences with folk here and there."

Sera took a closer look at the man she was putting so much trust in. She'd place him in his early sixties, with hands that bore scars and calluses that could have come from construction work rather than baking. Beneath the extra weight his pies had put on him, he looked solid, built like a bull. She could see him exchanging his apron for a tool belt. But there was no way to tell just by looking if he was as honest as he was strong. Sure, Asher had put in a good word for him, but how well did she know *Asher?* "Got references?"

"We-ell, that depends on what ye mean when ye say references," he hedged. "Ye want to see examples of my work, I've those a'plenty—and customers that'll swear by it. Ye want to hear some aspersions cast on my character... well, ye'll likely hear those, too, and from some of those same clients."

Sera considered it. "I'll take their names. Meet me at my place Tuesday afternoon, and we'll talk about installing your fixtures and supplies, and whether you'll be doing the work. I'll have made my decision by then." Sera passed Malcolm the address, and he passed her the names and numbers of several clients he'd hastily scribbled down. She'd spend the intervening time making calls and comparing contractors. She might have a good feeling about the irascible Mr. McLeod, but she wasn't stupid.

"Ye're new in town, am I right?"

She nodded. She must still have some New York clinging to her.

"How'd ye come to hear about me then?"

"Oh, my new landlord, Asher Wolf, told me I should come."

Without a word, Malcolm snatched the slip of paper with the number scrawled on it out of Sera's surprised hand. He crossed the figure out and wrote something in its place. "Any friend of Asher Wolf is a friend of mine," he said gruffly. "Give ye a good deal on the construction work, too."

Sera looked at the number and her heart did a happy little boogie. "One more thing, Mr. McLeod, before we seal the deal," she cautioned.

"What's that, lass?"

"When you come on Tuesday, bring pie. No pie, no deal."

Malcolm's guffaw followed her out the door.

"Another time, Highlander," Sera murmured, a broad smile lighting her face as she headed for her car.

Chapter Nine

There was something wrong with Sera's feet.

Or maybe they just knew something she didn't. No matter how she chivvied, cajoled, and commanded, they simply would not take her farther into the courtyard.

Seriously, feet? You're that afraid of a few sexually liberated ladies? C'mon, it's not like they're going to stage a production of The Rocky Horror Picture Show *and force you to play Janet.*

Or were they?

Since coming to Santa Fe, seeing the little plaza laid out before her had never failed to suffuse Sera with a feeling of excitement and satisfaction, but this evening her pleasure was tempered with anxiety. In fact, she'd approached *Placita de Suerte y Sueños* with something like dread. She'd spent the afternoon picturing the Back Room Babes' gathering as anything from a Roman orgy to a quilting bee—and unsure which would be worse. Pauline, damn her cowardly hide, had absented herself all afternoon—probably not wanting to face her niece's ire over her massive deception—so Sera had had no one to ask what to expect.

Thus, the stuck feet.

The *placita* seemed quiet, no ambushes or hazing rituals lying in wait for the unwary newcomer. Dusk was just falling, laving the adobe buildings in rose-colored light that painted them a deep mauve. A breeze murmured through the scattered shade trees and stroked Asher's extravagant botanical arrangements into a soft chorus of sighs. Even the earth mother fountain's cheerful splashing seemed hushed. The shops were shut down for the evening, but a blaze of warm light spilled out from P-HOP's front window, beckoning—or daring—Sera forward. A burst of feminine laughter erupted, Pauline's propped-open door funneling it out into the twilight.

Laughter is good, right? Just so long as they're not laughing at me. Sera took a deep breath, smoothed her outfit free of nonexistent wrinkles, and prepared to meet her new... well, she wasn't quite certain what they'd be. Friends? Clientele? Nemeses? *Feet, listen here,* she ordered. *We didn't get all dolled up to spend the evening rooted to the pavement. Besides, with those kicks on, you gotta want to show off a little, right?*

Not being sure whether the dancing shoes Aruni had recommended were meant for ballroom or mosh pit, she'd settled on a pair of calf-high black leather slouch boots that made her legs look good and had a low enough heel that she'd make it through whatever the night might bring. Since she was so short, she'd decided against a skirt, instead pairing them with leggings and a silky tunic in an azure hue that complemented her skin and lent the slate gray of her eyes a shimmering blue overtone. She'd belted the tunic with an obi-style leather wrap belt, feeling as though she were gearing up for battle. *Okay, I'm about as gussied up as I get. Hopefully these ladies don't eat me alive.*

Maybe I should have brought more treats, she worried. It never hurt to meet new people with a heaping handful of sugary delights, particularly since she no longer had the option of offering liquid social lubricants to smooth the way. Sera hefted the box full of Meyer lemon squares she'd whipped up this afternoon after her meeting with Malcolm. They might be humble, and hardly innovative, but nobody didn't like lemon bars. Three dozen ought to be plenty, unless the Back Room Babes were a veritable army. Granted, they *sounded* like quite a gathering, if the noise spilling from within P-HOP was anything to judge by, but the place couldn't fit more than a couple dozen full-grown adults, so...

"Wondering whether or not to go in?" an unmistakable voice called to her from beyond the fountain. Asher—once again wearing his adventurer's hat—leaned over his porch rail, keys in hand after having obviously just locked up his shop. Guadalupe, she was glad to see, was nowhere in evidence, and Sera very much doubted the snooty sales clerk was in Pauline's shop with the BRBs.

"Something like that." Asher's voice had unstuck her feet, and she ventured closer, fetching up at the base of his porch. Damn, he looked good. She hadn't seen her new landlord in a week—except in some rather embarrassing dreams—and he seemed to have grown exponentially more attractive in her absence. *Burnished blond hair: check. Lush lips: check. Glorious green eyes: double check.*

Asher pushed his hat back, like a real old-fashioned cowboy. But instead of spurs, it was the chain that held his keys that jingled as he stuffed them into his rear pocket. "Well, I can't speak from experience, as I have never penetrated the inner sanctum, but they seem like a harmless enough bunch."

Sera immediately began picturing Asher penetrating inner sanctums, and her cheeks reddened. *My God, this man makes me twelve years old again every time I see him.* And given that she was about as *talented* as a twelve-year-old when it came to romance, that was a road she'd best not tread. *I've got to get a grip. Find something innocuous to talk about, quick!* "I met your friend Malcolm today," she said, laying her box of goodies by her feet on the edge of the wooden porch, and noticing the pooches were nowhere to be seen tonight—Asher's doghouse was dark and silent. *Too bad,* she thought. *I'd love a little canine-inspired confidence right now.*

Asher noticed the direction of her glance. "Sascha and the pups are with a sitter. With Zozobra and all the festivities, there'll be too much going on in the streets tonight, and I don't want them that worked up."

The way he said "Zozobra" mesmerized Sera. It was as if his lips were weaving a spell, and its effect was to render her incapable of pondering anything but how those lips might taste and feel whispering similar mysteries against her mouth. Nuzzling the syllables against her neck...

"And speaking of excitable, how did you find our pie-making friend?" Asher cocked his head and studied her, as if wondering where her thoughts had roamed.

Sera snapped out of it as best she could. "I asked him to come work for me," she confessed.

Asher's laugh was a bark of delighted surprise. "You *are* an unusual woman, Serafina Wilde. But I think you may have done yourself a favor with that decision, though he may give you cause to question it now and then."

"Maybe we can talk more about it next week?" she asked. "I'm meeting with him on Tuesday afternoon, and before I do, I'd like to go over some details about the space and the construction."

"Not a problem. I'll drop by the store around noon."

"Thanks. Well, I should be going—I've been told I've got quite an evening ahead of me." She wanted to ask him if he was going to this mysterious Zozobra thing, too, but she didn't quite have the guts. His private life was really none of her business, and she didn't want him to get the idea that she was unduly interested in his comings and goings.

"Um, before I go, could I ask one more favor, Ash?"

"Name it."

Oh, lord. Those little crinkles around the corners of his eyes were going to be the death of her.

"Could you, ah, give me a push? I don't think I can move under my own steam."

Asher hopped over the porch rail in what she was beginning to think of as his signature move. Instead of a push, he did her one better—he took her shoulders in his large hands, squeezed gently, and captured her startled gray eyes with his depthless green gaze. "You're going to be the best of them, Bliss," he said.

And then he gave her a hug.

Sera was still wobbling on her feet long after he'd gone, enveloped in the afterglow of that embrace. She took a deep breath, perfumed with the blossoms of Asher's night-blooming flowers and the echo of his forged-metal scent. She felt strong, exhilarated—and yes, maybe just a little bit sexy.

All right, ladies, let's see what you got.

"Serafina!"

Now I know how Norm must have felt, coming into Cheers.

A rough dozen women were arrayed across the armchairs and atop the countertops of Pauline's House of Passion, but upon Sera's entrance, they straightened, raising glasses and whooping her name in a rousing chorus. Their boisterous clapping and waving filled the space as though they could boast twice their number. Out of the crowd stepped Pauline, resplendent in a flamingo pink belly-dancing outfit dangling scarves, coins, bells, and totems from every conceivable surface. Atop her head, in lieu of a veil, she'd plopped a Spaghetti Western–worthy sombrero. Yet despite the flamboyant getup, to Sera's eyes, Pauline looked a trifle off her stride. "Let me introduce you to the ladies!" she cried, threading her arm through Sera's and pulling her fully into the shop. Out of the side of her mouth, she muttered, "Hortencia isn't with you, is she?"

Sera shook her head, still taking in the scene.

P-HOP's cozy Victorian vibe had been replaced with a looser, though no less feminine feel tonight. The women inside ranged in age from their seventies all the way down to their early twenties, clad in festive fabrics and fascinating jewelry, sporting cowboy boots, Birkenstock sandals, and an array of hairstyles from the sober single braid to the teased bouffant. In every hand were glasses, though Sera was relieved to see they weren't all margarita goblets—at least half of the women were sipping kombucha or soft drinks—so she wouldn't stick out if she didn't imbibe. All had jazzed up their cups with Polynesian paper umbrellas, and several of the women sported feather boas, Mardi Gras beads, or Hawaiian leis about their necks. The room was steamy with body heat and fragrant with the scent of jalapeño-heavy nachos and cocktail weenies.

Pauline put her arm around her niece and began the introductions. "Sera, this is Bobbie, Crystal, and River Wind." Bobbie was a well-dressed woman of about fifty with a very businesslike hairdo who reminded Sera of a real estate broker, while Crystal was heavily tattooed, pierced, and had definitely served some time as a Brooklyn barista, if only in a past life. River Wind, an ageless raven-haired beauty, exuded the kind of serenity Sera strived for during meetings, and rarely found. She waved shyly at the three women. "I think you already met Janice, right?" Pauline continued. Sera nodded at the waitress, smiled, and smiled some more as more women crowded forward to greet her with robust shouts of welcome. Up next were a weathered, whip-thin woman who exemplified the ideal of the Western horsewoman in denim and riding boots, a cherubic redhead, and Sera's new favorite gal pal. "And that's Lou-Ellen, Syna September, and of course, Aruni."

"Hey, girl!"

Sera saluted, glad to see the yogini beaming at her. The rest of the names flowed over her in a wash of welcoming faces.

"Everyone, this is my niece, Serafina. As I mentioned, she's going to be opening a bakery here. It's called Bliss."

"To Bliss!" Much clinking of cups and applause ensued.

Sera blushed, squirmy at being the center of attention. "I brought lemon bars," she said lamely, holding up the box for the ladies to see.

"To lemon bars!"

The treats were lifted from her grip and passed around, to a wave of delighted moans and *yums* from lips soon rimmed in powdered sugar. Someone shoved a cup of kombucha in her hand, and just like that, Sera entered the whirl. She was hugged, mussed, and fussed over; toasted and roasted before she'd as much as had a moment to sit down.

And she realized something. She absolutely. Fucking. Loved it.

Serafina, who'd always needed a drink or several to get her to unbend enough to socialize at any gathering that wouldn't fit inside your average-sized closet, found herself sliding into being "one of the girls" so easily she was tempted to check herself for some of Pauline's back room lube. As she circulated about the room, she met women whose careers ranged from full-time mommy to part-time potter, plus a real, honest-to-goodness weaver, an event planner, and a tax attorney. Some of the ladies were local shop or gallery owners, who promised to stop by as soon as her bakery opened, and offered to steer business her way. Before she knew it, she was ensconced in a saggy armchair near the rear of the store, Aruni perched on one arm, Janice on the other, draped in Mardi Gras beads and lemon bar crumbs, while Pauline, with a little help from some of the others, climbed atop the mahogany counter at the front.

"Sisters!" cried Pauline, waving her leathery, scarf-swathed arms over her head for attention. Her bells and coins clashed, drawing what little attention the sight of her astonishing costume left unclaimed. "In honor of our newest initiate, I think it's time we go over our bylaws and mandate, don't you?"

"Bylaws!"

"Mandate!"

"What she said! Woooooo!"

"Okay, hush, you ninnies. Let me talk. Now Baby-Bliss, don't freak out. I made up all that crap about mandates and whatnot, just to sound fancy. Really, we've got just two golden rules. You ready?"

Sera raised her glass in acknowledgment, hoping Pauline wouldn't notice she'd yet to taste the foul brew within. "Hit me," she invited. Aruni and Janice high-fived over her head, then mussed her hair playfully.

"What's Rule Number One, women?" Pauline prompted.

"We don't talk about *Fight Club*?" piped up Syna. She ducked as Crystal lobbed an empty plastic cup at her.

"Anyone *else?*" A bit of the retired professor entered Pauline's voice.

"Rule Number One is, 'We support our sisters,' " a voice called from the doorway.

A hush fell over the women. Sera peered across the room and looked at the newcomer, who had spoken sharply enough to draw blood. It was Hortencia.

Pauline furled her gauze-draped wings like an exotic bird, costume jangling as she folded in on herself. Her face took on a pinched expression, and she sniffed disdainfully, but she refused to acknowledge her lover's arrival.

Hortencia was having none of it. "Isn't that right, Pauline?" she prompted.

Serafina wondered if she was going to be hearing about Rule Number Two at any point tonight.

The Back Room Babes had all gone quiet, and Sera had no doubt they were well aware of the rift between their founder and her beloved. Sera read sympathy, impatience, frustration in their eyes—like children watching their parents fight, all the while knowing nothing could be as important as the love that formed the foundations of their relationship. It touched her to realize these women felt as deeply connected to her aunt as she herself did. Pauline Wilde was an extraordinary woman, who had a powerful effect on others. Unfortunately, she was also extraordinarily *stubborn.* Stomping one Birkenstock-clad foot in pique, she climbed down from the counter, clashing and chiming as she strode up to her ex. "You should talk. You've got a funny way of showing support, yourself," she huffed.

"Me? It's *you* who's trying to bar me from the club—"

"All right, all right, ladies," Aruni interrupted, rising gracefully from the arm of Sera's chair and clapping her hands for attention. Her years of yoga teaching came in handy, providing the authority to wrangle a roomful of wayward women and realign their focus. "We're all here to have a good time and show Serafina how much *fun* the Back Room Babes are. *Fun*—remember? So why don't we take a nice, deep breath," she demonstrated, inflating her belly to almost comical proportions, then whooshing it out with exaggerated release, "and chant a friendly *ohm* to shake off any negativity and get us in the mood. Ready, gals?"

There were nods and a couple of isolated woo-hoos from the BRBs.

Aruni raised her arms as if she were conducting an orchestra. Her minions, well-trained and enthusiastic, rewarded her with a mighty *OHHHHHHMMMMMMM!* that fairly blew Sera's hair back.

Fetched up in the wake of the chant, Hortencia and Pauline both wore somewhat abashed expressions, but they still refused to look at each other.

"Fine," Pauline muttered, fiddling with the cord on her sombrero to tighten it around her neck. "She can stay. But I'll be damned if I demonstrate the sensual foot rub on her horny old toes. I don't care *what* tonight's agenda says."

"I wouldn't let you near my *perfectly bunion-free* feet if it was Maundy Thursday and you were channeling Jesus himself, you sour old shrew—"

Aruni raised her hands again, and the BRBs responded with another deafening *ohm* that effectively drowned out the women's squabbling. Their mouths snapped shut with identical clicks. They knew when they were outnumbered.

"Now then," Aruni said, dusting off her hands briskly. "Who's for more kombucha before we head out?"

Several hands shot up.

"Wait! Wait, 'Runi, you're forgettin' the best part." Janice was laughing as she gestured for attention. "Gals, put down the dang kombucha for a second, will ya? We ain't shared Rule Number Two with Serafina yet. And we cain't neglect that. Every newbie needs to know about Rule Number Two if they're gonna hang out with us Back Room Babes." She tunneled her arm behind Sera and urged her up from her seat, turning Sera to face the assembled *femmes.* "The thing ya gotta know, Sera, is that every time we meet, Rule Number Two states *someone* gets challenged to a dare. And you can't back down or say no if you're the one that gets herself picked."

"Um, like what kind of dare are we talking here?" Sera asked, her sense of the evening's fun suddenly wavering. *Please don't say demonstrating my oral skills by giving a banana a blow job. Or describing my favorite sexual position. Or, or...* The possibilities were terrorizing.

"Well, it has to be for the person's own good, ya know?" Janice explained. "Like, if you have a hang-up or something you're ashamed of, we give you a task that helps you get over it. For instance, last winter, Syna here shared that she wasn't too comfortable with her body. And just look at her!" Janice pointed at the other woman—a cute, zaftig mommy type in her mid-thirties. "She's gorgeous. So we dared her to go make naked snow angels on the plaza after midnight, and damned if she didn't have to do it."

"Nearly froze my bits off, but I made some kick-booty body sculptures," Syna September said genially. "Tourists were taking pictures of them for days. First time I was ever proud of my bod." She gave a little shoulder shimmy, flipping her auburn hair sassily.

"Anyhoo," Janice continued, "it wouldn't be a true BRB get-together without someone dolin' out a dare, and someone else having to fulfill it. Tonight's a little different, since we're straying from format to go see Zozobra instead of sticking around the clubhouse all night, but I still say we ought to let Sera have a shot at it. What do you gals think?"

Chants of "Dare! Dare! Dare!" ricocheted through the room.

Sera could feel herself stiffening up; wanting to retreat. This felt like too much attention, too much pressure from too many strangers. Her gaze automatically sought out the nearest exit. But then a wave of unaccustomed calm washed over her. This wasn't high school, or one of Blake Austin's premeditated humiliations. This was all just good fun, with good people who clearly harbored only good intentions. And hey, they were giving her the opportunity to dish it out, which meant she didn't have to *take* it—not just yet anyway. *You came here to try new things, to open yourself up,* she reminded herself. *Go ahead, Sera, live a little.*

"You want me to dare someone? Right now?" She plunked her hands on her hips, surveying the women.

"C'mon, Sera, show us what you got!"

Inspiration struck. As did the urge to giggle. "Well, I don't really know most of you well enough to venture a dare, but there is *one* I have in mind." A sly grin spread across her face, and the women cheered.

"Lay it on us!"

"Yeah, Sera, go for it!"

Sera held up a finger. "Just a sec, I'll be right back." And she headed right back—to the back room. It didn't take her but a moment to find what she needed. She tuned out the various rubber, latex, and realistic "vix-skin" toys, her eyes seeking humble steel (well, fur-augmented humble steel). She grabbed what she sought off a peg on the wall and hustled back to her new pals, who waited anxiously for her reveal.

"This one's for my aunt. Pauline," she beckoned with a grin. "Come on down." Jangling like a tambourine, Pauline sashayed forward to her niece. Her mien plainly said, *"Oh, please, you can't fluster* me. *I was sexually liberated before you were a zygote."* Sera took her hand, holding it up for the BRBs to see as if she were a referee proclaiming Pauline the victor in a prize fight. In a way, she *was* a referee, Sera thought, biting her cheek as she drew out her moment with unaccustomed showmanship. *Hey!* she marveled, *This is actually pretty fun!* "Hortencia, you're next. Get up here."

Hortencia looked as if she might refuse to come forward. "Dear, are you sure you've got the hang of the rules?" she prevaricated. "I'm sure it says somewhere that you can only dare one person at a time, and—"

"Horse hockey, Hortencia!" shouted Lou-Ellen. "There's nothing in the rules that says she can't dare two for the price of one. You're just chicken shit."

"Bwock, bwock, bocka-bocka-bwwwwwock!"

The Back Room Babes were convulsed with laughter. Kombucha and margarita mix sloshed over the lips of cups, and howls of hilarity hit the rafters. Sera herself was bubbling over with mirth. "C'mon, Hortencia. Show a little spine. I know you've had a tough day, being raised from the dead and all, but I promise this won't hurt."

"Oh, very well, if it'll stop you ladies from going any more *loco* than you already have..." Hortencia stepped forward. Sera took hold of her soft, crepe-skinned wrist, holding it close to Pauline's with one hand.

And with the other, clamped pink, faux-fur-trimmed handcuffs around both of them.

Pauline and Hortencia sent up instant squawks of protest, tugging at their wrists but finding themselves unbreakably bound together.

"Serafina Bliss Wilde!" shouted Pauline. "Unlock us this instant!" She tried for a stern, authoritarian stance, but the sombrero and belly-dancing outfit rather undercut her efforts. With a pang, Sera read a trace of real panic in her aunt's eyes. Yet even as she second-guessed herself for her impulsive act, Sera noticed Hortencia was biting back a reluctant smile, and she was reassured she was doing the right thing. The wink Hortencia sent sidelong in her direction further reassured her.

"These dares are supposed to be for the person's own good, right? Help you with your hang-ups and whatnot? Well, it looks to me like you two ladies have got one hell of a hang-up you need to hash out, and you don't show any signs of doing it on your own. Maybe this will give you the opportunity—and proximity—you need. Come see me for the key at the end of the night if you still want to be separated," said Sera, grinning fit to crack her face.

"Now, who's going to tell me about this Zozobra thing?"

Chapter Ten

"Where are we going again?" Sera asked Aruni. The Back Room Babes formed a noisy procession, strolling, staggering, and skipping down Santa Fe's sidewalks in the gathering gloom. They seemed to be heading north of the main tourist destinations, and as they walked, they slid into the slipstream of hundreds of other celebrants, citizens and tourists alike, festively dressed and visibly excited. Despite her request, no one had come forward with any information about the festival with the oddball name, and Sera wished she'd had the foresight to Google it before she came out tonight.

Aruni relented, but just a tad. "We're headed up to Fort Marcy Park for the burning," she said, chuckling at her own cryptic comment. "Then after he's toast, we'll be coming back to the plaza to eat and drink and dance the night away. Well, some of us will be drinking. Not me, though—pollutes the body, and besides, I want to save room for Frito pie!" She laughed at her own hypocrisy, and Sera spared a moment of gratitude that she wouldn't be the only one abstaining from alcohol this evening. "You got back just in time, girl," Aruni continued. "Tonight's not only Zozobra, it's also the first night of Fiesta. This town's been throwing itself a weekend-long party every September since 1712, if you can believe it. I'm told it's the oldest citywide celebration in North America. The whole city will be dancing and singing and stuffing their faces all night long!"

Aruni did a little jig, thrusting her arms skyward and twirling in a circle, unable to contain herself. But about this "burning" business, she would say no more, insisting Sera would have more fun if she waited until they got there to witness the event with unspoiled eyes. *Jesus,* Sera thought.

This town is like dry tinder. I hope, whatever's burning, it's far away from any buildings or loose brush.

They'd started out heading down West Marcy Street, just a block from where their little *placita* nestled, first turning onto Washington Avenue, which was one of Santa Fe's wider thoroughfares, then crossing Paseo de Peralta, where the hideous pink erection that was the Scottish Rite Temple (according to Aruni, owned and operated by a local Masonic sect) loomed over the neighborhood like a Pepto Bismol–colored cry for help. They soon passed the turnoff for Artist Road, where Pauline's house stood, and past which the ski basin opened up, though Sera had yet to visit it. As they walked, more and more people joined the procession, some holding flashlights, others drinking surreptitiously from concealed containers. Many families carried blankets and picnic baskets. With the crowd swelling and spilling onto the streets, it was impossible to take one's car out tonight, which pleased Sera's Manhattan sensibilities. She loved to walk, even if the thin air here did steal her breath.

Or perhaps it was the enchantment of the evening that was making her light-headed. Along the adobe outer walls of big hotels, museums, fancy restaurants, and modest homes alike, little brown paper bags lit from within by tea candles—*farolitas,* according to Aruni—added atmosphere along with twinkling light. Chile ristras—mostly deep red, but some with yellow or green dried peppers mixed in—hung from the patios, door frames, and fences of many buildings, a ubiquitous decorative accent here in New Mexico, though still foreign to Sera's eyes. Flags featuring Spanish heraldry from what must have been colonial days flapped in the light autumn breeze. Yet decked out as the city was in her festive best, her citizens shone brighter still.

Pauline was by no means the only one outrageously dressed. Bands of mariachis in tight toreador-style outfits competed with street vendors swinging glow sticks, their heads half-buried in bands of neon glo-tubes like Burmese women's necklaces gone psychedelic. Buskers and performance artists were sporting everything from conquistador outfits to traditional Pueblo Indian attire, reminding Sera that Anglos were relative newcomers to a city that had been old before America was even a nation.

At last they reached Fort Marcy Recreational Complex, where, Aruni informed her, there was a very nice pool and a ball field if she were ever in the mood for some exercise. Sera, whose idea of a workout involved deadlifting thirty-pound racks of steaming hot bread to and from her ovens, doubted she'd be seeking out softball leagues anytime soon, but she could appreciate the green space the park offered. At least, she assumed it'd be green. In the gathering darkness, surrounded by thousands of her fellow Santa Feans, it was difficult to tell what color the grass beneath all those shuffling feet might be.

At the gates, Pauline inadvertently yanked Hortencia's arm up as she reached to pull a pile of tickets from underneath her sombrero. *Guess belly-dancing costumes don't come equipped with pockets,* Sera thought. *Hope Pauline doesn't freeze her bits off later on, considering how much the temps drop at night around here in the autumn.* Hortencia shot her lover the hairy eyeball and ostentatiously rubbed her wrist, but Pauline was all cold shoulder—at least toward Hortencia. She had a bit more love for the rest of the Back Room Babes.

"Women!" she shouted. "Gather round. I've got our tickets here." The BRBs flocked to her side, taking their tickets and waiting their turns to funnel through the gate in the park's chain-link fence along with what felt like—and probably was—half the city. "If we get separated," Pauline called, "meet back at the plaza after the burn, ladies. And don't forget—have a goddamn *great* time!"

Sera followed Aruni closely, anxious that they *not* become separated. As far as her eye could see, swarms of people spread out, picnicking, meeting up with friends, laughing, blaring music. It reminded Sera of concerts she'd attended on Central Park's Great Lawn in summers past. Well, that was until she looked *up.* Sure, there was a stage, much the same as those shows she'd seen in New York. But Manhattan's stages didn't tend to boast fifty-foot effigies of what looked like the world's largest, ugliest waiter.

"What the fu—" Sera stopped stock-still, just yards inside the park's entrance. The colossal marionette took center stage, white-faced, huge-eared, with angry staring eyes and a long, white outfit sporting a painted-on black bow tie, black buttons, sash, and cuff links that looked fashioned from pizza pans. Actually, the effigy looked quite a bit like the Mr. Bill Play-Doh doll from old episodes of *Saturday Night Live*, to Sera's astonished eyes—if Mr. Bill's torture *du jour* were being stretched into Gumby shapes on a Spanish Inquisitor's rack. As if aware of Sera's thoughts, the figure's long, spindly arms began to wave in slow-motion distress, and amplified moans of distress started issuing from its wide, gaping mouth, echoing across the grassy field.

The crowd responded with a roar of delight.

Aruni and Janice swept their arms around her, laughing. "C'mon, girl!" Aruni cried. "It's starting! Let's get as close as we can. We don't want to miss the fire dancers or the little gloomies!"

Sera allowed the two women to tug her forward, vaguely aware of the rest of the Back Room Babes spreading out into the crowd. She saw Hortencia start determinedly off in one direction, only to be pulled up short as Pauline just as stubbornly headed along a different vector. Hortencia, on the right, yanked her handcuffed arm. Pauline glared daggers at her and planted her Birkenstocked feet. Then the crowd surged between them and Sera, and she momentarily lost sight of their angry tableaux.

"Um, guys..." Sera began, resisting the pull of her two new friends. "Is there supposed to be a moaning Mr. Bill looming over us like that?"

"Yup. Not to worry. He's an invited guest. That there's Zozobra himself," Janice said, following Sera's dumbstruck gaze. "His name means something like 'Old Man Gloom' in Spanish. He's supposed to represent all the negativity of the past year."

Sera could see why. He looked a lot like a grouchy neighbor she'd once had, whose greatest joy in life had been waving his tennis-ball-tipped cane at neighborhood teens for anything from littering to displaying their tramp-stamp tattoos too close to his front stoop.

"Um, what is the crowd chanting? I can't really make it out."

"They're shouting *'Burn him, burn him!'*" Aruni told her. "They're going to set him on fire pretty soon, purge all that bad energy. He's full of tax returns and divorce decrees and foreclosure notices. All that awfulness. I put a kiss-off letter to my ex in there myself. Had to slip the kid from the Kiwanis Club's Zozobra-decorating crew ten bucks to let me stuff it in there, but it was worth it."

"Nice," Sera complimented. She could think of quite a few negatives she'd like to see go up in flames, but somehow, she doubted the Kiwanis kid would be able to assist her in squeezing Blake Austin's bloated ego into the effigy. *Not that it would fit.*

"And what're those tiny figures dancing around the base all about?" They looked like they were practicing for a Casper convention.

"Those're the gloomies." It was Janice who answered, dimpling. "They're local kids picked to take part in the ritual. They're supposed to be ghosts of negative energy, if I remember right. Syna's boy Jimmy got himself picked to be one of them this year. She was so proud. Oh, and look, there's the fire dancer." She pointed.

Sera could just make out a figure in flame red, twirling and leaping around the base of the wailing effigy, waving a torch tauntingly. "I can guess what her job is," she said. The chants of the crowd were growing louder, fists pumping in unison in the direction of the stage, like protestors at a rally, or rock 'n' roll fans. No few of them held up lighters, showing their eagerness to help toast the grotesque figure.

"Yup. C'mon, Pauline's calling us." Aruni urged her to close the gap between them and the rest of the Back Room Babes. Janice gave Sera a wink and linked arms with her.

Despite the rowdy crowd, the BRBs were able to form a loose circle, and at Pauline's urging, they all clasped hands. (Of course, Pauline and Hortencia had little choice in the matter, but they seemed to be keeping their simmering dispute under a tight lid for the moment.) Sera's hands were taken by Aruni on one side, her birdlike fingers cool and serene, and Syna's on the other, warm and slightly sticky. Janice had moved farther down the circle, linking up with Crystal and another woman whose name Sera couldn't recall.

"Women," cried Pauline. "I'm so happy to be sharing this moment with you tonight." She had on her lecturer's bon vivant voice, Sera noticed with a smile—the one she'd perfected on NPR interviews and during commencement speeches at small women's liberal arts colleges, back in the day. "What we have here is a perfect opportunity to free ourselves of just about any damn thing that's been holding us back. You each joined the Back Room Babes because you were searching for fulfillment, something that was missing in your lives.

"For some of you, it was a disappointing marriage bed," she continued in her booming voice, oblivious to the grins and interested looks she was gathering from outside their circle. "For others, it was simply a desire for *more* desire, or to get to know and befriend your bodies better. And some of us—let's face it, we just needed a place to shoot the shit with other women." She jiggled her arms, sending a wave of friendly energy through the group's linked hands. "Zozobra's your chance to literally watch all those hang-ups go up in flames, and to chart a new course for your future. Now, I want you each in turn to get in the middle of our circle and share one thing that's been blocking you from being the ultimate, bad-ass woman you've always dreamed of being, and then tell us what you're going to do to change it. We'll hold space around you to honor what you share and help you focus your affirmation for change. Who'd like to be first?"

Syna let go of Sera's hand with alacrity, hustling her booty into the center of the ring. The other women closed ranks around her, with Sera now holding River Wind's callused hand. (River, she'd learned, was a local sculptress, and the one responsible for the earth mother fountain in *Placita de Suerte y Sueños*'s courtyard.)

"*My* biggest problem is my exercise equipment," Syna announced. "I spend hours every day wallowing in guilt over not using my stupid elliptical machine. I'm tired of hating myself because I don't want to get motion sickness wobbling away on that darn torture device for forty-five minutes a day, all so my buns will sit a quarter-inch higher in my ever-so-fashionable mom-jeans. So here's my Zozobra-resolution: that glorified clothes hanger is getting kicked to the curb! My butt is just fine, and anyone who says otherwise—including my husband—can just suck it!" She waggled her fist in the air, cheeks flushed.

The BRBs let out a lusty cheer. "No, elliptical!" they shouted, in unison except for Sera, who only caught on belatedly. Aruni leaned over to Sera and murmured, "Funniest part is, her husband *loves* her curves. She just refuses to believe him when he tells her so. He's absolutely crazy about her."

Sera smiled, touched. *What would it be like to have a relationship like that?* She had no real frame of reference. Her brief flings in college and culinary school had been... unsuccessful... to put it kindly, and her relationship with Blake... Forget burned; she'd been *incinerated.*

Syna stepped back into the circle, which opened to welcome her. Immediately, another woman stepped forward. *Not a bit shy, are they?* Sera thought, admiring the BRBs even as she began to dread her own turn in the ring. *Maybe I can arrange a fainting spell, or fake a nice seizure?*

"Harvey won't go down on me," Bobbie blurted as soon as she got to the middle of the group, startling Sera straight out of her reverie. The perfectly put-together woman smoothed her cardigan twin set and checked that her pearls were sitting straight. "I told him it's really *not* a cardinal sin to perform cunnilingus, despite what his ex-wife told him. I even begged him to ask his priest if he needed confirmation, but he keeps refusing. Well, if he doesn't at least give it a whirl *once,* I'm going to find someone who will!"

"Yes, cunnilingus!"

"Harvey's her new boyfriend," Aruni whispered in Sera's ear, after the giggles died down and Bobbie rejoined the others.

"I gathered."

"Wish me luck, girl!" Aruni dropped Sera's hand, squeezing her shoulder in passing as she strode gracefully into the ring. She plunked her hands on her lithe little hips. "I won't bore you guys carping about my *dummkopf* ex-boyfriend. We all know he's a sucking pit of negative energy." She tossed her curls. "Well, my Z-resolution is to wash that *schmoe* right outta my hair, as the song says." (Sera pictured a Yiddish grandma belting out Doris Day's tune, and choked on a laugh.) "He did what he did, but it's my choice to hold on to that bullshit or let it go. Tonight, I let it go. You'll never hear another word about that *yutz* from me again." Aruni pressed her palms together in prayer position, then opened up into a quick sun salutation. Unable to resist, she finished by flinging her arms wide like a child and letting out a whoop.

"No, *yutz!*"

One by one, the BRBs stepped forward and shared their secrets, their revelations sometimes touching, sometimes funny, and once, in the case of a woman who'd been molested in her youth, truly heartbreaking. All the while, the crowd's chant grew in volume, the gloomies bowed and swayed at the feet of Zozobra, the fire dancer twirled and taunted. The ground began to vibrate with the energy of the restless, eager throng.

At last, only Pauline, Hortencia, and Sera were left, and Sera certainly wasn't going to volunteer, despite the pointed looks and unsubtle head jerks her aunt was giving her.

"It's not gonna work, Aunt Paulie. I'm not putting my secrets on display until you two have laid all your cards on the table."

Pauline harrumphed, trying to cross her arms but being checked when she dragged Hortencia's along with hers.

"Oh, grow up, Pauline!" Hortencia snorted. "Let's get this over with. We swim together, or drown alone." She hauled Pauline with her into the ring, and the encircling women gave a ragged cheer. The chants of *'Burn him! Burn him!'* from the packed-in masses were growing louder by the moment. The BRBs looked from Pauline to Hortencia, wondering which woman would go first.

Pauline could have modeled for a new perfume called *Eau de Chagrin.* Under her jaunty sombrero and loud costume, she seemed smaller, more fragile than Sera could ever remember. Still, she wasn't licked yet. Squaring her shoulders with a determined shimmy, she took a deep breath. When she spoke, she addressed not just Hortencia, but all of the Back Room Babes.

"There's something I haven't told you, and I guess tonight's as good a night as any. It's been hanging over my head long enough, for fuck's sake, so maybe it's time to let Zozobra carry the burden from now on. Anyway, I'll get to the point." She cleared her throat. "Remember how I always tell you women to get to know your bodies, make friends with them, even cop a feel of your favorite bits whenever you won't get arrested for it? Well, one day I was saying hello to LuLu here"—she hefted her left breast demonstratively, setting coins clashing on her costume—"and I found something. A lump."

As if on cue, the mob's chanting paused, as on the stage, the Queen of Gloom stepped forward, making some proclamation that was inaudible from this deep in the crowd. In the relative quiet, the Back Room Babes' gasps were amplified theatrically. Sera felt a thrill of alarm, but Pauline was quick to soothe it. "It turned out to be benign. But it shook the shit out of my confidence, and it got me thinking about what's important to me."

"Pauline Wilde, how dare you not tell me about this right away!" Hortencia looked shocked.

"Let me get this out, Horsey. I need to explain why I've been such a pain in the ass."

Hortencia clamped her mouth shut, though she looked like it cost her.

"Anyway, the damn lump got me thinking about my mortality. I ain't the spring chicken I once was, though I've still got it where it counts." She performed a rather impressive belly roll, proving her costume wasn't just for show. "I started realizing I wanted to solidify the things that mattered to me, keep them close. I wanted some way to cement my relationships. That's why I asked you to marry me, Hortencia. I mean, domestic partnership's fine and all that, but I wanted it on paper if we need to be there for each other in a medical crisis, or, or... whatever might come. And damn it, woman, I just wanted the world to know you're the love of my life!"

Hortencia looked ready to cry. Her soft brown eyes were awash with sentiment. She clutched Pauline's hand, the cuffs forgotten.

"And, Bliss?" Pauline glanced over to her niece, her own sharp brown eyes damp. "I'm sorry I tricked you, kiddo. I just... I just wanted my darling niece by my side, and I wanted you to have the same chance I had to flourish in this magical place, the way you deserve. You're so talented, and you've had such a rough lot. Not too many women could handle everything you've faced with such panache." Unsaid but clearly telegraphed were the things Pauline left out—the death of Sera's parents, her struggles with addiction, Blake Austin, and all the fallout from her decimated career.

Sera appreciated her aunt's unusual discretion, even as her heart melted to see her so open and vulnerable. She'd never loved Pauline Wilde more, and that was saying a lot. She blew Pauline a kiss, telling her without words that all was forgiven.

"Anyhow, so that's why I did what I did. I lied to my only niece and I hurt the woman I love. And I'm sorry, both of you. I'll admit I freaked out when you said no, Hortencia. I shouldn't have dumped you just for refusing my proposal. I still don't know why you did, though. I know it can't be about my technique in the *boo-dwahhhr*..." she ventured, tendering up an uncertain grin and giving her hips a swirl that set her scarves fluttering.

The chants of *Burn him! Burn him!* began again, rolling across the field. The sky was completely dark now, and the crowd's lighters, flashlights, and glow sticks competed with the floodlights illuminating Old Man Gloom up on the stage. In the center of their own little assembly, Hortencia sighed. "If you're finished taking a bow over your prowess in the bedroom, Pauline, I'll *tell* you." She turned so she was facing her lover squarely, and the BRBs leaned in to listen. It was getting harder and harder for their little circle to maintain solidarity as the restive gathering of thousands surged and shifted, awaiting the main event. But Sera, enchanted as she was by the festival, was more interested by far in seeing her aunt's relationship mended.

"What first attracted me to you, Pauline, was how comfortable you were with yourself, how free you were in every possible way. And freedom was just what I needed. You know I was married—for years and years. Forty of them, to be exact. And when Carlos and I split four years ago, that was the first time in my entire life I'd gotten to do *exactly what I wanted.* Watch the damn dog show instead of football on Thanksgiving. Eat at a new restaurant every night of the week, instead of recycling the same menu of enchiladas, *calabacitas,* and his mom's awful *carne asada* over and over. *And for the first time in my life, I got to acknowledge that I loved women, not men.* Do you know how liberating that was?" Hortencia challenged. "Of course you don't. You crawled out of your cradle liberated. You flew from lover to lover like a hummingbird pollinating flowerbeds, and never looked back. But I...well, I came from a very traditional Catholic home. I married at twenty. I kept the house. I gave my husband three beautiful kids. And I waited until *they* had kids before I took back my life and claimed my freedom. That's why I never wanted to move in with you, Pauline. I loved having a space that was all my own. So when you asked me to marry you, I just...I don't know. It wasn't that I wasn't sure about *you,* and it wasn't some lingering desire for a heterosexual relationship. I just saw the walls closing in on me again, and I panicked. I'm sorry. And I'm sorry I tossed that perfectly lovely ring over the side of the balloon."

Pauline waved that away, as though diamonds plummeting out of hot air balloons were the least interesting thing in the world. She pushed her sombrero back off her head, letting it dangle down her back from its leather cord. Tears were streaming freely down her lined cheeks, but she looked radiant, her own personal gloom utterly banished.

"Oh, Horsey..." She trailed off.

Hortencia drew their clasped hands to her breast. "Pauline, if you still want to get married...I mean, if you'll still have me, well, I'd..." She choked up.

Again, Pauline waved impatiently. "Hortencia, you beautiful old bird," she declared, taking her beloved's cheeks in her hands and gazing fondly into her brimming blue eyes, "I don't care if we live in sin forever, as long as I'm with you." The two women kissed.

And kissed.

And kissed.

"Yay, living in sin!" howled the Back Room Babes, erupting in applause. Those nearby in the crowd paused in their pyromaniac chanting to clap along with them.

It broke the spell, forcing Hortencia and Pauline to finally come up for air.

"Oh, my. Ladies, we better hurry up. The burning's about to start, and we don't want to leave anyone out. It's your turn, dear," Hortencia prompted Sera. "Tell us what's been holding you back, and how you plan to change it. It's quite liberating."

"Yeah, kiddo," urged Pauline. "Give it up to Zozobra, let it all go into the fire!" The crowd seemed to agree, the frenzy of shouting and dancing kindling the night.

Both older women were grinning blindingly. But Sera's own smile fell away. She could feel all the eyes of the Back Room Babes on her as if they were literally pressed to her skin. She knew very well what her worst hang-up was, and she very much wanted to keep it to herself. The women were opening their circle for Sera, smiling and gesturing for her to take center stage. When her feet wouldn't move, Pauline and Hortencia came to her, taking her rubbery arms and drawing her into the circle in their place.

Maybe I should just talk about the alcohol, she thought desperately. *It's certainly done a number on my life.* But in her heart, Sera knew booze was a demon she'd already exorcised. The addiction would always be a part of her biology, but it no longer directed her behavior, and so long as she maintained her sobriety, it wasn't a source of shame. Her *real* problem *was*—and as mortifying as it was for Sera, it would simply *devastate* her aunt. *I can't do this, I can't do this... it would kill Pauline if she knew...* She opened her mouth to mumble some platitude about trying harder to meet a nice guy, or making more time for her social life.

Instead, to her utter horror, the truth flew out.

"I can't have an orgasm."

A howl erupted from the hysterical crowd.

Fireworks shot into the night sky, detonating with deafening booms.

And with a great roar and a whoosh, Zozobra burst into flames.

Chapter Eleven

For as long as she lived, Serafina would never be able to say exactly how she made it from the field where Zozobra had gone up in smoke, along with the last remnants of her dignity, to the citywide celebration that was toasting his fiery demise. One minute she was in the center of a circle of gaping, dismayed women; the next, she was spilling onto Lincoln Avenue at the entrance to Santa Fe's historic plaza, swept along on a tide of happy, party-hungry Fe-heads ready to get their fiesta on.

Sights, smells, and sounds assaulted her senses in the best possible way. The trees at the center of the plaza had been dolled up in festive colored lights, while tents, booths for food, games, and souvenirs as well as a bandstand crowded every inch of open space about the square, blocking off the streets to traffic. The mellow adobe facades of the buildings framing the plaza—the Palace of the Governors, restaurants, shops selling everything from tacky souvenirs to authentic cowboy boots and spendy sheepskin coats—were all decked out in lights and flapping fiesta banners. The Five and Dime General Store was closed for the evening. (Sera had asked her aunt when she'd first arrived how a sundries store had managed to co-opt such prime retail space, but Pauline had just shrugged and told her that, as far as she knew, it had always been there, and the tourists appreciated access to cheap sunglasses, sunscreen, camera batteries, and postcards.) The ice cream shop on San Francisco Street was doing a brisk business, however, as she suspected it always did—who wouldn't like an ice cream cone to stroll around licking while taking in the sights?

A relaxed, festive air had replaced the crowd's earlier frenzy. The faces around her were lit up with enthusiasm, purged of negativity just as Zozobra promised. Not Sera, though. As usual, she'd failed to ride the moment to its intended conclusion. She winced as she recalled how her awkward pronouncement had coincided with Zozobra's big flame-out.

On the one hand, it *had* been surprisingly freeing to finally cop to the truth. There it was, out in the open: *Serafina Wilde had never in her life, alone or with assistance, ever managed to achieve sexual fulfillment.* She'd buried that shameful secret since puberty, not even telling her doctor or best friends. She'd faked it with what few boyfriends she'd had up until Blake, and he... well; her pleasure hadn't been uppermost on *his* mind. All these years, Sera's inadequacy had weighed on her, nagging at her self-esteem and making her leery of relationships, until tonight, for the first time, she'd gotten it off her chest. And despite the fact that she didn't hold out much hope of ever "curing" her conundrum, it was a relief not to have to hold it inside any longer.

On the other hand, there had been the look on Aunt Pauline's face.

If she'd announced she'd run off to join a cult of burqa-wearing fundamentalists, she could hardly have stabbed Pauline Wilde more directly at her core. Everything she stood for—the freedom to express, demand, and receive pleasure from her own body—and everything she'd taught; all for naught with the one person who should have been her greatest success. Pauline had never had a daughter, but Sera knew she'd loved her niece as deeply as if she were her own. She'd tried her best to raise Sera, who'd arrived on her doorstep a shy and traumatized teen, to become a strong, confident woman. Now Sera had, by virtue of her sexual failure, called into question Pauline's very movement, her philosophy—hell, her technique!

What she'd seen in her aunt's eyes tonight had almost resembled... *betrayal.* And as much distress as her disability had caused Sera herself over the years, it was nothing compared to the dismay she felt at hurting her aunt's feelings so deeply. But she hadn't had a chance to express any of that to Pauline. Immediately after her admission, still embarrassed and a bit shocked at herself, Sera had been caught up in the crowd. She'd lost track of the rest of the Back Room Babes, apart from Aruni, and she hadn't reconnected with her aunt since. In fact, she had to wonder whether Pauline and her followers were avoiding her. From their expressions during her confession, it was obvious that whatever issues had brought *them* to join Pauline's club, no one else had her particular problem. Perhaps, in their pity, the BRBs were giving Sera some space.

Well, she could live with that, Sera told herself. She just hoped she hadn't spoiled Fiesta for everyone.

Then she shook herself—hard. *Really, how arrogant can I be!* Sera suddenly remembered her sponsor's characterization of the alcoholic ego. As Maggie put it, alkies tended to think of themselves as "the piece of shit at the center of the universe." *No one is worrying about my little "situation" right now,* she chided herself. *They're all having a blast, dancing, singing, eating, and drinking. Just as they should be. And as* I *should be, too. Well, except that drinking part. Tonight is a magical night, and I'm not going to ruin it by worrying about what others think of me.*

Much.

Aruni had gone off in search of the Frito pie she'd earlier mentioned, and judging by the many booths offering comfort foods from *chile verde* to *posole* with cornbread, *tamales* to *chalupas, chimichangas,* and *rellenos,* Sera doubted she'd have much trouble finding it. Aruni had promised to bring her back some Navajo fry bread drizzled in honey—giant, mouthwatering pillows of deep-fried dough which looked fit to beat any sort of fried bread Sera had yet tried (and Sera had tried a lot). For the moment, she was on her own in the square, though hardly alone. Kids ran about, dodging tourists, their scolding parents, and one another, giggling and shouting. Some were in regular street clothes, while others were dressed for the festival dancing, with girls in white peasant blouses and wide, colorfully ruffled skirts, and boys in white tunics and trousers, with sashes that matched the girls' skirts. Up on the stage behind the bandstand, some of their parents had already begun performing traditional New Mexican *ballet folklorico* dances, swirling and stomping to the tune of a huge troop of musicians that constantly swelled and ebbed as members joined for a jam session and then left to stroll the plaza with guitars and fiddles, bringing their joyous music along with them.

"Check it out, they actually serve it *in* the Frito bag!" Aruni shoved an exploded chip bag under Sera's nose, slit down the middle and gushing with shredded cheese, onions, sour cream, beans, and guacamole. She dug a plastic fork into the mess and shoveled up a bite, waving it in front of Sera's face. As advertised, Sera could see whole Fritos layered in with the rest. "Try a bite," Aruni urged.

"Um, maybe in a bit." Smiling her thanks, she accepted the paper plate of fry bread her new friend had kindly brought her, enjoying the greasy, sticky experience of street food, but finding it hard to swallow her earlier embarrassment. *Fuck it,* she thought. *I gotta know.*

"Aruni, do you think..." Sera struggled to finish her question. She looked down at her plate, wishing she had the stomach for the fried treat, then forced herself to meet the yogini's gaze.

"Hm?" Aruni's mouth was full of vegetarian chili and crunchy chips. Her eyes held nothing but innocent inquiry. "Do I think what?"

"Do you think the BRBs will ever invite me back?"

Aruni swallowed hastily, wiping her mouth with a flimsy paper napkin hardly up for the job. "Girl, are you kidding? This is exactly the sort of challenge we live for! I don't know the back story on this no-O problem of yours, but clearly you need our assistance." Her eyes sparkled. "We can be your coaches, you know?"

Sera could picture them with their heads together, muttering things like "Friends don't let friends fuck frigid" as they planned out her future sex life. "Any way I can stop that?" she ventured. "Nip that little idea in the bud?"

"Why would you want to?" Aruni looked bewildered. "Sounds like you've been held back long enough, if you ask me. I mean, I'm no guru like Pauline, but I gotta tell you, there's nothing like a good O to get you 'ohing,' if you know what I mean." She grinned, then sobered, seeing Sera's expression.

"Aw, hon, I'm sorry. I can see you're uncomfy, and that's not what anyone wants—in fact, I'm pretty sure that's why Hortencia is keeping Pauline occupied for you right now." She nodded over at the central dance area in front of the stage and bandstand, and Sera caught sight of Hortencia and her aunt engaged in a hip-wiggling Latin dance number. The two women were surprisingly agile, considering their age and the fact that they were still shackled to each other. As she watched, Hortencia looked up, caught Aruni's eye, and deliberately steered Pauline deeper into the crowd, away from the two younger women.

"Do you think I ought to go talk to them?" Sera asked reluctantly. "I've still got the key to their cuffs, after all."

"I suspect those two will do just fine tied together for the night." Aruni winked outrageously. "In fact, you better hope they're staying at Hortencia's place tonight if you don't want to get serenaded by a whole *lot* of O's overnight." She stuffed her yap full of the last bite of Frito pie. "Seriously, though, you've never thought of doing something about your prob? I mean, it must really be a bummer when you're in bed with a dude and he isn't getting you there... I know you said you're not seeing anyone, but what if you want to start?"

What if, indeed? Unwilling to explain the particulars of her problem, Sera started to brush Aruni's question aside with her standard line about focusing on her career, when her gaze was caught by something across the plaza. Or rather, some*one*. Someone with whom she would very much like to get "there," if her deepest fantasies be known.

Asher Wolf was sitting with a group of musicians on a bench under the portico shading the Palace of the Governors, hat half obscuring his face as he crowded in close, looking over the arm of one of the festively dressed mariachis at the fiddle in the man's lap. Sera wasn't sure exactly how she'd zeroed in on him among so many hundreds—it was, she thought with wry amusement, as though she had special Asher radar, allowing her to home in on her enigmatic landlord through any obstruction. As she watched, he lifted the violin with its owner's permission, cradling the neck in one careful hand and bringing the instrument to his chin, close to his ear. He tested the strings with his other hand, plucking at them and listening intently before tightening one of the pegs and listening again. At last, he nodded with satisfaction, then attempted to pass it back to the musician. The man clapped him on the back, shaking his head, and instead offered him the bow, urging Asher to play. The others, strumming guitars of varying sizes and shapes, also egged him on, but Asher just laughingly demurred.

"You know what, Sera?" Aruni asked, oblivious to the direction of Sera's gaze. "I think you should start taking some baby steps right away. Like, try some exposure therapy."

"*Who's* tryin' *what* kinda therapy?" Janice drawled, trotting up to them and throwing her arms across their shoulders companionably. "Dang, y'all, I thought I'd never make it through that crowd! Do not, I repeat, do not *ever* drink a forty-eight-ounce travel mug fulla Big Mama kombucha unless y'all wanna wait forty-five minutes for the chance t' experience the world's stanky-ass-est port-o-potty. Pee-uuuu!" She shook her head as if to rid her nostrils of the memory of the stench. "So, what-all are we talking about?"

Sera dragged her gaze away from Asher, but the picture of him, so at home here in the heart of Santa Fe's artistic community, stayed with her as she turned her attention back to her new friends. Before she could deflect the conversation onto more comfortable topics, however, Aruni jumped in.

"We're working out some of Sera's kinks."

"Yeah?" Janice looked impressed. "How're we doin' that?"

"We're not sure yet. We just decided to try. Right, Sera?" Aruni gazed expectantly at Sera, who gulped.

"Actually, um, I don't think we did decide that—"

"Count me in!" Janice cried. "Ooh, I got a great idea!"

"Awesomesauce! What is it?" Aruni's already wide eyes went manga cartoon-round. "Janice is the *best* at this kind of thing," she informed Sera.

"I am, ain't I?" Janice smirked. "So listen up. I got it. What our Miss not-so-Wilde needs tonight is a good old-fashioned Back Room Babes dare!"

"Who's throwing down a dare!?" came an outraged voice. The three turned to see Syna, Bobbie, Crystal, and Lou-Ellen had joined them. River Wind was close behind, carrying a picnic blanket. She sent Sera a quiet, commiserating smile and spread the blanket for the women on a patch of grass being vacated by a family with small children who looked tuckered out from the festivities. "No one's doing a dare without us to witness," continued Syna, flopping down gratefully on the blanket. She waved the smoked turkey leg in her fist regally. "We witness or it didn't happen!"

The others heartily agreed, plunking themselves down and pulling Sera with them.

Sera groaned as she sat cross-legged on the rough woolen blanket, but she was already cheering up. The faces of the women around her were lit up with goodwill and relaxed *joie de vivre,* inviting her to be part of the grand celebration taking place all around her. They didn't seem the slightest bit inclined to treat her like a pariah—in fact, just the opposite. It was like having a dozen sisters all of a sudden, and if it was a little weird, going from relative orphan to Brady Bunch so abruptly, it wasn't half bad. "Guys," she tried halfheartedly. "I'm fine. It's really not that big of a deal. Please don't make a big stink..."

But oh, yes, they intended to make a big stink. "Dare! Dare! Dare!" they chanted.

Sera covered her eyes, envisioning being stripped naked and chained to a giant Maypole-sized dildo in the center of the town square. "Have mercy," she squeaked. "Or...or I swear I'm never baking for a single one of you again."

That gave them pause.

"Okay, guys," Aruni said in the silence that followed Sera's threat, "let's just make it a little one, for tonight. How about...hm. I don't know. What about flashing your boobs?"

"Too many kids around," warned Syna. "Including mine. John's just over there with my son Jimmy"—she pointed across the plaza to where a sandy-haired man was herding a towheaded ten-year-old over toward a carnival booth, "and nice as your rack is, hon, I don't want him catching an eyeful before he graduates college."

"Thank God," breathed Sera. There was no way in hell she was letting any nip slip tonight, dare or no dare.

"Anyhow, no offense, 'Runi, but how'n heck's that supposed to help her with her little hiccup?" Janice wanted to know.

Yeah, how? Sera thought. *I'm already about as mortified as a woman can get.*

But she was wrong.

"I've got it!" Syna beamed. "Something wholesome *and* helpful."

"Dish it, Syna!" All eyes were on the curvy redheaded mom, eager for her answer. She did not disappoint.

"This one's perfect. It'll help her boost her confidence, and also practice letting loose, but it's not, like, dirty or anything."

"Spill it, sister. We're dying here," snickered Crystal, cracking her tattoo-covered knuckles.

Syna rose to her feet, her cheeks rosy with merriment. She swooped down and grabbed Sera's hands, tugging her to stand by her side.

"Serafina Wilde," said Syna September, "I dare you... to go ask a guy to dance!"

"Nice!" crowed Crystal.

"Sweet, but *could* be sexy," mused River Wind.

"I still say it's not as good as a flash," Aruni grumbled, "but whatevs. You'll have fun."

"Who do you think you'll pick?" Bobbie wanted to know.

"It has to be someone hot," Syna qualified. "No asking some Grandpa Magoo if he wants to cut a rug."

"Yeah," Janice agreed. "Definitely got t' grab yourself a stud, hon. But don't worry. From what I can see, there's dozens of guys finer'n frog's hair to choose from tonight. Maybe hundreds!"

There were, indeed, scores of eligible fellows out on the plaza that night. But there was only one man for Serafina.

"Would you like to dance?"

Fuck, fuck, I can't believe they got me to do this. What if he says no? What if... God help me, what if he says yes?

Asher appeared to consider it.

Sera fought the urge to scuff her toe in the dirt. She was already blushing like a nun at a burlesque show, simply standing here in the shadow of the wolf's wide, dreamy shoulders. She'd caught up with him just as he was leaving his mariachi friends, starting to thread his way through the crowd toward she knew not where—or whom. Perhaps a lady friend? *Well, I've put a kink in his romantic plans in that case,* Sera thought. *Or maybe just thrown him a curveball?* Sera was acutely aware of the Back Room Babes' stares from the square behind her, but it was Asher's green gaze that skewered her now. He seemed to be taking her request with rather intimidating deliberation. *Wondering whether I'll start stalking him if he throws me a bone? Or just worrying for the safety of his toes? C'mon, hot stuff, don't leave me hanging,* she silently urged.

"Yes, Bliss. I believe I *would* like that," he said at length. "Very much."

"Have you been drinking?"

Sera's hand flew to her mouth. "I can't believe I just said that," she gasped.

Asher's eyes crinkled at the corners, half-amused, half-puzzled. "Not yet," he said easily enough. "The lines for the beer stands are prohibitively long. Why, am I going to need something to fortify me? You're not wearing combat boots," he said, scanning his way down her figure until his gaze rested on her soft, slouchy boots, "so I think I am safe to accept your kind offer."

"Oh! Well, you know, the girls made me do it. Ask you, that is. I mean, I wouldn't have presumed... not that I wouldn't want to dance with you, but..."

Sera stumbled to a halt. "Damn it, let me start again." She risked a glance up at his face. Asher was trying to maintain a politely inquisitive expression, and failing. A grin etched its way across his mobile features, his eyes alight with curiosity, their green reflecting the fiesta *luminarias* in ways that set her heart—and her libido—hammering. "What I mean is, the Back Room Babes challenged me to ask a cute guy to dance, and, well, you were the cutest one I saw." *Can't believe I said that. Can't believe I said that! But hell, it's true, isn't it? And he's gotta know he's the hottest thing since Zozobra went kablooey.*

"Oh, well, in that case, I could hardly refuse." Asher's grin grew. "And, Bliss, as far as 'cute' goes..." He gave her another, warmer once-over, then stopped abruptly.

Sera held her breath. Was her Asher-ometer on the fritz, or did he appear suddenly uncomfortable? Did he think she was hideous? Was he some sort of George Washington I-cannot-tell-a-lie type who tripped over a harmless little social fib? But no, she wasn't getting that impression. Though his hat kept his expression partially shaded, she sensed Asher's problem wasn't with returning her compliment; it was with bantering flirtatiously at all. It was as though this expression of purely masculine appreciation were taboo—or if not taboo, at least extremely rusty.

At that moment, the band began to play a ballad—a very *romantic* ballad. On the stage, the fiesta dancers took a break, and a middle-aged gentleman with a barrel chest and a seamed, florid face took their place, backed by several musicians. He began to croon in Spanish, and Sera thought she recognized an old Gypsy Kings song. The crowd hushed to hear his mellifluous baritone, and couples began to stream to the area reserved for dancing in front of the stage. Asher doffed his hat, tossing it with a nod of thanks to one of the friends still sitting under the portico. He shook his head in an effort—only partly successful—to erase the impression the hat had left on his burnished gold hair. "Come, Bliss," he said, holding out his hand. "Let's join them."

Before she knew it, Sera was swept into the whirl.

And by damn, she was determined to enjoy it.

From her awkward teen years on, she'd hated dancing. Never once had she been able to relax and let a boy lead. She always second-guessed what the guy was going to do, worried he'd send her crashing into other couples or dump her ass-first during a dip. Worse, she dreaded disgracing herself with her own clumsy, unsure moves. Because of it, she was lucky if the worst that happened was zigging when she should have zagged, and rarely was she asked twice by the same guy. Which was fine with Sera. Dancing made her so tense, standing by the sidelines was preferable by far. Even alone, unless she was dead drunk, she'd had trouble letting go and allowing the music to move through her.

Not tonight.

Tonight, Sera vowed, she would be free. She owed it to herself to take in everything this one-of-a-kind festival—and one-of-a-kind guy—had to offer. No more would she paint herself the wallflower. Years of reticence, decades of self-consciousness—they'd all have to take a vacation. She. Would. Not. Miss. This. Moment.

Hear that, brain? she taunted. *You're not going to spoil tonight for me!*

And it didn't.

Her feet began to feel light, her head lighter, and her heart lightest of all, expanding with the sensation of being utterly, one hundred percent present in the moment. And what a moment it was. With the scents, sights, and sounds of Fiesta curling around her, Sera felt wrapped in a borrowed confidence she wasn't sure she'd ever give back. Was this what serenity felt like? She'd certainly said enough prayers for it over the past year. Her shoulders relaxed, her body took the lead, and her mind felt free to take it all in, marveling from the sidelines without trying to control. She twirled, glided, and swayed as if she'd been born to dance.

It wasn't Asher's doing, though he *was* a masterful dancer. He eased her through the throng with assurance, shielding and guiding Sera with instinctive courtesy as they melded with the others on the plaza. He had moves, too—no awkward high school boy, he. His arm was assured around her back, and his hand, callused and strong where it cupped hers, applied just the right amount of pressure to connect and direct them without overwhelming her. And his hips...*oh, man.* When Asher swiveled in time to the music, Sera had to force herself not to ogle their effortless roll and swing, imagining what *else* he might do with hips like those.

But delicious as he was, it wasn't her partner who made this dance perfect. Something had changed within Sera herself. She could feel the difference. It was like...well, it was like the feeling she'd had sometimes when she was drinking. That loosening of anxiety in the chest after the first swig went down, that feeling of "I can face anything." That social ease others seemed born with, but which she'd always lacked a full measure of, and lost even more after her parents' deaths. She felt as though she had found the elusive switch that could flip her feeling of being "less-than" off. From the moment the Back Room Babes had issued their dare, she'd known she was going to take it. Take it, and make the most of it. To do anything less would be to dishonor the kindness life was throwing her way. She'd had enough tough times in her past to know she'd better savor the good ones. *No matter what else happens from here on,* she thought, *tonight I am a lucky woman.*

And, perhaps, about to get a bit luckier.

As the song wound down and the singer began another ballad, Sera drifted back to earth, glancing up at Asher. He didn't seem inclined to end their dance just yet. In fact, if she had to guess, he seemed to be enjoying it more than a little himself. His face had relaxed, his shoulders loose but his arms strong around her. While the song segued, he tucked her a bit tighter to him and turned them gracefully, leading them to a spot on the edge of the crowd where they had a bit more room to move. Almost as one, they took a breath of the fiesta-scented autumn air. Again, his eyes took her in from head to toe. His focus had sharpened.

"That is a lovely color on you, Bliss," he complimented. His voice seemed a notch deeper than normal.

"This old thing?" Sera blushed, glancing down at the azure tunic she wore. She was suddenly glad she'd made an effort to dress up a little tonight. She spent so much time in chef's pants and flour-coated clogs, it was hard to remember the rest of the world tended to put in a bit more effort. Plus, after Blake, she'd had zero interest in attracting attention from the opposite sex, so her out-of-kitchen uniform of shapeless tees and battered jeans had suited her just fine. But tonight...

"Thanks, Asher," she said, just above a whisper. His regard was suddenly so overwhelming, she could barely remember to keep her feet shuffling along to the music. The air in the small space between them felt hot as one of her ovens, in contrast to the cool September breeze teasing her hair and fanning her flushed cheeks.

"I noticed you are wearing my earrings," he went on. His hand left the middle of her back to brush her lobe with exquisite gentleness, eliciting a shiver Sera prayed he wouldn't notice. "I hope it's not arrogant to say they suit you very well." His palm reclaimed its place at her waist... then slid just a touch lower, heating the small of her back through the silky fabric.

"N-No, not arrogant at all," she stuttered. Her breath didn't know whether it was coming or going, but her earlier serenity had definitely taken a hike. "You're very kind. I love them. I'm so glad I had an occasion to wear them tonight." Was it her imagination, or was her sexy landlord *flirting* with her? Just a little bit?

For the first time since they'd met, Asher's attention felt fully engaged, the distance he usually reserved for himself somehow breached. And the expression she read in his eyes as she dared another glance up...*wow.* It was as though he'd turned the light on behind those eyes, withdrawn the curtain veiling them. In that gaze, she read so much—almost *too* much. A soul that could contain great mischief, but also deep, deep sorrow. Intelligence, perception, and kindness; an acceptance of others' foibles even as he strove for perfection in himself. And a wound that had shattered him, utterly shattered him, somewhere at the heart of it.

It was like looking into the essence of a great symphony, all the elements of passion, playfulness, and exultation commingling. Sera stumbled to a halt, her feet no longer obeying the music, drowned out by what she saw in Asher's expression.

He came to a stop with her, but his arms kept their clasp about her body.

"I think..." A look not unlike consternation crossed Asher's face. He stared down at her, unwontedly solemn. "I think I would like to kiss you, Bliss. Would you...also like that?"

Would I like that? Would I like *that?*

"There's only one way to find out," she found herself saying with far, far more sassiness than she'd expected to be able to muster in a moment like this.

But Asher didn't smile. As momentous as this occasion felt to Sera—she hadn't kissed or wanted to kiss anyone since Blake had shattered her confidence (she had, in fact, never had more than a casual coffee date since getting sober)—it appeared to be even more fraught for Ash. His hand gently cupped her face. Sera registered its rough texture, its control and exquisite sensitivity. Its...*trembling?* His thumb traced her bottom lip, and Sera found herself trembling as well, her lips parting in anticipation. *When is it going to happen?* Is *it going to happen? Oh, my God, it's about to happen...*

And then his lips took hers, and her wits took off.

Chapter Twelve

Well, everything *looks* perfectly normal down here," said the voice between Sera's thighs.

Paper rustled, metal instruments blessedly retracted, and Dr. Flores, Sera's brand-new gynecologist, wheeled herself back on her stool and into visual range. "You can sit up now," she instructed briskly.

Sera did as bade. (There was nothing like a speculum to make a girl feel subdued.) She sat cross-legged on the exam table, disposable paper gown gapping in all sorts of unflattering ways, trying to tuck everything tuckable back into place. *I can't believe Pauline did this to me,* she thought for what had to be the hundredth time. *And I can't believe I* let *her. Hell, my last pap smear was less than a year ago. This* so *wasn't necessary.* But Pauline Wilde would not be denied. She'd spent the entire weekend peppering her niece with probing questions, poking her and eyeballing her like she was some sort of exotic specimen, then tut-tutting and exclaiming, "Why didn't you ever *say* anything?" at least once an hour. And come Monday morning, she'd been on the horn first thing, getting Sera an appointment with her personal gynecologist, whether Sera liked it or not.

"I don't see what the emergency was, frankly," said the doctor. She was a steel gray woman from top to bottom, neat but not militarily so from her wiry, short-cropped hair to her starched doctor's coat and gunmetal pantsuit. "The way your aunt made it sound, I thought we'd be admitting you to the ER. I don't usually offer appointments in this big of a rush. It normally takes weeks to get in to see me," she said with a hint of pride.

"I'm very sorry, Dr. Flores. I don't mean to waste your time," Sera said. "It's just that Aunt Pauline was very concerned, and I..."

Thought this would shut her up.

"Fine, fine," said Dr. Flores. "You're here now, and of all my patients, Pauline is probably the one I'm happiest to let call in a favor. So let's get to your symptoms, shall we?" She didn't wait for Sera to continue. "Are you having any burning sensations when you urinate?"

Sera shook her head.

"Pain during sexual activity?"

How to answer that? "Um, not exactly..."

The doctor pinned her with a slightly impatient look. "*What,* exactly?"

"Well, no, no pain, but also... no sexual activity."

The doctor's expression didn't change. "For how long?"

"Over a year," Sera whispered.

The doc made a note in her chart. "And over a year ago, when you *were* sexually active, did you experience pain during sexual activity?" she asked impassively.

"No... ah, not exactly." Sera looked wistfully over at her clothes.

The doctor cast her stainless steel watch an equally wistful glance before leaning back on her stool and studying Serafina from under knotted brows. "*What,* exactly?" she repeated.

"Not pain, but... not really pleasure either. And, um... you probably know how Aunt Pauline is about, um... pleasure."

Was it Sera's imagination, or had Dr. Flores's lip quirked?

The doctor scribbled another note, then slapped her hands down on her thighs decisively and rose to her Aerosole-clad feet.

"Okay, Miss Wilde. I'll send out the usual pap smear and do a urinalysis, but as I said, I can find nothing physically wrong based on your exam. Come into my office as soon as you're dressed," she invited, "and we'll have a little chat."

She might have said "chat," but Sera heard "firing squad." She gulped and did as ordered, wishing forlornly that she hadn't given up smoking along with drinking as she dragged on her T-shirt and jeans and slipped into her beat-up Dansko clogs. Now would have been a great time to smoke 'em if she'd got 'em.

Inside the doctor's airy, peach-walled office, O'Keeffe prints confronted

Sera at every turn. She squirmed down as small as she could into the doctor's little beige love seat, averting her gaze from the flowery vulvas and focusing instead on the anatomical models of ovaries and uteri that littered the woman's glass-topped desk. *I'll take anatomical over artistic any day.*

The doctor unfolded a pair of neat, wire-framed bifocals and propped them on her nose, glancing at Sera over them. "Now, Miss Wilde, how about you describe the *exact* nature of the problem that's brought you here today?"

Was it her imagination, or was Dr. Flores making fun of her, just a wee tiny bit?

Serafina took a deep breath. *Enough wasting this nice lady's time, Sera,* she chided herself. "I guess I better just come out and say it, huh?" She sighed, twisting her hands in her lap. "But that's the problem. I can't. Come, that is."

"Meaning, you can't experience orgasm?"

Sera nodded glumly.

"I see." The doctor jotted down another note in Sera's file. "Is it an inability to experience arousal, or is it more like arousal with anorgasmia—that's when your body experiences sexual pleasure but can't achieve climax," she added when Sera looked blank at the word.

You'd think I'd know all the words for my condition by now, Sera thought. *Blake certainly had enough of them, and "frigid" was one of the kindest.* "Ah... the second one, for the most part. I can get in the mood"—her kiss with Asher on Friday night had amply proved that!—"but I, ah... I've never quite gotten 'there.'"

"Never achieved climax." Dr. Flores looked a bit impatient with Sera's discomfort using the clinical terms. "Not even alone? When you masturbate?" the doctor clarified.

Yeah, I got that from the whole "alone" thing, Sera thought, blushing. She shook her head mutely. She'd given it a fair try—Pauline had practically given her a mandate to, once Sera had reached her mid-teens—but though things would start off well, they'd always end up the same way. *Failure. Frustration.* Eventually, the shame over her inadequacy had been too much, and she'd simply given up trying. "No. Once or twice I got pretty close—

or at least I think I did—but, um, there was a definite failure to launch." Having no frame of reference, and a distinct lack of desire to watch porn, Sera had had to rely on her friends'—and Pauline's—descriptions of what the climactic moment felt like. And based on their rhapsodizing (in Pauline's case, endlessly), she'd definitely missed the boat.

Dr. Flores steepled her fingers and frowned over them—not in a judgmental way, but rather as if pondering a perplexing puzzle. "If you had to guess, what would *you* attribute your sexual dysfunction to?"

"The lady in your waiting room," Sera blurted out.

"Your aunt Pauline?" One gray brow rose, Spock-like.

Sera nodded, wishing she hadn't spoken.

"What does your aunt have to do with the situation, if I might ask?"

How to explain this? "You know how Pauline has this Ourgasms movement, right?" She rushed on when the doctor nodded. "Well, I, um... I sort of watched one of her instructional videos once, when I was fourteen..."

Behind her shiny steel-framed bifocals, Dr. Flores's eyes widened just a tad.

Sera's cheeks flamed, and she felt just this side of nauseated. She didn't want to imagine what the doctor was thinking. "It wasn't my fault—the tape was in our *Princess Bride* video sleeve—but once it got rolling, I couldn't look away. And, um, it was pretty graphic, you know? And after that, whenever I'd get close to orgasm, I'd have a vision..." Sera couldn't finish.

"A vision?" The doctor looked vaguely alarmed.

"Not like a hallucination or anything," Sera hastened to explain before the woman could summon the men with straitjackets to come haul her away. "Just, um, in my mind, I always end up picturing Aunt Pauline. She pops up like a bogeyman just when I'm most in the mood, and... I, ah, lose it. The moment, that is." Serafina swallowed. "Sometimes I'll see what I saw in the video"—*so gross!*—"and other times, it's like she just shows up in my head and does one of her signature 'Helloooooo, Bliss!' greetings right when things are getting hot and heavy." *And now that I've seen Pauline in that fuchsia belly-dancing outfit, she'll probably be wearing* that *next time. If there* is *a next time.*

Now Dr. Flores showed some spark—a spark of asperity. "Let me get this straight. You're saying your aunt is to blame for your difficulty achieving orgasm. Your aunt, who has spent her entire life empowering women to do exactly the opposite."

"That's about the size of it." Sera squinched down lower on the sofa. "I mean, I'm not *blaming* her, I'm just saying she, ah...kind of gets in the way."

Dr. Flores set down her shiny steel Cross pen and squared Sera's folder on her desk with exaggerated precision.

"Miss Wilde, I sympathize with your position. However, I can personally vouch for Pauline's methods. That woman's got a pelvic floor like a trampoline." From her tone, Sera gathered this was a good thing. "She's my best patient, hands down. I wish they could all be like her—knowledgeable, responsible; hell, she's taught *me* a thing or two about female genitalia. Simply put, your aunt is a bona fide sexual guru. I recommend her unreservedly to many of my patients who need counseling in this regard. And I'm sorry, but if *she* can't help you, I don't think *I* can help you with your problem."

The doctor rooted through her desk drawer and came up with a business card. "However. If I might make a suggestion," she said, offering Sera the card, "I'd say give this person a call. It might take years to see results, but it's worth a try."

Sera stood, accepting the little rectangle of reinforced paper, as well as the doctor's handshake.

"Good luck, Miss Wilde. And give my regards to Pauline."

Sera didn't have long to wait to obey.

In the waiting room, Pauline leapt to her feet at the sight of her beloved niece. Her hair, barely confined in a messy braid, bounced down her back, trailing ribbons and tiny bells. Her breasts, even less fettered, jiggled gently against the worn green and yellow T-shirt she wore, emblazoned with "Hot Stuff" and an arrow pointing straight down. Her skirt was a calico tribute to Laura Ingalls Wilder. Her expression was anxious.

"So what'd Dr. Flores say? Isn't she great? I knew she could fix you up, kiddo." She patted Sera's shoulder gingerly, as if her niece were a terminally ill patient who would shatter at the slightest hint of rough treatment. "What'd she recommend? I can lend you my Kegel exercisers if you want, but really, I should just buy you a set. I don't know what I was thinking, I should have gotten you a whole array last Christmas!" Pauline was babbling a bit, clearly anxious.

Wordlessly, Sera handed over the card Dr. Flores had given her. Pauline took it, then blanched. "This can't be right," she muttered. "It says this guy is a clinical psychiatrist, specializing in Freudian analysis!"

With short, jerky movements, Sera gathered up her jacket and steered her aunt toward the door. "Not another word about orgasms, Aunt Pauline," she growled. "Or I'll scream. And not," she threatened, "in a good way."

Chapter Thirteen

It was just one kiss, Sera, she reminded herself as she drove the short distance from Pauline's house to the shop. *One kiss, no tongue, no reason you should have spent the last three days in a frenzy of breathless anticipation.*

But she had.

And don't forget, he practically dropped you like a hot rock afterward. If one could drop a hot rock *politely.* Asher had pulled away after leaving her lips in a state of emergency, his eyes shuttering and expression turning, if she had to describe it, rather mortified. He'd thanked her gallantly for the dance, even kissed her hand in a way that would have been utterly cheesy coming from another man, and promised to see her at *Placita de Suerte y Sueños* on Tuesday as agreed. And then he'd beat a hasty retreat.

Leaving Sera to wonder what it was about her that left everyone involved so unsatisfied.

The weather seemed to mirror her glum mood this morning. It had been showering intermittently since dawn—she'd been surprised to learn it did, in fact, rain in the high desert—and the air had taken on a distinct autumn chill. Clouds scudded across the sky, turning it a tumultuous gray as she pulled her aunt's crappy Subaru into a parking space just outside the little shopping center. Her rental car had become too expensive to keep, and Sera hadn't had a chance to look into a car of her own yet, though she, Hortencia, and Pauline had discussed shopping for one later this week. (Sera, who had never owned a car, was having mixed feelings of dread and delight over the prospect.) In the meanwhile, Pauline had been kind enough to lend her the shitheap, though she hadn't come along for the ride.

Sera had wondered why Pauline had refused to join her at the store today—she'd expected her aunt to be ecstatic at the chance to wade waist deep into the plans for renovations. When Sera expressed her surprise to Hortencia that morning, the older woman had given Sera a bit of insight. "She's letting you make Bliss your own, dear. She's afraid that if she comes with you, she won't be able to resist sticking her beak in your business and you'll feel obligated to go with her ideas rather than your own. The only way she can keep her trap shut is to plant her old butt at home while you draft your plans."

Touched, Sera had given her aunt an extra big hug on her way out, accepting Pauline's return squeeze and "Go get 'em, kiddo," with eyes that were just a shade misty. "I'll be really careful with your stuff, Aunt Pauline," she'd promised.

"Eh, junk it all, what do I care? Shovel that shit outta your way and get crackin', cutie. Just don't forget the back room—we agreed you'll be leaving that alone for now, right?"

"Right, Aunt Paulie. Let the boners be. Got it. Love you, see you later!"

Now it was time to beard the boners in their den.

Sera let herself in through the wrought-iron gate and walked through the short covered arch that opened out into the *placita,* dodging between droplets as she emerged into the open courtyard. She nodded a friendly greeting to the earth mother fountain, whose basin looked a little fuller this morning, and breathed deep of the morning air, trying to center herself. It smelled like damp dust, if such a thing were possible—rain on dry earth, piñon and sage, and a hint of Asher's flowering plants. Always, something of Asher seemed to find a way to insinuate itself into her awareness.

As she headed for P-HOP—*gotta remember to start calling it Bliss now*—Sera studiously avoided peering through the junglelike foliage covering Lyric Jewelry to see if her neighbor was around. It was early, but not too early for him to be at work. *Not too early for me to start focusing on my own business either,* she told herself firmly. They weren't scheduled to get together until closer to noon, and she had buckets of work to do before then. She hitched the bundle of moving boxes and cleaning supplies higher over her shoulder and made a beeline for her store. She needed to clean out the space as best she could before Malcolm arrived this afternoon, as she was hoping to have a clear plan, at least in her mind, for where the appliances would go, and what renovations she'd be asking Malcolm to make.

For indeed, she would be employing Mr. McLeod as her contractor. His references had checked out. What little time she'd been able to steal for herself between fending off her aunt's probing questions about her substandard sex life and trying to shut out the displays of lovey-doveyness from the recently reunited couple, she'd spent researching contractors. While there were several qualified companies in the area she could call upon, most were prohibitively expensive, and all had daunting wait lists before they could take on any new work. None could match Malcolm's offer, and few had had a better rep—at least where it came to the quality of the actual work—than the irascible Scotsman had turned out to have.

The people she'd contacted had had quite a lot to say about McLeod himself. "Grumpy bastard," "impossibly rude," and "breathtakingly arrogant" were just a few of the epithets she'd collected. However, each of them had to admit, he'd done the job as promised, fulfilling even the most persnickety of requests and finishing every little detail with a professionalism that had surprised them all. "McLeod's an evil genius," one woman had quipped. "He renovated my entire gallery from floor joists to rafters in half the time and with half the crew anyone else could have done it. Even helped rehang the paintings afterward. And then proceeded to insult every single work of art in the place." The woman had laughed. "I didn't know whether to thank him for the good work or sic my dog on him!"

Sera wasn't worried—about McLeod, at least. About hot, quickly regretted kisses with Israeli artisans... well, that was a whole other kettle of fish—one Sera didn't intend to stir endlessly for the rest of the day. She dug Pauline's keys out of her bag and threw open the door to her dream.

Which looked a bit of a nightmare at the moment. Kombucha cups, crumbs, and leftover leis were strewn about the place, victims of last Friday's BRB conclave. Sera sighed, flipped on all the lights, flung the drapes wide, and grabbed a garbage bag. Then she fished her iPod out of her denim jacket and started scrolling through her playlists for the peppiest, most obnoxiously clean-inspiring music she could find.

Ear buds securely screwed in, iPod tucked in back jeans pocket, Sera lost herself in the work.

A couple hours later, she'd managed to pack up most of Pauline's knickknacks, and she'd developed a light sheen of sweat from powering through the task with help from the Ramones, the Clash, and the Specials. Her spirits had lightened with the physical exertion, and her head was wholly focused on the job at hand and the future it promised, *not* on her neighbor. She'd pushed the furniture to the sides of the room until she could deal with what would stay and what had to go—a few of the armchairs were vintage cute, but most were vintage mausoleum—and she'd managed to scrub down most of the surfaces. *Why I'm bothering when we're just going to be tearing up the place, I'm not sure,* she thought ruefully. But she wanted to see the space as close to pristine as possible so she could start over from scratch. She was just looking around trying to determine what to tackle next when her eye was caught by a UPS box that had been left by the front door—probably the one Asher had mentioned the day they'd first met. "Might as well see what's in it," Sera muttered to herself.

She grabbed her pocketknife and headed for the cardboard container. For all she knew, it could be kombucha food, or maybe matching belly-dancing outfits for the rest of the Back Room Babes.

But no. It was weenies.

Knife in one hand, packing tape sticking to her fingers, Sera stared into a carton of cock. There were glow-in-the-dark vibrators shaped like Japanese manga figurines. Glass wands Glenda the Good Witch would have blushed to wave. Double-duty probes that looked more like Joshua trees than something one ought to be filling one's happy crevices with. Dildos, vibrators, and strap-ons packed the box to capacity. A note taped to the invoice read, in flowing cursive, "Dearest Pauline—Hope these keep you humming! (Batteries included, of course!) Love to the Babes—Your friends at the Ecstasy Emporium." The tagline beneath the wholesaler's logo read, "Premium Pleasures. Down and Dirty Prices."

"Dildos," she muttered. "Why did it have to be dildos?"

Abruptly, Sera was back in high school. Tenth grade, to be precise. Friday night, the night of the Spring Semi-Formal.

In her new flower print Betsey Johnson minidress, fishnet stockings, and favorite beat-to-shit fourteen-hole Doc Martens, she was about as fashionable as her grunge-meets-Goth sensibilities allowed her to get. She'd been primping for hours, listening to an old Alanis Morrisette CD while she tried on liquid liner (disaster) and dithered over whether the dress was too much or too little. (The way it rode up the backs of her thighs made her self-conscious, but it was that or her empire waist velour, and she'd gotten *that* stained with ganache when she'd foolishly chosen to wear it while baking for a class fund-raiser.)

Sera *had* to look her best, because tonight would officially be her first real date.

She still couldn't believe Robbie Markham had asked her out. Robbie was *cool.* Robbie was an upperclassman and played for practically all the varsity teams. Robbie had a coif of floppy black hair that shaded one soulful brown eye, and when he flipped it back in that signature Robbie Markham way, all the girls would sigh. What's more, Robbie Markham had, until this week, never deigned to notice Sera was alive. When he'd asked her to be his date to the semi-formal, Sera, who'd planned to boycott the event in favor of a night spent attempting to break the hard-crack boundary on her so-far-spotty candy-making efforts, had literally looked around behind her. But she'd had a wall of lockers at her back, and Robbie, smiling his crooked Robbie Markham™ smile, had filled her field of vision, waiting for her answer with the cocky assurance of a guy whose face was likely to appear on nearly every page of the upcoming yearbook.

"So, um... Sarah, right?"

Sera had nodded, not daring to scare him off by correcting him. Her palms felt sweaty, so she hid them behind her back, pressed flat against the cool blue-painted metal of the lockers.

"You, ah, wanna hit the semi with me?"

Sera had felt like she'd been hit *by* a semi. She honestly wasn't sure if she wanted to go. She didn't know Robbie. Dancing made her queasy. And damn it, she'd really been looking forward to seeing if she could get those caramels to firm up properly. But one didn't say no to a date with Robbie Markham. It was a once-in-a-lifetime experience; even Sera could see that. Caramels could wait.

"Sure," she'd croaked. She'd really, really wanted to throw up.

But she'd said she would *show* up, and now Robbie would be meeting her at the school in less than half an hour.

Wonder if Pauline will notice if I take a nip from her liquor cabinet, Sera thought as she made ready to leave. Pauline kept some Kentucky bourbon and a bottle of single malt around somewhere, she knew from previous raids. While a shot of sour, fiery Maker's Mark was more likely to set her stomach roiling than settle the butterflies currently occupying it, Sera was willing to risk it.

Pauline, unfortunately, was blocking the booze. When Sera emerged from her small bedroom into their living room, she found her aunt sprawled out on her settee, a big Victorian affair draped in lace doilies and tassels, reading her tattered copy of Simone de Beauvoir's *The Second Sex* for the fourteenth time. Seeing her niece decked out in gay cotton print and dark, dramatic makeup, she leapt to her feet.

"Rite of passage!" she cried, throwing her hands to the sky and planting her bare, toe-ringed feet in a wide stance. "Don't move a muscle, kiddo. Let me get my camera. I gotta record this for posterity." Pauline dashed to her bedroom, returning almost instantly with the battered Nikon she'd toted across four continents in her days as a cultural anthropologist. She fiddled briefly with the lens cap and the focus. "The lucky man's not picking you up?" she asked, pouting, though Sera had already told her as much at least twice.

"Guys don't *do* that anymore, Aunt Paulie," she said, rolling her eyes. "We're meeting in front of the school."

"Shame," Pauline continued, clicking her tongue. "I'd have loved to get one of those cheesecake prom night pics of the two of you, even if it is horribly 1950s of me." She sighed and shook her head. "Oh well. This'll have to do. Strike a pose, Baby-Bliss. Make like it's the luckiest night of this young fella's life—because with you as his date, he damn well better think so."

Sera managed a pained grimace for the camera.

"Um . . . Aunt Pauline?" she ventured when the Nikon was safely stowed again. "Can I ask you something?"

"Sure, Baby-Bliss, anything," her aunt replied, giving her a squeeze as Sera reached for her denim jacket and checked her reflection one last time in the mirror by the front door. *Is my eyeliner still crooked?* she agonized briefly, but decided she couldn't afford to start all over again. By the time she was done, Robbie would have given up on her and gone inside, and she really didn't want to look like the lonely dork wandering the halls seeking her date when he'd probably already be hooking up with somebody more popular. Still, her uncertainty was so paralyzing it was hard to get her feet to move. She needed help. She *wanted* her mother like never before, but her mom had been gone for three years, and she couldn't help Sera now. Now there was only Aunt Pauline, who tried hard but who had the maternal instincts of a burlesque queen.

Oh, Mom, she thought, aching. *What I wouldn't give for one of your hugs and pigtail pulls right now.* Sera's eyes stung with sudden longing, but she refused to cry and ruin her eyeliner. She'd wept for her parents long enough—so long she'd missed a good portion of her freshman year, and been so mute with grief even after she returned to school that she'd barely managed to make friends. Things had slowly improved and, Sera hoped, were about to get even better now that she'd been noticed by one of the most popular boys at school. She couldn't afford to mess this up.

But Sera didn't know how to ask Pauline, who had been born bursting with sexuality, what she wanted to ask. So she just blurted it out.

"Aunt Pauline, what do I *do?*"

Pauline's hawklike features crinkled in surprise before realization set in. "You mean, when you're with the boy? Oh, that's simple. You do what you *want* to do, Bliss. No more, no less." She touched her niece's cheek fondly. "You don't need a refresher on our safe sex talk, do you?"

Sera frantically shook her head. That'd been one conversation she wouldn't soon forget. Souvenirs from that discussion had included a rainbow assortment of condoms, a semester-long self-defense class, and a prescription for birth control pills Sera had no intention of filling until she was in college.

"Don't forget you're a strong, confident, beautiful young woman," Pauline reminded her, resettling Sera's denim jacket collar so that it lay properly against her neck. "You deserve the best. After all, kiddo, you're *my* niece." She drew Sera into a fierce, patchouli-scented hug. "Go get 'em, Tiger."

But it was Robbie who turned out to be the tiger, growling and nuzzling her neck like a wild animal the minute he'd shuffled her through their obligatory first dance. In an alarmingly chaperone-free corner of the gymnasium, he boxed Sera in and began smothering her surprised mouth with deep, slurping, porno-inspired kisses. In the background, Hanson's "MMMBop" played at deafening volume, further nauseating Sera.

Sera pulled back. "Robbie—Robbie, whoa!" She grabbed his hand, shocked, and yanked it away from where it was crushing her breast. "What are you *doing?*" Robbie's fingers abandoned the battle for her boob and swooped down to make a grab for her butt. Before she could so much as gasp her shock, he'd gotten a handful and squeezed—hard. His mouth dive-bombed her neck, sucking in a way she was sure must leave hickeys.

Hickeys! she thought, horrified. *God, everyone will see!* She'd always found love bites revolting when girls walked down the halls proudly displaying them like brands of possession by the strutting, preening boyfriends who strolled beside them. And though most girls at their school might kill to sport a Robbie Markham™ hickey, Sera was becoming surer by the moment that she wasn't one of them.

Robbie began pressing his lower body against hers, and Sera grew even uneasier. There was a hardness there, poking her, and she didn't think it was his belt buckle.

"Robbie, stop it!" she cried, pushing against his chest. It took almost all her strength to create some breathing room between them, and his hand was still kneading her ass like a baker with a vendetta against his dough. "What are you doing?" she asked again. She swiped a trembling hand across her slobber-spattered lips.

"What's wrong, babe?" he asked glassily.

Sera had already tasted the stale malt liquor on his breath, so she guessed he'd been hitting the forty ounces from the corner bodega pretty hard. *Maybe if he'd offered* me *a forty,* she thought, *I'd be enjoying this more.* What was wrong with her? Shouldn't she be thrilled to have the hottest boy in school mauling her—and what's more, mauling her in public where everyone could see? But she wasn't. "Skeeved out" was the term that came to mind. Of all the romantic fantasies she'd entertained—Robbie parading her down the halls proudly, Robbie dipping her expertly in a dance—*this* definitely hadn't been one of them.

"Um . . . could we, just, you know . . . slow things down a little?" she squeaked.

Robbie looked confused. "Why would we want to slow down? Speeding up is the fun part." He bumped his crotch against hers illustratively. Those dreamy brown eyes—eyes all the girls sighed over—were glazed over in a way Sera didn't like. "I know *you* know what I'm talking about." He smirked. "Don't worry, babe. I'm all about giving a girl like you what she needs."

"A . . . girl like me?" she sputtered.

"Yeah. A girl with *experience.*" He squeezed her butt meaningfully, trying to move in close again.

"Experience?" Sera's brow furrowed. "What the hell are you talking about?" she demanded with a bit more heat.

Robbie's confused expression was darkening to sullen as the wheels turned visibly in his mind. *Why did I never notice how* dumb *he is?* Sera wondered. "Come on, babe," he pouted. "Don't go all frigid on me. Everyone at school knows you're that sex professor's kid. Bet she taught you some *hot* shit. Show me what you got, sex kitty," he muttered, making little *"meow"* sounds Sera found revolting. "Give me what I came for. C'mon, kiss me." His lips loomed, wet and reddened.

Sera shoved harder. "Get *off* me, Robbie," she hissed. She looked around, not wanting to call attention to her predicament—the whole school would be gossiping about it if they saw her wrestling with Robbie like an outraged virgin—*never mind that I* am *an outraged virgin,* Sera thought hysterically—but hoping for a chaperone who could break things up without making it her fault. Then his words began to really penetrate.

"Wait a minute, what do you mean, what you *came* for?" she asked. She tried to make her voice firm, but it wouldn't fully obey her. She pried his hand off her ass and took a step sideways, out of his grasp. "I thought..." Sera wasn't sure how to finish that sentence. She darted a glance her date's way, and her stomach clenched. Robbie looked pissed. No, he looked *thwarted,* and from the tightness in his face, it wasn't an experience he was used to. When Robbie Markham made a pass, girls were supposed to swoon.

"What, you thought I *liked* you?" he sneered, looking her up and down disdainfully. Sera felt every imperfection cataloged in that stare, from her short stature to her less-than-skinny frame and hair that just wouldn't "do the Rachel" no matter how hard her stylist tried.

Then Robbie did something that hurt worse. He started to laugh.

He guffawed in big, incredulous whoops that began to draw looks from across the dance floor. "You thought—what, that you were going to be my girlfriend now? Oh my God. *Seriously?* Get over yourself. I don't even remember your name, freak show. I just want what you give up for all the guys." He grabbed her crotch, and Sera's mind went blank with horror. Her knee, however, had absorbed Pauline's lessons in self-defense well, and it gave Robbie Markham's balls the kiss he'd been asking for—times a hundred.

Sera left Robbie squealing on the gymnasium floor, clutching his family jewels and encircled by a crowd of gawking classmates.

Returning to school on Monday was the hardest thing she'd ever done. She'd spent the weekend avoiding her aunt's avid questions about her date and obsessing over whether she'd committed social suicide as badly as she feared. But all seemed well; no one harassed her or even mentioned the incident...

Until she opened her locker after third period.

Only to be deluged by a hard rain of dildos.

Dozens upon dozens of them poured from the small space out onto the linoleum floor, bouncing and rolling as, behind her, Sera heard her fellow students howling with laughter. Her face flamed bright red and she spun around.

Robbie stood surrounded by a gaggle of his groupies, arms folded over the front of his letterman jacket. What felt like half the school had gathered in that third-floor hallway, apparently alerted ahead of time that something was afoot. Some of them were laughing so hard they had tears running down their cheeks. But Robbie just glared at her. "Figured these must be more your style, freak show," he taunted. "Well, have fun with them. Sure as shit no boy at this school's ever going to ask your frigid ass out again."

For the rest of her high school career, Sera had been known as *The Ball Buster,* and true to Robbie's prediction, no one had asked her out. She had, however, delighted her girlfriends with buckets of delicious, perfectly formed caramels.

She had also developed a lifelong aversion to sex toys.

Just then, Sera's iPod took it upon itself to start playing Billy Idol's "Dancing with Myself," jolting her back to the present—the store, Santa Fe, the fact that she was twenty-nine years old and no longer thought Betsey Johnson the height of fashion. It was a good feeling. Hell, it was the best feeling ever. *That's not me anymore,* she reminded herself. *I'm sober, I'm strong, and no asshole guy's ever going to intimidate me like that again.*

Ba-dadadadada-DA-da…

The old familiar guitar riff spiked her adrenaline. *Damn straight. I'm a woman of substance, about to be a small business owner. And Robbie Markham is probably fat, bald, and addicted to Cialis.*

Without volition, Sera's head started bobbing and her shoulders started wiggling. As she rose to her feet, her toes tapped in the scuffed combat boots she'd worn for cleaning today—grandchildren to her old high school clompers. She started humming along with the lyrics.

"When there's nothing to lose, and there's nothing to prove…," crooned Billy.

Nothing to lose, indeed. But perhaps quite a lot to prove.

"Fuck it," she growled.

Sera grabbed the nearest dildo—a massive, fleshy pink dong studded with what she assumed were pleasure nubs, though they looked more like alien warts. She cranked up the volume on her iPod as high as it would go and started belting out the words to the song.

Using the wiener as a microphone.

"Oh, oh, oh, oh!" she yelled along with Billy, making a brat-punk face. And again, *"Oh, oh, oh, oh!"*

And suddenly Serafina was dancing. With herself.

The shop's newly cleared floorboards served as her stage, and Sera let her freak flag fly. She strutted and whirled, doing her best Billy Idol impression. Lip curl: check. Head bob: check. Fist pump: oh *hell* yeah. It was just her, Billy, and the empty store, having a private moment. Sera's chin-length hair flew about her sweat-dampened cheeks as she rocked out with her cock out. Dust rose in little puffs around her despite the sweeping she'd done, and the sun, breaking out from behind the clouds, speared in through the front window, giving Sera her own personal spotlight.

She shimmied her shoulders, raised her fists, and pumped her arms above her head until she was sweating as her Idol commanded. Billy reached the chorus, rasping and growling into her ears, reminding Sera she didn't need anyone's approval; she could meet her own needs. *"With my record collection and the mirror's reflection...,"* she howled into the dong.

At the mention of mirrors, Sera's glance caught the one along Pauline's back wall. She strutted over to it, channeling Billy's mojo, wailing the words of his hit into her improvised mike.

Its reflection, however, showed she was *not* dancing with herself. She was performing for an audience of two.

Or at least, one human, and one very curious puppy.

Asher and Silver were arrested just inside her doorjamb, both sets of eyes wide, both jaws unhinged.

"Ahhhhhhhh!" Sera screamed as she spun to face Asher. The dildo, sweat-slicked from her impromptu performance, slipped the bonds of her surprise-slackened fingers and went sailing across the store.

Smacking her landlord—*bull's-eye!*—right in the chest.

Chapter Fourteen

Plunk! With a rubbery plop, the dong bounced off Asher's pecs and landed on the floor. Silver—who seemed to have grown at least six inches since last she'd seen him—growled and pounced on it with delighted fury, grabbing it in his tiny teeth and gnawing for all he was worth. His husky head shook happily as he did his doggy damnedest to subdue his prey.

Sera yanked out her ear buds and came to a crashing halt in the middle of the store. Her hands flew to her lips in horror. Of all the ways she'd envisioned her next encounter with Asher Wolf occurring, this hadn't even made the top five hundred.

"Don't stop on my account," Asher said mildly.

"Jesus, Asher," she swore, "don't sneak up on a girl like that!" Her cheeks bloomed with color, as they seemed so wont to do in his presence. She slunk over to where Silver was enjoying his unexpected snack. "C'mere, boy, drop the weenie," she cajoled, but the pup was having none of it. He growled again and bared his teeth around his prize, backing up behind Asher to ward off her incursion.

Sera gave it up as a bad job. No way was she going to have a tug of war over a wiener with a half-pint puppy in front of her gorgeous—and too damn kissable—landlord. She pushed her unruly hair out of her eyes and dared a look up at Ash. He appeared to be biting his lip to keep from cracking up. An answering grin snuck up on her own lips. "Aw, shaddup," she said finally, though he hadn't spoken. "Let's just pretend you never saw that, okay?"

"I'm not sure I can ever forget such an... impassioned... performance,

Bliss," he said, crossing his arms as though to keep the chuckles contained within his chest, "but I'll do my best to keep it to myself."

"Fair enough. You want something to drink?" she offered, heading behind the counter to give herself some space and let her blush die down. Her heart was hammering, and it wasn't just from dancing. She felt giddy and awkward at the same time; less embarrassed about the performance Asher had just witnessed than the kiss on Friday that had sent him fleeing into the night. Still, on the whole, she had to admit she was glad to see him. "I've only got bottled water, unless you're into Big Mama..."

She had to smile at his quick, alarmed shake of the head. He was hatless today, his old-gold hair cropped closer than it had been last week, very butch. Her fingers itched to test the fuzz on the back of his neck, feel the rough/smooth texture of that buzzed cut. "I'm fine, thank you, Bliss," he said, crossing the room to stand closer. Only the mahogany cabinetry kept them apart, and he narrowed the distance by leaning his hip cozily against it. *Lucky cabinet,* Sera thought.

"I'd offer you a seat, but I'm afraid they're all taken," Sera apologized, gesturing at the armchairs that were occupied with the boxes and bags she'd packed up. She grabbed a bottle of water and guzzled to cool herself down, wetting a paper towel and running it across her cheeks to calm the fires raging there.

"No problem. I shouldn't stay long in any case," said Ash. "I've got a special order to finish for a customer who's coming by this afternoon."

"Oh," she said, trying to keep the disappointment from her voice. She leaned her elbows on the worn countertop. His mirth at her Billy Idol imitation notwithstanding, she could tell Asher was uncomfortable with her today. He wasn't meeting her eyes the way he used to. And she had no doubt about the cause. *No way am I bringing up our kiss. Or his freaked-out reaction. Let* him *stew over it,* she thought. *I've got nothing to apologize for.*

Apparently, Asher felt *he* did. "Bliss..." he began. Like a sudden storm cloud obscuring the sun, his expression grew somber, the light fading from his eyes. He looked harsher, older. He also looked more awkward than she'd ever seen him. Sera's stomach clenched.

"Yeeesss..." she drawled when he didn't continue. She tried to keep her teasing smile in place, but she had a feeling it was about to be dashed.

She was right.

"I'm sorry I kissed you," Asher blurted out. He pushed away from the counter and started pacing, running a hand through his hair. "I should never have done that."

Ow.

"Don't worry," Sera said through lips that had gone stiff. "I didn't have any expectations." She was shredding the paper towel unconsciously between her fingers. "I'm sorry for asking you to dance. It was inappropriate and you probably didn't feel you could say no..."

She looked away, desperate to be anywhere but here, reminded of how much she was lacking as a woman. She recalled how she'd clung to Asher during their kiss, and how he'd been forced to gently but firmly disentangle himself from her clutches. Apparently, one kiss from her was enough to send her landlord racing for the hills, if his pained expression were to be believed.

By the open door frame, Silver whined, locked in a death match with the dildo. He'd wrapped his front paws around the dong and had the head in his mouth, while his back legs kangaroo kicked the shaft. *I know a certain shithead chef I'd like to see receive that treatment,* she thought, momentarily distracted. But thoughts of Blake only sent her mood crashing further. He'd always said she was a lousy lay—a lousy everything, except when it came to pastry. And it seemed he'd been right. Asher had found her kiss repulsive.

Tears burned behind her eyes. She clenched the damp paper towel in her fist, crushing what was left of it. She wished he would just leave. She wished a drink—or several—were still an option for her.

Asher ceased his pacing, his gaze arrested on her face. It must have been showing something of what she felt, because he lurched forward without a hint of his customary grace. Before Sera could react, he was catching her surprised hands in his rough, callused ones. Sera dropped the paper towel as her heart thundered.

"No," he said. Forcefully. "No." More gently this time. "Bliss, I don't

know what you are thinking at this moment, but whatever it is was not my intention."

"I..." She didn't know how to continue. His intentions, her perceptions, both were in a muddle and she wasn't sure how to find her way back out. "Asher, I don't know what to say here..."

"I had no idea I would upset you so much." His hands tightened around hers. "I knew I shouldn't...but I couldn't help myself. I didn't realize how badly it might affect you. Damn it, I can't believe I took such advantage!" One hand left hers to spear through his hair again, as if forgetting he'd shorn it short. He looked ready to tear hanks out.

"Advantage?" she ventured. Sera couldn't fathom what that meant. She'd never met a man who was more of a gentleman than Asher Wolf.

"Yes. It was wrong of me to impose upon your good nature. You were merely fulfilling your friends' dare by dancing with me, and I had to take it further and ruin everything by kissing you. It was inexcusable."

"*Inexcusable?* C'mon, Ash, it wasn't *that* bad of a kiss—was it?"

"Because of our respective positions here," he explained, seeing her befuddled expression. "And no—it wasn't bad at all, Bliss. In fact"—the hand that still covered hers moved in a caressing gesture that sent streaks of sensation up and down her arm—"it was just the opposite. For me, at least. But I should never have taken such advantage."

Sera was catching on. "Because you're my landlord?"

"Just so."

"And you think I felt obligated to—what, put out?—because of that?"

His lean cheeks reddened. "Well..."

Sera burst out laughing.

Really, really hard.

Maybe it was the relief that he hadn't hated her kiss, but she could not seem to stop *ha-ha*ing and *ho-ho*ing, especially when she saw the chagrined expression that spread across his handsome features. Typical macho male.

"Oh, Ash," she said when she could breathe again. "Don't worry about it—really, it's no big thing. And believe me, if your kiss had been unwelcome, I wouldn't have accepted it—*and* reciprocated the way I did.

I'm a big girl. I'd have made my boundaries clear if you were crossing them. You were a perfect gentleman, every step of the way."

"You made it hard to be," Ash admitted. "It was the first time..." He broke off, eyes turning inward. "Anyway, the first time in a very long time that I've had such a delightful evening with a woman. I'm glad to know I wasn't trespassing into inappropriate territory."

You can trespass like that anytime you like, Sera wanted to say. But she didn't quite have the gumption.

"So...we're good?" she asked instead.

"Yes, I believe so," Asher agreed. He dropped her hands abruptly. He seemed to be scrambling for a neutral topic. "So, ah...was your weekend...pleasant?" He winced a bit, as if aware his segue left something to be desired.

Sera had a moment of *schadenfreude* at his discomfort. It was such a novelty to be the one not left tongue-tied in their interactions that she took a second to savor it, having a feeling she'd be back to blushing and stuttering before long. "Nice enough," she allowed. The change of subject was welcome. "I spent a lot of time on the phone, chasing leads about contractors, actually."

"And did you find one?" Ash asked politely.

"I'm thinking of going with your friend Malcolm. I meant to ask your feelings on the subject, since it'd be your walls he'd be tearing down and your floors he'd be ripping up. It's the reason I wanted you to come by today." *Not because I wanted another taste of those freakishly delicious lips.*

Whatever Asher might have said on the subject was drowned out by a shriek coming from the courtyard.

"Oh my gawd, what *is* that *thing?*" a woman's nasal voice pierced the still-damp morning air. "It's growling at me! I think it's going to attack! Don't let it near me, Stanley!" Another high-pitched shriek. "What is that in its *mouth?!?*"

The absence of puppy in the shop registered with Serafina and Asher simultaneously.

"Silver!"

They ran for the door. Skidding to a halt on the porch beside Ash, Sera took in the scene. Asher's little husky had cornered a couple of tourists by the fountain, new chew toy firmly wedged in his drooling muzzle. Tail wagging frantically, he was the picture of friendly curiosity. But apparently Stanley and his wife were getting a different impression. The lady, a woman in her early sixties with a weathered face and a lot of black eyeliner and brittle dyed black hair, was visibly trembling and clinging to her husband for support at the sight of Silver, who didn't come up even as high as the top of her posh leather cowboy boot. Her husband, short and pudgy, with ears as whiskery as the pooch's, looked closer to fainting than she did.

Not dog lovers then, Sera surmised.

"Mister, is this your animal?" the man—Stanley, it seemed—called out.

Silver shook his little head, sending doggy drool flying.

The woman squeaked and clutched her husband's arm tighter. Asher started down the porch steps. "I have that honor," he said lightly. "He won't harm you."

Sera snickered. The worst Silver could do to the tourists would be to cover them in puppy slobber. *But then, if I were wearing a brand-new full-length hand-embroidered shearling that still had the price tag dangling from it, I might consider that a calamity, too.*

Asher stepped forward to defuse the situation. Sera watched admiringly from the porch, resting her elbows on the railing.

Silver, however, wasn't done playing. As Ash reached to scoop him up and away from the treed tourists, the puppy scooted out of reach, barking around his latex prize and wagging ever more furiously. He glanced back at Asher, inviting pursuit. Asher had no choice but to oblige. Enthralled with the game, Silver took off. Asher broke into a lope, even as Sera broke into a grin. Her landlord's lean musculature was a pleasure to watch as he dodged and wove in his impromptu rugby match with the husky. She knew she should help him, but really, it was so much fun to watch...

She wasn't alone in her sentiment, she saw. Across the courtyard, she glimpsed Aruni poke her head out of Tantrastic to see what the yelling was about. The class she was teaching had given up all pretense of maintaining mountain poses or sun salutations or whatever they were doing, crowding the plate-glass window to watch the goings-on. On the *placita*'s opposite side, Mr. Yazzie, who ran a sculpture gallery that specialized in fantastical—and fantastically expensive—glassworks, had also emerged, squinting to see what was up. He pulled his baggy maroon cardigan closer around his stocky body, nodding in response to Sera's friendly wave. Pauline had introduced her to the gallery manager her first week here, and she'd found the older Native American gent very kind and charming, especially when he shyly confessed a penchant for sticky buns. Sera had assured him they'd be on her menu. Now she saw he had a bit of a sense of humor, too. "Five dollars on the puppy," he called. "Care to match it?"

"I've gotta go with the Wolf, George," she shot back. "And make it ten."

George gave her a thumbs-up gesture of acknowledgment.

Asher was rounding the fountain again, Silver in the lead, while the tourists yelped and plastered themselves against the porch railing of Asher's shop. A series of joyous barks erupted from the doghouse, where Sascha and the other pups rested, and the terrified couple squealed and backed away. Sera covered her mouth to keep from giggling.

Silver was barreling toward the *placita*'s entrance, and Sera had a moment's fear he'd get out into the street. He disappeared into the covered archway, Asher steps behind. She heard a yip of doggy dismay, a Scottish-accented "Gotcha!" and then a bark of a laugh. Seconds later, Asher emerged, *sans* puppy but with a huge grin on his face. Behind him, a red-faced Malcolm McLeod trailed, puppy tucked firmly under one arm and dildo pinched gingerly between two fingers.

The tourists skedaddled the moment the way was clear, muttering about wild, depraved beasts and vowing to go in search of more civilized shopping. The *placita*'s front gate clanged pointedly behind them. Aruni and her class gave the dog wranglers deep bows from prayer position, while Mr. Yazzie clapped politely.

"Which one's yours, lass?" Malcolm asked as he reached Sera's front porch, hefting both pup and prop.

"Um, neither, really," she said with a blush. "But I'll take that one from you," she said, nodding for the toy.

Malcolm's mustachios twitched. Sera couldn't tell whether it was irritation or amusement. "Guess that makes the pooch yer property, Asher my boy," he said, passing the panting pup to the taller man.

Asher accepted the runt, crossing quickly to deposit him in the doghouse with Sascha and the others. Sera saw Lupe peeking out from one of the shop's windows, her pouty lips pursed as she caught sight of Serafina. Sera saluted the saleswoman, struggling to keep the snark out of the gesture. *Bet Asher never kissed* you *during a magical evening of dancing under the Fiesta lights,* she thought smugly. But then again, maybe he had. Sera had no way of knowing what sort of romantic escapades her landlord got up to on his own time. He might mumble cryptic hints about his lack of recent action, but how could she tell if he was being honest? Blake Austin had once had her convinced of his fidelity, after all. She wasn't exactly the world's best judge of character when it came to men.

Sera's smile faded, and she forced herself to focus on her new pie maven/construction foreman.

"Thanks for coming, Mr. McLeod," she said, reaching to shake his hand.

Malcolm didn't take it. Instead, he brushed right past her, entering Bliss without a backward glance. "So this is the space, is it?" he asked.

She followed him inside, tossing the toy back in the box with its brethren and wiping her slobbery hand on her jeans. She slanted Asher a raised eyebrow over her shoulder at Malcolm's rudeness. His reply was a rueful shrug as he entered after them. Malcolm was stomping about, his wavy white hair trailing down the back of his weather-beaten coveralls, portly belly proceeding him. He knocked on the mahogany counter, wiggled the recessed shelving, and banged on the whitewashed adobe walls, muttering to himself. After a minute, he gathered himself and leapt into the air, coming down hard with both feet on the scuffed pine floorboards.

Sera gaped. He looked like one of the Mario brothers trying to smash a Yoshi. "What are you doing?" she gasped.

"What's it *look* like I'm doing? I'm checking the floors for soundness. If I'm to be taking this shop from dump to dream, I'll need to know what we can count on, and what'll need replacing."

"Well, *count* on is fine. *Pounce* on is something else," Sera replied. She stuck one hand on her hip and gave Malcolm her best *you're not bossing* me *around* glare.

"Who's the expert here, girlie? Me or ye?"

"Did you just call me *'girlie'*?" Sera hissed.

Asher stepped between them. "Play nice, Malc," he warned. "Remember what I told you."

Sera reminded herself of the vow she'd made to herself not to let the pie maker get under her skin. "What exactly did you tell him, Asher?" she asked.

Malcolm's face reddened even more, but Asher's eyes were innocent. "I told him you were a nice lady who knew what she was doing and that he was a...how do you call it? A dipshit, and one who didn't know when to keep his mouth shut."

"Ah." Sera felt herself grow warm. "And when did you tell him this?"

"We had a quick chat over the weekend," Asher said, waving as if to say it was nothing.

Sera wondered if anything else had come up during their "chat," such as that stunning—and stunningly awkward—kiss she and Ash had shared. She decided she didn't want to know. "Right," she said briskly, hopping up to sit on her counter and give herself some height and distance from the men. "So, guys, I asked you here to talk logistics and make sure what we're planning is kosher with everybody. Can we get down to business, Mr. McLeod, or do you have any other obnoxious remarks you'd like to offer that'll make me reconsider my decision to hire you?"

Malcolm scowled, crossing his arms combatively but keeping a lid on his comments. "Let's talk turkey, lass. I've got a rented lorry full o' fixtures and it's costing me a bloody fortune by the day. I'm no more eager to pussyfoot about than ye are."

"Okay then. Let me show you what I had in mind."

And Sera outlined what she wanted done. She'd drawn up diagrams as best she could, showing where she envisioned her ovens and storage areas, where the prep counters should be, and how she planned to partition off the working areas from the serving and dining spaces. Both men listened intently, Asher taking a backseat while Malcolm put in far more than his two cents.

"I want a wall here," Sera said, gesturing demonstratively. "It should separate the prep area from the front. And I want a giant window in it, with one-way glass so we can see what's going on up front and still maintain a bit of privacy while we work. I want to be able to keep an eye on my customers and counter help, without them having their eyes on me."

Malcolm chewed on his yellowish mustache and made a *"hmphing"* noise. He eyeballed the space. Took out an electronic tape measure from one of his overall pockets. Strode over to one side of the store and aimed the device's laser sight across to the other. Made a note on one of his crinkly order pads. "With the light streaming in, it won't be completely one-way," he warned. "At least in the afternoon, that glass'll let folks see in somewhat."

"That's okay," Sera decided. "It'll give people a taste of what we're up to back there without letting them gawk *too* much. And the mornings are when we really want to focus on working undisturbed. Afternoons, we'll probably be up front half the time anyhow, or just frosting cakes and such in the back."

"Or cleaning," Malcolm muttered. "Feckin' dishes never do themselves, do they?"

"I plan to hire help for that," she assured him. "And a barista for the coffee bar, who can help out at the register. But my aunt Pauline will be the main counter person."

Malcolm's face reddened again.

"You mean to have some doddering old tart bumbling about while we're working the breakfast rush? Are ye daft?"

Sera drew herself up, taking a deep breath to remind herself—*again*—of her vow not to let Malcolm infuriate her.

"There's a lot you need to know about my aunt Pauline, Mr. McLeod. So listen up." Sera stared him down until she was sure he was paying attention, obscurely comforted to catch Asher's smile out of the corner of her eye. "Pauline Wilde is an extraordinary woman, capable of just about anything. She's no more in her dotage than you are, and twice as energetic, if that gut of yours is anything to go by. Not to mention, she's light-years more charming. And yeah, maybe just a little bit of a tart." Sera let a grin peek through her stern demeanor for just a second. "Anyhow, my hiring her isn't a matter for debate—though my hiring *you* is. Got it?"

Malcolm looked as if he might roll up his mustachios and storm out, but Asher slapped him on the back and gave his shoulder a companionable shake. "You'll love Miss Pauline, Malcolm," he assured the stubby Scotsman. "She's one of a kind, just like you. The two of you will get along beautifully."

Sera privately doubted that. "Back to the plans," she said. "Now, Asher, you're okay with us installing the ovens and sinks and refrigeration units along this wall, is that right?"

Asher nodded. "I can show Malcolm the electrical grid and get him the specs he'll need to learn the wiring before he goes knocking holes in the walls."

"Great," said Sera. "I'll also want a second bathroom installed and the one that's there now renovated to accommodate greater traffic."

"What about back there?" Malcolm asked, pointing toward the bead-shrouded back room. "Why not just put the loos in the rear?"

"Unfortunately, that area is sacrosanct." Sera put on her no-negotiating face to cover the mischief that wanted to shine through. "Why don't you go have a look at what's back there," she invited, waving Malcolm toward the beaded curtain.

Malcolm went, muttering about women and their cryptic ways.

He returned with a pinched look on his face.

"I dinna want tae know," he said tightly, his brogue thickening to porridge-like consistency. His red-apple cheeks were fairly glowing. "I kenned ye were a strange bird the minute ye darkened m' doorstep, lass. But if yer money's green and yer cookin's half as good as ye boast, ye could stable a barn full o' leather-clad llamas back there and ol' McLeod wouldn't blink. Just *dinna,* for the love o' heaven, be asking me to bake ye any o' them... *ahem*... anatomically shaped desserts. We clear?"

"We are clear, Mr. McLeod," Sera assured him. "Crystal clear."

After that, the plans went smoothly. Less than a half hour later, they were rolling up their drawings and Sera had sealed up Big Mama for the trip to her temporary storage at Pauline's. She felt fairly confident she'd gotten her ideas across to the irascible Scot, and Asher appeared on board. Her heart lifted and a thrill of excitement raised goose bumps on her skin. *It's really starting to happen,* she thought. Her heart did a happy dance.

"So what's next?" she asked, stuffing her notes back in the messenger bag that served as her purse.

"What's next is *ye* make yourself *scarce,*" Malcolm said, already turning back to his graph paper and pencil stub, measuring tape in one hand.

"Excuse me?"

"Ye heard me. Get out. Come back in six weeks, and I'll have something to show ye." He scratched his thick mane of hair with the blunt end of the pencil stub. "More'n like, I'll have finished the whole works by then. But don't ye be bothering me before then."

Sera stiffened. "You want me to leave."

"Ye slow, lass? Be *gone.* Vamoose. Take a hike. Literally. Yer surrounded by mountains and trails here, so why don't ye get lost along some of them, and find yer way back here 'round the first week of November, like. I won't have ye hovering over me like a hen with only one egg the whole time I'm working in here. I don't work well around persnickety women."

Persnickety? Sera thought. *Is he kidding with that shit?* "And I should—what, just leave the store to your tender mercies during that time?"

"Something like that, aye." Seeing her ire, Malcolm sighed. "Look, lass. Ye just got to our fair city a wee bit ago. Ye probably haven't had much time to sniff around; get to know what she's all about. But ye need to understand this place to become a part of it. Ye need to feel it in yer bones and yer heart. Ye can't do that while yer breathing plaster dust and getting in my way."

"Wow, that was...unexpectedly poetic, McLeod," Sera said with a grudging grin. "But I'm guessing you're a lot more concerned about me being underfoot than fearful for my spiritual welfare."

"Believe as ye will," Malcolm grumbled. "Just don't be blundering about whilst I'm working."

"And you?" Sera asked, looking over at her landlord. He stood slightly to the side, with his arms crossed over his chest, making his knit shirt pull indecently across his corded arms and pecs. "What do you think about all this?"

"I think Malcolm has a point, actually," Asher said mildly. "This may be your best chance to acquaint yourself with your new home before you become too busy to take advantage of its offerings. Besides, there's little you can do to help with the renovations, Bliss—unless you're adept with power tools or drywall?"

Sera had to admit she wasn't.

"Then I suggest you go explore our fair city. I'll happily keep an eye on our contractor friend, since I'm just next door. And of course, I'm sure you'll be stopping in frequently to check on Malcolm's progress. Malcolm, surely you have no objection to that?"

"I suppose not," he grumbled. "So long as the lass ain't planning on telling me how to install my own ovens."

Sera stopped to consider. She'd pictured herself wading knee-deep in the renovations, maybe wielding a hammer or painting walls—at the very least, supervising the contractor and his assistants daily. But she had to admit, she'd probably be more in the way than helpful, considering her utter incompetence with power tools. Maybe her pie Nazi did have a point. Maybe she *could* afford to take a small step back here, just for a little while. Once the bakery opened, Sera would be on her feet night and day, baking and serving from 4 a.m. 'til 4 p.m., then handling shop business until she collapsed. She was more than willing to put in the hours to make her dream come true. But Malcolm was right. She knew less than nothing about drywall, nail guns, and electrical engineering. If she hovered over the construction like a hen with just one chick, she'd only get in the way. For sure, she didn't intend to traipse off on a Caribbean cruise for the next month and a half while her half-crazed contractor bashed down walls willy-nilly, but he was right—better take advantage of this last hurrah to see some sights and get to know her new home.

"You'll really help me keep this wild man on a short leash?" she asked Asher.

"I will—if you'll promise to take his advice and go explore Santa Fe while you have the chance." He drifted closer, until Sera could smell a hint of that special Asher scent—clean cotton, hot metal, and man, man, man. "Perhaps you'll let me show you some of my favorite spots," he offered. "It would be my pleasure, Bliss."

Sera's face warmed. Oh, she'd like to explore some of Asher's favorite spots, that was for sure. And maybe she could introduce him to a few of her own...

Focus, fool, she told herself sternly. *You're here to start your life over, not blow it all to hell again over a guy who'd be way out of your league even if you* didn't *have that pesky no-O problem.*

Sera slung her messenger bag more securely across her body and hoisted Big Mama onto her hip. She turned away from the men, heading for the door.

"I'm gonna need some wheels," was what she said.

Chapter Fifteen

"There are times in life, Pauline, when a woman just needs a man."

Hortencia had been arguing as much to her lover for the last twenty minutes. It wasn't going over well. If they hadn't had an audience, as a matter of fact, Sera feared it might have come to blows. Fortunately, they were at Hortencia's place of business, and even Pauline had enough decorum to keep her outrage at a simmer within the hushed confines of the yarn shop.

As Hortencia and Pauline bickered, Sera busied herself examining a ball of something that looked remarkably like one of the Tribbles from *Star Trek*. Orange, fluffy, and incredibly soft, the mohair puffball perched on the top of Hortencia's counter among dozens of its friends in a rainbow array of colors. She wondered if it would start cooing if she petted it, as she was tempted to do. All around her, similar poofs in all shapes and sizes crowded bins and shelves, threatening to tumble forth in an avalanche of crafty softness.

Hortencia was one of three employees at Knit-Fit, all comfortable-looking women in the fifty-plus age bracket who took their art with deadly seriousness. Today, Hortencia was sporting one of her own creations: a cable-knit Aran sweater of astonishingly intricate design in a soft salmon shade Sera wouldn't personally have chosen. She also had a little crocheted flower brooch in a slightly rosier hue pinned to her bosom, and her homemade socks, peeking out of her sage green Merrell mules, were an alpaca blend in complementary tea rose ripples. She looked utterly at home in the shop.

She also looked pretty pissed off.

"We *need* a man," she was insisting to Pauline. "I've been buying my family's cars for decades, and I'm telling you, you get a better deal if you go with a *caballero.*"

"I am physically *nauseated* that you would suggest such a thing, Hortencia Alvarez." Pauline made a gagging sound, grabbing up a ball of yarn and squeezing the fiber until it bulged out between her fingers. "What did our sisters march for, what did we sacrifice and fight for all these years if, here and now in the twenty-first century, we're still depending on men to do our haggling?"

"Which do you think *Sera* cares more about? Her principles or her bank balance?" Hortencia shot back.

Both women turned their attention to Serafina, who was suddenly very busy examining the wool-to-alpaca ratio on the label of a ball of worsted weight.

"Well? What do you say, kiddo? Do you want that knuckle-dragging Malcolm McLeod along to infantilize and disempower you, or can you stand on your own two feet and make your own bargains?"

Sera smothered a grin. "Oh, I don't know, Aunt Paulie. I think I could use all the help I can get." She gave Pauline's shoulder a squeeze to mitigate the sting of her betrayal, taking a moment to appreciate her aunt's T-shirt du jour, which was silk-screened with a faded image of Helen Reddy in her heyday. Underneath, someone—undoubtedly Pauline—had scrawled a caption in Sharpie marker: "I am Woman. Hear me r-O-ar!"

"See?" Hortencia indulged in a moment of genteel gloating. "Sera sees the sense in what I'm saying. We need a man for this mission, and Mr. McLeod was available—*and* suitably threatening-looking. So quit your bitching, drop that stitching, and let's get on the road already."

"You just like the way he flirts with you," Pauline grumbled to Hortencia, arms crossed beneath her braless breasts, innocent yarn skein squashed in the grip of her white-knuckled fist.

Sera smothered a grin. It was true, Malcolm *had* looked a whole lot more amenable to the suggestion of playing token Y-chromosome for their car-shopping expedition once he'd caught his first gander at Hortencia. In fact, when she'd introduced them the other day, it was the first time she'd ever seen her pie Nazi completely bereft of his customary bluster.

Pauline, who had already taken a deep dislike to the Scotsman when *she'd* met him a few days earlier, had been quick to notice his uncharacteristic pleasantness. She'd been even quicker to disparage the Scotsman's character, appearance, and capabilities both culinary and contractorial once McLeod was out of earshot. Though she was raring to take on her new career as late-in-life counter commander at the new bakery, Pauline wasn't at all keen on working with a "chauvinistic, unkempt caveman" who saved his only sweetness for his pies—and her life partner. Hortencia had pooh-poohed her disparagements, claiming to find McLeod a rather winning individual. That, of course, had set off a whole new round of arguments between the lovebirds, which they appeared to have resolved in the privacy of Pauline's boudoir. Sera was just glad the house's adobe walls were a foot thick.

In truth, Sera didn't know whether to be amused at or envious of the two women's closeness. What, she wondered, would it be like to have someone—Asher, for instance—jealous over her?

Don't be ridiculous, Sera, she chided herself. *Who's his competition? The last man you dated was so fond of you he's spent the last year trying to ruin your life and crush your career. You're not exactly a man-magnet. You're lucky Asher's as kind to you as he has been, but you better forget any fantasies that he's suddenly going to develop a mad, passionate crush on your sorry self.*

Then Sera shook herself mentally. *Whoa. Who hit the bummer button? It's too damn nice a day to go feeling sorry for yourself,* said the healthier part of her mind—the part she'd been working on developing since she'd stopped pickling it with booze. *Think about it. Maybe you've had a few romantic disasters. Maybe relationships aren't your forte, but you've still got a lot going for you. You're young (well, youngish), you're free, and you're about to buy your very first car. Stop being a dweeb about your landlord and get with the program.*

For a wonder, her brain actually behaved. Sera refocused on the day ahead of her and the women she was with. *Gratitude,* she heard Maggie's voice remind her. *Think about where you've been, and feel blessed at how much better things are* now. She brought herself back to the present—the brisk, sunny day, the woolly-smelling, colorful yarn shop, and her family. Nutty as they were, she wouldn't change them for the world.

"For the *last* time, you ludicrous woman," Hortencia was saying as she gathered up her windbreaker and tugged it on over her sweater, "we are not having this argument again." She slung her handbag over her shoulder. "I swear to God, you'd think I was Miss America if you listen to that one," she said to Sera, winking. "Just this morning she was ready to belt the bag boy at Trader Joe's for offering to double bag my groceries."

"I'm *sure* there was a *double entrendre* in there," Pauline muttered, lobbing the well-squeezed skein into a bin of matching yarn. "You should have seen the outrageous wink he gave her, Bliss," Pauline insisted. "Like I wasn't standing *right there!*"

"He had an eyelash in his eye, fool," Hortencia snickered, chivvying them out the door and waving good-bye to her coworkers, who were sipping Earl Grey and poring over a pattern book at the back of the store. The door closed behind them with a jingle as light as Sera was determined to keep her mood.

The three women walked the block and a half from Knit-Fit to *Placita de Suerte y Sueños,* and Sera was pleased to hear the sound of hammering and saws from within her half-baked store by the time they passed beneath the portico and caught sight of the earth mother fountain. Things had been going well with the renovations as far as she could tell. She was no expert on demolition, but Malcolm seemed to have done the deconstruction in record time—probably eager to get his fixtures out of storage in the moving truck and installed in their new home. Aruni, she imagined, was probably a bit less pleased, as the commotion was sure to be harshing the mellow of her students' yoga classes at Tantrastic. The yogini had assured her everything was fine, however. "Every time I hear the hammering," she'd chirped, "I just think, "we're that much closer to homemade croissants and cupcakes!" Sera had been keeping Aruni's students in yoga-suitable treats as a special thank-you for their patience with the construction. Though multigrain energy bars sweetened with brown rice syrup were personally not Sera's bag, she was more than happy to whip up a batch now and again for a good cause.

"Why we couldn't just ask Asher is beyond me," Pauline was saying as they passed Lyric Jewelry. "If you're so fired up to lug along a Y-chromosome on this mission, you could have at least gone with someone easier on the eye. I'm sure he'd be happy to help us..."

"We're not asking Asher," Sera said quellingly, keeping her voice low as they brushed past the extravagant foliage that shaded his shop. It wasn't the first time she'd vetoed the idea. "The man's done enough for us as it is, and I'm not taking advantage of his good nature for every little thing," she insisted. What she'd *like* to take advantage of was hardly his good nature, but Sera wasn't about to cop to that. She kept her eyes studiously averted from his shop windows. Though things had been cordial between them since the kiss incident, Sera hadn't wanted to push her luck, and she still wasn't sure what the deal was with her and Asher. Was he interested? Was she?

Oh, c'mon, you liar. You're interested.

But Sera had decided that, interest or not, she wasn't going to pursue her sexy landlord. Even if she *could* catch his fancy—and she wasn't at all confident of that, kiss notwithstanding—things were simply going too well in her life right now to take such a risk. She'd rather focus on what she could control, rather than her unmanageable attraction to a man who was way out of her league, and whom she could never hope to satisfy.

Speaking of things I can't control... Sera's eyes widened as Malcolm barreled out of the store, dusted head to toe in white plaster and cursing up a storm.

"I canna go w'ye today, and that's all there is to it," he blurted out, his brogue thicker than the dust that blanketed his coveralls. "Damn plaster won't set right and these idjits"—he waved back toward the shop, where his crew of day laborers were doing their best to ignore him—"wouldn't know spackle from shite if I dunked their fool heads in a bucket of it. So dinna give me no grief, woman. 'Tis impossible." He stopped short when he saw the two older women. His florid face was all set to fall into a scowl at the sight of Pauline when his gaze was arrested by the shorter, grandmotherly Hortencia. Malcolm rocked back on his heels, one hand self-consciously moving to dust off his long ponytail and smooth stray strands back from his whiskery cheeks. "Och, sorry, Miss Alvarez. I dinna see ye there."

"Hello, Mr. McLeod. Do I take it from your disheveled appearance that you need to reschedule?" Hortencia was cordial, no more, but Sera could see even that much warmth was too much for Pauline. Sera's aunt moved closer, slinging an arm ostentatiously around her lover's shoulders. Hortencia shot her a disbelieving look and shrugged out of Pauline's clutches.

Malcolm's eyes traveled back and forth between the two older women, assessing. "Afraid so," he allowed. "I hope ye'll not hold it against me."

Sera was more worried about flaky plaster than flaky contractors. She took a step forward to see what was going on inside the store, but Pauline grabbed a handful of the back of her jean jacket. "Certainly not," Pauline said crisply. "I'm quite sure we can manage without your"—she looked the dusty Scot up and down—"assistance."

Sera had never heard Pauline sound quite so schoolmarmish. She gave her aunt a smooch on the cheek for being so cute—and for keeping her from obsessing over what was going on inside her half-demolished place of business. "I'm sure we'll be fine on our own," she said. "C'mon, ladies, let's get a move on."

"Did you need help with something, Bliss?"

Asher's voice brought Sera up short. But then, she always felt she came up just a little bit short when her landlord made an appearance.

It was Pauline who answered Asher. "Hey there, hot stuff. As a matter of fact, we *could* use a little help here, if you've got an hour or so to spare."

"Oh, no, Pauline, really," Sera protested. She turned reluctantly to face Asher. Sometimes just the sight of his handsome face socked her in the gut with a feeling she could only describe as "sucker punch." Today was one of those days. Asher stood leaning on his porch rail, sporting a white linen shirt, untucked, collar open to reveal the heavy silver chain around his neck. If there was ever a man born to wear white linen, Sera thought, it was Asher Wolf. Khakis and scuffed motorcycle boots completed the look, and his hair was an artless tussle of gold-bronze spikes. Tucked under one arm was Silver, tongue lolling. The puppy barked a greeting.

"Ash, Sera needs a man. Today."

Even Hortencia winced at Pauline's pronouncement, shooting Sera a sympathetic look.

Her landlord straightened up. Was it her imagination, or did he look alarmed?

"Aunt Pauline!" Sera cried. "I do not!" She turned to Ash. "Seriously! I'm all good. No man required. Happily man-less here!" Her voice was a squeak, her face redder than a chile ristra.

One corner of his generous mouth quirked up. He hefted the pup higher, and Silver, snugly ensconced in his master's grip, gave him a snuffly puppy lick on his ear.

Sera understood the impulse.

"Nonsense," Pauline snorted, slapping Sera on the back rather harder than necessary. She shot her niece a look Sera wasn't the least tempted to try to interpret. "Weren't we all just saying how important it was to have a swinging dick around on a mission like today's?"

"Actually," Hortencia began, "you were pretty firmly *against* the whole 'swinging dick' agenda, if I remember back as far as fifteen minutes ago."

Sera felt a little faint. Was there something about passing through menopause that made women unutterably crass?

There was nothing for it but to grab the . . . well, grab . . .

"Ash," she blurted out, striding up to the railing between them, "I'm trying to buy a car. These two got it into their heads that we should ask a man along, to help us check out the vehicle and make sure the dealer doesn't take us for the proverbial ride. McLeod was going to tag along for backup, but he's, ah . . ." She looked at the pie maven, who had turned back to the store and was gesticulating rudely at some of the workers inside. "Occupied," she finished lamely. "Anyhow, it was just a thought. We should be fine on our own. I'm sure you're far too busy . . ."

And I'm far too dizzy, when you're around . . .

"Nope," he said cheerfully. "Never too busy to help a friend, Bliss. Lupe can mind the store."

"I can?" The sylphlike saleswoman stood in the doorway of the jewelry store, hands on annoyingly curvy hips. The glare she shot Sera could have curdled lemon mousse.

"I'm more than confident in your ability to run the shop for the rest of the afternoon, Lupe," said Asher, giving her a warm look. "You have such a way with the tourists." Sera privately doubted that, but was glad to see Lupe's mollified expression. She didn't need to go accruing enemies out here—the one she had back in New York was enough to last her a lifetime. "You won't mind closing up the shop for me this evening, will you?" Asher asked his assistant. His green eyes were limpid, innocently inquiring.

Lupe wasn't immune to their blandishment. She drew herself up to her full height, dwarfing Sera, at whom she shot a "my boss trusts me with important matters" expression. "You can rely on me, Asher." She gave him a molten look. "Always."

"That's great, Lupe, thank you so much." Asher was already turning away. "Hey, Malc!" he called. Malcolm left off berating his day laborers and turned around. "Can I ask you to drop off Sascha and Silver at my place on your way home? Key's under the mat."

"Aye, if ye'll promise the little runt won't take a shite in my truck."

"He won't," Ash called back with a grin. "I hope," he muttered too softly for Malcolm to hear, winking at Sera.

"What happened to the other pups?" Sera asked, noting their absence for the first time.

"They were old enough for their new owners to take them home, so I had to let them go." Asher sounded a bit wistful. He ruffled Silver's gray-and-white fur and plopped an unself-conscious kiss on the top of the pup's head. "It's just him, his mama, and me now, until we find just the right person to take our little rapscallion in."

Sera reached out a tentative hand to pet Silver, and received a generous tongue bath for her reward. "I'm sure you'll find someone soon," she said, feeling a pang at the thought of no longer seeing the little pooch around.

"Are we petting puppies or buying cars here?" Pauline's voice interrupted them. "C'mon, before all the hybrids are gone."

Sera sighed, knowing a nice, sensible vehicle—probably a Subaru, if Pauline had anything to say about it—lay in her very near future. And while she was excited about owning her first-ever automobile, she couldn't say she was psyched that she'd be buying something so boring she'd probably have trouble picking it out in the parking lot. *Still,* she reminded herself. *This is what sober people do. They make sober-minded life choices, and buy sober-minded cars. Suck it up, Sera.*

"Right." She hitched her shoulders into something resembling decent posture. "Let's go."

Next thing she knew, Sera was smushed up next to the very manly Israeli in the backseat of Pauline's beat-up old Impreza, while Pauline and Hortencia chattered away up front. They could have been discussing anything from presidential politics to the best way to prepare gumbo, for all Sera paid heed. Her senses were centered squarely on the man pressed against her right side.

Fuck, he smelled good. Like, slather-me-in-butter-and-call-me-a-biscuit good. His hot-forge scent, in the confines of the suddenly tiny Subaru, was positively overwhelming. *Would it be too obvious if I rolled down a window?* she wondered. *Because if I don't do something to distract myself from those fantastic pheromones, I might start licking him. Right there in the hollow of his throat, where his collar is open just that tiny little...*

"So," Sera asked, trying to breathe shallowly. "Guess you know a lot about cars, huh, Ash?" But she wasn't really focused on his answer. *If I could make a dessert with a scent like that,* she was thinking, *women would be stuffing themselves silly with it.*

"Almost nothing," Ash replied blithely.

"Really?" she asked, distracted despite herself. "I would have pictured you as some sort of mechanical savant. You're so...crafty, after all." Sera winced, aware of how dumb that had sounded.

"Not at all." He smiled. "In the army, I drove a Jeep, and we were taught to keep our equipment in good order, but beyond that, I never bothered much with the workings under the hood. I was always more interested in the mechanics of organic materials—growing things, the flex and give of wood, the alchemy of molten metal under my tools. Electronics, hoses, and combustion engines never appealed to me the same way."

Sera was caught up in the vision of Asher wearing fatigues, probably toting an Uzi or something. She remembered all Israelis were required to serve in the military in their youth, but it was hard to see Asher in that light. Manly, yes. Militant—no. He was far too full of kindness and appreciation for life to strike her as a warrior.

She basked in that kindness whenever he turned it her way, but she knew if he ever learned the truth about her, it could easily turn to pity. A lump formed in Sera's throat, all unexpected. If he looked under *her* hood, he'd find her as defective as they came.

An addict. A failure in her career. And less than a woman in the way that counted most.

She had no business fantasizing about... wait, what the hell *was* she fantasizing about when it came to Asher? Marriage? Babies? Mad, passionate, and most of all, *fulfilling* sex?

Sera was very much afraid the answer was "yes" to all three.

You're buying a car, girlfriend, she scolded herself. *Not a lifetime in some adobe dream house with a coyote fence and two-point-four unexpectedly attractive offspring. Stop daydreaming before you come to grief.*

Sera inched away from Asher and stared out the window, hoping this mission would be quick.

It wasn't.

Despite the earlier coolness of the day, it was hot out at the Auto Park, perhaps because there were no trees or any other sort of cover. The sun was beating down, *Good, Bad and Ugly* style upon the asphalt-paved lot, a hundred mini suns bouncing back at Sera from the hoods of highly polished vehicles, making her wish she hadn't forgotten her sunglasses back at Aunt Pauline's. She'd taken off her denim jacket and tied it around her waist, but sweat was still trickling down her neck and pooling uncomfortably in her cleavage (as she hoped Asher hadn't noticed). A headache had started just above her brows, and she thought she might be a little dehydrated.

No one had told her buying a car was such hard work.

Then again, it probably *wasn't* such hard work for normal people. But Sera had been struck with an attack of circumspection, balanced uncomfortably against the deep, dark desire to do something truly dumb. For an addict, accustomed to acting on impulse and regretting it later, it was like stomping on the gas and brake pedal simultaneously. Her adult, sober mind knew the smart thing to do. But her lizard brain was demanding its due—loudly.

The lot was full of perfectly nice cars. Her budget and business needs *demanded* a perfectly nice car. But she didn't *want* a perfectly nice car. She wanted a badass car. Or maybe a truck. A big, honking pickup truck with scary, nubbly tires that came up to her waist and a corrugated steel bed just begging for a dusty old dog, hopefully wearing a bandanna around its neck and panting up a storm. It would bounce up and down dirt roads just like trucks did in commercials, spitting gravel and roaring. It would cart tons of whatever the hell it was asked to cart (never mind that Sera's desserts were so light and airy the biggest cake in her repertoire barely weighed ten pounds). And it would say, loud and clear, "I am not a wimp. Put that shit right out of your mind. I am a confident, strong, undefeated woman. And I am every bit as badass as my truck."

In the course of trying to talk herself out of this impractical longing, Sera had driven half the cars on the lot. Half of *those* were too expensive—far beyond the range of a baker just beginning her own business. The other half were divided into the practical—*yawn*—and the even more practical—*coma.* Subarus, Sera had discovered, were apparently the vehicle of choice among the green-chile-eating set. "Hippie liberal Dukakis–voting cars," she could hear Blake's voice in her head, clear as a bell and disdainful as always. He had driven a succession of flashy BMWs throughout the time Sera had dated him, looking down that long, aristocratic nose of his on "rice burners," as he dubbed the whole range of modest, unassuming Japanese automobiles.

Almost, but not *quite* enough reason to buy one.

While Serafina had no problem with hippies, liberals, or those optimistic enough to have supported Dukakis, she simply wasn't finding anything that spoke to her. Her aunt and Hortencia had had the good sense to step back after the first hour or so, when their well-meaning suggestions ("Oh, you don't want the dark blue one, dear, you'll roast!") and helpful hints ("Baby-Bliss, you can't buy that one, it barely has a backseat. How will you get your rocks off in a car like that?") hadn't brought Serafina closer to a decision. They'd retreated into the cool of the dealership's interior. Sera could see them through the glass, pretending to be fascinated by a display of Chevy Tahoes that positively dwarfed the two women.

Asher had hung in there with her, however, even through several abortive test drives. Sera glanced at him, then quickly away, her cheeks flushed from more than sun. She'd seen how he clenched his knuckles white on the armrest a few times as she had taken a curve too quickly in an unfamiliar vehicle. But he'd maintained his cool, not commenting on her questionable driving skills. He hadn't tried to influence her decision either, though she rather wished he would. Otherwise they might both grow old here. Even the leathery, sunglass-clad salesman had wandered off after a while, sensing he wasn't going to hook this fish anytime soon.

"Damn it," she muttered. "I can't do this." She turned back to Asher, looking up at him with a grimace of apology. "I'm sorry for wasting your time, Ash. I guess I'm just not ready to buy a car after all." Stupid tears were pricking at the corners of her eyes, and Sera pretended it was just the sun, shading her face with one hand to hide them from the tall Israeli. "We should collect the ladies and go, I guess."

Asher stopped her with a hand on her shoulder as she began to trudge toward the dealership. "Bliss," he said. Then he put a hand under her chin and lifted her face to meet his gaze in a way that would have been patronizing coming from any other man, but was impossibly hot when he did it. "What is it you really want?"

Aside from you?

"I don't know." Sera shook her head to dissipate the tears before they could fall. She plunked her hands on her hips and took in a deep breath, not wanting her landlord to see her so vulnerable. Experience had taught her it was a poor idea to let the male of the species catch her anything less than fully composed. Then she blew out the breath, deciding to let him in, just a little bit. "You know what, Asher? Actually, that's not true at all. I know *exactly* what I want, I just don't think I should want it."

Asher merely looked at her with one brow quirked, not helping, not judging. His hand had fallen away from her face, but she could still feel its heat against her skin. Would probably be feeling it when she tucked herself into her lonely bed tonight.

Sera sighed. She'd better fess up. "It's stupid. But I want... that one." She pointed.

The car of her dreams sat on the edge of the lot, exiled with the used—excuse her, "pre-owned"—cars. It was not cute. It was not fuel-efficient. And Sera was fairly sure it wasn't even an automatic. The powder blue pickup was at least a decade old, rusting around the edges, and absolutely perfect.

"The Dodge Ram 2500?" Asher sounded a bit incredulous.

"Is that what it is?" Sera was already drifting closer to it. Up close, it was even bigger, and she could see that someone—clearly not at the factory—had painted jaunty flames along its haunches. *Man, this baby has it all,* she thought. Big-ass tires? Check. Massive engine? If the hood was anything to go by, a whole herd of draft horses probably lived under there. Canine-friendly bed? Sera peeped up and over the flank of the blue beast and saw someone had left a blanket with some ready-made dog hair already on it. Never mind that she didn't even have a dog. Maybe Asher would let her borrow his when Silver got old enough. She looked back at the Israeli, who had followed her to inspect the monstrous truck.

"I must be crazy to even consider this," she murmured.

"Quite possibly," Asher agreed.

"I mean, you practically have to wear a Stetson to even get behind the wheel of this beast," she continued.

"I'm sure we can borrow one for the test-drive," Asher replied. "I believe I saw a gentleman wearing one enter the dealership just a few moments ago. I bet he wouldn't mind..."

Sera swatted Asher's arm, her mood swinging dizzily with his teasing and her own swelling case of the fuck-its. "C'mon, Ash, you're supposed to be talking me out of this."

"Is that what I'm supposed to do?" he asked, feigning surprise. "I was under the impression I was here to help you buy a car."

"A car, yes. A monster truck I probably can't even drive, no."

"You can't drive? Ah, that explains a lot..."

Sera shot him a dirty look, then spoiled it with a rueful smile. "Well, I mean, of course I can drive. I passed my test and everything; I have a license—thanks to Pauline. I just never got that much practice living in New York City, you know?"

"What does Pauline have to do with your driving license?" Asher wanted to know.

"She gave me the advice that helped me pass my road test," Sera said, uncomfortable now. *Why did you have to bring* that *up, big-mouth?* she chided herself.

"And what advice was that?" Asher's eyes were alight now.

She squirmed a bit. "Well, I was really nervous the day I had to go take the test. I must have been seventeen or so. So I asked my aunt what I should do. She said, 'I only got one piece of advice for you, kiddo.'" Sera imitated her aunt's intonation with the ease of a lifetime's familiarity. "'You wanna pass your test, wear a tight shirt.'" Sera shrugged. "It worked."

"I can see why it would," Asher said, eyeing Sera's cleavage, showcased by her V-necked white tee.

Sera flushed. *You're probably reading him wrong, Sera,* she told herself. *That, or you've been in the sun too long. He is* not *flirting with you.* "Yeah, well, anyhow...I don't really drive that much, but I always had this fantasy..." She should really *not* be discussing fantasies with this man. "This, dream, rather. That one day I'd have myself a really, I don't know... *unladylike*...car. And that I'd totally own it—master it, if you know what I mean." Sera rambled to a halt.

Asher's eyes crinkled at the corners. "I think I do. And speaking of 'mastering'..." He stepped closer to Sera, and for a moment she had the crazy idea that he was going to snatch her into an embrace like some sort of movie brigand...until he reached around her and levered open the truck's enormous steel door. "I think you should take your fantasies seriously, Bliss. Why else have you come here, if not to live your dreams?"

The abyss yawned, tempting. Sera took a leap...

Up, and into the truck's cab.

Oh yeah. The view from up here made her feel instantly more badass. Taller. Stronger. And prepared to take a whole lot less shit. A smile tugged at the corners of her lips. Her heart rose, and she couldn't resist beaming down at her landlord.

"I'll go get the keys from the salesman," Asher said.

Chapter Sixteen

It was a bare half hour before sunset when Sera roared down the gravel-strewn road toward Asher's house in Arroyo Hondo, proud owner of a 1999 Ram with one hundred and fifty-seven thousand miles on it. Pauline and Hortencia, lips zipped against leaking disapproval, had headed home in the Subaru, leaving Sera to give Asher a ride back to his house.

Which she was doing to the best of her ability.

Thank God Asher had had all that military training, she thought. Had he not, his nerves might not have survived Sera's maiden voyage in the truck she'd named, with some irony, "Cupcake." But all things considered (and a few chamisa bushes notwithstanding), she'd done pretty well, following Asher's instructions to the little community tucked away in the hills just south and east of Santa Fe proper. With the small part of her attention not engaged in keeping the one-and-a-quarter-ton truck on the rutted track, her eyes took in the environs—rolling hills, endless vistas stretching nearly a hundred miles into the mountains that limned the horizon like construction paper cutouts in varying shades of gray and blue, the clouds above orange and purple and rose with imminent dusk. Short piñon trees and scrub brush characterized the landscape, which felt somehow both wide open and strangely sheltering. Then Sera turned her attention back to the road, which was a bit too twisty for gawking greenhorns to take for granted.

At length, with *almost* no new scratches on her not-exactly-direct-from-the-factory paint job, they turned down Asher's drive. Sera's face broke out in a grin—one part pride that she'd wrangled Cupcake into doing her bidding, one part delight at the sight of the place where Asher lived.

The patio alone was worth the price of admission. Native stone paths embedded in fine gravel twined whimsically between garden beds bursting with lavender, rosemary, and sage bushes, forming a graceful trail leading guests to the front door. The door itself was an intricately carved Balinese design of birds and flowers, mellowing into obscurity against warm adobe walls. Beside it, a rustic portal of weathered poles gave shade where it leaned against the side of the house, several bird feeders swinging from its upper reaches. A ladder to nowhere—a phenomenon Sera saw nearly everywhere in Santa Fe—angled itself against the wall farther toward the back of the house. A brick-paved porch encircled by a low adobe wall created a welcoming space for an outdoor meal or a quiet moment of contemplation. All this Serafina took in with a sweeping glance that told her her landlord's home was something special.

Sera's breath caught as she turned the clunker carefully into the guest parking slot, trying not to slay any shrubbery as she muscled the truculent truck around the gravel turnabout. The turning radius on the old behemoth was... less than ideal. But she got the darn thing in Park and it either stalled out or turned off, she wasn't sure which—and didn't much care. She let out her breath in relief.

"Made it!" she said brightly.

Asher gave her a look she couldn't quite place. Then he leaned over, across the gear shift, and dug one hand into her hair. He pulled her close to him, making Sera gasp, then planted a kiss...

On her forehead.

A brotherly—perhaps even patronizing—kiss.

Before Sera could react, he'd hopped from the truck, motorcycle boots kicking up little puffs of dust. "Come, Bliss," he invited. "You must stay for dinner. After your adventure, you've got to be starving. I know I am." He flashed her a grin as he slammed the truck's door and came around to her side.

Is he really going to... Yes, he really was going to open her door for her, all chivalry, never mind that she was driving a truck so butch it practically took testosterone instead of gasoline.

Sera didn't try to protest. She *was* starving, and besides, she was dying to see where Asher lived—and not so incidentally, to spend more time with him. Brotherly kiss or not, her heart was racing far more than her recent ride could account for. "Wow, um, sure," she said, hopping the considerable distance down from the driver's seat to the ground and reaching up to slam the door. "Dinner sounds awesome, if it's not too much trouble. I mean, if you didn't have any other plans or anything..."

"No other plans, Bliss," he said, leading the way. "I'm all yours tonight."

If only...

She trailed after him, clutching her keys in one hand and surreptitiously trying to smooth her disheveled hair with the other. Dinner with Asher was unexpected—intimidating, but so enticing she simply had to accept. "Just a sec," she said, pausing on the patio. "Gotta check in with Aunt Pauline so she doesn't worry." Quickly, she sent her aunt a text message letting her know where she'd be and that she hadn't had a gruesome accident in the "monstrosity," as Pauline had dubbed her new truck. Almost instantly, Pauline flashed back a winky emoticon that Sera could swear was a leer, along with a message saying, "Atta girl! I won't wait up." Shaking her head at her aunt's incorrigibility, she looked up at Asher. "Okay, all good now. Lay on, Macduff."

With a small flourish that reminded her of the first time they'd met at P-HOP, he invited her to precede him, and Sera smiled as she passed before him into the house.

Her smile grew as she took in the interior.

The entire right side of Asher's living room was one long wall of glass. Floods of evening sunshine slanted in from the patio, filtered through passive solar windows and the leaves of his ever-present plants. Everywhere, foliage made itself at home, trailing vines, poking up proudly from pots, hanging from rafters. The perfume of growing things scented the air with a subtle, earthy tang and provided a trace of precious humidity. To the left, a galley kitchen with acres of polished wood counters branched off from the living room. A wall of built-in bookshelves, packed to capacity with novels and biographies in both Hebrew and English, was tucked to one side, with doorways leading out of sight to the left and right. Sera's eyes took in waxed brick floors, heavy viga beams, skylights, and at the far end of the room, a woodstove. To her, the very thought conjured images of Laura Ingalls roughing it on the prairie, but even Aunt Pauline had one, so she supposed it was a legitimate method of heating out here in the high desert.

A magnificent walnut and hickory dining table set took pride of place near the front of the living room by the kitchen, glowing with polish and looking like the heirloom it surely was. The rest of the room was strangely empty however, Sera noticed. There were no pictures or personal mementos. For someone who took as much care with his shop environs as Asher did, the unfinished quality of his house was marked. As though, Sera thought, his heart was more in his work than in his home. The only seating, aside from the elegant dining room chairs, was one old corduroy-covered armchair slouched in a corner by the woodstove, begging for a cat or a dog to flop down on its saggy cushions.

As if she knew she was wanted, Sascha trundled out from around a corner, tongue lolling and doggy lips turned up in a grin. When she saw her master, she gave a soft woof, quickened her pace, and hastened to stuff her long gray nose right in his chino-covered crotch.

Sera's cheeks burned, but Asher just gave the bitch a scratch behind the ears and gently shooed her away from his family jewels. "Sweet Sascha," he murmured, "we have a guest. Be polite."

Sascha obligingly turned to Sera and gave her the same treatment.

Sera was saved from death by dog-induced embarrassment by the arrival of Silver, who galloped into the room and playfully latched on to his mother's plume-like tail. Sascha nipped remonstratively at her offspring, then both pooches sat on their haunches and looked up at Asher, plainly expectant.

"I believe refreshments are in order, if I'm any judge of canine communication," he said lightly. "Come! Dinner!" He strode off into the kitchen, huskies scrambling after him in their haste to be fed. Sera snapped to attention and nearly followed along before she realized he hadn't meant her. She smiled sheepishly.

As he poured kibble into a bowl, Asher called back to Sera, "May I offer you something to drink, Bliss? A glass of wine, or a beer?"

Oh God. Here it came. That awkward moment every sober alcoholic faced a thousand times. Maybe she could finesse it. But instead of her usual "I'm on antibiotics" or "I get migraines," Sera found herself blurting out, "Um, I don't drink anymore. That is . . . I, ah, quit a while back."

Her whole psyche cringed. *Way to blow it, Serafina,* she groaned inwardly. Asher seriously didn't need to know about her struggles with the bottle. *I might as well have worn a T-shirt that says, "Boozer on Board,"* she thought grimly. But somehow she hadn't been able to lie to Asher.

Asher didn't blink. "How about a soda or an iced tea?" he asked mildly. "Or I can make coffee, if you prefer."

Whoa. He wasn't going to ask? Sera was as taken aback as she was relieved. Experience had shown her that people either got really squirrelly and awkward when she copped to her alcoholism (often the ones with drinking problems themselves), or they peppered her with uncomfortable questions she wasn't prepared to answer. Or worse, tried to convince her she didn't need to quit drinking—she didn't *look* like an alcoholic, after all. But Asher did none of those things. He simply accepted what she said, and moved on.

Flustered by the warmth that blossomed in her chest, Sera shifted her weight and crossed her arms under her breasts. "Maybe just some ice water? Driving Cupcake is thirsty work," she joked lamely.

"Coming right up. Please, have a seat," he invited, gesturing to the dining chairs. "I'm sorry I can't make you more comfortable, but the puppies pretty much ate the couch, so I had to toss it. I don't have much in the way of furniture left."

"Except this gorgeous table," Sera said, stroking her fingers across the fine-grained walnut and tracing the seamlessly inlaid diamond patterns worked in lighter hickory as she seated herself. "Wherever did you find such a beautiful dining set?"

Asher busied himself taking a glass down from a cabinet and filling it with ice. "It was a wedding gift from my father-in-law," he said, not looking at her. "He was a woodworker, and he made it to surprise my wife and I . . ."

Asher stopped, as if the memory were too painful.

"Oh," said Sera. Her heart ached for him, but there was a small, petty part of herself that ached for a different reason. Clearly, her landlord wasn't over whatever event had scarred his past—and he wasn't over the woman he'd lost. If she were a truly decent person, she would be comforting him, not lusting after him. *But what if I make it worse?* She *did* want to ask him about his wife—*was she dead, had they divorced, had she run off?*—but she wasn't prepared to ruin the evening by gauchely blundering into Asher's private pain, as she feared she might. Besides, she sensed very clearly that he wished he hadn't brought up the subject. She had to respect that, even if it left her burning with questions. When he set the water down in front of her, Sera guzzled it a bit too fast, spilling some down her chin. Her cheeks flamed. "See? Told you I had a drinking problem," she quipped, hoping for at least a chuckle.

Asher didn't laugh. Instead he leaned down and traced his thumb along the path the droplets had taken, wiping her skin of stray moisture. Sera gulped as their eyes met. An instant surge of desire rocketed through her system, nearly taking her breath away. Did he feel it, too?

He wasn't admitting it if he was. He pivoted back to his kitchen, calling lightly over his shoulder, "Let me see what I can scrounge up for us to eat."

God, he was the perfect man. An artisan, a musician, a wizard with plants and animals. And now, her own personal chef.

Ten minutes later, Sera learned that wasn't *quite* true.

Asher was a hopeless cook.

He was all sound and fury, banging pots and sizzling pans, but if the acrid smoke and the muttered cursing in Hebrew were any indication, her landlord's talents did not extend to the culinary arts.

"Need any help there?" she ventured after he slid the unidentifiable results of his efforts straight from the frying pan into the trash—for the second time. "It *is* what I do for a living, after all."

Asher turned to face her. For the first time since they'd met, his cocksure composure had slipped just a crack, and there was a harried look on his face. "I'm a bit nervous," he confessed.

"*You're* nervous?" her voice went up a notch in disbelief.

"I haven't cooked for a woman since my wife..." He stopped, looked chagrined. "Well, not for many years. And never for a famous chef," he said more lightly. "I can only imagine what standards you're used to."

"Mr. Wolf," she said with mock solemnity. "Let me make a suggestion here."

"By all means," he said with the same seriousness.

"Get your buns out of the kitchen and let a professional take over."

In the end he didn't leave the kitchen, but he proved to be as good a sous chef as he was lousy at taking the lead, culinarily speaking. At her direction, he washed, sliced, and diced meekly, if less than deftly. There wasn't much to work with—typical male, his fridge was pretty barren—but Sera managed to unearth some tomatoes (homegrown from his garden, of course), mushrooms, a hunk of mozzarella, some avocado and basil (also from Asher's garden), and a half-dozen eggs. With practiced movements, she built two respectable omelets and, within minutes, slid them onto the stoneware plates Asher provided. "There," she said. "Not fancy, but they'll do."

"They're beautiful," Asher said, with a bit more admiration than Sera thought was warranted. He held up the plates and examined them from every angle, as if they were a set of sculptures on Canyon Road he was considering buying. "I could never master such a fantastic omelet; not with a hundred years of practice."

She flushed at the compliment and immediately tried to deflect it. "And here I thought omelets were the one food every man knew how to make. Isn't it, like, in the guy handbook that you're supposed to be able to make morning-after eggs?"

"I would hate to fail you so egg-regiously on so important an occasion as the morning after," Asher said with a grin at his own pun.

Sera looked down, more flustered by the thought of a "morning after" with Asher than amused at his wordplay. To him, it might just be light banter, but to her...well, *hell.* She could feel herself falling for this delightful, inscrutable man in a way she simply couldn't afford to allow... but couldn't seem to prevent either. All she could think was that the morning after with Asher would be...glorious.

Maybe for most *women, Sera,* she told herself flatly. *For you, it would be an exercise in humiliation. You'd have to sneak out like some college kid doing the walk of shame after you disappointed him in the sack the way you surely would. Remember how Blake used to look at you after sex? Like he'd just been forced to ingest Starbucks instead of his usual Jamaican Blue Mountain? You can't forget that, or you're in for a world of hurt. Don't ruin things here the way you did back home.*

"Shall we eat?" she said, rather too abruptly. Sera practically snatched the plates from Asher and set them down on the table. She was relieved to discover she hadn't lost her touch—and if Asher's happy moans were any indication, he thought the same, wolfing the simple omelet down with alacrity. In fact, he looked so mournfully at his empty plate when he finished that she ended up making him a second helping. It did her heart good to watch him gobble her cooking. She so rarely had the opportunity to cook for just one person—and never for a person as fascinating as Asher. At least in this, Sera knew she shined.

"I could make dessert," she offered. "I thought I saw some stuff in your fridge that might make a nice crème caramel. Or I could whip up some cookies..."

Asher shook his head, placing a hand lightly over hers when she made to rise from the table. She couldn't help noticing the fine shape of that hand—long, lean fingers and raw knuckles, calluses and faint scars. A man's hand. And it lay over hers on the table where he and his wife had shared so many meals. Sera gulped.

"You're not here to work, Bliss," Asher said. "You're my guest, and it is I who should be serving you. But since I am, as we have seen, a disaster in the kitchen, I'm afraid we'll have to forgo the sweets." He flashed a grin. "I can, however, offer you some rather decent coffee—I promise you, my coffee is far better than my cuisine." He rose lithely to his feet, headed for the percolator, giving her a questioning look over his shoulder. "Will you have a cup?"

"Yes, please," Sera said gratefully. "I'd love some."

"Since I am *sans* sofa at present, let's take our coffee outside," he suggested when the pot had brewed and he'd put their plates in the sink (not before running a finger along his to catch the last savory lick). "It should be warm enough if I bring a blanket, and the stars look to be fierce tonight. There's no better way to enjoy after-dinner coffee in New Mexico."

Sera felt a little faint, thinking of sharing a blanket with that much manly goodness. Was it her imagination, or was Asher inventing reasons for her not to leave? She couldn't quite read him, but she was getting the definite sense that he wanted her to stay...almost as if he had something he wanted to say to her. Even as her sober instincts were screaming caution, some part of her—the part that had recently purchased a two-ton truck, probably—was telling her to let this play out. Something big was in the wind. "I can only stay for a little while," she hedged. "Then I really should be heading home. Pauline will worry." *Like hell,* she thought privately. *If I come home too early,* then *she'll worry—that I'm not getting laid.*

Asher turned toward what Sera figured was his bedroom. "I'll just go grab a blanket then, if you'll carry the coffees?" Was it her imagination, or did he seem a tad edgy, too? He was back, carrying a fluffy white comforter under one arm, before Sera could consider the ramifications of that question too closely.

Sascha and Silver preceded them out, tails wagging as they disappeared into the gloom. True night had fallen while they ate their simple meal, Sera saw. As her eyes adjusted, she noticed a two-person glider tucked away at the back of the patio. She saw two side tables, one on either end of the glider, and carefully set their coffee cups down. Gingerly, Sera set herself down on the padded cushion, as far toward her end as she could manage. She didn't want to presume anything. Silver pawed at her leg through her jeans, whining until she helped him up into her lap. The puppy provided a welcome distraction, and Sera petted his soft fur gratefully until he grumbled with pleasure and rolled himself into a contented ball, tiny head resting on comically big paws.

Asher folded himself down next to her with seemingly no thought for her personal space, his big, loose-limbed frame warming the length of hers even before he spread the puffy down coverlet over both their laps (and Silver, who had instantly fallen asleep on Sera's). Sascha rounded out the tableau by flopping down on the bricks at her master's feet, her thick coat providing all the warmth she needed to combat the October chill.

This must be what family feels like, Sera marveled. She hadn't truly had one since her parents had died, so many years ago. Pauline had done her best, and her best was damn good, but Sera had always felt something was missing. A wholeness, a sense of completion. Now, her heart felt full, though her belly felt like a meadow full of butterflies had taken up residence. Alarmed at the fanciful direction her thoughts were taking, she took a sip of the coffee Asher had made, breathing steam out into the brisk night air. He was right—the coffee was delicious. And as promised, the stars were shining fiercely in the achingly clear sky, blazing down like pinpoints of celestial mystery. But Sera barely saw them. There was a terrestrial mystery stealing all of her attention. A mystery she desperately wanted to solve.

Who was Asher Wolf, deep down at the heart of him? Was he someone who could...

Who could what, *Sera?* her inner voice asked caustically. *Overlook your shortcomings? Love you?*

"It's definitely cold tonight," Sera remarked, plucking at the blanket to cover herself a bit more. "Wonder if we'll have snow in time for Halloween next week." She winced, embarrassed at being reduced to talking about the weather. Asher smiled gently, as if he sensed her discomfort, and tucked the blanket more securely around both of them. He left one arm across the back of the glider after he finished, nearly touching her shoulders but not quite. With his other hand, he placed his own coffee down on his side table after a single sip. Inside the cozy down nest, heat began to blossom, suffusing Sera and evidently overwhelming Silver, who burrowed his way out of the covers until he plopped out at her feet. Yawning, he trundled over to curl up next to his mother.

Asher set the glider going with a push of one foot.

Sera finished her coffee in three quick gulps, setting the mug down rather too hard on her own side table. "Sorry." She winced at the clatter.

"It's all right, Bliss," he said. "I'm nervous, too."

"That's the second time you've said that tonight," Sera blurted out. "What do *you* have to be nervous about?"

He slanted her a sidelong look, those green eyes of his almost black in the darkness. He ran a hand through his short hair, then laid it back across the glider, this time touching her shoulders—deliberately, she thought.

"Bliss," he said gently. "Do you know you are the first woman I've invited to my home here in Santa Fe? Since I moved here four years ago—since my life fell apart back in Tel Aviv—I've been content to move slowly, collecting myself, letting this place heal me and my needs make themselves known to me in their own time. At first, I simply needed everything to be different, to remind me of nothing from the past, so I built myself a new business, honed a craft I'd only ever practiced as a hobby before. Nothing truly touched me, except my memories—both good and bad. I drifted in this beautiful dream of a city. For a long time, it was enough, and eventually my heart became quiet. But now those needs... they're awakening." He leaned closer, impressing her with his earnestness. "What I mean to say, Bliss, is that *you* are awakening them."

Sera's heart was suddenly thrumming like a hummingbird's wings. She sensed he was about to open up in a big way, and that perhaps he'd spent a lot more of his time focused on her than she'd ever imagined. Could she handle what he had to say? His hand was gently stroking her hair, toying with the lock at the front that never behaved itself, fingers skimming her cheek. Sera trembled, hardly daring to breathe.

Asher spoke softly, but with conviction. "What I'm talking about, Bliss, is the need to know another person... to hear her, and understand what drives her. The need to see her grow and challenge herself—even if it is sometimes in ways that make her uncomfortable."

For an unhappy moment, Sera wondered if he were just speaking generically, but what he said next dispelled any question—Asher meant *her.*

"I need to watch her dance with abandon when she thinks she's alone—and to hold her close while we dance together under the Fiesta lights. To watch her blush—far too often—at every little thing." He smiled, stroking Sera's cheek as if to note how flushed it was even now. "To watch how she gives love to those who are important to her, and witness her kindness when she offers others a new start. To see her smile"—he traced her lips with one featherlight finger—"and to know that, just maybe, I had something to do with that smile..."

Sera trembled, and tears threatened to overflow her lashes.

"Asher..."

"I find myself with the most powerful need to taste the confections that come from her kitchen, and to see her master a monstrously big truck. And most of all, I have the need to do *this*... "

This time, the kiss was *not* on her forehead.

It captured her lips, hot and urgent, but what it stole was Sera's soul. The feeling was like a sob, a deep, ache-from-the-bottom-of-your-guts sob, only it was good, so good, both desire and admiration intermingled. The desire was for his body—*and how*—but the admiration was for his *personhood,* in some intangible way.

She couldn't help but respond. Overwhelmed, afraid, and dizzily flattered, Sera once again felt her wits skip town under the influence of Asher's kiss. But for once in her life, her body seemed to know just how to respond. As their lips and tongues tasted and tested one another in the cold, clear night, she was overcome by the essence of Asher. It was all-encompassing. Like a drug, like the drink she'd given up, she longed for more of this man. He was so immensely promising, so tempting in the most primitive way...

Never in her life had Sera felt such a surge of straight-up passion. It flooded her loins and quickened her breath until she was dizzy with it. All she could think was *more. Give me more, and more, and more again.* She moaned, and his mouth took hers more deeply. She tasted coffee, fresh and deep, and man...and longing. Unbelievable longing, both hers and his.

It was that longing that stopped her.

Sera ripped herself from Asher's embrace, leaping to her feet and nearly tripping over the comforter in her haste to get away. Silver yipped sleepily as she lunged over him and Sascha, scrambling to achieve some distance.

"Bliss, what's the matter?" Asher rose to his feet in a hurry, but Sera waved him away.

"You don't know what you're saying, Asher," she warned. "You don't know me."

"I know enough—" be began.

"You *don't* know enough, Asher. You don't know the first thing about me. If you did, you wouldn't be kissing me right now." She drew in a sharp breath and wiped her lips, as if she could erase the feel of him so easily. "Truth is, Ash, I've been a first-class mess for most of my life, and I'm only just starting to sort myself out now. I'm an alcoholic; a failure in my career. Back in New York, my very name is a joke in some circles." Sera's voice broke, and tears began to fall in hot streams down her cheeks. "I'm glad you're getting over whatever it was that hurt you, Asher. You deserve all those things that you want—that you *need* from a woman. Most of all, you deserve happiness. You're an amazing man. But I'm *not* an amazing woman—not yet. I'm still trying to get my shit straightened out, and I'm so far from where I want to be that some days I can't even see the goalposts. And there are *some* things"—*like my problems in the bedroom*—"that I'm probably *never* going to overcome. You won't find what you need with me, much as I wish I were all those things you think you see right now. I wouldn't bring you happiness, Asher—I'd only fail you, and humiliate myself in the process. So let's just nip this thing in the bud, okay?"

Sera didn't wait to see whether Asher agreed. She ran for her truck and hauled ass out of there, leaving a trail of smashed lavender and sage in her wake.

And one very disappointed Israeli.

Chapter Seventeen

"You two should fuck," Pauline announced.

For emphasis, she stuck her spade in the pile of freshly turned earth she was fertilizing, propped her elbow on the handle, and gazed at her niece and her guest with a beatific smile that encompassed them both.

"Whaaaaat?" Sera squealed. *Oh no, you did* not *just say that out loud… right there in front of Asher!* She cringed behind the flower bed she was, with no great conviction, attempting to weed.

"You know. Bone. Bang. Bump uglies. Make the beast with two backs. Shag each other silly. That whole thing." Pauline waved the spade back and forth between Sera and Asher, then made an obscene, impossible-to-mistake finger gesture.

Serafina didn't know whether to throw up or die. *Oh, my God.* A third option—blushing herself into a coma—appeared to be her body's instinctive answer to the conundrum.

She'd begged Pauline not to ask Asher over. Barely two days had passed since their disastrous dinner at his house…two days during which she'd dodged his calls and stayed away from the *placita,* claiming she had to meet with restaurant suppliers (which was true) and didn't have time to drop by the store (which was not). She wasn't ready to deal with her landlord yet—if she ever would be after his romantic revelation and her cowardly absconding act.

Pauline, however, wasn't concerned with Sera's finer feelings, as today's awkward get-together proved. She'd asked some rather pointed questions of her niece when Sera had arrived home the other night, tear-streaked and still visibly trembling. Sera, having no intention of telling her aunt what had happened, had merely assured her that Asher had done nothing wrong, and that Pauline could put away the ball-skinning knife. When Sera proved stubborn in her silence, Pauline had turned crafty, inviting the Israeli over to help bed down her garden for winter. Never mind that Hortencia had volunteered for the job (she was no slouch with a spade, and had been tending her own gardens for fifty years); no one would do for Pauline's little patch of earth but her favorite foliage whisperer.

Sera didn't know what to make of Asher's apparent eagerness to take up that invitation. He'd arrived mere hours after Pauline's call, with mulch and gardening tools in the back of his meticulously maintained Land Rover. Sera had planned to invent an errand and escape before he got there, but Pauline had foiled her—she'd told her niece Asher was coming at two, but asked Asher to show up at *one*.

So now the three of them were gathered in the little adobe-walled garden behind Pauline's house; Sera wondering if she could successfully disappear down a gopher hole, Asher looking impossibly manly with a rake in one hand and his leather hat shading his eyes as he surveyed the little plot of land, and Pauline sitting on a stump, wearing a set of Hortencia's knitted leg warmers (and a pair of arm warmers as well) along with her faded "Professors Do It in the Classroom" sweatshirt and a much-patched calf-length denim skirt. It was a bit of a Mexican standoff, Sera thought—Asher at one point of the triangle, Sera and Pauline staking out the other two, as if none of them quite trusted what the others might get up to.

Well, that wasn't quite true. Pauline could be trusted to thoroughly embarrass her niece.

Sera shot her aunt a fulminating glare. "Aunt Pauline, I swear I will never forgive you if you don't shut your trap," she growled. "I'm really sorry, Ash," she muttered, barely able to look at him where he stood beside a pile of pungent compost, clad in ancient jeans and a soft heather-green V-neck that complemented his eyes absurdly well.

But Asher seemed okay with it. "It's all right, Bliss." He turned to her aunt. "Miss Pauline," he said gently, "I think that's something the two of us can sort out on our own. We're grown-ups. And besides, I think your niece appreciates a bit of delicacy in these matters, if I'm not mistaken."

My hero.

Sera shot him the most grateful look of her life. Still, her blush, if anything, only intensified...because he hadn't denied the possibility of them "bumping uglies." But incredible as it was that Asher really, sincerely seemed interested in her, she couldn't risk their budding friendship—or her delicate, still-healing self-esteem—on a fling that was destined to end badly. Facing him day after day at the *placita* once he learned how lacking she was as a woman...Sera shuddered at the thought. *Oh, Ash. Don't you understand, I'm no good for you?* She thought she'd made that sad fact abundantly clear the other night. *How many shrubs must a girl slay before a guy gets the hint?* She still owed him a lavender bush. Now, if she could only convince her aunt to let it alone, she could go be miserable and unfulfilled in peace.

"Yes, *please,* Aunt Pauline," she gritted out. "A modicum of delicacy would be nice."

"Harrumph," Pauline harrumphed. "Well, I'm just concerned for your health. It's not good for you to go as long as you have without a nice, thorough climax, kiddo. And I suspect it's been awhile for you, too, handsome." She jerked her head toward Asher, who shifted his weight and tried to look as though people commented on his climactic status every day.

Unexpected tears flooded Serafina's eyes. Maybe it was her aunt's well-intentioned humiliation, or perhaps it was the certainty that she'd never know what it was like to "shag" a guy like Asher senseless, but suddenly she couldn't stand to stay in that garden another second. "Excuse me," she said in a small, choked voice, rising from the flower bed and bolting for the house.

Asher caught up to her in the kitchen. Sera was scrubbing blindly at the dirt under her nails, shoulders stiff, water running full blast. But she sensed him coming anyway. Lately, she'd had Asher-radar so acute she felt like she could pinpoint his location with GPS accuracy, any time of the day.

He put his scarred jeweler's hands exactly where the tension resided, where her shoulders met her neck, kneading with a gentleness that only made her want to cry more. Sera shrugged away, refusing to look at him.

"She means well, Bliss."

"Stop calling me that," she mumbled.

"What, 'Bliss'? But why?"

"Because I don't know the meaning of the word!" she wailed, half-angry, half-despairing. She flung herself around, grabbing a dishtowel and wringing it between her hands as if it were her aunt's meddling neck.

Asher didn't understand. "Of course you do," he chided. His hand rose to push back the errant lock of hair that teased her cheek, then fell away as she flinched from the gesture. He'd removed his hat and left it on the tile-topped island in the center of the kitchen. Sera could see the faint indentation the band had left along his hairline, and she had the absurd urge to smooth it. His long, lean frame edged closer, subtly crowding Sera against the counter by the sink as he took the towel from her hands and set it aside. "You're here, aren't you?" he pointed out. "Pursuing your dreams. Opening that bakery is all about bliss. One taste of your confections, and that's all a man needs to know about satisfaction..."

For some reason, his kindness set off her anger. "*Satisfaction?* Ha! You don't get it, Asher Wolf," she interrupted. "Just like *I* don't get it. There's no such thing as satisfaction with me. You wanna know why? Because *I can't have an orgasm.*"

"You can't..." Asher looked disbelieving. Or perhaps aghast was more like it.

In for a penny, in for a pound. Serafina had totally lost her cool. And though she knew she was dooming any chance of ever hooking up with this delectable guy, she plowed on. It felt good to get the source of her shame off her chest. Liberating. "That's right. I'm goddamn frigid. Never had a climax. Don't know what all the fuss is about. My hoo-ha is *broken,* get it?"

Asher appeared to be mouthing the word "hoo-ha" to himself. Perhaps they didn't have it in Hebrew.

"You know, my vagi—"

"Yes, I *get* it, Serafina," he said quellingly. "I simply don't believe it."

And with one whirlwind swoop, he grabbed her up and set her bodily on the counter. His body followed hers, lean hips crowding into the space between her jeans-clad legs, one arm clasping her back to hold her steady and keep her as close as two people could get. Sera could hear the furious beating of his heart—or was she feeling it? She smelled again that wonderful Asher smell—earth and fire, pure intensity. His breath was hot against her face, a vein pulsing in his neck where she could almost reach it with her lips. His eyes, green lightened almost to gold now with emotion, searched her startled gray ones.

Searching for what?

Permission? If so, he had it. Sera couldn't deny him, even if she must ultimately disappoint him. Her lips opened, trembling, but she couldn't seem to speak.

Still he sensed the moment she surrendered, and he took full advantage of it.

The hand Asher buried in her hair was gentle. The kiss he slanted across her mouth was anything but.

Oh, fu...

And suddenly, Sera was someone else: a sexually charged woman in the arms of a man so hot he seemed to singe her straight through her clothes. She was not awkward. Not a failure. Not *frigid.* Asher wouldn't allow it. In his grip she was bliss, indeed; swept with sensation that left no room for second thoughts, hang-ups, or hesitation. His knowing hands guided her, molded her body to his. His stubble scraped her cheeks, her ear, her throat, while his lips, tongue, and teeth branded her skin with delicious sensation. Sera found herself clutching him to her, vaguely aware of the cool tiles against her backside, the cabinet behind her shoulders, a patch of sunlight illuminating the gold in his hair. Her hands, used to kneading malleable dough, found his shoulders and their unyielding musculature, reveling in his heat, his solidity. He'd yanked her forward so the apex of her thighs was pressed directly against the heat of his loins. *Wow,* she thought faintly. When Asher went from cool, debonair landlord to passionate lover, he really didn't hold back. As a man, he was gentle; full of humor and wit and a kindness that wouldn't quit.

As a lover, he was a hurricane.

No second-guessing, no insecurity. Asher was all primal male, demanding and eliciting a feminine response from Sera she hadn't known she was capable of. With quick, expert strokes of his tongue, he claimed her mouth. With firm, possessive sweeps of his hands, he delineated her curves, bringing her nerve endings to life like Times Square lights. When he molded the contours of her breast, even through her bra and shirt, Sera felt the streak of sensation zinging directly to her core. And when he pressed against her *there,* her mind froze.

She wasn't thinking about Blake, or her failures in his bed. Sera wasn't thinking, *period.* Her body had taken on a life of its own under Asher's expert tutelage. And right there in her aunt's cozy kitchen, she was galloping rapidly, heedlessly toward that moment she'd dreamed of, and believed was beyond her reach...

Until Asher pulled back on the reins.

"Bliss."

It took Sera a moment to register that he'd pushed back from her. Was, in fact, holding her at arms' length. Her body missed the heat of his, as if he'd stolen her clothing on a cold winter night. Her brain couldn't comprehend why he was over *there,* when her need was *here.* She reached for him, but he caught her hand in both of his and kissed it gently.

"Bliss," he said again.

Her eyes began to focus, and she noticed his had returned to their normal moss green, though his chest was still rising and falling fast with his labored breathing. "Um, yeah?" she said a bit dreamily. She brought his fingers to her mouth and began nibbling one, running her tongue along its length in a way that was both wanton and totally unlike her.

Asher snatched it back, gasping slightly. "Bliss... we have to stop."

"We do?" she asked foggily.

"Yes," he said, and Sera got the gratifying impression that he'd rather have said no. He made a gesture of frustration, pleading for her understanding, then stretched out his hand to stroke her cheek. "Beautiful

Bliss, you deserve more than this. Your satisfaction is something I want to give you with every fiber of my body. But not"—he gestured about the kitchen, and they could both hear, outside, the sound of Pauline singing off-key as she bashed about in her garden—"like this. Not for your first time."

"It's not my first time," Sera objected, reaching for him again. *What a time to play gentleman,* her aching body groaned. "I'm a grown woman, Ash, and I've got plenty of experience."

Asher took her cheek in one callused hand, drew close, and kissed her with heat tempered by gentlemanly consideration. His lips left hers reluctantly. "Neither of us have *this* experience," he contradicted. "And I want us to experience each other properly, so you'll understand how much this means to me, and so that I may have the honor of showing you just how *satisfying* I find you."

Sera let him go. The fire he'd ignited was cooling, her thoughts coalescing once more.

"So what are you saying?" she asked.

Asher ran his hand through his hair in that agitated way she was beginning to love. "What I'm saying is this: You are the most passionate woman I have ever met, Serafina Wilde. You're fiery, you're gutsy, and you're more alive inside than most women even dream of being. There is absolutely nothing wrong with you. I don't know who has convinced you otherwise, but we are going to sort this out, you and I. When I return, I intend to take you out on a real date—a proper, old-fashioned date—and then..." He paused. "Then we'll see where the night takes us. Do you understand?"

His intensity should have frightened her. Instead, it only turned her on more. *Come back and finish what you started,* she wanted to plead, even though she wasn't at all sure where that might lead. It had *felt* like she might get there...felt so incredible she couldn't believe he was denying her now.

"Do you understand?" he demanded a second time, those green eyes going gold again. He stepped closer, took her chin between his fingers, and brought that incredible heat of his once more within reach.

Sera gulped, nodded.

"And do you agree?" he asked, more gently and with a touch of his regular humor.

Sera didn't trust herself to speak, so she nodded again, against his hand. She noticed she was running her own hand down the contours of his back, stroking lower to trace his hips, his buttocks. Her hand wanted to grab hold, and *keep* hold of that prime male real estate... but he was still talking, and his expression told her she better pay attention.

"Good. I'm glad. Because I'm going away, Bliss—going home to Israel. I'll be back in a week, perhaps ten days, and then we'll revisit this. But first"—he lowered his head and kissed her again, at first gently, and then not at all gently—"first, I've got to go speak to my wife."

With one final, brief kiss, he donned his hat and left Sera there, sitting on the counter by the sink, closer to orgasm than she'd ever imagined, and more befuddled than she'd been on her last epic bender.

Speak to his wife?

Chapter Eighteen

If you're finished ignoring me like a pouty teenager, kiddo, there's someone who wants to talk to you," Pauline said. She pointed to the phone, which was lying off the cradle on the mosaic-topped telephone table by the sofa.

Sera rolled her eyes at her aunt. She hadn't been *ignoring* Pauline; she'd been *punishing* her for this afternoon's boorish behavior. There was a difference. But she supposed her affronted act had gone on long enough. Pauline couldn't help herself—she was congenitally uncouth—and if her interference was playing merry hell with Sera's love life, well . . . it hadn't turned out *all* bad.

Maybe. The jury was still out on that one.

The jury, and Asher's wife, Sera reminded herself. Apparently that mysterious paragon wasn't as out of the picture as she'd assumed—and what it meant for her and Asher, she had no idea. *Asher wouldn't dally with me if he was still married, would he?* Somehow she couldn't picture her landlord as a philandering cheat. She had to have a little more faith in him than that. But still . . . She shook herself to bring her thoughts back to the present.

"Weird," she muttered to herself. "Who would call me at Aunt Pauline's number?" Those few folk she kept in contact with from New York all had her cell number—not that it had been ringing off the hook or anything. She approached the old-fashioned, chunky telephone (which Pauline had bedazzled with flecks of turquoise and fossils she'd picked up in the desert) and gave it a tentative "Hello?"

"What's going on over there, Serafina?" Margaret's somewhat nasal, unmistakably New York accent cut through the miles. "Your aunt called me up, all in a lather, and told me I wasn't 'doing my damn job.' You okay?"

Sera glanced disbelievingly at her aunt, who was leaning against the archway that connected the living room and the kitchen, leg-warmered ankles crossed, shamelessly eavesdropping. "You called my *sponsor?*"

Idly, Pauline began to pick at the unraveling edge of one of her arm socks. "You bet your bippy I did," she said. "Seemed to me you needed some good advice, and you're too pigheaded to take it from me. Figured I'd give that Margaret woman a try, since you speak so highly of her, and she's supposed to be such a font of wisdom and all."

"How did you even get her number?"

Pauline plucked Sera's cell phone from her arm warmer, into which Sera could now see Hortencia had knitted little pockets. She waved it demonstratively. "I'm not fooling around here, kid—though I wish *you* would."

"*Hellooooo.* Earth to Serafina Wilde," Margaret's impatient voice cut through Sera's irritation with her aunt's meddling. "What the heck's going on out there, Sera? You staying sober? Making meetings? What's the deal?"

"Sorry, Margaret," Sera apologized, focusing her attention back on her sponsor. "Yes, I'm fine—still sober, getting to meetings pretty regularly, and doing my program reading at night like you taught me. Everything's fine—my aunt's just turned into a busybody in her old age." Sera shot a baleful look Pauline's way and deliberately turned her back on her.

"Well, since we're both here on the phone, you might as well get me up to speed, Sera," Margaret said. "Clearly something's got you in a froth, and we both know it's not good for people like us to get too frothy. Why don't you start with why the Wilde-Woman took it upon herself to reach out to me, *ex parte.*"

"I will," Sera promised. "Just give me a sec." She spun around and skewered her aunt with a look even darker than the last one. Pauline mugged an innocent expression, whistling at the ceiling and swinging one foot like an overgrown kid. Sera rolled her eyes. Pauline was hopeless—and so was trying to change her. She sighed, her annoyance fading. "You've got me where you wanted me, Aunt Paulie," she pointed out. "Now how about some privacy?"

Pauline looked like she would protest, but at Sera's scowl, she decamped to her bedroom, muttering about finding the sweater that matched her knit extremities, as it was getting "a wee bit nipply" outside.

"Okay, sorry," Sera said into the phone. "So what's happening is, Pauline's decided to take a stab at running my love life, and she gets testy when she doesn't get her way. I liked it better when she was only worried about her own O's and left mine out of it."

Margaret laughed. "When did she ever do that?"

"Never," Sera admitted. "Anyhow, it looks like I've gotten into a bit of a romantic entanglement, and Pauline just doesn't know when to quit pushing."

"Hm," said Margaret. "What kind of "romantic entanglement" are we talking about—the good kind, or the Blake Austin kind?"

Sera sighed and rubbed her temples, where a rather fierce tension headache was gathering. "The kind that *could* be really good—or *would* be, if I were the right woman for this guy." She proceeded to spill the whole story—all about Asher (whom she deliberately hadn't mentioned in any of her previous calls to her sponsor), how attracted she was to him, and how, unbelievably, he seemed to like her, too. She finished by spelling out how disastrously their dinner had ended the other night and detailing a rated-G version of their subsequent encounter in the kitchen today. She skipped the part where she'd confessed her broken hoo-ha, but did tell Margaret about Asher's promise—or was it a warning?—that he wanted to take her out when he returned.

"So anyway, Maggie, I don't know whether to jump the guy's bones or hold back in case the whole thing blows up in my face. I mean, after all, I'm supposed to be opening my dream store in a couple weeks, and I really ought to be a hundred percent focused on that. Plus, apparently right now Asher's winging his way to Tel Aviv on some mysterious mission to make things right with his wife, and he wants to take me out for what he calls 'a proper date' when he gets back—" Sera would have kept rattling on, but Margaret interrupted.

"Wait a minute, Sera," Margaret commanded. Sera could almost see her making the "roll that shit back a bit" gesture she always did with her hands. "Go back to the part where you told this Asher guy you were no good for him. You really said that?"

"Uh-huh," Sera said, mentally preparing for a lecture. She twirled the old-fashioned phone cord between her fingers.

"Let me get this straight. You told the guy—this guy you describe as practically perfect, and hotter than New York in July—that you didn't deserve to be with him because you were an addict and a failure?"

"Well, ah..." Sera chewed on a lock of hair. "Yeah, I might have said that."

"If you were here, I'd give you such a smack on the ass right now," Margaret swore. "*How* many times have we read the Big Book together? *How* many meetings have we sat through? You calling all those people in the fellowship failures?"

"No, of course not..." Sera said meekly. Her fellow alkies were some of the folks she admired most. Hearing their stories of how they'd scraped themselves out of life's gutters and pieced themselves back together into some of the kindest, most responsible people she'd ever met had inspired Sera herself to stick around and give living sober a chance.

"Damn right, Serafina. As well blame the cancer patient or the diabetic for their disease. You—well, you may have drawn the short straw when it comes to addictive propensities, but it's what you've done to *overcome* that condition that defines you, not the addiction itself. I mean, how many alcoholics do you know who *couldn't* get sober?"

Sera had to admit, she knew a lot. Only a small percentage of addicts ever managed to get—or stay—in recovery.

"And of the ones you know who did succeed," Margaret continued relentlessly, "how many of them had it easy?"

"Um, none?" Sera forced herself to stop chewing her hair and twisting the old-school phone cord around her fingers. Both were nearly in knots, just like her guts. But Margaret was right, she *had* come a long way, and she had a lot to be proud of. She couldn't let this absurd insecurity left over from the Blake years continue to cast a pall on her life. She felt herself standing straighter. "So if I get you right, what you're trying to say is that I should be proud of my past, not ashamed—or at least, proud of my progress."

"That's right," Margaret said, satisfaction coloring her voice. "You can't control the way you were born, but you *can* control how you handle life's challenges. Now you...you've done a pretty damn fine job, if what Pauline was telling me before she put you on the phone is true. Your store's nearly ready to open. You've met a nice bunch of gals. Apparently you even got yourself some kind of badass monster truck. You're really making a life for yourself out there. Why *shouldn't* you have a gorgeous guy in it?"

Because I'm a dud in the sack, Sera wanted to say, but she'd told too many people about her no-O issue and she really didn't want to go over it again. She had enough people out here hovering over her and monitoring her erogenous zones as it was.

"There's no guy in the world so great you don't deserve him," Margaret continued. "I'm serious, Sera. Don't blow your chance at happiness because of some outdated idea you have of yourself. You're a new woman, and you've got everything it takes to achieve the life of your dreams. Just don't let your disease talk you out of it, and you should be okay."

Sera smiled. "Thanks, Margaret." She was starting to feel better. Maybe, just maybe, her two favorite female advisors had a point. She should stop assuming she knew what was best for Asher, stop assuming she wasn't good enough for him, and just let things play out. Asher was no Blake Austin. No matter how badly things went, he would never be deliberately cruel to her. The worst that could happen was that Sera would wind up humiliated—and she was no stranger to humiliation. The *best* that could happen, however...well, *hell.* The best would be very good indeed.

She forced herself to listen to her sponsor, who was still talking.

"You want my advice, I think you should lighten up, like your aunt says. That old broad's got a lot of wisdom in her. Listen to her, and I think you'll be happier for it."

Serafina knew better than to argue with her sponsor—a formidable woman who just *might* come out to Santa Fe to deliver that ass-smacking if she wasn't satisfied Sera was following her suggestions.

"Yes, ma'am," she said. "I'll take that advice."

Which was how Sera found herself spending the next two weeks on a bona fide Orgasm Quest.

Chapter Nineteen

"I can't believe I let you talk me into this, you guys. I *hate* sweating."

The four women sat around a brazier in the dim light of a mud-brick Navajo torture chamber. Pan flute music was being piped in from some unseen corner. Clouds of sage incense wafted to their nostrils, while waves of heat billowed from the brazier, like cushioned fists thudding against their overheated skin.

You better believe you're in New Mexico now, girl.

Sera felt as though the walls of the sweat lodge were closing in on them.

"Just relax, Baby-Bliss," Pauline advised. "Try to focus."

"I *can't* focus, Pauline," she snapped. "I'm *naked* here."

"Naked is natural, dear," put in Hortencia. "Look at me. I'm perfectly at ease with it." She gestured languidly. Her plump, seventy-year-old frame was nearly boneless with relaxation, parked against the log-and-mud-brick wall of the lodge like she'd grown from it. Her white hair had gone a bit limp, but soft tendrils curled charmingly about her apple cheeks, which were rosier than ever. She'd brought along a home-knitted throw cushion for her bum, Sera saw, protecting her from the ground.

Beside her, Aruni settled her well-toned legs more comfortably into lotus position in her own corner of the hut. Her back was ramrod straight, but her curls were kinkier than Hugh Hefner. "Me, too," she piped up.

Sera fought the urge to stick her tongue out at her friend. Sure, *she* had no problem being naked, because *she* had a perfect, years-of-yoga-toned body. And she had nothing to stress about—Aruni already *had* an orgasm totem. A fox, she'd said. A nice, fluffy red fox.

What am I *gonna get?* Sera wondered. *A beaver?*

Aunt Pauline had been adamant they attempt this adventure. "We're going on a vision quest, kiddo," she'd said that morning after rousting Sera out of bed and tossing her a towel. "Nothing else has worked, and Asher will be back any day. Forget all that other stuff we tried. I don't know why I didn't think of this before! What you've got to do, Bliss, is find your orgasm totem. And there's no better way to invite a visit from your orgasm animal than a nice, naked sweat ceremony. Once you find it, I'm sure it'll show you the way. God knows *I've* tried," she'd muttered. "But you, my darling niece, are one tough nut to crack."

So here they were, two weeks into the great "quest for the holy wail," as Janice had laughingly dubbed it, and no closer to climax (at least in Sera's case) than they'd been a fortnight ago. Aruni, Hortencia, and Pauline were her fellow pilgrims today—the others had wanted to come, but the only time Pauline could reserve the sweat house up at Ghost Ranch had unfortunately conflicted with most of their work schedules.

Ghost Ranch, Sera had learned as they drove, had been expatriate New York artist Georgia O'Keeffe's spiritual home. And as they'd arrived at the vast, empty space north of Abiquiu, she'd thought she understood why. Red sandstone cliffs rose out of the desert floor, painting the land with stunning color. Swaths of flat terrain were broken by mesas and rock formations that seemed carved by a capricious hand, bold and fierce. There was a hush surrounding the place, as if the very earth knew it was sacred. Here, O'Keeffe had let her creativity spread wide as the horizons, fearlessly exploring her artistic limits as well as her frank sensuality. If ever *she* was going to find hidden depths of passion within herself, Sera had thought, it would be in a place like this.

She'd continued to think so up until they'd arrived at the hexagonal hut they'd reserved on the back end of the sprawling property. Looking at the squat, crumbling structure with its weather-beaten door and bare-earth base, she'd begun to have second thoughts.

Now she was having third and fourth thoughts—most of them about how she could escape without upsetting her aunt and her well-meaning friends. Sera dug a stone out from under her butt, trying to shift in such a way that she could conceal as much of her nakedness as possible. Even among other women, all this bareness was giving her the heebie-jeebies. And the heat! She'd baked bread in cooler ovens.

Oblivious to Sera's distress, Hortencia ladled water from a bucket by the brazier onto the hot stones it was warming. Immediately, the heat in the hut intensified, and with a sizzle, more clouds of steam erupted.

"Seriously, guys, is it supposed to be this hot?"

"No sweat, no sex life," Pauline said peaceably.

Sera moaned.

Aruni giggled. "I'm *so* resisting the urge to make a joke about chefs not being able to stand the heat in their own kitchens."

"Try harder," Sera advised, panting. She'd broiled steaks under cooler conditions than this. And she hadn't been nude. "You probably do that hot-lava yoga all the time, don't you?" she accused.

Aruni fluffed her hair, which had curled so tightly in the humid air that it resembled uncombed sheep's wool. "Of course. Bikram is about the most cleansing feeling you can experience without a colonic. I'll reserve you a spot in our next class if you want, Sera," she offered.

"I don't think I'm going to survive that long," Sera gasped. She curled up on her side, laying her cheek against the packed earth floor. The ground was mercifully, if only minimally, cooler, and she'd take what she could get. Besides, fetal, she felt slightly less naked.

"Try to envision your totem, Bliss," Pauline encouraged. She was sprawled indecorously across the dirt floor, wearing nothing but a string of marigolds around her neck and a serene smile. "Just imagine yourself inviting the spirit to join you, with kindness and love, asking for its guidance but demanding nothing in return. Remember," she teased, aware of her niece's discomfort, "the sooner you see your orgasm spirit, the sooner you can put your clothes back on."

I think I am *seeing visions,* Sera mused dreamily a short while later, cheek sticky with sweat and dirt. But it wasn't some animal guide come to take her to the brink—either sexually or otherwise. Instead, what Sera saw was a nice tidy recap of her failures over the past two weeks.

Thanks, brain. I needed another reminder of how hopeless I am.

Pauline had called upon the BRBs for assistance, and they'd been more than glad to help—especially after they heard about Sera's upcoming date with Asher. "Honey, you don't wanna hook up with the Wolf until you've sorted out your hoo-ha hiccups," Janice had advised, and the rest of the women had nodded wisely. They'd compiled a list of "orgasm encouragers" a mile long, and they'd been determined to guide Sera through each and every one of their dubious schemes. Sera, equal parts touched, intrigued, and skeptical, had agreed to play along. *What's the worst that could happen?* she'd figured.

She'd found out the hard way.

First, there'd been the "sensual hiking." According to the Back Room Babes, nothing was guaranteed to boost one's confidence—as well as bring blood to the extremities—like a nice, brisk walk in the woods. After gasping and wheezing her way up a trail whose undeniable beauty Sera might have appreciated more had she been able to breathe, Sera had joined Pauline and the others on a ridge to spend an uncomfortable half hour rhapsodizing about how connected to their physical bodies the exertion made them feel, how the trees and the earth and the sunshine brought them closer to nature and their own natural urges. Sera, a Manhattan girl to the core, had spent the time scanning the underbrush for mountain lions, squealing every time a bee buzzed by, and wondering if she was going to be able to make it down to the parking lot without needing a medic. Orgasm had been the farthest thing from her mind.

After the hiking, there'd been the sensual bread baking—Pauline's idea, naturally.

"C'mon, kiddo. If you can get a loaf to rise, you can get a rise out of anything—including your libido." They'd come together in Bliss's half-completed kitchen, the scent of fresh plaster in their nostrils and identical wads of basic hearth bread dough on the counter before them. It was just the two of them, as it had been when Sera was a teen and her aunt was teaching her to love the alchemy of baking in Pauline's cramped Washington Square kitchen. "Have you never noticed how baking bread and making love are very similar skills?" Pauline had continued, in her happy place as she mused about her favorite topic. "It's all just kneading and fondling, coaxing and rising . . ." She demonstrated, shaping her dough into a long, thick loaf with deft strokes of her floury hands. She even gave it a nice, bulbous head so no one could mistake what she was crafting. "Just close your eyes, imagine you're in bed with Asher, and let the feelings flow . . ."

All those years she was teaching me to bake, she was really preparing me for this . . . Instead of "flowing," Sera found herself squishing her loaf into a pasty splat on her end of the stainless steel counter. She, whose utterly perfect *boules,* baguettes, and *bâtards* were the envy of half of Manhattan's French bakeries! She loved the feel of living dough under her hands, the tender give, the saucy resistance . . . yet none of it made her feel horny. In fact, to Sera, the whole exercise felt vaguely as though they were profaning her still-unfinished kitchen. She sighed. "Sure, there's fondling and coaxing. There's also punching, and slapping, and slashing . . . and pinching and deflating . . . Come on, Aunt Paulie, it's not the same thing at all."

Pauline heaved a huge sigh, setting her perfect loaf to rise again under a damp towel and wiping her floury hands on her apron. "Maybe not *exactly* the same, kid. But you can't tell me baking bread isn't about the most sensuous thing you can do outside of the boudoir."

Sera sighed and chucked her own mangled wad of dough into the waste bin. "Enough already," she'd said. "Not to hurt your feelings, Auntie, but I don't want to be battling visions of your penis-shaped hoagies every time I use my own kitchen." She'd let Pauline bake up her cock-shaped loaf, mainly to test out whether Malcolm's ovens were as good as promised (they were), but she'd refused her aunt's offer of a hot, steamy slice slathered in butter and dripping with honey. "Bread and bootie just don't mix," she said firmly, and nothing Pauline said was going to change her mind.

After the bread, there'd been the hula hooping. Aruni had been responsible for *that* travesty, inviting all of the BRBs out to her studio one evening after regular classes and passing out plastic hoops to the women. In full teaching mode, she'd called out suggestions for them to improve their form through her headset, demonstrating technique and urging them all to feel the sexual vibes in their pelvic regions.

Janice and Crystal had gotten into a competition to see who could keep their hoops spinning the longest while Hortencia cursed up a storm, claiming her "dang hooie-hoop" must be defective since she couldn't get it higher than her knees. River Wind had done respectably, until she'd pulled her back out and had to call it quits. Pauline, naturally, maintained perfect rhythm, whizzing her hoop about her old hips with proficiency and an occasional exclamation of gutsy delight.

Sera, somehow, had given herself a fat lip. Which hadn't been much of a turn-on.

About the midnight moonlit drum circle, the less said the better. With unerring skill, they'd managed to cop a squat right on a red anthill, and then, once they'd managed to sort *that* stinging situation out, the BRBs had woken every dog in the neighborhood with their bongo slapping and drum whapping. It was a wonder no one had called the police, what with all the ruckus. Sera, who had the well-developed aversion for drum circles of someone who had oft attempted to relax in Central Park's Sheep Meadow, had not changed her mind about the milieu.

And she hadn't come a whit closer to climax.

The next week, Crystal, that evil wench, had dared them all to a chile-eating contest. She and the others swore by the aphrodisiac properties of the local hot peppers, so they'd tromped out to a famously sadistic dive called the Horseman's Haven for some burgers smothered in nuclear meltdown chile, washed down with kombucha they'd snuck in themselves. There'd been a fair amount of gasping and wailing with that activity, but most of it had been Sera bemoaning the loss of her taste buds and the time it would take to regrow them.

The worst part, for Sera, had been disappointing her new friends. They took such joy in their excursions, be they silly, sweet, or utterly unhinged. These women just let it all hang out, whooping with laughter and living in the moment, even when it made them look goofy or exposed their weak spots. But Sera just... couldn't. The harder she tried to let go, the tighter she got wound up. And the more she saw the crestfallen expressions on the BRBs' faces after each failure, the more conspicuously "broken" Sera felt. But she couldn't bear to disappoint her aunt, and so she'd pasted on a smile and sworn to keep on trying.

Yet her lack of progress was straining even Pauline's vast reserves of optimism.

In the end, Pauline had clapped a stern hand on Sera's shoulder and marched her into Bliss's back room, which Malcolm, true to his word, had not touched. "Look, kiddo," she'd said rather grimly. "I know you're kind of a prude. So I tried to think outside the cocks. I thought maybe we could find a gentle way to ease you into things. But maybe the 'hard' way is the only way." She'd ordered Sera to pick out a selection of machinery, imagery, and "facilitating lotions," then take her loot back to the house. Then she and Hortencia had taken themselves off, loudly announcing their intention to take in a new German art-house film at the Lensic—a *three-hour* German film.

Sera was embarrassed to admit, she'd actually given it a whirl. Yet no matter what aids she employed, nor what pleasant memories of Asher's embrace she conjured, the result was...disappointing. She kept picturing her aunt tiptoeing up to the window to see how she was doing, or pressing a glass to the door...or worse, offering a tutorial on the proper usage of her "tools." In the end, almost without conscious design, Sera had found herself in her aunt's kitchen, baking up a half-dozen almond *galettes* she had no good home for. She hadn't been able to look either woman in the eye after they'd returned from the theater, merely serving them up the delicious dessert with a side of *crème fraîche* before retiring to her room to nurse her shame.

Now, melting to death in the ever-increasing heat of the sweat lodge, Sera knew she could never tell Pauline that the real reason she couldn't achieve orgasm was Pauline herself. Her aunt would be devastated. *Maybe I should just fake it,* she thought. *It's worked for me before... and it would get me the hell out of this convection oven.* But Serafina believed in rigorous honesty—it was one of the tenets of her recovery program. And so she sweated it out.

At least the lighting was nice and low, Sera thought hazily. And the sage was actually quite pleasant, once her nostrils got accustomed to it. The rosy glow from the brazier was...hypnotizing. The heat curled around her, lulling her, though she fought to stay alert. *This isn't so bad,* she told herself. *It's just like a sauna.*

A very steamy sauna.

Curtains of white condensation swirled about the hut, obscuring Sera's vision. Somehow, as the mists parted, Sera wasn't surprised to see the sweat lodge had admitted another guest. A very ugly, odd-looking guest, about a foot tall and walking on all fours. It trotted right up next to her in the hut, bold as it pleased. The other women had faded from Sera's awareness, banked in clouds of steam, and it was just her and the wrinkly, vaguely phallic-looking beast.

"What are you supposed to be?" Sera, somehow unsurprised, asked the creature.

"Can't you tell? I'm an armadillo," the armadillo said proudly.

"Sorry," Sera apologized. "I'm more used to subway rats and pigeons. I don't think I've ever seen an armadillo in real life before."

"And you ain't seeing one in real life now, hon," said the armadillo, which for some reason was now sporting a cowboy hat. And chewing a hayseed. "I'm not supposed to be purple. And my tail is a lot longer than this in real life. Plus, mostly I live in Texas, not so much New Mexico. Watch a nature show once in a while, won't you?"

"Sorry," Sera said again. "So, are you, like..." She couldn't say it.

"Your orgasm totem? Your cum-critter? Your arma-dildo? Nah. I'm just a hallucination. But if you like, I could give you some advice."

The armadillo trundled up closer to Sera, and she noticed that it was thick-skinned, yet naked, as she was, with a soft underbelly. Its eyes, half-buried in armor, were sharp and bright, its nose long and twitchy. It looked at her as if she were infinitely amusing, but also perhaps a tad pitiable.

"Sure," said Sera, who at this point wasn't above taking advice from purple fantasy animals. "Lay it on me."

The armadillo pushed its rhinestone-spangled hat back on its tiny head. "My advice?" the beast mused. "Don't worry about what these dopey broads tell you. When the moment comes, it's just like sneezing. You know what I mean?"

"Um, not really," said Sera, who appeared to be floating about six inches above the floor of the hut now. "Sneezing?"

"Ever tried to hold back a sneeze?" her not-totem asked.

"I guess," said Sera, who had never thought about it before.

"How'd that work out for you?"

Sera considered it. Her mind was strangely languid. "Um, I sneezed anyway, but it was kind of bunged up. Not very nice."

"Uh-huh. And ever tried to *make* yourself sneeze?" The armadillo didn't wait for an answer. "Can't do it, can you? It's not something you can force, and it's not something you can fake—not properly. You can't stop it and you can't control the timing. Just like climax. Also," it paused and said thoughtfully, "I'm pretty sure you can't do either with your eyes open." The armadillo gathered itself, settling its hat more firmly over its brow with one tiny claw. It patted its nonexistent pockets. "Anyway, lady, that's about all I got on the subject." It started to walk away, toward a little hole Sera hadn't noticed before in the mud-brick walls. Then it stopped and turned back for a final word. "Oh, yeah—one more thing. You may never have sneezed before, but I have a feeling you're gonna be developing some severe allergies pretty soon. Anyhow, take it easy!"

"You, too, Mr. 'Dillo," said Sera, who had decided that was her new friend's name. She smiled and waved, feeling mellower than she'd felt in a long time. "Byeeee!"

❧

"I think we left her in here too long. Damn it, Pauline, you and your *loco* ideas. Look at her, babbling and muttering like that. We cooked her darn brains!" Hortencia sounded halfway between scared and exasperated.

A hand was patting Sera's cheeks, none too gently. "C'mon, kid-bean, snap out of it."

Her aunt's voice, Sera thought dreamily. Pauline sounded worried. But why? Everything was going to be just fine.

"Pauline?" she murmured, coming slowly to awareness. The door to the hut had been propped open, and someone had draped a fat, fluffy towel over Sera to shield her from the chilly breeze drifting in. The brazier had been banked, the steam dissipated. The others were dressed, and had donned concerned expressions along with their attire. Sera sat up and looked around, feeling calm and slightly out of focus, as if she'd smoked some really nice pot—another thing she didn't do anymore. "Hey, guys. Are we ready to go now? Don't let me forget to stop at the drugstore on the way home. The armadillo told me to stock up on tissues."

After that, the Back Room Babes decided to give it a rest.

A good thing, too, because the next day, Sera's contractor called and told her she'd better get her ass down to Bliss, *tout de suite.*

Chapter Twenty

Sera rushed down to the *placita* all in a lather upon receiving McLeod's curt message, nearly mowing down a troupe of late-afternoon tourists as she gunned Cupcake through the streets of Santa Fe's chi-chi shopping district. Inexpertly parallel parking the beast, she leapt out and dived for her place of business, *tout de suite* indeed.

She found her contractor waiting outside the shop, wearing a thunderous scowl.

"Now look, woman," he greeted her, "I don't want any fuss or shenanigans when ye see what I done inside. Promise me ye won't have a fit of the vapors or nothin', or I won't let ye in."

Momentarily, Sera wished for a weapon. Perhaps the tire iron from Cupcake's rusty bed. But not having thought to bring one, she realized it would be faster to agree than to argue. She could always renege and strangle her contractor with his own ponytail later if necessary. Right now she had to see what he'd done to her store. She nodded tightly, swallowing a tight breath.

Malcolm ushered her in ("shoved" would have been more accurate) and flipped on the lights.

"Oh," she said, a mere breath of sound.

Malcolm had made her dreams come true.

The shop was exactly as she had envisioned it, from countertops veined in creamy white marble to cabinets of white-painted wood that were both cozy and contemporary. Stoves, ovens, and refrigerated storage had been installed and partitioned off with the two-way mirror that would allow the bakers in the back to see their customers while retaining the privacy to swear, sweat, and slave away unobserved. Up front, there were stations for cake decoration (a concession to those who loved to watch while the finishing touches were put on their delicacies) and shelves with cardboard boxes in various sizes for packing them up when they were complete. Display cases gleamed under fluorescent lights, aching to be filled with brioche, cookies, and cakes. Coffee and espresso machines gleamed with the promise of steaming caffeinated joy, just where Sera had pictured them, with enough room for a barista to maneuver and yet not get in the way of the counter help at the register.

The little touches they'd gone over—incorporating Pauline's Victorian lamps, burnishing the pine plank floors to waxed golden perfection—were all in place. For customers wishing to linger awhile over their goodies, comfortable yet durable wingback chairs cozied up next to an eclectic assortment of shaker-style stools and ladder-back dining chairs, clustering around small, marble-topped tables the perfect height for resting a drink or a pastry on while one read the paper. (Sera had very much enjoyed the estate sales and antique store hunting that had gone into their purchase.) Hooks for coats and a stand for umbrellas stood ready by the front door. The stout log vigas had been sanded and were glowing with new life after her brilliant contractor's attentions. Even the windows had been washed, the sills painted a cheerful turquoise against the diamond-finished white stucco interior of the shop. Outside, Asher's plants, newly trimmed, framed the windows nicely without overwhelming the space. Inside, the overhead chandelier in brass and crystal Sera had special ordered from a supplier in New York sent light sparkling across the counters and seating arrangements.

As for the back room... well, it was discreetly curtained off, barred with a little silver chain like they used at movie houses, and labeled with a small, handwritten sign saying "Over Eighteen Only," the way Sera had directed. Pauline had wanted to paint a lurid sign over the lintel calling attention to her lair of sultry delights, but Sera had nixed the idea, reminding her aunt that children would no doubt soon be running around the bakery, poking their noses into everything. She had no desire to spend the next sixty years of her life fending off lawsuits from outraged parents.

Everything was as she'd envisioned it—or better. Sera spun in a circle, taking it all in.

They were ready for business.

"McLeod, you're a goddamn genius!" she crowed, throwing her arms about him and giving him a hearty kiss on each of his bristly cheeks.

"Och, ye promised me, no womanly theatrics," Malcolm swore, but Sera could tell he was pleased with her reaction.

"It's beautiful," she breathed. "Thank you so much."

Malcolm stuffed his hands in the pockets of his coveralls, rocked on the balls of his feet, and cleared his throat. "Nothin' to it," he muttered, but Sera saw the pride in his eyes when he looked about at what he'd wrought.

The perfect place to make sweet dreams come true.

Too bad Asher's not back yet, Sera thought. *I'd have loved for him to see this before anyone else.*

But Asher was still in Israel, at least as far as Sera knew. She'd had no word from him since he'd left her high and dry in Pauline's kitchen, and she was beginning to wonder if she'd imagined the whole incident. Certainly, his professed passion hadn't sent him winging his way back to her with any great haste. Perhaps he was having too much fun with his *wife.*

Never mind your landlord, Sera, she told herself. *It's go-time. Best get your head in the game.*

Malcolm apparently agreed. "We can open anytime now," he said. "Once we get to baking, that is." Under bristly white brows, the look in McLeod's eye was challenging, as if he still didn't quite believe Sera could cook.

She smiled. This was one challenge she had no fear of facing.

"Just let me get my apron," she said, and ran back to her truck.

⁂

They were alone in the bakery, and it was an hour before dusk. Sera was wrapped in her favorite warn-to-thread linen apron, a hair net, and all the determination at her command. Malcolm had just arrived to do his part, his "proprietary" pie-making tools in a sack over his back, making Sera think of a chef-coated Santa. She herself had been cooking 'round the clock since yesterday, prepping doughs, double-checking menus, timing out recipes to maximize oven space and temperature like the seasoned campaigner she was. Icings, fillings, and delicate decorations were complete, resting in refrigerators and on out-of-the-way shelves for the moment when they'd be called upon. Sponges and bigas bubbled away in rising buckets, while prepared dough, tightly wrapped in plastic wrap, awaited the magical moment when it would be set free to become fragrant, crusty bread. Quiche ingredients were laid out ready to hand in Sera's *mise en place,* and flaky croissant dough beckoned, waiting to be folded into beautiful crescent shapes or wrapped around chocolate sticks for *pain au chocolat.*

Tomorrow was opening day, and she still had an avalanche of baked goods to prepare. Back home, Pauline was busy putting together her famous almond tarts and several types of cookies, saving Sera time and space to work on the main events—the cakes, macaroons, mousses, and tortes that would soon fill Bliss's display cases to mouthwatering effect. Hortencia was baking up a batch of her *abuelita*'s famous *biscochitos,* the recipe for which she'd promised to share with Serafina. Now Malcolm would add an array of his famous pies to the offerings.

Since they'd agreed on opening the bakery right away—Sera had placed a standing order with a supplier for her baking supplies weeks earlier, and arranging delivery was the work of a phone call—there was nothing to hold them back. An ad in the local weekly, the *Chile Paper*, and one in the *Santa Fe New Mexican* had pretty much maxed out her promotional budget. Since the decision, Sera had been running on adrenaline, excitement, and nerves. Neither she nor Malcolm would likely see their beds before tomorrow night—if then—but Sera was prepared for that. Hell, she'd been preparing her whole life for a moment like this. Sleep could wait. She took a deep breath and turned to the man at her side—pie maven, contractor, and—she hoped—friend.

"What do you think?"

He was looking around, obviously impressed with how much she'd accomplished since last they'd met. "Ye done a lot," he conceded. "Looks like ye might just pull this off, lass."

Sera grinned. "Damn straight we're going to pull this off. You ready for the final push?"

"You just stay on yer side o' the counter, keep yer mitts out of my piecrust, and we oughta do fine."

Fourteen hours later, bursting at the seams with carbohydrate-rich delights, Bliss opened for business.

Chapter Twenty-One

"Why the long face, kiddo? You don't like the balloons out front?"

"The balloons are great, Aunt Paulie," Sera assured the older woman. And they were—once she'd popped the cock-shaped ones (which Pauline had got from the Ecstasy Emporium) with a cake tester while her aunt wasn't looking. She'd also taken a spit-dampened finger to the chalkboard sign Pauline had, with great zest, inscribed with the words "Cum in! We're wiiiiide open!" and replaced the missive with a more decorous invitation for customers to attend the store's grand opening.

"Then what? You look like someone swapped salt for sugar in your favorite recipe." Pauline leaned against the counter, examining her niece with narrowed eyes.

Sera sighed. "I don't know what I was expecting, Auntie. I suppose I was being unrealistic, but I had this fantasy that we'd be swamped from minute one. An addict's grandiosity, I guess."

Pauline gave Sera a squeeze that threatened to bagpipe all the air out of her. "It'll happen, Baby-Bliss. Give it time. It's early in the day." She patted Sera on the shoulder.

Sera sighed. As grand openings went, she'd seen better. She'd also seen much worse. Or so she reminded herself throughout the day as she, Pauline, and Friedrich, the tongue-tied young barista they'd hired from the local liberal arts college, managed the steady trickle of customers who filed in and out of her new shop. She told herself to be patient, be realistic. Yet as the day progressed, there was no stampede for fresh cupcakes, no run on the croissants. Tourists wandered in, murmured appreciatively over the bright, cheerful décor, then bought a latte and a bear claw or two. Sometimes they stayed awhile. More often they moved on to the next stop on their agenda, be it museum, gallery, or boutique. Mr. Yazzie from next door came in around midday for his promised sticky bun and a minute of friendly chat. Even Lupe had wished them a sulky "good luck" on her way to opening Lyric Jewelry. And of course, Aruni was her biggest champion, not only dropping by for a green tea and a veggie breakfast mini-quiche first thing in the morning but sending all the students from her midday class over to check Bliss out after they'd finished twisting themselves into pretzels of serenity. Hortencia had bustled in toward three when her shift at Knit-Fit ended, carrying a hand-crocheted cozy for Big Mama's container, along with a hug and a kiss for Sera and Pauline. The Back Room Babes had made a point of popping in for cups of kombucha, scones, and slices of pie, bringing a smile to Sera's face with their cheerful greetings and loud exclamations of delight as they bit into their treats.

Overall, as the day went on, Sera found herself reasonably pleased, if not giddy with the triumph she'd secretly envisioned.

Her aunt, however, seemed to have developed some of Sera's earlier malaise. Pauline had started out happily enough, decked out in her favorite rainbow-colored skirt, a screaming yellow bandanna, and a shirt that proudly proclaimed "Bakers Like It Hot and Steamy!" Between ringing up customers at the front register, she'd amused herself asking Friedrich all sorts of impertinent questions about his love life and clucking over his blushes and stammers. But as time went on, she'd soured. For Pauline, who stood at the ready, positively panting to show folks the "other side" of the business, had had *not one customer.* Sera could tell she was getting miffed. She kept glancing from the roped-off back room to the last customers lingering over their pastries, then over to Sera. But Sera had, in no uncertain terms, forbidden Pauline from evangelizing about the wares behind the curtain if customers didn't specifically ask about them. Sera had no intention of becoming famous for peddling sexual aids—at least not before she became the toast of this town's culinary culture.

At this rate, that might take awhile.

Maybe I should have spent more on advertising, Sera thought as she wiped down the counters and counted the leftover croissants she'd be donating to the food depot on Siler Road if they didn't sell out. But she'd done what she could afford, and she knew she'd have to rely on word-of-mouth from satisfied customers to begin building a loyal fan base. *I just need patience, and a little faith,* she told herself. Of course, a nice review wouldn't hurt either. But Sera's polite message to the food editor at the *Chile Paper*, inviting him to check out her new business, hadn't been returned.

And speaking of returns, Sera was still awaiting Asher's. It had been over two weeks now, and even Lupe, whom Sera had risked cold shoulder-itis to ask, had no firm ETA for the enigmatic Israeli. She couldn't help feeling he should have been there for her grand opening, though she had to concede that wasn't quite fair—it wasn't like she'd told him when she intended to open. Still, his absence hurt—more than she liked to admit.

Maybe he's not coming *back,* thought Sera. *Maybe that wife of his convinced him to stay, or...* Sera had no answers.

But she *did* have one more customer, as she saw when she looked up in response to the chiming of the bell Malc had fastened over the door. A painfully thin young woman, perhaps mid-twenties, with the look of a computer sciences major entered the shop. The woman stopped, sniffed, and coughed, as though the scents of cinnamon, butter, and sugar were disagreeable to her. Then she lifted her chin and marched up to the counter, stiff-legged. She pulled out a pad and scanned it, then fixed Sera and her aunt with a gimlet glare.

"Are you Ms. Wilde?" she barked.

Both Pauline and Sera started. "Yes," they answered in unison, then glanced sheepishly at each other. Pauline grinned, slung her arm around Sera, and elaborated. "I'm Pauline Wilde, and this-here genius is my niece, Bliss, the mastermind behind this oasis of oral delights."

Sera winced.

The young woman coughed another dry cough, peering at the two of them as though they were specimens in a not particularly fascinating zoo. "So you're the owner," she said to Sera, who nodded.

"Proprietor anyhow," she agreed. "Pauline will always be the real boss around here."

The woman didn't smile or acknowledge Sera's distinction, except to scribble a note in her little pad. *Awkwaaard,* Sera thought. But she couldn't afford to alienate someone who might be a local. "What can I get for you?" She gestured at the display cases. "The *tarte tatin* is very nice, and the chocolate ganache cupcake is, if I do say so myself, completely out of this world." She smiled warmly at the woman. It had been awhile since she'd dealt with difficult customers, but her old skills from her days catering to some of New York's finickiest foodies hadn't completely left her.

"I'm not hungry," the woman said flatly. She cleared her throat again, as if the very notion of cupcakes made her gag. "I came because I was called."

"Called?" Sera ventured. She could well believe the woman wasn't hungry—she'd seen the type before: the soulless, hardly human sort who had no interest in food beyond how it might sustain them. The type, frankly, that gave Sera chills. Sera looked her over more closely. The woman's face was startlingly square, with nearly no chin but incredibly wide jaws, like a living Lego action figure, or a less attractive Betty Boop. Her throat was so gaunt Sera could see the rungs of cartilage beneath the skin, and she could only imagine how skeletal the rest of her must be. Her long, mousy brown hair was tied in an untidy bun. It, too, looked thin. *Eat a cupcake, lady,* she wanted to scream. *It's obviously an emergency.*

"Yes, *called,*" Lego-head said. She sighed irritably. "I'm Marnie Pyle. From the *Chile Paper*?"

In her excitement, Pauline elbowed Sera in the ribs hard enough that Sera yipped. "From the *Chile Paper*, you say?"

"Yessss," the woman hissed impatiently. "Someone called the food section about this bakery, wanting a write-up. I'm who they sent."

"Oh!" said Sera, her focus sharpening. "But we called Burt Evans, the regular reviewer. We never heard back, so we figured he wasn't interested."

"Burt's got gout." The woman's disgusted expression clearly said, *Serves him right, the fat bastard.* "I'm planning to go into investigative journalism," she said importantly, "but my editor seems to think I've still got some dues to pay. So I got assigned to cover this"—she looked around the bakery dismissively—"story."

You don't always get to choose your angels, Sera reminded herself. *But once they arrive, it can't hurt to roll out the red carpet.* She exchanged significant looks with her aunt, who was squirming with barely suppressed excitement. Sera winced internally. An excited Pauline was a garrulous Pauline—and lord only knew what she might say. "I got this, Aunt Pauline. Think you can man the register alone for a bit?"

Pauline, standing in the nearly empty shop, gave her niece a disbelieving look. "Did I suddenly go senile in the last twenty minutes?" she muttered. Sera ignored her. Much as she didn't want to offend her aunt, she *really* didn't want Pauline's unfiltered outrageousness to affect Ms. Pyle's write-up. Sera came around the counter, ushering the woman gingerly over to a table. "Please, let me offer you a cup of coffee—Friedrich, would you make our guest whatever she'd like? Anything you want, Friedrich can make it—we rescued him from Starbucks and he's still in the honeymoon phase," she joked.

Lego-head didn't smile. "Coffee, black," she said.

Friedrich nodded and wordlessly poured a cup of joe—from the freshly brewed pot, Sera was glad to see. Sera brought it over to her "best" table, a lovely little inlaid marble square parked between a pair of squishy antique leather armchairs she and Malcolm had carefully Scotchgarded. She glanced back at her aunt, who was fulminating not very quietly by the register. Friedrich kept his head down, wiping up stray coffee grounds with a rag. "Maybe you could bring us an assortment of pastries, Aunt Pauline. You know all the best ones—not that there are any bad ones," she added hastily, glancing at the reporter.

"Let me see if I can get my feeble old brain to work well enough to pick a few," said Pauline, sniffing.

Sera wiped the wince off her face. "So!" she said brightly, watching as her guest settled stiffly into an armchair, "you're here to write a review of Bliss?"

Marnie Pyle coughed. "Less a review than a brief puff piece on the opening. When Burt's feeling better, he may drop by for a more thorough story." Her tone told Sera not to count on it.

"Right, well..." Sera trailed off. "Uh, so what comes next?"

The reporter dug into her messenger bag and placed a digital recorder and her notepad on the table between them. "I'll ask you a few questions, then you answer them," she said, her expression indicating Sera had been on the waiting list for a brain transplant too long. "I'll try to make this quick." Sera could almost hear the unspoken, *For both our sakes.* Marnie coughed; a single, Gollum-like bark. "So, we'll start with your background as a baker, and then talk a bit about what brought you to Santa Fe from wherever it is you're from." She leaned back in her chair—a pose not so much receptive as infinitely weary.

Sera hit all the high notes, weaving a highly sanitized version of her story for the bored reporter. Neither her education at New York City's preeminent culinary school nor her experience in some of Manhattan's finest kitchens seemed to impress the woman. *She probably wouldn't know Jacques Pépin from Jacques Cousteau.* As she watched Lego-head's eyes glaze over like honey dip on a donut, a thrill of panic swept over her. A bad review could spell the end for them before they'd barely begun. Sera well knew the effects of negative publicity—back in New York, Blake Austin's smear campaign had effectively ruined her. But nothing she said elicited more than a sigh or a brief scribble on the reporter's pad.

Sera tried harder. She hadn't slept for two days, and she was running mainly on sugar and caffeine. But she'd be damned if she didn't give this interview her utmost. Forcing animation to replace her exhaustion, she rhapsodized about Santa Fe's spectacular climate and bemoaned the kinks the high altitude had thrown into her well-rehearsed recipes. She shared how her aunt had invited her to set up shop, and how it had always been her dream to become a *pâtissière.* She talked extensively about their menu, being sure to mention McLeod's famous pies. Still, nothing seemed to capture her guest's attention.

Until her aunt stepped in.

"Here we go!" Pauline sang out, swishing over to their table with a swing in her hips and a plate piled high with samples of Sera's treats in her hand. With a flourish, she set the plate down and plunked her bum on the arm of Sera's chair. "My Bliss here is hands down the best baker in New Mexico—New York, too, I bet. I taught her everything she knows," she confided.

Sera tried not to wince. *Please, please don't embarrass me*, she silently pleaded, remembering other times over the years when she'd futilely sent up this same prayer. It would be just like Pauline to start babbling about Sera's orgasm quest...or the back room. Under the table, Sera crossed her fingers.

Lego-head looked dubiously down at her plate. Pauline had arranged perfect bite-sized samples of some of Sera's greatest hits—from a classic Napoleon to a hazelnut-infused *mille crepe,* plus a petite triple-chocolate mousse (the same that had first garnered Blake Austin's attention) and the green chile quiche Sera had added to the menu as a concession to the locals (she had experimented with green chile cupcakes but had given it up as a bad job). Everything looked exactly as Sera would have hoped—mouthwatering, elegant, and fresh.

Lego-head took a tiny bite of the mousse. Her mouth screwed up and she took a quick sip of coffee.

"Is something wrong?" Sera couldn't stop herself from asking.

Lego-head coughed. "I'm sure it's fine. I just don't like chocolate." Her scrawny fingers fumbled for her pen, and she wrote herself a note. She tried the quiche. Made another face. "Or eggs." Another scribbled note. She sampled the *mille crepe,* its dozen delicate layers parting with a ghost of a sigh beneath her fork, oozing hazelnut crème and hours of effort. "Very rich," said Lego-head, but not in a particularly approving tone.

Sera shot her aunt a look. *We're dyin' here.*

"Did my niece tell you about the back room?" Pauline asked brightly.

Oh, no. No, no, no, no, no...

"Back room?" asked Lego-head, eyes sharpening.

Now it was Sera's turn to elbow Pauline, which she did sharply enough that the older woman nearly lost her seat on the arm of Sera's chair.

But the reporter's investigative instincts had kicked in. And Pauline's pride in her life's work would not be stifled—no matter how hard Sera prayed. "Oh, yes, it's the real secret of this shop. We don't call it 'Bliss' just because the baked goods are out of this world. Our mission is to offer sensual pleasures of *all* sorts—fulfillment for the senses, the earthier the better."

Ms. Pyle stood up. Her ennui had vanished, and Sera, to her horror, saw visions of bylines dancing in the woman's unfortunately shaped skull. "*Now* we've got an angle," she barked. "Show me this back room of yours."

Pauline was more than happy to do so. And Sera, sensing she ought not body-slam her last living relative to the ground in front of witnesses, was powerless to stop her.

❧

The headline in the *Chile Paper*'s next issue read:

Cupcakes and Climaxes: New Bakery Offers More Than Just Taste Sensations

The day after the issue dropped, they were swamped.

The day after that, a chance tweet from a certain vacationing celeb whose Twitter following exceeded half a million took the tale of Santa Fe's new "dessert and dildo place" to the web. (Apparently, said celeb's assistant had stopped by the store and brought her master—er, employer—a few treats and some spicy stories.) The celebrity thought his followers might get a giggle, and he was right—but so did the national news media.

Because the day after that, the film crew from CNN arrived.

And the day after *that*, her nemesis returned.

Chapter Twenty-Two

Oh, shit. Asher's back.

His figure was unmistakable—long, lean, and purposeful, edging his way through the throng of customers that had lined up outside the door and half filled the courtyard. His destination was clear...he was making a beeline for Serafina herself.

Sera froze. The world went a bit wonky, time slowing while the space between them seemed to wobble and shimmer. Sera gave up breathing as a bad job, had to lean her butt against the counter behind her lest her legs betray her.

He looked good. *Damn* good. Tanned, burnished, fair glowing with good health and a lightness of presence she couldn't fail to notice, even as she wondered at its cause. It was as though he was lit up from within—or, more accurately, that the fire she'd always sensed in him, banked, had flared into full-throated life. She guessed she had about forty-five seconds before he finished wending his way to the front and they were reunited. Her heart began to thrum like the harp in an angel's chorus, her breath coming quick and shallow.

"Hellोooo...Peanuts?"

"What?" Sera blinked, brought back to the customer in front of her with a start.

"It doesn't have any peanuts in it, does it?" repeated the anxious mother whose five-year-old was doing his best to get his grubby prints all over Sera's nice clean display cases. "Billy's allergic to peanuts. Well, not *allergic,* but his pediatrician says peanut allergies are very common among boys his age, so we don't want to take any risks! So no peanuts. Does this have peanuts?"

Sera collected her wits as best she could. "Um... it *is* a peanut butter pie, so yes, I'm afraid it does contain peanuts," she said with an apologetic smile. She squelched the desire to point out the display card that clearly pronounced the nature of the confectionary beast, right in front of the woman's nose. The mom had "frazzled" written all over her as it was.

She wasn't alone. Since the CNN crew had taken the story of her "salacious" new bakery national, interviewing Sera, Pauline, and their neighbors for a piece that had elicited a raised eyebrow from Anderson Cooper himself, tourists and locals alike had been flocking to Bliss, and the phone had been ringing off the hook. Sera was running out of brioche faster than she could bake. She was worn to the bone, practically swaying on her feet.

And it was, hands down, the most fun Sera could remember having, drunk or sober.

Even Malcolm, who'd sworn never to do customer-facing work again, had been drafted to do day shifts baking, prepping, and packaging in the back. Up front, Sera and Friedrich were being run off their feet, helping Santa Feans shop for Thanksgiving treats, birthday cakes, and *pain quotidian* alike. The tables were full, the armchairs overflowing, and patrons were wedged in every available space, munching, sipping, chatting, and comparing notes. Their cheeks were flushed, their eyes bright from sugar, and the din of the crowd was stadium-loud. Their energy fed Sera as if she were plugged directly into it with some psychic extension cord. It was like the very best buzz she'd ever had on booze—exhilaration, exultation, and ego keeping the need for sleep at bay and her reflexes sharp. But this high wasn't about self-destruction.

It was the fulfillment of a dream.

Pauline's dreams, too, were coming true. She had set herself up on a stool by the back room like some flower-child nightclub bouncer, and was taking numbers for customers curious about her little corner of the Bliss empire. Today's T-shirt read, "Ask Me About Our Ben Wa Balls!" and she was sporting a purple felt beret angled jauntily over her salt-and-pepper hair. The line for the back room was nearly as long as that for the baked goods, but Sera couldn't begrudge her. Not only had Pauline's indiscreet comment garnered Sera the publicity she needed to make a go of her bakery, Sera had, quite simply, never seen her aunt so joyfully in her element.

Solicitously, Pauline led those with a prurient interest into her domain of personal empowerment, guiding them through the purchase of pleasure-enhancing accoutrements, and then (on Sera's recommendation), discreetly packaging their newfound treasures in opaque plastic bags printed with the store's name in flowing pink script. She'd already had to place several orders with the folks at the Ecstasy Emporium to keep up with the demand.

It was pandemonium—wonderful, glorious pandemonium.

It was also just about all Sera could handle at the moment.

Apparently, Asher Wolf hadn't got the memo.

"I *so* do not need this right now," she muttered.

"*Excuse* me?" the mother said sharply.

"Oh, not you, you're fine," Sera said, waving distractedly. *But I, on the other hand, am most definitely* not *fine right now. Even if* he *is the finest thing I have ever seen in my life.*

Part of her wanted to shove the lady's cookies at her, vault over the counter, and launch herself into Asher's arms. Another part wished he'd just disappear—at least until she had time to process her feelings. But Asher obviously wasn't going away—in fact, he'd edged himself to the front of the crowd now, so close she could smell his signature, sigh-inducing pheromones. *What'm I going to say to him?* she fretted. It had to be something casual, something that wouldn't reveal how much she'd missed him, how often she'd thought of him since he left, and damn it, how much sleep she'd lost replaying, over and over, their spectacular make-out session.

Be cool, Sera, she warned herself.

"Where have you *been?*" was what came out of her mouth.

Loudly.

Titters, snorts, and muffled laughs erupted from the crowd waiting their turn at the counter. Sera's face flushed a painful near-purple, and she debated whether the storage cubby at her back might be generous enough to accommodate her.

"I'm sorry, Bliss." Asher's eyes were earnest, his whole face radiating regret. "I would have returned sooner if I could. I had...obligations...to attend to back home."

Obligations like his wife? Sera wondered.

"I see," she said. She turned to her customer. "How about I arrange an assortment of those *palmiers* and some chocolate-dipped meringues? No peanuts, I promise."

"Fine, fine," murmured the mom, stroking little Billy's tousled hair as she gazed hungrily at the man Sera very much wanted all to herself.

"I just got in less than an hour ago," Asher explained. "And, ah...I brought you something," he continued with unusual shyness. He reached behind him, and for the first time Sera noticed the long canvas sack slung over his shoulder, like a rifle case or a really, really big yoga mat holder. He swung it around front and reached inside, stripping the cloth away to show her what lay beneath.

"Oh." Sera's hand flew to her mouth. Tears pricked her eyes.

It was a sign for her store. A big, metal sign with "Bliss" forged in the most elegant calligraphy against a chased background of fanciful designs inlaid in silver, copper, and brass. Amid flowing abstract renderings of what looked like flowers and mountains, Sera picked out delicate little cupcakes, tiered party cakes, éclairs, cookies, and even...was that?... yes, a tiny chocolate babka. It must have taken him days, if not weeks, to create.

"It's wonderful," she said.

It was Asher's turn to blush, just a tiny hint of rosy color staining those tanned cheeks. "It was the only thing missing," he said. "Before I left, Malcolm showed me the store, and I thought, 'It's perfect, it has everything—except a way to let customers know how marvelous it is inside.' So"—he shrugged—"I made this."

"Nice going, guy, but could you woo your girlfriend some other time? Some of us are crying for a latte and a cinnamon bun here."

The suggestion came from a burly, cowboy-hatted mountain man with a beard Grizzly Adams would have envied and a grin that took the sting from his words.

"I've come at a bad time," Asher said, reddening further as he took in, seemingly for the first time, just how crowded the shop was.

"No...well, yes," Sera admitted. "It's a bit hectic right now, but I do want to talk to you, Ash." *And kiss you, and lick you, and make myself at home stark naked on top of your body...*

"After closing, then?" he asked. "I'll just go and retrieve the dogs from the kennel, and check on Guadalupe in the meantime—she's been managing the shop on her own far too long."

"Yeah, that'd be great—just maybe give me an hour after closing to set the place to rights," Sera said, wondering if she'd have time to scrub off the sweat, sugar, and sinful thoughts she'd be accruing in the meanwhile. "You know where to find me."

"Until then."

Sera's sigh was echoed by half (primarily, though not entirely, the soprano half) of her customers as Asher sauntered out of the store. And as the door closed behind him, Pauline experienced a sudden run on the back room that made her smile quite, quite broadly.

Chapter Twenty-Three

At the last second, Sera snatched the forgotten snood off her hair and gave her head a shake, hoping she'd achieve "sexily tousled" rather than "bag lady chic." Knowing her hair, she figured her chances were about fifty-fifty.

An hour after closing, Bliss was empty, tidy, and gleaming with readiness to face the next day. *What a change from earlier today,* Sera thought, feeling a strong sense of satisfaction—and yes, pride as she surveyed her store. It was a feeling she'd yet to get familiar with. She still tended to see herself as a failure—an addict, a washout in her career. *But look at me now,* she marveled. A so-far successful store. A sweet little bungalow she shared with her aunt. New friends. Glorious sunsets every night, fresh mountain air, and chile-smothered Southwestern food to eat pretty much any night of the week. *And* an incredibly hot guy about to walk through her door.

Just. Don't. Fuck. It. Up.

"Fuck what up?" Asher asked as he poked his head through the door.

Did I say that out loud? "Oh, I was thinking of including a special later this week—it's this little turkey-shaped *fleur de sel* caramel truffle that'd be perfect for people's Thanksgiving tables. But it's been awhile since I made them and I was worried about how they'd come out. The molds can be a bit tricky." All true, *if* he'd interrupted her thoughts ten minutes earlier.

"I've no doubt they will turn out brilliantly, given who's making them," Asher opined, edging the rest of his easy-on-the-eye frame into the shop.

Sera shrugged off the gallantry, uncomfortable with such ready praise. *Blake would've been on my back, breathing down my neck about how those little suckers better pop out perfect or my ass could find another line of work,* she couldn't help thinking. But Asher wasn't Blake. Oh, boy, was he ever not Blake.

"Come in, come in," she said, wiping her hands nervously on her jeans and turning for the back. "I was just closing up. Let me double-check that everything's off in the kitchen." She disappeared behind the glass wall, feeling the need to avoid Asher's gaze. *How'm I supposed to feel; a guy like that walks in all windswept and sexy? After* three weeks *with not a word?!* She wanted to lob day-old bagels at his head. But not nearly as much as she wanted to tackle him to the floor, slather him in homemade buttercream, and lick it off inch by inch with her tongue.

Down girl. She retreated to her happy place—the store's commodious kitchen.

"Bliss," said Asher.

When she turned around, he was much nearer than she'd expected—had followed her into the kitchen and was standing so close she could feel the heat radiating off him despite the Navy peacoat and olive wool scarf he'd worn against the late November chill.

"Bliss," he said again. Deeper.

"Hm?" Her voice was a scant breath, her whole being mesmerized by the intensity of his scrutiny.

He gathered her, quite suddenly and quite thoroughly, into his arms. She squeaked, but had time for nothing more before his lips claimed hers.

It was—or at least *felt*—about ten minutes later when he let her go. Stroking Sera's hair back from her flushed cheek, forehead pressed against hers, he was murmuring something over and over. It took Sera's scrambled brain a while to parse it out.

"I'm sorry, I'm sorry."

"For what?" she asked. *Giving me hope? Or giving me a case of the screaming "I-gotta-have-ya's"?* Sera pulled back to study his face. Green eyes shot through with golden spikes, brows that knit appealingly, lips that were slightly swollen from their kisses and so, so enticing...

"For taking so unforgivably long to return to the best thing that's come into my life in many years."

"Oh, *that.*" Sera crossed her arms under her breasts, reminding herself not to succumb to his apology without at least token resistance. But token resistance was pretty much all the resistance she could muster. "Yeah, Asher, what was all that about? I thought you said a week, maybe two. It's been *three.* And the last words you left me with weren't exactly reassuring."

His features creased with confusion. "What, that I wanted to take you out?"

Scratch that. Now Sera really *was* ready to nurse a grudge. "Um, *no,* Asher. I believe you muttered something about *having a little chat with your wife* before you disappeared for nearly a month."

Asher's hand scrubbed at the stubble that scruffed up his perfect jawline. "Oh, *chara,*" he swore in Hebrew. He had the same look he'd worn the day she'd dinged him with the dildo—the day he'd been worried about taking advantage of her.

Hangdog. Ashamed.

Good.

"Come here," he entreated, holding out his hand.

Sera debated, but she couldn't resist. He enfolded her hand in both of his, drawing her close as he backed up until he hit a countertop. With a lithe movement that would have done a dancer proud, he grasped her by the waist and twisted to deposit her, light as a feather, to sit atop the stainless steel counter. Sera could feel the coolness through her jeans, and then Asher's heat as he crowded up close to her. Somehow, her legs were spread wide, and he had wedged himself between them. His fingers speared into her hair, cupping her face and turning it up to his. Even atop her perch, he towered over her. "Bliss. My wife has been dead for four years. I went to make my farewells, make peace with my memories of her. I did this because, after you came into my life, it became clear that I had met a woman with whom I could perhaps make a future. Before I could pursue this—pursue *you*—in good conscience, I had to say good-bye to my past, and so I went to visit her grave."

Tears stung Sera's eyes, threatening to spill over. Her own hands rose to cup his cheeks in return, and she leaned forward to bring her lips to his, telling him wordlessly that she witnessed his pain; honored it.

"I'm a dumbass."

That startled a laugh out of him. "Your ass," he said with a twinkle, "is smart enough to fascinate me on quite a regular basis." He demonstrated by sliding his hot hand up her leg until he reached the portion of her anatomy in question, wedging his hand between it and the counter to give it a squeeze.

"It's I who have been the 'dumbass,' Bliss," he continued more somberly. "And I'm sorry for it. I had no business being so cryptic, and then not calling...It was wrong of me." He shook his head. "I thought I'd be gone just a few days, that I'd have plenty of time to take care of my business and get back to you to explain more fully why I'd gone. However, when I returned to Tel Aviv, I found my family in a bit of disarray." He stroked Sera's leg absently as he spoke, perhaps taking as much comfort as he was giving.

"My father is getting on in years, and his health has been declining for some time. Whenever I would call, my mother and sister always assured me it wasn't serious, that they were looking after him and there was nothing to worry about. Yet less than a week after I returned home, he had a stroke." At Sera's stricken look, he hastened to reassure her. "It turned out to be very minor—some kind of infarction, I believe they called it—but he was in the hospital for several days and I needed to be there. And after that I stayed to help my mother and sister settle him back at home, to be sure they had all of the support they needed."

"Of course," Sera said, feeling daring enough to run two fingers down the side of his face in a gentle caress. "I'm so glad you were able to be with your parents at a time like that." Her own parents were long gone, but Sera remembered how devastated she had been at even the hint that her aunt might be sick, when Pauline had told her and the BRBs about the lump in her breast.

Asher caught her fingers and kissed each one. "I think my family has been shielding me too much. Since my wife's death, they've tried to keep things light and respect my need to process my grief in my own way—even to moving halfway across the world. Perhaps they thought I couldn't handle another illness, and so they played down my father's condition. When I saw the reality...well, I'm afraid I became a bit caught up in family concerns.

Still, Bliss, I should have called. But somehow . . . I just wanted to wait until I could see your face again . . . touch you . . ." Asher suited actions to words as he stroked one callused hand down her arm. ". . . gaze into those pretty gray eyes. And tell you . . . how much I've longed to be with you."

"Asher, you really need to stop talking now."

Sera very much enjoyed the look that crossed her handsome suitor's face.

"I'm sorry?" He took a step back, leaving her bereft of his warmth.

Sera grabbed his hand, reeled him back in. "You should be. I went to a lot of trouble to put on this mascara"—she pointed to her lashes—"and I don't think you'd enjoy seeing it decorating my cheeks like a bad batch of icing. So please, spare us both and come here and kiss me, before I start to blubber."

Asher was nothing if not obedient.

From there, things took a rather delicious turn. Sera couldn't keep her hands off her lovely landlord, and he seemed to feel the same. Between lush kisses and caresses that sent her pulse soaring higher than the Santa Fe ski basin, he murmured words that were music to her ears. "I thought of you all the time I was away. I wondered how you were faring; whether the store had opened yet, and how you were getting along with Malcolm and Pauline. I pictured how delicious you looked the last time we were together, flushed and wanting atop that countertop in your aunt's kitchen—much as you are now. Hell, much as *I* am right now." He grinned, framing her face in both hands so she couldn't look away despite the fresh blush that bloomed across her cheeks. "I couldn't wait to get back to you, Bliss. And I can't wait to take you out—on a real, true date."

I can't wait either, Sera thought. *I don't care how badly this ends. I want to follow this fantasy as far as it takes me—to smile with him, hold hands with him, and hell, yes, make love as best I can with him. So what if I'm destined for the worst case of female blue-ball syndrome in the history of the world? I'm not giving this up one minute before I have to.*

She kissed him for all she was worth.

Asher kissed her back as if she were priceless.

I've never been happier in my life than I am right at this moment, thought Sera.

The universe thought that was very funny indeed.

Chapter Twenty-Four

"Well, well, well."

The words, uttered in tones of mockery so saturated as to drip disdain, came from the doorway that led to the front of the store.

Sera knew that distinctive blend of derision. She'd endured it day and night for years; had lived and breathed it for the better part of her career. She gasped and pulled back from Asher.

Yup. There he was. Blake Fucking Austin, haunter of nightmares, squasher of livelihoods, eviscerator of egos.

Was it possible to go from passion to projectile puking in one point two seconds? Sera was afraid she was about to find out.

I shouldn't be so shocked, thought a tiny part of her brain that was in fact very, very shocked. *He's managed to ruin every other moment of happiness in my adult life. Why* shouldn't *he pop up, like the rotten little troll he is, to destroy this one?*

"Serafina Wilde," drawled her nemesis. "And right where I last left you. Spreading yourself like second-rate caviar on a cracker for the kitchen help." That laugh. That bastard, horsey laugh that scraped her spine like harpy claws. "I can't say I'm surprised. You've quite the penchant for canoodling in kitchens." He eyed Asher, who had swung around, every muscle tense, to size him up.

Sera tried to see Blake as Ash might see him (rather than with the devil horns and cloven hooves her imagination always supplied). Powerfully built, but with the beginnings of a midlife paunch. Craggy features and thick, slightly oily black hair that waved back from a high forehead to brush his collar. Cashmere blend Burberry overcoat, white silk scarf tucked just so against the lapels. Loafers that were very likely Ferragamo. A smile that defined *snide*.

"What are you *doing* here?" Sera gasped. The hand Asher laid on her shoulder steadied her, but did nothing to dispel the atavistic horror that erupted in her belly. "What the fuck, Austin, didn't you get enough of making my life a living hell in New York? You had to follow me two thousand miles just to make sure I was still properly miserable?"

God, when would the bullying *stop?* When she was reduced to flipping burgers in some truck stop in rural Iowa? Sera hopped off the counter, keeping Asher close by her side but needing her feet on the ground in this moment. Yet even with feet firmly planted, shoulders squared, she still felt about a foot shorter than her already meager stature; as if she'd withered from the sheer proximity of her ex. She was keenly aware of Asher observing this confrontation, of the questions that must be swirling in his mind. *God, I hoped I'd never have to tell him about Blake...* Her heart was racing, her palms sweating. She wiped them surreptitiously against the legs of her jeans. She *had* to keep it together. The only thing keener than Blake Austin's palate was his ability to sense—and exploit—fear. "When's it going to be enough, Blake?" she demanded, hating the slight quaver in her voice. "When are you finally going to leave me alone? You're obsessed!"

Blake let another smile slither across his lips, leaning familiarly against the frame that supported Sera's two-way mirror wall. "Egotistical as always, aren't you, pet? And every bit as deluded as you ever were. As if I'd bestir myself such a distance merely to get reacquainted with your pathetic self." He snorted. "No, I'm here in this *quaint* little town for a different purpose—utterly unrelated to your presence, I can assure you. I'm overseeing the opening of a new restaurant I'm backing on Canyon Road." He ran a lambskin-gloved finger down the edge of the freshly painted doorframe, as if he expected to find grime. "I'd heard about your little porn-themed pastry shop, and as it was already along my route to dine with my investors tonight, I decided to pop by and see for myself just how far my former protégé had fallen. Really, Serafina." He shook his head. "Selling novelty penis cakes and boob-shaped bonbons? Even I had no idea you'd sunk so low."

Why did we have to sell out of pie, today of all days? Sera had a blinding, breathtaking need to plant a lemon meringue square in Blake's smirking puss. Her fingers clenched into fists, and she realized she hadn't exhaled in far too long. *Probably breathe flames if I did,* she thought.

Asher brought Sera back to her senses, wrapping an arm around her and squeezing gently. "Bliss, who is this incredibly rude little man? I would very much like to rearrange his face." Sera could feel his muscles bunch, practically smell his testosterone go into overdrive. "Do I have your permission?"

Sera *almost* said yes. Very little would have given her more satisfaction than to watch the powerful, tender man she loved wipe her nice kitchen floors with her sadistic ex-boyfriend.

Holy shit, wait... I love *him?*

Yes, Sera marveled: *indubitably and irrevocably, I love the hell out of Asher Wolf.*

A lightness blossomed in her chest. The sick knot in her stomach unraveled, replaced by a wonderful, calm warmth that stole over her. She felt her confidence swell, grow steadfast—something she'd never been able to sustain in Blake's presence before. A part of Sera marveled as she realized what had happened. *I... I actually care about myself. I care enough about myself to give my heart to a* good *man, a* kind *man. I am done with all that self-destructive bullshit I sought out for so long—no more booze, and no nasty, belittling boyfriends to make me feel second-best. Hell, I don't care if I can't have a stupid orgasm. I don't care if I screwed things up in the past. I deserve better than to be treated the way Blake treats me.*

All the years of living small, of curtailing her dreams in favor of her fears—she'd come to Santa Fe to put that negativity behind her. And this—realizing she'd fallen for Asher—confirmed she'd really started to do it. *I am done being treated like dirt. Done being intimidated by mean-spirited bullies like Blake Austin and Robbie Markham. I'm never going to be the scared little girl who kowtowed to those jerks again.*

"Bliss?" Asher prompted. "What do you say? Shall I teach this oaf some proper manners?"

Sera started to smile. And once she started, that smile just grew and grew.

Blake didn't like the look of it. "Setting your goon on me?" he sneered, but she could tell he was uneasy. Asher was younger, fitter, and at this moment, bristling with a menace Sera had never before seen in her easy-going landlord and soon-to-be-lover.

My lover. My champion. The guy I adore.

I am one lucky woman.

Sera had to laugh. She turned to Asher. "Sorry, goon." She grinned. "This is one demon I need to slay myself." She stepped up on tiptoe to plant a kiss on Asher's scruffy chin, seeing his features soften as he searched her eyes for confirmation she was all right. "Really, Ash. I've got this. But thanks for the offer. You'll never know how much it means to me."

At least, I think *I've got this,* Sera thought as she turned back to Blake. Even now, infused with the delicious, pink-cloud-inducing knowledge of her love for Asher, Sera wasn't quite as confident as she pretended. Blake had been the stuff of her sweat-drenched nightmares, the source of her deepest insecurities, for far too long. He'd ruined her reputation, nearly put her out of business. Worse than that, he'd made her doubt everything from her talent as a chef to her desirability as a woman. Still, she'd be damned if she'd let the bastard bully her in her own goddamned kitchen. His very presence was threatening to soil her beautiful new business, and God knew what he had in mind when he really got going.

For, whatever he claimed, Sera knew Blake hadn't flown all the way to Santa Fe to manage any grand opening. Not one so coincidentally timed anyhow. No, her ex was here to snuff out any happiness she might have created for herself, just as he'd done so many times in the past. He must have seen the news coverage of her new bakery and decided it behooved him to smash her chances of success here as he'd done so thoroughly back in New York.

She'd better smash first.

Her new solid marble rolling pin seemed a likely weapon. It was in her hand before she even realized she'd swiped it off the counter. Blake watched her movements, black eyes narrow. A look of amusement—she couldn't tell whether real or feigned—stamped itself across his louche features. Sera planned to wipe it off, one way or another.

"Listen to me very closely, Blake," she said softly. "You are not welcome here. I want you to vacate my property—right fucking now. If you don't leave—and *stay* gone—I'm going to call the police." Sera waved the pin threateningly as she approached her nemesis, stopping with a few feet still between them. "Do you understand me? You're trespassing on private property and I'd be within my rights to use this in self-defense. So unless you want me to make *pâté brise* out of your ugly mug, I suggest you go meet those investors of yours—if there even really *are* investors—and Get. The. Hell. Out. Of. My. Shop!"

Blake shrugged upright, casting a derisive glance down at Sera, rolling pin and all. "I've seen what I came to see, Serafina. There's nothing of any appeal to me here." He dusted his sleeve, as if it had been contaminated by contact with Sera's walls.

A horrible thought crossed Sera's mind. She advanced once more toward Blake, pin at the fore, until the tip stopped just short of his chest. "Don't even think of pulling any of your bullshit out here, Blake. Badmouthing me and bullying the local business community to get me blackballed won't get you anywhere. *I* have friends here. *You* don't."

"Don't fool yourself. I have friends everywhere, Serafina." Blake gave the lip twist that served him as a smile. "Better than that, I've people who *owe me favors.* Best not be threatening me, or you'll find your third-rate tart shop going out of business before you can blink. A word to the media—*my* word as an internationally renowned chef—and you'll be finished. In fact..." He trailed off, seeming to consider something. "What was the name of that local rag that passes for a weekly around here? Something awfully kitschy—ah yes, *Chile Paper*, was it? I really must be in touch with them. About my new restaurant, of course."

Another über-smirk.

Sera's blood boiled over. "Asher, I've changed my mind," she growled. "Would you please bash the living shi—"

But Blake was gone.

Into the night like the creature of darkness he was.

Sera hustled to the front entrance—which Blake had left swinging open, naturally. She didn't see him in the courtyard, but a streak of silver—of

Silver, actually—caught her eye as Asher's puppy came barreling toward them, his mama Sascha remaining more discreetly behind near the *placita*'s fountain. The pup, who was growing by the day, launched his gleeful, barky self at Sera, and she barely managed to catch him in her arms.

His tongue bathed the hot, angry tears from her eyes. *Thank you, pooch,* she thought fervently. *I really don't want your master to see me lose it over that sleazeoid.* Rage, a sense of injustice, and adrenaline all coursed through her system, making her shake with reaction. And in their wake came a second round of doubts. Sure, she'd run her demon off—for now—but had she really slain him? Sera sank her trembling fingers into Silver's coat and rubbed her cheek against the top of his head, breathing in his doggy smell. She felt Asher arrive at her side before she heard him.

"Bliss," he said quietly. "What was all that about? Are you all right?"

She turned, pooch and all, to look up at him. *My mascara is probably halfway to my chin, if Silver hasn't licked it all off.* Oh well, what he'd just seen in the kitchen was worse than a little Tammy Faye facial action.

"Yeah, I'm all right." *No, I'm not.* "That was just a bit of my baggage, coming back to haunt me. Sorry it ruined our evening." Silver whined and placed his paws on either shoulder, as if giving her a hug. He continued to lick her chin.

"That looked like more than just 'baggage' to me, Bliss," Asher argued gently. "Who was that?"

She sniffed, staring out into the night. "That," she said with a sigh, "was the man who convinced me I better quit drinking."

She put the puppy down, where he happily began to do battle with Asher's motorcycle boots. "I'm sorry, Ash. I think I'd better go home now. I'm exhausted, and I need to be up in a few hours to start baking again." She glanced up at him, feeling tentative, shaken in the wake of tonight's tumultuous events. Suddenly, being with Asher, being *happy* with Asher, seemed a lot less possible. *Sure, I love him, but when he knows everything about my past, will* he *ever be able to love* me*?* Blake had brought with him a bitter reminder of who she was—who she *used* to be—and it was a sobering feeling. She didn't want to be that woman anymore. She hoped she'd changed enough to escape the old Sera. But whether Asher could handle the truth of who she'd been... well, that remained to be seen. "I... I think I need some time alone."

Asher's green eyes searched her face with concern. "You'll be all right? Would you like me to drive you home?"

"I'll be fine." Sera laid her palm against his stubbly cheek, feeling a pang. "Thanks for having my back, Ash."

"I'd like to have your front, too," he teased, a twinkle in his green eyes.

That surprised a watery laugh out of Sera. She ran a hand down his coat front, tracing the buttons, loving him even more for trying to cheer her up at a time like this. "We'll see about that one, handsome," she said.

"Will we? I'd still like to take you out, Bliss."

"That," she sighed, "is the nicest news I've had all day."

She left him after a kiss that went a long way toward soothing the upsets of the last hour.

Silver barked softly at the first flakes of snow that sifted down into the courtyard as Sera turned her back on her future, and went home to contemplate her past.

Chapter Twenty-Five

"He did it. That snake really went ahead and did it!"

Pauline slammed the newspaper down on the counter as she swept into the store, fuming. Having been filled in by Sera when the snake in question first slithered into town, three nights ago now, she was well aware of Blake's descent upon the otherwise delightful City Different, and she was about ready to blow a gasket. Or had been, before she saw the paper. Now, "supernova" might better describe her aunt's combustible attitude, Sera thought.

"Did what?" she asked, gingerly unfolding the paper. It was about a half hour before opening, and she was just getting the shop ready for the influx of Thanksgiving Day customers who'd be wanting to pick up their orders before the store closed early for the holiday. Pauline, who had flatly refused to let Sera do any cooking, had left a turkey in the oven back home and had prepped all the makings for a delectable feast in advance. Hortencia was over at the house making sure pots didn't boil over and getting the place prettied up for the occasion. Tomorrow, with customers in a food coma, Sera would have her first day off since Bliss had opened.

She *also* had a date, formally confirmed, to spend the evening with Asher.

For now, though, she still had four hours of retail chaos to get through. She'd *thought* herself well prepared for any eventuality. Boxes stood at the ready, ribbons all set to wrap them. Cookies, pies, and cakes sat proudly in their cases, waiting to be taken home to a lucky family for the holiday. Her advance orders alone ensured Bliss would be in the black for a spell.

She ought to be rejoicing. But when Sera saw what her aunt, trembling with ire, pointed out with one stiff finger, she found herself in no mood for celebration.

It was another article by substitute food writer Marnie Pyle.

She scanned down the page. "Son of a bitch!"

It was ostensibly about Blake's new venture, a swanky new Southwestern fusion affair with appetizers in the $40 range. Ostensibly... until she got to the part where he just "happened" to mention his former protégée. Sera read aloud, her voice rising with outrage.

> "Yes, I've heard about that odd new pastry venture down the road. I knew its proprietor, Serafina Wilde, back in New York. She used to work for me, for a short while."

"A short while! Try four of the longest years of my *life,*" she seethed.

"Look what else he said, that rat fink," Pauline commanded. Her hands were knotted into gnarled fists atop the counter and her long, wiry hair fairly crackled with outrage.

Sera placed a comforting hand on her aunt's shoulder, then continued reading. Despite her efforts to remain calm, her own voice played the scale of outrage with every sentence.

> "However, neither her cooking nor her conduct were really up to my exacting standards. I found her disappointing, if I'm honest. And I don't mind telling you, I was rather surprised to discover Miss Wilde had opened an establishment that went by the name of 'Bliss,'" Chef Austin informed this reporter. "My experience of Miss Wilde was that she knew very little of bliss, culinary or carnal. Back when I knew her, she had a bit of a reputation as a... well, suffice it to say she wasn't known for her comfort within the realm of the sensual." Asked what he meant by this statement, Chef Austin refused to comment, beyond saying, "There was a reason we ended our association. Best of luck to her, of course. But one has to wonder if she's

really being up-front with her customers by peddling them the promise of some confectionary Kama Sutra, considering her personal shortcomings in that milieu."

She flung the paper across the shop. "*Shortcomings!* He's one to talk. The man couldn't boil an egg without an assistant! And that's only his professional shortcomings. Don't get me started on the size of his—"

Friedrich, who'd been wiping the spigots on the already clean espresso machine, coughed sharply. Both women turned to look at the young man they'd practically forgotten was with them in the shop. Blushing, the slight, dark-haired youth mumbled something in the general direction of the brass-fitted machine's innards. It was so unusual to hear him speak that both women stopped, mid-rant.

"What was that? Speak up, kid," Pauline demanded.

Friedrich swallowed and found his rarely used voice. "I said, it sounds like libel to me. Maybe you should sue."

"I'll do one better," Sera vowed. "Get that Pyle woman on the phone, would you, Pauline? I've got a few choice words for that chick."

In the end, Sera had to settle for arranging an interview for the Monday after Thanksgiving—even the skeletal Miss Pyle, it seemed, took time off for turkey day. The reporter had grudgingly agreed to reinterview Sera, though she'd refused to apologize for printing Blake's words without referring back to their object for comment. *Journalists today,* Sera reflected as she served her last customer and prepared to go home to her own well-deserved dinner. *They'll print any old gossip, never mind the damage they're doing.* She couldn't help wondering if she'd soon see a drop-off in business as a result of what the paper had printed. Certainly, Pauline hadn't done much trade in the back room this morning, but Sera told herself she was being paranoid—Thanksgiving weekend just wasn't the right time, probably, for people to focus on their sexual gratification—they were too busy gratifying their gullets.

That was what Sera told herself—and reassured Pauline—with as much conviction as she could muster. But Blake's opening salvo had her more nervous than she let on. A few innuendos might not be enough to keep people from shopping at Bliss, but who knew what he had planned next? Blake's takedown back in New York had started similarly. And the worst of it was, the article had mentioned he was still in town—intended to stay through the holidays, apparently, to see his new venture through its maiden voyage. He could do a lot of damage in that time.

She'd never been able to figure out exactly why he was so relentless, so ruthless in his pursuit of her downfall, until a former associate had explained it to her after apologetically turning her down for a job.

"Look, Sera. I'd love to hire you," the burly executive chef at a certain Midtown staple had said to her one afternoon. His ruddy face turned ruddier as he spoke, and he couldn't quite look her in the eye. Instead he fiddled with the salt and pepper shakers that graced the linen-draped two-top he'd invited her to share with him between the lunch and dinner shifts. At least he'd given her the courtesy of an interview—few others in his position had been willing to do as much, as Sera had learned to her chagrin over the months since her showdown with Blake in the Hamptons. "Meltdown at the Maidstone," they were calling it, or so she'd heard from those few friends whose loyalty she'd managed to retain. Ever since, she'd been pounding the pavement like nobody's business, and getting nothing but doors slammed shut in her face.

"But you're not *going* to hire me, are you?" She'd gulped the tepid water from her glass, wishing it were wine—or hell, a whole flock of Grey Geese—but knowing she was through with all that. Pauline hadn't gotten her into that twelve-step program for nothing, and Sera was clinging to her new sobriety with all ten claws. But at times like these... well, a double vodka would go down pretty smooth. She fiddled with the stem of the glass, daring a glance up at the chef she'd always admired for being a straight shooter as well as a damn good cook.

"No, I'm not," he said. "You're talented as hell and any kitchen in this city would be lucky to have you—but I'm sorry. I just can't risk it. Chef Austin's put the word out that you're untouchable, and he's got too much clout for me to go against him. He could have health inspectors on my ass. He could get me negatively reviewed. He could pressure my suppliers to stop selling to me. Hell, I once saw him get a fishmonger barred from the Hunts Point Market just for selling his mahimahi to another customer instead of saving it all for one of Blake's restaurants—when Blake didn't even have an order in that day. And that ain't the worst of what Austin's done when he's out for blood. Sorry, Serafina. You're a great pastry chef, but no dessert, no matter how delicious, is worth that kind of grief."

"I…I don't understand," Sera had whispered, hating the break in her voice that betrayed her. "Why is he *doing* this?"

"Way I see it, it's pretty simple," the chef said with a sympathetic grimace. "I know Chef Austin, and that is one bastard who does *not* like to be crossed. I heard all about that day—hell, half the kitchens in Manhattan are *still* buzzing over it—and bad as that whole business was for you, it's been a slap in the face to Austin, too." At Sera's uncomprehending expression, he explained. "Honey, you're the only woman—hell, the only *person*—who's ever managed to make a fool of Austin. He's a man who expects complete loyalty, blind obedience, and most of all *worship*. Hooking up with another guy, right there in his own domain in front of all his minions, was the ultimate humiliation, even if he would never cop to it in a million years. And when you dared to yell at him afterward, you challenged his rule. You showed spine, if only for a second. He can't have that—his whole reputation is built on being an iron-fisted tyrant. If girlfriends start sassing him, if fellow chefs mutiny, his whole empire could crumble. Or at least, that's how he sees it."

"That, and he's a total freaking psychopath," Sera had muttered.

"Yup." The chef had patted her hand sympathetically. "There's definitely a screw loose with that one—or maybe one that's wound too tight. Dangerous either way. Once Austin locks on to a target, he doesn't stop until it's utterly annihilated. But hey." He brightened. "Maybe you should try catering. I bet you could fly under the radar, and the money's not bad." He'd hesitated, calculating. "I could put in a good word for you with a coupla places. I can do that much, at least. But stay away from Blake

Austin—seriously, Serafina. The guy's like a pit bull, and I don't wanna see you get mangled."

Too late.

But a year was long enough for Sera to spend rolling over and showing her belly in submission. It was time to put this rabid dog down.

She still had no idea what she was going to say to the reporter on Monday. She only knew she had to cut Blake off at the knees, before his slanders ruined the fledgling happiness she'd carved out for herself here. But she had all weekend to dream up a scheme, and Pauline had promised to convene the Back Room Babes to help them brainstorm after work on Monday evening. Tonight, she told herself, was for turkey.

And tomorrow, her date with destiny...

If by "destiny," one meant the scrumptiously fine Asher Wolf.

Chapter Twenty-Six

"You look lovely."

"I believe that's *my* line, Bliss," Asher said with a smile.

Sera blushed, wishing her internal censor hadn't chosen tonight to take a hike, allowing her to blurt out her admiration for her new beau like the dork she profoundly didn't want him to know she was.

Asher didn't seem to mind. He leaned in and kissed Sera's cheek, stroking it, as was his wont, with a gentle caress of his fingers. Despite the chill in the air, the inch or so of snow that had fallen over Thanksgiving Day, his hand felt hot to her as he stood in her doorway, tall enough so Sera had to crane her neck to meet his gaze. "I hope you won't mind if I borrow the sentiment back from you. You are stunning this evening."

"Thank you, Asher," she said, feeling absurdly formal. In honor of the occasion, she'd worn the earrings he'd given her, along with a forties-style V-neck dress in cherry red that managed to look retro-cute while not being too costume-y. She'd found it in a boutique on Water Street this morning after the belated realization that her regular uniform of jeans and a ratty tee probably wouldn't cut it for tonight's big date. Wrapped in the dress's flattering folds, she was fairly confident she looked her best. She just wasn't sure her "best" put her in the same league with her dashing landlord, who looked effortlessly elegant in a black button-down and black slacks that showed off his lanky frame to mouthwatering effect. He had the peacoat on again, open despite the cold, and she saw that he wore a sharp black corduroy blazer beneath it.

He did say we're doing it up fancy—or at least as fancy as Santa Fe gets. Good thing I took him seriously. She'd even dug out a pair of black pumps from deep in her wardrobe, and was glad of the extra couple inches they added to her less-than-towering physique.

"You want to come in?" she asked, gesturing behind her to the living room, where Pauline was doing her unsubtle best to eavesdrop while pretending to point out items from the Ecstasy Emporium's catalog to an indulgent Hortencia.

Asher shook his head. "Normally I'd love to, but I'm afraid we're on a tight schedule." He waved at the two women on the sofa. "Hello, Pauline. Hello, Hortencia."

"Heya, studly," Pauline called out, dropping her pretense of catalog shopping. "You got that little item we talked about?"

"Got it," Asher called back. "Your aunt's a lifesaver," he said with a wink for Sera, ignoring the look of alarm she shot in his direction.

Pauline better not have slipped Asher any of her darn sexual aids, Sera thought darkly. The potential for humiliation was practically limitless. *Then again, if things get hot and heavy, this date is about 99 percent likely to end with me in a state of extreme mortification anyway. Why worry about a few stray sex toys?*

Asher had refused to tell Sera where they were going tonight, promising that she'd be well fed and pampered but denying her any details. *My mystery man.* Sera wasn't sure she liked surprises, but if she couldn't trust Asher, whom could she trust?

Trust yourself, *Sera,* said a voice in her head that was part Margaret, part Pauline, and part finally growing-up Serafina Wilde.

"Are you all set?"

His question jolted her out of her thoughts. "Ready as I'll ever be," Sera said, giving him a smile that was only half bravado.

⁂

"Ohhhhhhh!"

Sera clapped her hand over her mouth, ashamed of the frankly carnal noise she'd just emitted. But seriously, how could she help it?

"This is delicious!" She put down her fork and looked around. "Wait, where are we, and how did I just put such a fantastic piece of food into my mouth without knowing it?"

Asher laughed. "I must be slipping. I can see I've failed to capture your attention."

Quite the opposite, in fact. Her attention had been *so* focused on her date that she'd failed to notice where he was taking her.

The short journey in Asher's Land Rover from Pauline's place to the restaurant on Canyon Road had passed in something of a blur (caused, in large part, by the kiss her landlord had laid on her just as he was helping her into the car). She remembered being ushered inside a farolito-lit adobe compound that looked like it must be a historic property, then sitting down and folding her napkin in her lap automatically, but she'd barely taken note of their surroundings as the hostess seated them. She'd been too homed in on Asher—his attentive behavior, the hand he'd placed on the small of her back. Now, mouth full of lingering delight from the delicate truffle-infused *amuse bouche* their waiter had started them with, Sera gathered her wandering wits and gazed about her.

Freshly whitewashed adobe walls and gauzy cream draperies gave Sera the impression of having alighted in some ethereal haven, far from the ordinary concerns of life. The high ceilings were graced with discreet fans, stilled now that it was nearly winter. Wall nichos boasted tea lights that flickered romantically, and piñon logs crackled merrily in the kiva fireplace. Stark, modernist art installations and dried floral arrangements lent an embarrassment of elegance to the dining area. It was unlike anything one would see on the New York dining scene, and yet, based on that first fantastic bite Sera had just enjoyed, this place could go head-to-head with some of the top restaurants in Manhattan and come out with nothing to be ashamed of. In fact...

"Oh God, this isn't Blake's new restaurant..." she blurted out.

Asher hastened to reassure her. "This place has been here for years, and believe me, after the other day, I went out of my way to make sure your... ex...had no stake in it." The way he said "ex," Sera knew there was much more he would have liked to say—or ask.

"About that, Ash..." Surely, he had to be wondering what she was doing with such a skeevy ex-boyfriend in her not-so-dead-and-buried past. Asher deserved to know the truth—especially if Blake decided to rear his ugly head again. Since Ash was her landlord, anything Blake did to ruin her business could end up having an effect on him, too. *So much for small talk,* Sera thought. *We're headed right for "nasty revelation city" before we've even ordered our main course.* "I don't want to bring up unpleasant business in such a beautiful place," she said, "but I should probably explain..."

"Bliss." Asher's hand covered hers, and Sera forced herself to stop straightening the already perfectly aligned silverware that gleamed against the snowy table linen. She dared a glance up, finding Asher's gaze warm and kind—no judgment in evidence. Sera forced her shoulders to relax, willing them down from somewhere in the vicinity of her ears. Asher had never given her reason to fear mockery—unless it was of the gentlest kind. "You don't have to tell me anything, Bliss. You owe me no explanations."

"But I want to," Sera demurred. "Remember that night at your house a few weeks ago...how you said you liked what you knew about me, and I told you you didn't know anything at all?"

"How can I forget?" He laughed ruefully. "My lavender bushes still haven't recovered after the way you tore out of the driveway."

Sera colored. "Yeah, well..." She looked down, hesitating.

"I'm only teasing you, Serafina. Please, continue."

Hearing her full name coming from his lips stopped Sera short. Somehow it felt even more intimate than his nickname for her. It was an intimacy she desperately feared losing. "I want to tell you about my past, Asher—and there are some things you probably need to know—but I'm scared that after I do, you'll...that you won't..."

"Won't what?" He stroked the back of her hand with featherlight fingers.

"Won't want to be around me anymore," she whispered. She looked away, blinking rapidly. It was times like these that Sera really regretted not being able to have a glass of wine—or ten—to take the edge off. But she knew that without her sobriety, she'd never have found herself in this moment—this potentially magical moment—with a man as wonderful as Asher. And she knew enough about herself to know that, even if he rejected her, she'd be okay—eventually. She wouldn't need booze to help her get over the heartache. She'd just *want* it a whole lot.

She made herself look up and meet his gaze.

His angry gaze.

Not a *lot* angry, from what she could tell, but definitely a wee bit pissed. Or perhaps exasperated, she wasn't quite sure. All she knew was that his green eyes were shimmering with turbulent emotions, tender and fierce by turns.

"Bliss," he demanded, "do you think I'm a bad judge of character?"

"What?! No, of course not!"

He cocked his head to one side. "And do I strike you as self-destructive?"

Sera wasn't sure where this was going. "Definitely not," she said. Asher was the liveliest, most engaged man she had ever met. Nothing about him spoke of dark, twisty bits. Sadness, sure. Heartache, perhaps—in his past. But not in such a way that he would want to harm himself, or make bad choices.

"Then please, do me the courtesy of assuming that I would not ask a lady to dinner if I believed her to be of less than sterling character."

"Oh," she whispered. *He thinks I have "sterling character."* Tears stung her eyes, and tenderness melted her heart. *Remember that mascara, Sera! Keep it together.* "Good point. Sorry about that, Ash. I didn't mean to insult you. I just hope you don't change your mind when I tell you the rest..."

Asher leaned in and kissed the hand he was holding. "After all the lovely qualities I have seen in you, Bliss—your courage, your kindness, your humor—I doubt there's anything you could tell me about your past that would make me turn away from you. I'm not so faint of heart as all that—and you need to know that about me." His hand tightened around hers, firm and urgent. "You must *trust* that about me, if we're to make a go of what's between us. And, Bliss, I very much want to make a go of things with you. So," he challenged, "whatever it is, why don't you try me?"

Sera could not deny him. After a speech like that, he could have demanded a kidney, and she'd have handed it over on her great-grandmother's prized silver chafing dish. So she took a deep breath and, in a torrent of words, told Asher everything. How the famous Blake

Austin had recruited her, wide-eyed and painfully shy, right out of culinary school. How she'd lost herself under his influence, lost herself even more under the influence of alcohol. How he'd found her wanting, how she'd found the solace of vodka. Sparing nothing, she described the humiliating Meltdown at the Maidstone, Blake's vendetta, and her slow crawl back to respectability in the year since. She left out only Blake's recent comments in the *Chile Paper* this week, not wanting to dump her drama on Asher lest he feel a need to get involved. *Blake is my problem, not Asher's, and I'll be the one to face him down if it comes to that.*

Appetizers came and went as Sera spilled her story, Asher refusing the wine list in an act of solidarity she didn't fail to notice.

At length Sera stumbled to a halt. "Anyhow, that's about it. The whole sordid story. My failures, my shortcomings, and the chef-shaped monkey that just won't get off my back." She stared down at her barely touched plate. *What a waste of foie gras,* she thought, apropos of nothing. She wasn't sure if she felt liberated or nauseated. Or maybe liberation itself was a bit of a queasy thing. It all depended on how Asher reacted.

Her date leaned back in his chair, crossed his long legs at the ankles, and folded his arms across his chest. "I'm disappointed, Bliss."

"I'm sorry?" *Oh, crap-covered-crap. He's totally disgusted now. We probably won't even make it to dessert. And I so wanted to know how the sweets in this place would stack up to my own...* But it wasn't the potential loss of pastry that had Sera's heart squeezing painfully in her chest.

"I don't see why you should be," said Asher. He saw her look of confusion and unfolded his arms, reaching forward to touch her again. This time it was her wrist he captured in a gentle vise. "Don't see why you should be *sorry,* that is. I'm only disappointed because, after all that buildup, I expected you to tell me you smothered kittens for a hobby or baked straight razors into your layer cakes." He shook his head, speaking urgently. "Bliss, from what you've described, you've done nothing to be ashamed of—nothing that you could help anyway—and the things you couldn't help at the time, you've since put to rights as best you could. You've been paying penance for events that happened long ago, and paying far too much, if you ask me. Isn't it time to let them go?"

Sera sighed, turning her hand over in his, tracing her fingers across the jeweler's scars and calluses that marked his sensitive flesh. She'd thought the Blake years were behind her, that she was no longer the sad, messed-up woman she'd once been. Yet when Austin had showed up, he'd brought with him a whole lot of baggage she'd hoped to leave behind forever. Part of her still feared Asher would see her as Blake always had—someone pitiable, flawed. Someone who couldn't satisfy.

"I'm trying," she said, giving Asher a wobbly smile. "But there are times I still feel...I don't know...*wanting* somehow."

"Let me tell you something," said Asher. "That was one deeply petty little man I met the other night. He cannot steal what you possess now." His grasp tightened. "Bliss, you've got a spirit that shines out, that's so infectious I smile each time I see you coming. That is the woman with whom I want to dine—and not just dine, if I'm fortunate, but laugh, and chase dildo-thieving dogs, and slay my unfortunate shrubbery. *That's* who you are to me, Bliss. Not a failure. Not *wanting.*"

"That's where you're wrong, Asher," Sera said, letting the tears spill, and damn the mascara. Her voice caught. "There's something I'm 'wanting' very much right now."

She stood up, came around the table, and showed Asher exactly what—and who—she wanted, making herself at home in his lap and giving him a deep, wholehearted kiss.

Their server waited as long he could, but eventually the strain on his arms began to take its toll. He cleared his throat politely. "Ah, sorry, hot plates over here..."

Sera blushed, removing herself to the correct side of the table. Asher discreetly adjusted his napkin over his lap as the embarrassed waiter placed their entrées on the table and made himself scarce.

"Hungry?" Sera said a little too brightly.

"Ravenous," said her date.

They dug in with a will.

"Perhaps you will tell me something of how you came to be a chef," Asher suggested once they'd sated the only appetite that was polite to attend to in public. As soon as the plates were removed, he'd returned his hand to hers, absently tracing the bones beneath her sensitized skin, drawing swirls across her knuckles.

Sera smiled, the outstanding elk tenderloin in peppercorn sauce having mellowed her mood. She was high on a cocktail of *haute cuisine* and hot date, and it felt fantastic. "It all started with bundt cake," she said.

"I'm sorry?" Asher looked blank.

"It's a type of pound cake that's made in a tube-shaped mold," she explained. "The pan can be anything from a simple ring to a fanciful castle complete with turrets."

"Ah," said Asher, not looking particularly elucidated.

"Anyhow, when I was a little kid, like barely five or so, I discovered this old bundt cake mold in our kitchen cabinet. I think it was a gift from some Austrian great-grandmother, but no one could really remember how it got there. At first I thought it was something you used for making sandcastles in the playground, but my mom showed me how you could bake a cake in it. I was so fascinated by the *precision* of the cake, how it came out so perfectly shaped, I got hooked. I mean, it was food, but it was also a toy! I guess most five-year-olds go through a phase like that. I just never grew up." Sera smiled at her own silliness. "I started begging my mom for Jell-O molds, mini tart pans—anything that could bake up into a cool shape. Mom was kind enough to indulge me. I loved the flavors, too, of course—I didn't get these curves from eating salad," Sera said, gesturing dismissively at herself, "but it was the *architecture* of pastry that really roped me in. Maybe a little bit like the work you do with metal," she said.

Asher nodded his understanding. "Perhaps," he said, smiling. "Though I don't often get to taste my work when I'm done. But go on, Bliss. Where did the bun cake take you?"

Sera didn't correct him; she thought "bun cake" was adorable. "Well, from there, Mom started helping me bake everything from whoopee pies to meringues, even though I have a feeling Aunt Pauline was actually more interested in cooking than Mom was. Still, she always indulged my obsession. It was one of the things I remember best about her—standing in the kitchen by her side when I was little, testing out recipes and frosting cakes. She always made time for us—'kitchen time,' she called it." Sera smiled wistfully at the memory.

Asher turned her hand over delicately, beginning to trace the lines of her palm and draw idle patterns up her wrist and forearm that made Sera shiver. "I've never heard you speak of your mother before," he noted.

"She and my dad died when I was just a teenager, and Pauline raised me after that," Sera said, hating and simultaneously soaking up the flash of sympathy she witnessed in his eyes. "It was a car accident. A cabbie fell asleep after a too-long shift and plowed right into them as they were crossing Third Avenue. It was instantaneous."

"I'm sorry," he said softly.

She'd heard as much from dozens of people over the years. A simple sentiment, easily expressed. But when Asher said it, she truly felt his sympathy, and more—empathy.

"You know something of that pain, don't you, Ash?" she ventured.

"I do," he admitted. "My wife died of ovarian cancer four years ago. I thought I would die with her."

Sera's eyes filled. She clasped her other hand around his, stilling his abstract tracings. "I'm glad you didn't, but I can understand why you wanted to." She paused. "Do you want to talk about it? I don't want to ruin a lovely evening with more heavy conversation, but..."

"It's all right, Bliss," he assured her. "I would have brought it up in any case, because I wanted to be sure you fully understood why it was so important that I went to Israel when I did."

He'd spoken of it, that night together in her store, but she sensed he had more to say. "You mentioned needing to make peace with your wife..." She trailed off delicately.

"Yes," he said softly. "As I said, I went home to lay my wife's spirit to rest, at least in my heart. When I met you, I knew it was time. My world had been about her loss for so many years—my art, my work; everything suffered. I left Israel to escape my memories, running from all our mutual friends, family—anyone who had known our life together. I came here hoping to hide from the pain, but of course, it traveled with me.

"I suppose that's why so much of my jewelry looks the way it does," he mused, as if it were occurring to him for the first time. "Maybe I was trying to recapture some of the music and harmony of that time. My wife had been a violinist, you see—a very accomplished violinist with the Tel Aviv Symphony Orchestra. We met when she commissioned a new instrument from my workshop. I was a luthier, and an amateur musician myself. We fell in love almost immediately, and for a time our life was full of music and laughter. We envisioned our future, planned out the names of the children we'd have. In fact, when Tali's belly began to grow, we thought at first that she was pregnant. We were so happy. But our happiness turned to horror when we learned the truth."

Asher's eyes were unseeing, lost in memories. "The tumor spread quickly, and there was nothing anyone could do. Tali was gone in months. And I..." His voice thickened. "I could no longer make music. I couldn't even listen to it, or be any part of its creation. I had no trade, and everything in our home reminded me of what I'd lost. So I left. I came to the American Southwest looking for spaciousness and a place where no one knew me; where I could let the past go. Eventually, I discovered I could parlay my skills with woodworking to metal smithing, and with my jewelry business and managing the other properties I'd purchased as an investment, I made a life for myself here." He rubbed his jaw, thoughtful. "I have been content. But now..." His green eyes sharpened, locked on to Sera's gray ones. "Now... I think I can be *happy.*"

Their waiter chose that unfortunate juncture to bring out the dessert tray. He was forced to cool his heels for quite some time as Sera made *her* happiness known to Asher with another passionate kiss.

She thought nothing could top the delight of this moment.

But their date was just getting started. For a nightcap, Asher took Sera to Japan.

Chapter Twenty-Seven

Well, Japan by way of the Sangre de Cristo Mountains.

Still savoring the lingering flavors of some desserts Sera had to admit were *nearly* as good as her own, Asher drove them up the winding mountain road that led, eventually, to the Santa Fe ski basin. He wouldn't say where they were going, only that it was a can't-miss destination for tourists and locals alike.

They turned off the road into a driveway with a sign that read "Ten Thousand Waves." "I'd be impressed with *one* wave," Sera commented as they pulled into the parking lot and drove up a ramp lit only with Japanese paper lanterns, "considering how far we are from any ocean. You want to give me a hint where we're going, Ash?"

Asher only smiled. Apparently, he was a guy who loved surprises, and Sera was discovering she didn't mind being on the receiving end of them, provided they came from this one-of-a-kind man. Certainly, tonight's were turning out to be pure pleasure. The delectable meal, the free and open confidences he'd shared...the way he'd reacted to her confessions.

She hadn't dared hope Asher would take her past in stride the way he had. She'd known he was kind, that he seemed open and accepting, but now he knew the worst—her years of drinking, how she'd let Blake bully her...hell, he even knew her deepest, darkest secret, thanks to the way she'd blurted out the truth about her anorgasmia. Yet he still seemed to want her. Asher was like the proverbial dream come true.

And now, he'd taken her to this amazing hidden oasis.

A slice of old Japan had been transported to the snow-dusted New

Mexican mountains. Under a star-strewn sky, breath steaming in the chilly autumn air, they trekked up a long, winding stairway cut switchback-style into the side of the hill. Zen-looking stone steps and frost-touched wildflowers interspersed with more paper lanterns lit their path. At the crest, they were greeted by a tranquil, pagoda-style building of mellow aged wood illuminated gently from within. "What is this place?" Sera asked softly. It seemed appropriate, somehow, to speak in hushed tones.

"It's a spa," Asher answered. He put a gentle hand on Sera's lower back and guided her within. Inside, a koi-pond fed by a rushing waterfall made a susurrant sound, disappearing beneath a weathered plank walkway. Up a short flight of rustic wooden stairs, the interior opened out into a warmly lit building with a curved front counter to Sera's left. The lobby boasted a discrete space for purchasing lotions and potions, a small snack bar, and a spacious waiting area. This last, she observed, was occupied by a dozen or so almost laughably relaxed patrons wearing kimono robes and dreamy smiles, sipping cucumber water and chilling out on wooden benches. Beyond the glass rear doors, Sera caught sight of another, larger koi pond and waterfall, as well as a traditional rice paper–walled building nestled among the pine and spruce trees.

"Wow, I'm impressed, Ash. I didn't expect you to take me all the way to Asia on our first date," Sera teased. Privately, she wondered what he had in mind. Were they getting matching mani-pedis? Facials for two? Or perhaps massages? Somehow, she wasn't quite keen on the idea of a masseuse's hands all over Asher's oiled-up body...

"I think you will really enjoy this, Bliss." Asher gently tugged her up to the front desk, but Sera barely noticed what he was saying to the clerk, beyond noting that he was claiming the reservation he'd called in earlier. She was too busy looking around—and sniffing around as well. Her keen nose scented cedar, lemon, and a sweeter fruity smell she identified as yuzu, a Japanese fruit she'd sampled occasionally and even incorporated into a dessert or two. The effect was lulling... so much so that it wasn't until the clerk asked her to sign a release promising she wasn't pregnant or likely to have a heat-induced stroke that Sera realized what kind of spa this must be.

"Hot tubs?" she asked Ash. Her pulse began to pound.

He beamed. "Among other things."

"*Naked* hot tubs?" Sera's voice was a bare squeak.

"Is there another kind?" he inquired innocently.

Sera scanned Asher's face, but he seemed quite sincere. Maybe in Israel, these paratrooper types bared their bods *sans* shame, but Sera wasn't at all sure she was up for that amount of intimacy. Not that she hadn't considered getting naked with Asher, but somehow she'd envisioned circumstances a little less... outdoorsy... for the exalted occasion.

He seemed to sense her uncertainty. "I've reserved us a private tub," he assured her.

"You mean there are *public* naked tubs?" Sera asked faintly. Her lips felt numb. *Maybe I'm having a stroke right now,* she thought. *I shouldn't have signed that waiver.*

"A women's-only tub and a coed public bath, I believe. They're less expensive than the private baths, so they're very popular with students and the like. But we'll have a tub all to ourselves tonight."

Yipe. Sera gulped. She wasn't exactly wild about mooning the Wolf on their first date. She'd pictured a little under-cover action, sure; but bathing together in the buff? He might have the chiseled physique of a Greek god, but Sera worshiped the goddess of butter, flour, and sugar—and it showed in her comfortably curvy frame. *Thank God I remembered to shave, at least,* she thought with a tinge of hysteria. *But man, this is all moving just a little fast.*

She wasn't sure quite how she felt... disappointed, perhaps? She'd thought better of Asher somehow. She knew from things he'd said that he was interested in getting intimate. She hadn't exactly put the kibosh on that notion herself, with the way she'd been climbing all over him at dinner. Yet the idea that he'd planned ahead for their rendezvous—that he'd taken them to a place he knew they'd be getting undressed from the get-go—it bothered her, a little. She told herself she was being silly. They were both adults—adults who had expressed their attraction quite openly in the past. But she still felt a bit queasy about the whole thing. Did she really know Asher well enough for this... and was their first time together going to be in some sauna? She fiddled nervously with her hair.

"So, um . . . are these tubs, ah . . . well lit?"

Asher burst out laughing, pulling Sera close for a hug that did more to disorient her than did his sudden mirth. "I'm sorry, Bliss. I'm afraid I was having a bit of fun at your expense." Letting her go, he reached into the shoulder bag he'd carried in from the Land Rover, pulled out something that looked like—no, *was*—Serafina's trusty one-piece swimsuit. Her extremely frumpy, boy-short-bottomed, pink-polka-dotted one-piece swimsuit. Seeing its homeliness in Asher's manly grasp was almost as mortifying as if he'd pulled out her period panties.

"That's my . . ." Sera stared uncomprehendingly. "How did you . . ."

"I asked Pauline to sneak into your things and grab a bathing suit for you. She passed it to me on the sly yesterday. I didn't want you to catch wind of where we were going ahead of time and spoil the surprise."

"But I . . . You said . . ." Sera looked around. It didn't look like anyone else was wearing a swimsuit under their kimono.

"Most people do bathe nude, Bliss. But I would never presume like that on our first date. I brought one for myself, see?" He held up another scrap of spandex he'd dug out of the bag.

Dear lord, a *Speedo.* Probably quite common for Israelis, who seemed far less body-conscious than their American counterparts. *What was I hoping for, board shorts? Or am I actually bummed he's not going full Monty?* A blush flamed across her cheeks. Asher had never had any intention of putting the moves on her. While she'd been picturing the sex scene from *Showgirls,* he'd had a G-rated kiddie pool romp in mind. She felt sheepish for her unworthy thoughts—of course Asher wouldn't subject her to some sleazy setup on their first date. Yet now that she knew he hadn't, there was a small part of her that wished he *had.*

Asher put his arm around her. "Come," he said, drawing her toward the rear exit. "There are women's locker rooms to the left, over there." He pointed. "The men's are upstairs. I will meet you at the bath—see, the symbol for ours is on the key." He pointed to the Japanese character inscribed on the big wooden key fob in his hand. "We've got the waterfall tub. Since I'll probably be ready before you, I'll go in and leave the door unlocked—all right?"

"Yup, meet you there," she said, pasting on a smile.

Hot tub, here I come.

~

Wrapped and double wrapped in the capacious kimono, feet sliding a bit in the rubber sandals the spa provided, Sera tiptoed through the thoughtfully landscaped grounds, nodding politely to other guests as she went. *A bathrobe isn't exactly my best look,* she fretted. Thank goodness it was dark, and the lighting was as discreet as the location was elegant. She moved through gnarled trees that looked like supersized bonsai, passed paths inlaid with slate paving stones and bordered with weathered wooden beams, noting how the spa's architects had created private enclosures through creative use of the mountainous terrain and discreet fencing, along with climbing vines and trees. Almost too soon, she located the symbol for the waterfall tub and eased the sliding door open.

As Sera's eyes adjusted to the gloom, she saw she was in a spacious outdoor enclosure, walled to her right by the side of the main building, and on the left, screened by a coyote fence from the prying eyes of other guests. At the back was a sauna with a small closet for robes and towels, and nearby she spied what must be a cold plunge with a tiny waterfall splashing into it. *No, thanks,* Sera thought. *I've got cold enough feet as it is.*

The center of the space was occupied by a capacious, sunken hot tub carved from natural stone, steaming gently against the rapidly falling nighttime temperature. It was perfectly landscaped into the native stone tiles that covered the ground, with a pleasingly curved lima bean shape to it and several benches at different depths for bathers.

Asher was waiting in the deep end.

"Hi," she said shyly.

"Hello again, Bliss."

He wore the wet look well. Even with the meager lighting, Sera could make out beads of moisture running down his chest, spreading a sheen across his shoulders and arms, which he'd draped across the back of the tub. Crisp bronze fur dusted his chest just the right amount, and his damp blond hair was appealingly disheveled. Beneath the gently roiling water, Sera could only imagine the rest—Speedo and all. Her mouth went dry.

Ready or not, here I come. She wondered how Asher would react to her "suit."

For, somewhere between stuffing her shoes and stockings into her cubby and taking a deliciously hot, yuzu-scented shower in the locker room, Sera had come to a conclusion. She was, metaphorically speaking, about as "in Rome" as a girl could get. There would never be a better time to do as the Romans did. Asher might be a gentleman, but that didn't mean *she* had to be a lady—not if she wanted to challenge herself to get over her past. At the last second, she'd stashed one final item in her locker before heading out to meet her destiny.

Now, aware of Asher's studiedly polite gaze, Sera sucked in her gut, straightened her shoulders, and slid her robe off. She paused for a beat to let him get a gander...

Then jumped, full Monty, into the tub.

"Hoo! Hah! Hot, hot, HOT!" she shrieked.

Stunned by the sizzling heat on her autumn-chilled skin, Sera thrashed over to a bench near the shallow end. She was caught between wanting to stand up and cool off in the nippy night air, and a belated attack of modesty that had her needing to shield her more... buoyant... assets from her date's interested eyes. She elected to endure the heat, scrunching down as low as she could get on the stone bench.

"It takes a bit of getting used to," Asher remarked, half walking, half swimming to her end of the pool. Smiling, he tucked a strand of wet hair behind Sera's ear as he loomed over her, sending hot water lapping up to her shoulders. "So, Bliss... either you forgot your suit or I'm overdressed," he said, brow quirked inquiringly.

"I... uh..." Suddenly, all the lines she'd practiced in her head melted like snowflakes in the steamy air. She ducked her head, pretending to study the jet system set into the stonework at her side.

Asher tilted her head back his way, forcing her to look him in the eye. "Listen, sweetheart... I didn't bring you here for this." His fingers stroked lightly down her neck, across her shoulders, making her shiver and belying his words. "I only wanted you to enjoy this very special place. I never intended or expected that we should..." He left the rest unsaid.

He called me "sweetheart"! Her heart did a little happy dance. *Yeah, Sera—and then he said he didn't want to fool around,* the Negative Nelly part of her mind reminded her. The bottom dropped out of Sera's stomach, and suddenly she felt very, very naked indeed.

"I'm sorry," she whispered, sinking lower in the steaming water. "I shouldn't have...I'll go back and get my suit..."

"Please don't," said Asher, coming to rest beside her on the bench—close, but not touching. "I only meant..." He stopped, sighed. "Bliss, I want very much to be with you—be *naked* with you—but I remember what you told me, and I didn't want you to feel any pressure..." He slid away to dip his head under the water. He let the steaming liquid sluice his hair back from his forehead, as if it would help clear his thoughts.

"What I told you?" Sera ventured. She had an uneasy feeling she knew what he meant.

"About your, ah...condition." Now it was Asher's turn to look uncomfortable. "I didn't want to rush you into anything, but believe me, Bliss...this Speedo doesn't fit quite as well as it did before you left that robe behind."

"Really?" she said, smiling just a bit. His confession pleased her inordinately, even as his thoughtfulness calmed her nerves, reminding her *this was Asher.* Asher wouldn't ever embarrass her, or shame her the way Blake so often had. She could afford to be a little daring with him, to experiment with her wild side. Maybe things wouldn't work out, but then again...she was in the land of enchantment now. Maybe a little of that magic would wear off on her.

Pauline would be so proud, she thought with a touch of humor as she stared up at the impossibly handsome Israeli. *Now, if she'll just stay out of my head for the next several hours...*

"I would never joke about something as serious as a Speedo, Bliss," Asher assured her, belying his words with a broad smile.

Sera floated closer. "I hope you don't mind if I don't take your word for that," she grinned. "Because I really think I need to find out for myself."

❧

The gentle chime of a bell interrupted what was proving to be a very magical moment. Gasping, Sera pulled away from Asher, who was nibbling her neck in a way that made her nerve endings trill like a chorus of songbirds. Since she was perched atop his lap and his arms were tightly banded about her waist, she didn't get far.

"Waterfall tub, this is your five-minute reminder," came a polite voice over the intercom.

Sera groaned. *And things were going so well.* No intrusive visions of Aunt Pauline. No yips, stutters, or stops. Only mounting passion more intense than anything she'd ever experienced. Asher had been so gentle, so thorough, stoking her desire with exquisite slowness, taking his time to treat each inch of her skin to the touch of his lips, tongue, and hands, getting to know every curve in a way that was both respectful and deeply, deeply intimate. No matter how she panted and pleaded, he wouldn't speed up either, murmuring Hebrew words she suspected meant "whoa, girl" even as he made her pulse race faster and faster. Had the bell not rung, she marveled, he might very well have rung *her* bell. *I never thought it could happen. But with Asher, everything feels so natural. I'm not self-conscious. I trust him. And more, I trust* me.

"Can we ignore that?" Sera asked, nuzzling closer.

"I only booked the tub for an hour," Asher said regretfully. He kissed the juncture where her neck and shoulder met, soothing the sensual fires he'd started, then eased her off his lap as though it was physically painful to part from her. "Come, Bliss. I'd better take you home."

"Darn right," she said, taking his face in both hands and kissing him deeply. "*Your* home."

Asher studied her seriously. "You're sure?"

Nothing ventured, nothing gained. Maybe the elusive orgasm would finally be hers. Maybe it wouldn't. Either way, she wanted to be with Asher tonight. "Mr. Wolf, I have never been more sure of anything in my life."

Asher abandoned the tub in record time.

Chapter Twenty-Eight

Moment of truth.

Standing with Asher in his sparsely furnished bedroom, lit only by the moonlight streaming through the skylight above them, Sera expected to find herself fairly coming apart at the seams. Always in the past, she'd been uptight, anxious in intimate moments. The few boys she'd been with in college had been about as clueless as Sera herself, and with her native shyness, she'd never really managed to relax and enjoy their ministrations. She'd get so far, and then just... freeze up.

And then would come the visions.

Pauline, watching expectantly over the boy's shoulder. Pauline, shaking her head at Sera's awkward caresses. Pauline, wearing pom-poms and a cheerleading outfit, doing cartwheels and chanting fight songs that ended in "cum, cum, cum" instead of "go, go, go." And worst of all, Pauline, demonstrating clitoral stimulation techniques.

The harder she'd try to tune out her aunt, the more intrusive the images would become.

She'd figured she'd eventually warm up, get over her awkwardness, and—*please, God*—stop being haunted by Pauline's passion pep talks. But then came Blake.

The charismatic chef had instantly attracted her. She'd craved his admiration, his affection, and at first, when he'd hit on her, she'd thought *she'd* hit the big time. A worldly, experienced lover. So debonair, so exciting. Surely, *now...* She'd had high hopes. But Blake hadn't been overly interested in Sera's satisfaction. He'd been a "wham, bam, thank-you-ma'am" sort of lover—only without the "thank you." And when Sera—tentatively, shyly—had gotten up the nerve to ask him to slow down, maybe try a few things she thought she'd like, he'd practically tossed her out of bed on her keister.

And then he'd mocked her.

Frigid. Hopeless. Deadweight. Those were just a few of the taunts he'd hurled at her during the time they had dated. He'd made her feel she was lucky he even tolerated her presence in his bed, given what a lousy lay she was. But in hindsight, Sera had to wonder—who'd really been the one with sexual shortcomings? Hadn't it been Blake who was impatient and selfish? She'd tried her best, but after a time she'd come to realize he actually *preferred* it when she lay there like a dutiful fifties housewife, letting Blake take, as he put it, "what little satisfaction he could." That way, she realized, he could concentrate on what Blake liked best—Blake.

The part that shamed her, to this day, was how long she'd let him.

She'd let Blake make her feel fearful, inadequate. But tonight, with Asher, she felt neither. What she *felt* like was grabbing her date's nice button-down shirt and rending it open in one great rip.

So she did.

Or tried anyway.

The first button popped off easily enough, but the rest, well . . . "Whoever sewed these on must have had serious OCD," she muttered, yanking futilely at the fabric.

Asher laughed and laid his hands over hers to still her pillaging. "Slow down, Bliss," he said. "We have all night."

"You don't have to treat me like some delicate virgin, you know," Sera said. "It's very gallant, Asher, but right now . . ." She trailed off, eyeing him with a sidelong smile.

"Right now?" he asked. He ran one finger down the V of her dress's neckline and watched the goose bumps rise in its wake.

Sera could see his chest rising and falling rapidly, sensed his barely leashed energy even as she inhaled that uniquely Asher smell—hot metal, rampant male. She felt intoxicated; drunk with delight, with anticipation, with giddy knowledge that this delicious man wanted to be her lover as much as she wanted to be his. He'd primed her past the point of performance anxiety, and now she wanted only to feel his naked skin against hers, his heat and desire matching hers.

"Right now...I'd rather you ravished me senseless." She backed him up against the bed with hands on his chest and a predatory leer. "And be warned, Asher...if *you* won't, *I* will."

He would.

❧

As it happened, Sera *did* have a visitation just as she was approaching the much-anticipated moment of her bliss. As Asher carried her ever closer to the edge, doing extraordinary things with his talented craftsman's fingers even as his body, so hot and sensual atop hers, drove her nearly mindless with desire, Sera saw a vision coalescing behind her closed eyes.

Please, not Pauline, she thought. *Don't let anything ruin this...this...oh, God, what did he just do with his tongue, that ought to be illegal...Please, just let this happen, I can't believe how good this feels, oh...oh,* wow, *there's no way a man ought to be able to...holy wow...*

But what swam into focus as Sera soared close to climax wasn't her aunt.

It was purple. It was petite. And...it was wearing what was undeniably a rhinestone-studded cowboy hat.

Hey! It's my armadillo! Sera marveled.

It nodded at her, tipping its hat.

"Gesundheit," it said.

And Sera's world changed forever.

Chapter Twenty-Nine

"You've made Pauline a happy woman," Sera said, rolling over atop her lover and planting a kiss on his smiling lips.

Asher, quite naked and quite obviously glad to be smothered in a blanket of Bliss, chuckled as he reciprocated. "Pauline, eh?" he said. "And what about the younger Miss Wilde?" He nudged her suggestively with his hips.

"She's living up to her name, for once," said Sera.

"Wilde or Bliss?" he teased.

"Both." She giggled, wriggling playfully.

"Don't start that up, my lovely one, or Pauline may overdose," Asher warned.

"Oh, I think the old gal's earned a reward," Sera murmured. "Let's see how happy you can make her..."

But Pauline had nothing to do with what came next—and what had already come (three times!) during one unbelievably blissful night.

An hour later, staring into the predawn sky through Asher's bedroom skylight, Serafina began to contemplate baked goods. Malcolm had first shift, and Pauline had promised to overcome her antipathy for the pie maven and help him open the store, but Sera didn't like to leave them alone together for too long. Besides, she had cupcakes, cookies, and tarts to create.

"Not to reverse a cliché, Asher, but I should probably sneak out in a few minutes," she said with regret. "I've got to get baking pretty soon."

His arms tightened around her, pinning her to his side in a manner that was not at all unpleasant. "Wait, please, Bliss. Before you go, there's something I need to know." He looked a bit chagrined. "I don't quite know how to ask this without sounding like a heel."

Sera was intrigued. "Give it a whirl," she said, snuggling close with her head pillowed on his shoulder. She studied the uncomfortable expression that stamped his strong features, loving how she was learning to read his emotions. "I've handled a few heels in my time."

"Bliss..." He paused, squeezed his eyes shut as though his own words pained him. *"Oy gevalt,"* he muttered. "I can't believe I'm going to ask this, but after what you told me about your troubles with your...well, with your previous attempts at intimacy...I wanted to be sure...that is..." He visibly pulled himself together and just blurted it out. "Bliss, was it good for you?"

Sera paused a beat.

"Honestly, I don't know what all the fuss is about," she deadpanned, then burst out laughing when she saw the look on Asher's face.

Asher growled, tickling her sides mercilessly until she shrieked.

When she could breathe again, Sera stretched up and kissed his chin, mirth fading from her eyes. "Asher, 'good' doesn't even begin to describe how I feel. You've given me a gift—one I won't ever forget. You've...I don't know...freed me, I guess. And it feels amazing."

Asher looked pleased with himself. He stroked one finger along her spine, sending thrills down Sera's back and all the way down to her toes. "You have freed me as well. I was frozen in the past for such a long time, but now I'm very much looking forward to my future. And..." He looked uncertain. "I know it's probably too soon to speak of such things, but...Bliss, I very much hope you will be a part of that future."

If there was a better feeling than orgasm, Sera had just discovered it. Screw chocolate. Screw winning the lotto. *This* was the jackpot.

"I am going to bake you *such* a babka," was what she said.

Chapter Thirty

Monday evening after work, the Back Room Babes piled into Bliss, took one look at Sera, and shrieked with delight.

"He's done it!" howled Aruni.

"That's our boy!" squealed Syna.

"Hurrah for the hot landlord!" Janice did a little dance, pumping her fists over her head.

Pauline plopped down on one of the shop's overstuffed armchairs, letting her minions settle about her with pastries and hot cups of joe. "I take complete credit, of course," she said. Her smile was pure smug.

Sera tried to take the ribbing with grace, topping off cups and handing out napkins for her friends as they made themselves at home in the shop. After all, for the past three days, she had spent every waking moment not otherwise occupied with hot ovens over at Asher's house learning just how hot and steamy *he* could be. The BRBs weren't the only ones who wanted to crow over Asher's prowess. Sera just wanted to do her crowing *privately.* And she preferred to think of it as "expressing her passionate delight." Decorously, of course. Never mind that she'd been expressing her delight so passionately since Friday night that Silver had taken to howling in solidarity from his kennel halfway across the house.

"Everyone got what they need?" she asked, scanning the women who'd been able to make it tonight. Bobbie, Syna, Janice, Aruni, Hortencia, and Pauline made a comfortable sextet (or sex-tête-à-tête, as Pauline had quipped) in the now-empty bakery. Sera was touched that, with only a phone call, so many of her new *compadres* had mobilized in her defense—

and they didn't even know what was up yet. Pauline had simply said Sera needed them, and they'd dropped everything. She couldn't remember the last time she'd had a group of friends so fiercely loyal—even if they did insist on embarrassing the hell out of her.

"We know y'all got what *you* need, mama!" Janice joked. "One look at your face, and I can tell you're a changed woman."

"Yeah, sister, you *glow.*" This from Syna, who was beaming rather brightly herself.

Sera suspected they were confusing "glow" with "mortified flush."

"Tell us everything, girl!" Aruni folded her legs lotus style, her slight figure barely making a dent in her armchair. "Was he gentle? Or did he go all Israeli commando on you once you hit the sheets?"

Friedrich, who'd been polishing counters with a rag as he helped close up shop, dug his ear buds deeper into his red-tinged ears and spun the dial on his iPod until Sera could distinctly hear Wagner's *The Ring of the Nibelung* leaking out. He kept his eyes downcast, but Sera caught him sneaking glances at Aruni. And though the yogini tried playing it cool, Sera definitely saw Aruni peek back at the barista from beneath her unruly curls when she thought no one was looking.

A little young for her, but hey, Sera thought, smiling inwardly. The kid was reliable, diligent, and as far as she knew, not at all a *putz* like Aruni's ex. *Maybe mine's not the only romance that could bloom around here, given a little attention. Hmm, maybe if I can get those two together, the BRBs will drop the topic of* my *love life...*

Sera perched gingerly on the edge of the coffee table around which the BRBs had gathered. Beads of sweat formed at her temples as she pictured Asher overhearing the Babes' raunchy conversation. Things between them were so new, so extraordinary, she didn't want to sully her memories of their time together with graphic girl-talk. "Guys, thanks for the vote of confidence, but, um, I'd really rather not go into our private business..."

She clapped her hands over her ears against the wave of boos and hisses that washed over her.

"All right, all right! Listen *up,* ladies," Pauline hollered, waving a chocolate éclair like a conductor's baton for silence. "Much as I regret my niece's continuing reticence in all matters carnal, I didn't call you over here to congratulate her on her initiation into the Big-O Society. Fact is, women, we are at war, and we must gird our loins for battle!" She bit off half the éclair in one ferocious bite. "Bls's brstid e-byfred's oofer bld, ah we gorra schtup 'm."

Blank looks met her pronouncement.

Hortencia harrumphed, tossing a look of mild disgust at her partner. "What this glutton over here's trying to say is, Sera's rotten ex-boyfriend is in town, and he's trying to ruin her life—and not for the first time. We've got to figure out how to stop him before he succeeds."

Pauline swallowed the bite of gooshy pastry, choking a bit. "Right. What Horsey said."

Sera handed her aunt a glass of water, addressing the ladies *en masse.* "It's true," she said glumly. "Blake's back, and he's up to his old tricks." She explained, in as few words as possible, what Blake had done a year ago, and what he was up to now. "Anyhow," she finished, "he's here in Santa Fe and he's already started the smear campaign." She handed around a copy of the *Chile Paper*'s article. "So, if you guys have any ideas about what I should do, I'd love to hear them."

There was a silence as the four women who were new to the situation huddled close to one another to read. Hortencia and Pauline sat back, waiting for them to finish, while Sera rubbed her temples, where a headache was starting to set in. Asher was coming to pick her up in a little while, and she just wanted to forget what had happened with Blake last week and enjoy her lover's company. Yet she knew she couldn't let Blake's perfidy gain momentum—the longer she let it lie, the more time he had to prepare his next salvo. She needed help, and the Back Room Babes were her greatest allies. They had deep roots in the community. They knew people; owned businesses, some of them. Hopefully, they'd be able to come up with some creative solutions to counteract Blake's slurs before they could cut into Sera's business.

Or if it comes to that, there's enough of us to tackle him in a dark alley, Sera thought darkly. *Wonder if they'd be game for a little skullduggery?*

It didn't take long for the BRBs to show how "game" they were.

With claws extended, they tore the tabloid to shreds.

"What a dick!" Aruni was incensed.

"I'll let my pet rat Rudy loose in his restaurant," Janice vowed.

"Let's stage a protest outside and let everyone know what a bully he is," Syna suggested. "I've still got a set of bongos left from the Occupy protests."

"String him up by the balls, is my vote," Pauline growled. "I've got the twine all ready. The *scratchy* twine."

"I've told you a hundred times, Pauline, barbed wire's *much* better in cases like these," Hortencia argued as she fastidiously gathered up the shreds of newspaper. "Really gets caught in the—"

A sharp, Gollum-like cough rattled the shop's windows, announcing the arrival of Ms. Marnie Pyle.

Six hours late, and less than excited to be there, if her expression was anything to go by. The reporter lethargically fished her notepad and digital recorder out of her messenger bag as she eased the front door shut behind her with one foot.

That woman needs an enthusiasm transplant, STAT. "Guys, this is Marnie Pyle," Sera said formally. "Since she wrote the, ah, profile on Blake's new restaurant, as well as the original article on Bliss, we asked her to come over so we could address some of the issues Blake raised in his quotes." *Like how he basically called me a frigid hack who wasn't qualified to serve snack cakes at a supermarket, let alone run my beautiful Bliss.* "Marnie, thanks for coming. We expected you a bit earlier, or I would have had my friends come by another time." Sera rose to shake the woman's hand, trying not to shudder at the dead-fishiness of her grip.

"Good lord, what's wrong with her *head?*" Syna whispered to Aruni as she gawked at the skeletal newcomer. "It looks like one of my son's Lego action figures!"

Aruni shushed her, smothering a grin.

The reporter barely acknowledged the other women. "Sorry," Marnie muttered, retrieving her hand as though Sera's were crawling with cooties. "I was hoping to catch you after hours. I didn't realize you'd have company."

"We weren't sure you'd make it," Sera replied neutrally, "so we decided to go ahead and have our get-together."

"I can come back another time," Marnie offered. Plainly, the prospect pained her.

"Please stay," Hortencia interjected, switching on the apple-cheeked charm. She turned to the BRBs, who were giving Marnie slitty-eyed stares. "Let's make Miss Pyle welcome, shall we? She's here to set the record straight about Blake's recent remarks," Hortencia reminded the women pointedly. "Isn't that right?" Now her gaze skewered the reporter.

Marnie cleared her perpetually clogged throat. "Well," she demurred, "I'll take Miss Wilde's statement anyhow. I can't promise we'll publish anything. We've got very limited space each week, and we have to save it for original stories. If anything, Miss Wilde's rebuttal might make a sidebar in the food section, but we'll see."

Janice's waitressing instincts kicked in. "Miz Pyle, take my seat, why don'cha," she said, hopping up and dusting off her chair for the reporter. "I'll just cop a squat over here." She plunked her butt down on an ottoman a little out of the circle of women. "Unless... Serafina, you want us gals to leave so y'all can have your interview?"

Pauline answered for her. "Women, you're staying. I want Miss Pyle here to understand what my niece is up against, and to hear in front of witnesses—just how she's been slandered."

"Libeled," muttered the reporter. "Nobody ever gets that. It's *libel* when it's in print—not that that's what the *Chile Paper* did. We just quoted the chef's remarks," she grumbled. "We're not responsible for their content."

With another dry cough, Marnie took the seat Janice had vacated and pulled out her digital recorder and pad. Aruni made way for Sera to sit across from the reporter, strolling with studied innocence to stand near where Friedrich had started bussing tables at the rear of the store. She struck a stretchy yoga pose that just *happened* to show off her lithe figure to good advantage, smiling sidelong at the barista until he blushed and busied himself with a tub of dirty cups and plates. On Sera's left, Hortencia patted her knee comfortingly, while Pauline, on her right, chucked her on the shoulder, muttering, "Go get'r, Tiger!" far too loudly in Sera's ear.

"So," Marnie said. "You wanted to respond to Chef Austin's comments, Miss Wilde?"

Shit. What am I gonna say, "Blake's a big fat liar, waaah?" While that pretty much covered it, Sera didn't think Lego-head would be any too impressed with the "he pushed me on the playground" defense. She should have been planning her rebuttal to Blake's slander—excuse her, *libel*—all weekend, but she'd been a *tad* distracted by the man she'd fallen crazy in love with. Now was her chance to fight back, and she'd better grab it, prepared or not. *Put on your big-girl panties, Serafina,* she commanded herself. *Say something dignified.*

Sera cleared her throat. "Well, yes, I—"

"Hello, ladies," called a voice from the front of the shop. "Hello, Friedrich."

All heads turned. Chins rose, bellies sucked themselves in, and hairdos found themselves fluffed.

"Asher!" cried the women.

"Yo, Ash," Friedrich mumbled, deigning to remove his ear buds and give the taller man a shy smile. There was a definite hint of hero worship in the kid's expression.

Sera couldn't blame him. Her heart was suddenly beating a whole lot faster, and a goofy grin spread itself across her face without asking permission. She waved shyly.

Asher strolled over and the BRBs parted, Red Sea–style. He made himself at home on the arm of Sera's overstuffed chair, stroking her cheek with a fond finger and gifting her with a smile that made her lungs forget how to do their job. In his eyes, Sera could see memories of the weekend they'd shared...and the promise of more pleasure to come.

"Hey, Ash," she said, voice huskier than normal. "You know all the BRBs, right?" At his nod, she continued with the introductions. "And this is Marnie Pyle, a journalist from the *Chile Paper*."

"Pleased to meet you, Ms. Pyle," Asher said politely, though his eyes never left Sera. His clever fingers began tracing the length of Sera's arm from wrist to elbow. Sera shivered happily, his caress momentarily hypnotizing her into a pleasure daze.

A sharp cough jolted Sera out of her reverie.

Oh, right. Introductions are supposed to go both ways. But should I introduce him as my landlord, or… Sera decided to keep things simple. "Marnie, this is Asher Wolf."

"You're Miss Wilde's boyfriend?" Marnie asked, displaying the first honest interest she'd shown since she walked in the door. The wide-jowled journalist eyed the tall Israeli speculatively. A bit *too* speculatively.

Her taste buds might be dead, but her libido's still kickin'. Sera winced, silently cursing the reporter's question. Men hated labels. Labels made them squirm and twitch—and sometimes run for the hills. Asher wasn't a runner—by now Sera knew that much—but despite three unforgettable evenings of romantic dates and nights of passionate lovemaking, they'd yet to have the dreaded, "let's define our relationship" talk. Sera held her breath, blanking on ways to head disaster off at the pass.

But Asher appeared unfazed.

"Yes, I am," he said cheerfully. "Or at least, I'm working toward it." He gave the nape of Sera's neck a kiss that managed to be both gentle and wildly stirring. The BRBs sighed. Sera turned pink as a Valentine's Day Peep, feeling a rush ten times headier than sugar flood her system.

Lego-head fiddled with her digital recorder, pointing it toward Asher. "Interesting," she grunted. "So, as Miss Wilde's significant other, what's your reaction to the comments made recently by Chef Austin?"

"Comments?" Asher looked puzzled, glancing down at Sera for an explanation. She tried not to squirm. *Maybe I should have told him. But I just couldn't bear to drag him into this. It's so ugly, and it shouldn't have to be his fight.* "Bliss, what is she talking about? What has that man said to you?"

"It's not what he said to Sera, studly, it's what he said to the world," Pauline huffed before Sera could begin to explain. "That rat slandered my Baby-Bliss to this"—she glared at the reporter before seeming to recall that alienating her would be a poor idea—"to this *fine journalist* here. Half the town probably read what she printed. We're trying to set the record straight."

At her side, Sera could feel Asher stiffen. "What *exactly* did Mr. Austin say about Serafina?" he asked very quietly.

The BRBs looked at one another, then at Sera, uncomfortable.

Marnie's eyes lit at the prospect of conflict. She emitted a teeny smile. "Miss Wilde hasn't shown you the article? *Interesting.* Well, I have a copy here in my bag." She dug in her messenger tote for the latest issue of the *Chile Paper*. She handed it to Asher, who received the newspaper as though it had been marinating in a storm gutter for a week. "Here, take a look."

Asher took a look.

With each paragraph his eyes scanned, his expression turned stonier. Sera found herself wanting to comfort him, though it was she who'd been maligned. *Now he's really finding out what he's gotten himself into with me,* she thought, feeling sick. *Damn Blake to hell. If he ruins this, too, I'll gut him and make a fricassee out of his kidneys.*

The reporter didn't miss Asher's expression. "Would you care to make a statement?" she asked, waving her digital recorder in Asher's face. "After all, you'd be best qualified to rebut some of Chef Austin's more, ah, personal accusations about Miss Wilde."

Asher snapped the paper shut. He was breathing with great deliberation, Sera saw, and his eyes had gone from green to golden, as they did only with strong emotion. He rose to his feet and towered over Marnie as he very deliberately handed back the offending tabloid.

"I have no intention of commenting on my girlfriend's personal business. No man of any worth whatsoever would do so—not in private and sure as *hell* not in public." His tone was so clipped, so fiercely leashed, that all the women held their breath, wondering when he'd lose it. "You want a statement? Print *this,* Ms. Pyle: It takes a man of extremely questionable character to say something of this nature in a public forum. Anything that comes out of Mr. Austin's mouth is to be examined very closely as to motive. If he slanders Miss Wilde—"

"Libels," muttered Marnie.

"If he speaks ill of her," Asher said quellingly, "it's due to some sick 'shortcoming' of his own. And while I won't discuss the intimacy I am honored to share with Miss Wilde, there is one thing I *will* say—and say without hesitation. This woman I love is the finest pastry chef this city has ever seen—and there is no doubt in my mind that she can outbake Blake Austin any day of the week."

Pauline stood up and cheered. "You tell 'er, hot stuff!"

The Back Room Babes clapped and whistled, stomping their feet.

"Ooh, hey!" cried Syna, shushing them with an impatient gesture. "That's totally what we should do! Have a bake-off! We'll teach that scuzz Blake a lesson *and* prove Sera's the better chef!"

"Hells yeah, girl!" Aruni squealed, grabbing Friedrich's arm hard in her excitement. She beamed at Sera. "You could *so* take that dude down in the kitchen! We'll show everyone he's full of shit *and* prove your baked goods are out-of-this-world orgasmic!"

Friedrich did not seem to mind Aruni's viselike grasp, though he blushed at the word "orgasmic."

The BRBs started throwing out ideas for how Sera could show up Chef Austin. Pauline and Hortencia got in a squabble about who got to be Sera's trainer for the big showdown. But Sera couldn't think about bake-offs or getting back at her ex-boyfriend. She was still reeling from what Asher had said—in front of all her favorite people *and* the press.

This woman I love.

Did he even realize he'd said the words? She dared a glance up at her newly designated boyfriend. He had eyes only for her, ignoring the fluttering BRBs and the avidly observing reporter. His gaze held everything she loved best about Asher: honesty, tenderness, and a wide-open window to his truly spectacular soul. And what she saw when she peered inside made her catch her breath.

Yup, he realized.

Sera's eyes welled. She couldn't look away, only blink rapidly as Asher returned to her side, kneeling at the foot of her chair. "I love you, Serafina Wilde," he said. His eyes were molten gold with emotion. "I am very angry with you right now for not telling me about this business with Blake Austin, but I do love you, and I want to help you face whatever comes. Please don't keep something like this from me again. Promise me, Bliss."

Sera snarfed back a sob. She couldn't stop herself from reaching out to cradle his face with both hands. "I promise. And, Asher..." She smiled tremulously. "I love you, too."

When he captured her lips with his, it felt like fate.

When she turned back to the BRBs, she found her fate had already been sealed.

❧

"Ladies, I can definitely make this happen." Bobbie, looking self-satisfied, was patting her already perfectly curled bangs into place.

"How?" Hortencia wanted to know. "Austin's not likely to accept Sera's gauntlet just because she throws it down. What's in it for him, besides total humiliation?"

"Don't be a downer, Horsey," Pauline scolded. "That's where Ms. Pyle comes in."

As one, the women turned to stare at the reporter, who wore a wary but intrigued expression. Conflict was her stock-in-trade, after all, and a feud between foodies was sure to spur circulation. As a springboard into investigative journalism, this wasn't exactly the sort of story that got one nominated for the Pulitzer, but anything that increased her readership was a plus. Marnie cleared her throat. "What do you have in mind?"

"We want you to print a challenge to Chef Austin!" Aruni chirped, bouncing over to join the ladies with a sassy backward glance at the flustered Friedrich. "Right, ladies?" She checked with her sisters, who nodded confirmation, then plunked hands on hips and gave the reporter a gamine grin. "You send that windbag a straight-up dare to meet Serafina in the kitchen and she'll prove once and for all who's the best."

"Where would you have this showdown?" Marnie wanted to know. "And when?" She was scribbling notes on her pad.

"That's where *I* come in," Bobbie said proudly. "I'm an events planner for the Santa Fe Winter Fiesta, which as you know is running all next week. I can absolutely slot in a cook-off, even last minute, and I'm sure we can sort out a venue. If you print the challenge, I'll publicize the heck out of it all over town and let people know where to show up. It'll be a sensation!"

"Yeah!" Syna chimed in. "Bill it as the great Cupcake Conflict or something. We can even get a production crew from Santa Fe Studios to come film it. My hubby works with a lot of those guys. Heck, the local news might even want to cover it. Or maybe it'll get picked up by one of those reality TV cable channels!"

"Dear, I'm afraid there's already a show like that," Hortencia informed Syna. "Several, in fact."

Pauline raised an eyebrow at her partner.

"What? I watch the Food Channel."

"Hasn't helped your cooking," Pauline muttered.

"Anyhow," Janice said. "Like studly said, our gal can beat the britches off that slimy scumbag when it comes to cookin'. Miz Pyle, all ya gotta do is print an item that invites people to judge for themselves who's the better chef, promise lotsa free treats, and we're in business. He won't dare refuse, or he'll look like he's scared to face our Sera."

Marnie coughed contemplatively. "Well, that would certainly address *some* of Chef Austin's accusations, especially if Miss Wilde wins the contest. But I don't see how it would counteract the comments about Miss Wilde's more... *personal*... issues."

The BRBs put their heads together, whispering.

Sera surfaced at last from Asher's drugging kiss to the sound of some seriously intense muttering from her friends. From their expressions, they might have been debating anything from the right way to disable a nuclear reactor to the best brand of lube in Pauline's back room.

"Wait, maybe we could..." murmured Syna, the gist of her suggestion inaudible to Sera.

"Nah, we'd probably get arrested if we tried that, but wouldn't it be awesome if we could?" Aruni said *sotto voce,* shaking her curly head regretfully.

Bobbie touched her pearls and squinched her well-plucked brows together in consternation. "C'mon, Pauline, you're our resident evil genius; help us out!" She gazed expectantly at their fearless leader.

But Pauline just flapped her hands at her minions. "Hush, women." She flopped back in her armchair and gave her niece an assessing look that was nevertheless rich with pride...and respect. "I don't know what you're fretting about, you ninnies. You can quit your scheming. My Baby-Bliss has got this one in the bag."

Oh, Pauline. Sera's heart overflowed as she looked from the man she loved to the woman who had raised her to know she deserved it.

I'm damn well gonna give it my best shot.

Chapter Thirty-One

The mixer blades beat with agonizing slowness.

Whomp.

A lifetime.

Whomp.

Two lifetimes.

Whomp.

Galaxies were born and died.

By contrast, Sera's heart was pummeling her ribs like an overzealous karate instructor. Sweat beaded her upper lip, and she glared into the brushed aluminum bowl as if her will alone could froth the egg whites into the nice, stiff peaks she was after. But no matter how she fiddled with the switches on the stand mixer's sides, the blades would not speed up. Her whites refused to foam. The pinch of salt she'd added did nothing to help. Or wait, had she accidentally used sugar? There was no time to start over. *The meringue has to be ready in five minutes, and I still have to brown the tops! Shit, did I even set the oven?*

She turned in a blind panic, flinging open the Blodgett's gaping maw. *No racks! What am I supposed to do without racks? I've got a hundred mini meringue pies to dish up, and no way to caramelize the crusts!*

Wait...a *brûlée* torch! *Gotta be a* brûlée *torch around here...*

She patted her apron, she flung open cabinets. Not so much as a cardboard safety match to be found in the whole goddamn kitchen! Ever more frantic, knowing her whole career, her very happiness, depended upon success, Sera searched the space for something—anything—she could use. Her gasping breaths were the only sound, until...

Wham!

A booted foot sent the kitchen's double doors swinging violently toward opposite walls. Into the breech stepped a figure in a billowing leather duster and a hat to match. From halfway across the steam-shrouded room, Sera could see Blake's black eyes narrow with malice as he caught sight of her. His lip curled derisively. In slow motion, one hand rose lazily, brushed aside his heavy coat, and revealed the holster at his hip.

Heart pounding, Sera lunged for the gun belt she was somehow unsurprised to find strapped to her own side...

And came up holding a half-squashed chocolate éclair.

A sinister grin spread across Chef Austin's face as he raised his pistol...

And Sera shrieked as she came suddenly, violently awake.

A yawning maw met her gaze.

Fortunately, it was Silver's yawning maw, smelling somewhat unpleasantly of puppy chow and all too full of tongue, which he proceeded to slop across her face as he barked, happy to see Sera awake. He pranced all about the bed, tail wagging frantically, spent a moment tunneling into the mussed bedclothes in case he'd missed any excitement, then flopped on his back in the warm spot Asher had left, paws up and begging for belly rubs.

Sera ruffled his fur absently, grateful for the wholesome enthusiasm of the puppy. It went a long way toward dispelling her nightmare—though not far enough. His master might have done a better job, she thought with a mental pout, but Asher was nowhere to be seen. *Shower? Coffee run?* He must have already walked the dogs, because Silver wasn't whining to be let out, and Sascha wasn't pacing at the half-open bedroom door the way she did when things got urgent. It warmed Sera's soul a little to realize she was learning the Wolf household's rhythms and routines, and even—maybe—beginning to find her own place within them. She turned her attention outward, smiling ruefully as a god-awful clanging and a raft of Hebrew curses informed her Asher was in the kitchen attempting to make breakfast.

She appreciated his efforts, but there was no way she'd be able to eat this morning, even had her otherwise lovely new boyfriend not been a horrendous cook. Her stomach was too busy putting on a Cirque du Soleil interpretive performance—theme: petrified pastry chef.

Today we settle the score, Blake, Sera thought with a certain grim determination. *Once and for all. I may not have dreamed up this cockamamie scheme, but now that I'm committed, I am damn sure going to give it everything I've got.*

Marnie had baited the trap well—and with rather more pizzazz than Sera had expected.

New Mexican Standoff!

Break out your dessert forks, Santa Feans. In response to recent comments made by celebrity chef Blake Austin, Ms. Serafina Wilde, proprietor of Bliss, a newly opened bakery known for more than mere culinary delights, is calling out her former mentor. Mr. Austin, in town to oversee the opening of his newest investment, the Blue Coyote on Canyon Road, had called into question Miss Wilde's competence in the kitchen, among other, more personal complaints. Miss Wilde now invites Mr. Austin to a "battle of the baked goods" at next week's Winter Fiesta.

"Let the fine folks of Santa Fe be the judge," said Miss Wilde. "I'm confident my confections capture the true essence of bliss. But if Blake thinks he can do better, he's welcome to give me a run for my money."

When the *Chile Paper* reached out to Mr. Austin for comment, the chef had only two words for Miss Wilde.

"Bring it," said Mr. Austin.

Readers are invited to visit the Winter Fiesta's website for more details on this sure-to-be epic culinary clash.

Uncharacteristically terse as his official reply had been, Blake's *un*official response had been classic Austin.

He'd sent Sera a dead fish.

It had arrived at the shop wrapped in newspaper, with a note that read,

Nice try, Sera-frigid. You, my dear, have as much chance of revitalizing your career with this little stunt as this fish does of swimming back to the ocean. But since you choose to invite your own ruination with such a spectacularly desperate ploy, I am more than happy to provide the final nail in your culinary coffin. I shall look forward to witnessing—and indeed, causing—*your utter and irrevocable humiliation.*

It was a nice fish, though. Alaskan king salmon, if Sera wasn't mistaken, twenty dollars a pound and no easy feat to acquire fresh in landlocked New Mexico. She'd been tempted to poach it with a light creamy dill sauce, but she wouldn't put it past Blake to have poisoned the poor thing. Its cold, staring eyes had seemed to pierce her, asking mutely, *You sure you want to go toe-to-toe with this dude? You don't want to end up like me, do you?*

Yet, outlandish as the Back Room Babes' plan to take Blake down was, Sera had to agree it was her last, best hope to keep her ex at bay. She had to fight back, fight hard, and fight *publicly,* or he'd continue to whittle away her reputation for as long as he cared to carry on his crazed vendetta. And as far as Sera could tell, that would be all the way to the grave. She would never have a better opportunity to stop him in his tracks than today's bake-off.

I feel like a gladiator facing my fate in the coliseum, she fretted. *Wonder what's the Latin for "We who are about to bake salute you"?*

Sera told herself it was a good thing that he'd taken up her challenge. Of course he'd done so only on *his* terms—and his terms, as it turned out, were many.

With Blake's fuck-you fish thawing on the counter and the BRBs gathered in the "war room" (Bliss's comfy armchairs) for support, they'd dialed up the chef's hotel to hash out the details of the duel. Sera had stayed out of it, feeling a bit like a boxer when her "trainers" started massaging her shoulders and pressing little sips of water on her (Aruni even offered to rub aromatherapy oil on her temples). Pauline had done the honors, punching the buttons on the store's phone hard enough to make Sera wince. However, when she started rummaging in the prep area's drawers for "the scratchy twine" after about a half second of conversation with Sera's ex, Hortencia had snatched the phone away. Then the real haggling had begun.

Despite Sera's admiration for her aunt's life partner, she had to admit Blake had gotten the better of the old gal. The "quaint contest," as he put it, had to take place in his restaurant (conveniently providing free publicity for the newly opened eatery). He required an assistant to help prep his creations (Sera could have one, too, he ever-so-generously allowed). And it would all be filmed by a crew of his cronies from the Food Channel. It didn't surprise Sera. When his ego was at stake, Blake Austin played to win. No doubt, he expected to crush her in spectacular fashion, show off his new restaurant, *and* dazzle his loyal fans with his overhyped culinary skills, all while turning a tidy profit by televising the event for the content-craving cable network.

The only concession Sera's team managed to wrangle was that the competition would focus *solely* on dessert. In no uncertain terms, Hortencia had told "he who shall go straight to hell" that, since it was Sera's baking credentials he'd so classily called into question, it was baked goods they would battle over. He wasn't lacking the talent to whip up a few measly tarts, was he?

Sera could hear Blake's response from halfway across the shop.

And so it came to be that Santa Fe's weeklong Winter Fiesta added a last-minute event.

Bake-Off at the Blue Coyote! ran the headline on the Winter Fiesta's website.

Famous chef takes on former protégée, and Santa Fe decides the winner!

Pastry chef and proprietor of Santa Fe's newest sensual sensation "Bliss" invites visiting celebrity chef Blake Austin to show who's really got the spice with a bake-off at Austin's newest venture, the Blue Coyote. Come by Canyon Road Friday starting at noon to witness these two highly skilled chefs showing off their sweetest creations. Then judge for yourself who makes you moan most with delight!

Bobbie had really done an amazing job of pulling the event together and publicizing it to the hilt. From what she'd told Sera, the cooking contest was the talk of the town, sure to be packed with locals and tourists seeking sugar rushes and a glimpse of the world-famous chef facing off against the City Different's newest bakery owner.

Whom they'd be rooting for was another matter.

Oh God oh God oh God... this is really happening. Today!

Sera pulled the covers over her head, resisting Silver's attempts at playing sheet-peekaboo by yanking at the fabric with his teeth. She wasn't worried about being outbaked by her former boyfriend—not in a fair fight anyway. She knew she was the better chef—hell, the last time that bastard had actually sweated it out on the line, his customers had been wearing Members Only jackets and neon Scrunchies. But really, what was the likelihood Blake would play fair?

Her stomach roiled.

The acrid aroma of burnt toast heralded Asher's arrival. Sera let Silver tug the sheet off her face, hoping her hair looked more "JBF" than "just been mangled." She blinked up at him. In his low-slung jeans, barefoot and bare-chested, hair adorably mussed, the tall Israeli was a powerful incentive to call off the contest and spend the day in bed.

"Good morning, lovely man," she said, submerging her fears in favor of savoring a few more minutes of pleasure.

"Good morning, lovely woman." Asher proffered a plate of what was ostensibly breakfast. His eyes lit with appreciation as she threw back the covers, revealing that the T-shirt she'd borrowed from him as a makeshift nightie had ridden up to the tops of her thighs.

Tugging the tee down out of a vestige of modesty, Sera swung her legs over the edge of the bed. She accepted the plate, which appeared to be the backdrop for a new work of black-and-yellow abstract art, and casually laid it on the nightstand where Silver could get at it. Nervous as she was about today, just seeing Asher lifted her spirits. *No matter what happens this afternoon,* she marveled, *this guy's got my back. I won't lose* everything *if I lose to Blake today.*

But Sera didn't want to lose *anything.*

I've earned this, damn it. My shop. My place in this town. My bliss. And I'm gonna fight to keep them.

"Thanks, Ash. Breakfast looks yummy. I think I'll wait until after my shower to eat, though. I've got a nervous stomach this morning."

He grimaced sympathetically. "I'm not surprised, given what you're facing today," he said, tracing the line of her cheek with a comforting finger. "By the way, did I hear a shout a minute ago?" He eyed Sera with mild concern.

She felt a pang, not wanting Asher to worry for her. Blake was *her* demon to slay. "Would you like to?" Mustering up a lascivious leer, she moseyed up to him and wove her arms around his waist. "I do seem to get pretty 'shouty' when you're around."

"Mm, yes, that you do." His smile crinkled the corners of his eyes appealingly. "I think my eardrums could do with another assault. But do we have time?" Asher was already nibbling her neck.

"Probably not." Sera sighed. She pulled away reluctantly to study the man she was growing to love more each day. Though they'd only been together a short time, she felt strangely secure in their fledgling relationship—serene, even—and excited to see where it would go. Artist to artist and healing heart to healing heart, they simply *got* each other. His support had given her so much strength, his faith in her had bolstered her confidence and made her future seem so much brighter. She would never be readier to face down her past. Sera's hand rose to cup his cheek, and she stretched up to give his chin a grateful kiss. "Much as I'd rather let you rock my world all day, I've got someone else's world to rock first. But trust me," she vowed, "*he's* not going to enjoy the experience."

Chapter Thirty-Two

What a circus.

Sera stopped stock-still a few feet inside the restaurant, letting her rucksack of culinary tools slip through nerveless fingers and clunk to the floor. Behind her, Malcolm, carrying the rest of their gear, harrumphed as he nearly plowed into her.

"Mind where yer gawkin', girlie," he growled.

Though he'd agreed to be her second in this duel, Malcolm was not best pleased to be spending his Friday subjecting himself to scrutiny by the "idjit unwashed." Once he'd heard a bit of Sera's history with Chef Austin, Malcolm had been more than ready to release his inner Highland warrior on her behalf, but he hadn't dropped his dislike of the general public or his disdain for their "criminally ignorant palates." Being judged by a bunch of "gastronomic ignoramuses" in this contest was the ultimate affront for the prickly Scotsman. Sera couldn't blame him; she was feeling unnerved herself at the prospect of letting the city of Santa Fe decide her fate. Fleetingly, she wished she'd taken Asher up on his offer to accompany her, but she'd wanted no distractions while she was getting her head in the game. She'd asked that he, Pauline, Hortencia, and the BRBs not show up until the contest was under way, so she could focus solely on the task at hand.

Focusing in *this* environment, however, would be anything but easy.

The Blue Coyote had been transformed from posh restaurant to public tribunal, with tables cleared away to leave a wide semicircle of space for the audience. The open-plan kitchen had a long, quarter-moon-shaped bar that allowed patrons to ogle the chefs across the pass while they worked (a fad the rather introverted Serafina had always loathed). The bar's countertop was set up with two sets of mixers; copious trays, tins, and molds; and matching *mise en place* containing ingredients from shaved Belgian chocolate to unsalted Irish butter, and everything in between. Tablecloth-shrouded trolleys at either end of the bar held more mystery items for the great bake-off. *Probably full of "challenging" ingredients like sea cucumber and monkey's knuckles, if the Food Channel people have had any say in it,* Sera thought, grimacing. They seemed to have taken over the place; camera jockeys and PAs with walkie-talkies stringing wires and testing light levels while the anxious restaurant staff looked on, wondering if they'd be able to clean up the mess in time to open for dinner.

Outside, Canyon Road reveled in a rare warm winter day, the sun blazing merrily in a poetically blue sky. Tourists were strolling up and down the winding street in just their fleeces and down vests, stopping to snap photos of the whimsical sculptures that graced practically every storefront. "Santa Fe's answer to Madison Avenue," Sera had heard it called, and she had to agree. The exuberant art scene showcased in Canyon Road's many galleries was at the core of the City Different's charm—and brought in a great proportion of its tourism dollars.

Already, people were peeking their heads in the Blue Coyote's main entrance and peering through the wall of French doors that would be thrown open in an hour when the contest began. Food Channel production peons were keeping the gawkers at bay as politely as they could.

Her opponent in this contest, however, felt no need for politesse.

In the center of it all stood ringmaster Chef Austin, looking tall and leonine in a royal blue chef's coat custom-embroidered in gold on the breast with his name and the steaming serving dish that was his trademark. *He's a steaming pile of something, all right,* thought Sera, straightening her own plain white jacket self-consciously. Supremely confident, Austin was ordering the staff and TV crew about with equal abandon, and they were hustling to accommodate, fearful expressions in their eyes that Sera remembered well from her days in his kitchens. Her stomach tightened.

The only way out of this mess was to win, and win big. If she beat Blake, the publicity would ensure her bakery became a real destination for tourists visiting Santa Fe. But if she lost...

If she lost, she could kiss her Bliss good-bye.

Oh, God...

Hey. Don't freak out just yet, she rallied herself. *Blake may be in his element, but I'm not entirely unarmed. I've got my recipes, my equipment, and one highly volatile Scotsman.*

At Sera's side, Malcolm oozed culinary menace, armed with camo-print apron, a special-order utili-kilt bristling with tools from pie crimpers to spatulas, and a hairnet that barely contained his snowy, waist-length locks. His mustaches had been braided, Gimli-style, giving him a truly ferocious look. *If I can channel all that ferocity into wowing the crowd with our desserts, we've got a chance at winning this thing. But if he goes off the rails... yeek.*

"That's the man, is it?" Malcolm growled, giving Blake the hairy eyeball from under furry brows. "Och, that preening popinjay dinna stand a chance against us, lass. Look at 'im, lording it up like 'e owns the place."

"He does," Sera reminded him, smiling despite her nerves as she noted how prominent her pie maven's brogue had grown since arriving in enemy territory. "Or at least, he's the largest stakeholder, so he may as well. C'mon, the contest's going to start soon, and we need to get set up." She started tugging Malcolm toward the prep stations.

"First I want tae size up th' competition. Let's go hae' a word wi' Chef Snottypants."

Before Sera could demur, Malcolm was marching, kilt swaying, over to her ex. "Hold your nose, Malc," she called, trailing behind him. "Blake's attitude stinks worse than a durian."

Apparently the threat of behavior more putrid than death-scented exotic fruit wasn't enough to put the Scotsman off.

"Austin!" Malcolm snapped, stomping to a halt beside the celebrity chef. Sera fetched up in his wake, stomach souring as she caught wind of Blake's obnoxious cologne.

Her ex didn't bother to acknowledge either of them, continuing to bark orders at his staff as if his opponents didn't exist. At his side stood a young man with a long-suffering expression, who was taking the brunt of it. Sera recognized him as Samuel Everett, one of the Southwest's more prominent up-and-coming *pâtissiers.* She'd seen him featured in several industry magazines, all of the write-ups glowing. Sam must be the pastry chef here. *Naturally,* she thought, *Blake drafted someone who can actually bake to be his assistant, since he's still reading the back of Duncan Hines boxes himself.* Under other circumstances, she'd have loved to swap techniques and gossip with the young chef over coffee. But no doubt Blake had filled his head with lies about her, and he'd probably run screaming even if they weren't on opposite sides of today's bake-off. It reminded Sera of why she needed so badly to win today.

No more, Blake. No more. You're goin' down.

"Oi! I'm talking to ye, ye arrogant shite," Malcolm snarled. A vein began to pulse at his temple.

Austin took his sweet time turning to face them. His eyes flicked wearily over Sera's short frame first, from sturdy clogs to the sparkly snood Hortencia had crocheted for her. Only then did his gaze turn to Malcolm, and Sera saw his eyes widen for a moment before they became hooded with his habitual ennui once more.

"Is this your second, or is it a sasquatch, Serafina?" Blake ogled Malcolm from kilt to hair net. "A bit... hairy... isn't he? With this one around, you'll want to check for stray fur balls when you plate your desserts."

Instead of swinging a cleaver at Blake, as Sera half feared, Malcolm merely planted his hands on his hips and eyed the other man for a moment. "What kind of accent is that yer sportin', mate?" he asked, a trace of amusement coloring his brogue. "I canna quite place it. Sounds t'me a bit like Brighton—by way o' Brooklyn."

Blake's eyes bulged. His jaw worked furiously. His true origins were a mystery even to Sera, who'd spent more years by his side—and in his bed—than she cared to remember. But it was obvious he didn't appreciate the Scotsman calling his ancestry—or his mystique—into question. "I won't stand for being insulted in my own restaurant by some *skirt-sporting savage,*" he began, taking a menacing step in Malcolm's direction. Malcolm met him halfway, the light of battle in his eye, issuing a growl that would have done a real sasquatch proud. But before either man could take a swing, Sera stepped between them.

It wasn't that she didn't want Malcolm to pummel her ex. She simply wanted to do the honors herself.

All the rage she'd felt through the years—the humiliations Blake had put her through, the dismissive, derisive way he treated her, and the ugly insinuations he'd spread all over town—*two* towns now—boiled to the surface in a blast of fury that had her face flushing brick red and her fingers balling into fists. Bad enough he'd poured his poison on her. How dare he insult her friend? She wanted to knee him in the balls. She wanted to channel Moe from the Three Stooges and fork him in the eye with two stiff fingers.

Instead, she would show him up, but good.

"Still a bully and a blowhard, I see," Sera growled through gritted teeth, glaring up at her nemesis. "You might as well skip the convection ovens today, with all the hot air you spew." She planted her hands on her hips and gave her ex a once-over as dismissive as his own had been, reveling in how *freaking great* it felt to stand up to her tormenter. "But your bullshit's not going to hide the fact that I'm still the better chef—*and* the better person. By the time I'm done wiping the floors with you today, everyone's going to know it."

Out of the corner of her eye, she saw Sam Everett's lip twitch before he wiped his face clean of expression.

"I hardly think so." Blake scoffed, sneering. "You forget: I know what you're made of, you pathetic *child,* and I know you haven't got the sauce to best me. I can't wait to watch you choke, Sera-*frigid.* It's what you're best at, after all."

Maybe at one time, but Sera wasn't that woman anymore. She didn't freeze up. And she didn't *give* up just because some mean, nasty bully pushed her around.

"Let's get this show on the road, Austin," she said tightly. "The next time I lower myself to talk to you, it'll be to accept your concession speech after I kick your ass all over this kitchen." She looked around for the person she'd been told would be shepherding the showdown—some woman from the Food Channel apparently, whose job it would be to lay down the rules and make sure the contest ran smoothly.

The hostess wasn't hard to find, seated in one of the restaurant's semicircular blue velvet booths. Her face was obscured from Sera's gaze by a team of makeup artists and hair stylists who were buzzing around her like highly paid mosquitoes, making sure every lock was coifed, every lash lengthened. Her dress—a clingy red spaghetti-strap number more appropriate to a sultry Miami night than a chilly December day in Santa Fe—fit her with almost embarrassing intimacy, delineating a physique that spoke more of long hours in the gym than at the dining table. Blonder than Gwyneth Paltrow's blondest day, tall and statuesque, she was everything Sera wasn't as a woman.

Sera's wrath-born bravado wilted like radicchio over a high flame. *Wow. It's like we're not even the same species,* she thought. And then the woman rose to greet her, and Sera realized that wasn't quite true. They had *one* thing in common.

They'd both bedded Blake Austin.

True, the last time they'd met, the blonde had had her mouth full, but Sera couldn't fail to recognize the woman who'd sent her off on her final bender. *Add one of my old chef's hats and put her on her knees, and... yup, that's the chick that was blowing Blake right before he blew my career to shreds.*

Sera's heart sank as the woman shed her entourage and drifted over to greet them, her walk willowy as a finishing school graduate's. By contrast, Sera felt like some uncouth barbarian. A *short,* uncouth barbarian.

Of all the hostesses on all the reality cable shows, why did it have to be *her?*

"Let me introduce a *dear* old friend of mine, Vanessa Hurley, host of *Hot Chef!*" drawled Blake, slinging his arm familiarly about the TV star's rather bare shoulders as she came to stand beside them.

To her credit, Sera noticed Ms. Hurley eased away from Blake's embrace, looking uncomfortable.

Then again, she appeared equally queasy at the sight of Serafina.

Does she remember me from that night? Sera wondered. *She seemed rather... preoccupied at the time, but if she can multitask as well as she...* Sera mentally shook her head to dispel the image that lingered there. "Pleased to meet you, Vanessa," she said, swallowing bile. "I'm a big fan of your show." Actually, she avoided it like *E. coli,* but the blonde didn't need to know that.

The look of unease had disappeared from the hostess's eyes so completely that Sera had to wonder if she'd imagined it in the first place. "That's awfully sweet," said Vanessa, offering a smile so sincere Sera could easily understand how she'd made it on TV. *This lady could sell barbeque sauce to the Neelys.* The TV host stuck out her hand for Sera to shake. It was cool, her grip firm with just the right amount of pressure. "I'm pleased to meet you, too. Good luck today, Serafina." Was it Sera's imagination, or had her grip tightened for just a moment, like she was trying to tell Sera something?

I don't have time to worry about subtext, Sera reminded herself. *I've got a dish of whoop-ass to whip up.*

"Let me show you where you'll be stationed and explain a few of the rules my producers may not have gone over with you on the phone." Still talking, Vanessa led Sera and Malcolm away from Blake. Sera was glad to follow, though she was so busy running through potential recipes in her head she heard only a little of what was said. As they set their things down on the leftmost of the two identical workstations, Sera scanned the prep area—digital scales, good; sheet pans, good; pastry bags, excellent. She'd brought her own sugar spinner, favorite molds and chocolate melting pots, not wanting to rely on the Blue Coyote's resources—or on Blake to apportion them fairly.

"So, you're all set?" Vanessa gave Sera a serene smile, adding a more reserved one for Malcolm, who was eyeing her like she was a weevil he'd found in his favorite flour container.

"Yeah, I think so," Sera said, preoccupied. Chitchatting with the fellatrix wasn't on her top ten list at the moment. But Vanessa seemed to want to linger for some inexplicable reason. Sera found herself a bit impatient. She laid down the chef's kit she'd been unpacking. "I'm pretty sure I got it all, Vanessa—no outside ingredients, don't look directly into the camera lens, don't dunk my mike in anything. Was there something else?"

"Just one thing. A personal favor, if I might make a small request." She spoke low enough that Malcolm, rummaging in the cabinets at their knees, couldn't hear.

"Um, sure, I guess." Sera was startled enough to meet Vanessa's eyes. Gone was the treacle-sweet persona. Underneath, Sera saw a woman of steely determination—a smart, tough professional who'd worked hard to get where she was. And perhaps, a woman with some of the same regrets Sera herself had. "What can I do for you?"

"You can kick Blake Austin's ass, Chef Wilde."

"What? But I thought...I mean, I assumed you two were, ah, friends..."

Vanessa colored becomingly. "You're not the only one who's ever made a bad choice. And believe me, he's never let me forget it. That man needs to be taken down a peg or five. You'll be doing every woman in this industry a favor if you beat him today. So give him hell!"

And Vanessa swished off, calling for a lipstick touch-up.

I'm damn well gonna try, lady, Sera silently promised. Heads down, she and Malcolm got to work, unloading their supplies, locating staple ingredients, checking ovens, and making sure her trusty equipment was close to hand.

She didn't look up again until a dinner gong *bonnnnnnnnnnged.*

"Holy shite," muttered Malcolm.

Sera started, gazing around the restaurant for the first time in nearly an hour. Holy shite was right. The Blue Coyote was packed to the rafters.

Her heart squeezed with stage fright. It was one thing to bake anonymously, barricaded behind cooling racks and in one's own element. It was another to perform like a trained monkey in front of a hundred strangers and with TV cameras angling to capture every move.

Do not fuck this up, Serafina Wilde, she told herself sternly.

To Sera's right, Blake and Chef Everett stood behind their portion of the counter, arms crossed casually over their chests, looking out over the crowd with every appearance of confidence. Into the semicircle of space taped off between the chefs and their audience, Vanessa strode with equal panache. Her charisma instantly captured everyone's attention—or perhaps it was the clingy red dress. The crowd quieted. Cameras zoomed in to catch every nuance of her stride, her smile, her flowing golden mane. The host hit her mark like a fashion model, paused, and tossed her hair over her shoulder.

"Good afternoon, Santa Fe!" Vanessa crooned. The mike discreetly clipped to her bodice made her easy to hear, even for those taking in the contest from the sidewalk outside the open French doors. A round of enthusiastic applause greeted her. "Welcome to the Winter Fiesta's most delicious event! We're so glad we were able to bring the Food Channel here to capture every moment of what is sure to be a baking battle royale. Is everyone excited?"

"Yeah!!!! Woooo!!!" cried the crowd. The cameras panned around to take in the reaction. Sera saw fluffy-haired Texan tourists rubbing shoulders with aging hippies, parents with their little ones on their shoulders, and a German tour group discreetly snapping pics with their mobile devices, despite the admonishments of the Food Channel producers. A cadre of curious shopkeepers had abandoned their stores to take in the contest as well. Sera recognized several of them from the neighborhood.

And right up front, grinning proudly, stood a wall of women Sera knew quite well.

Aunt Pauline, her arm about Hortencia. Aruni, bouncing on her toes with excitement. Janice, hands on hips and a grin on her lips. Syna, Bobbie, River Wind, and the rest of the Back Room Babes. All of them had come.

As one, seeing Sera had noticed them, they threw open their jackets to reveal matching T-shirts.

"Team Bliss!" their chests announced in giant pink sequined letters.

The BRBs pumped their fists and hooted. "Bliss! Bliss! Bliss! Bliss!"

That was when Sera noticed Asher, standing directly behind her aunt and Hortencia. She did a double-take when she saw he, too, was sporting a sparkly pink-lettered "Bliss" T-shirt beneath his navy peacoat. Somehow, he managed to pull it off without losing an iota of masculinity. Asher grinned broadly as he caught Sera's eye, puffing out his chest and chanting her name with the rest.

Beside him, Guadalupe was examining her perfect manicure and trying not to look bored as she balanced on five-inch stilettos. Mr. Yazzie from next door had donned his best cardigan for the occasion. He gave Sera a shy wave. Even Friedrich, sidling close to Aruni and looking nervous in such a large crowd, had come, though in lieu of pink sequins, he'd worn his usual uniform of ratty Nietzsche T-shirt and black skinny jeans.

Sera felt a wash of love for her Santa Fe family. *I'm not letting you down. Not any of you.*

Across the counter from Sera, Blake rolled his eyes and sighed as if physically pained, before seeming to realize the Food Channel's cameras would catch every expression. He pasted an indulgent expression on his craggy features.

Vanessa took the shenanigans in stride, giving them all a gracious smile. "All right then," she said when the noise died down. "So, does everyone want to hear how today's contest is going to work?" she asked.

Of course they do, thought Sera. *When it's you talking, they want to know the precise rate at which plaster dries.*

The crowd gave her the love she was looking for, and Vanessa accepted it graciously. "There'll be three rounds; the first featuring our chefs' best interpretation of local flavors, the next representing a taste of New York City, since that's where Chef Austin *and* Chef Wilde both earned their whites; and the last, a freestyle, no-holds-barred chance to completely knock your socks off." She gave the audience a smile that reminded Sera of Glenda the Good Witch.

If her eyes twinkled any more, I'd swear she had glitter in her contacts.

Vanessa continued. "There's only one judge today—and that's you! Everyone here is going to get a taste of each dessert, and the winner of the challenge will be decided by acclaim." Again, that cheerful twinkle. "That means whoever gets the loudest applause wins!"

If that were the case, Sera thought, Vanessa herself would be declared the champion without having to lift a spatula. *Can we just get on with this?* she fretted. At her side, Malcolm was shifting from foot to foot like a caged beast, and she wasn't sure how much more patience he'd have for the Food Channel's theatrics. *Me either, dude,* she thought, shooting him a tight smile and a prayer for patience.

"Now, we don't want anyone perishing of hunger or getting restless, so we've made it a rule that the chefs have a mere forty-five minutes to come up with each creation, start to finish, oven to garnish. And meanwhile..." She smiled like Oprah about to give away a fleet of cars. "While they work, we'll be serving everyone small plates from the Blue Coyote's kitchen and passing around hot toddies and mulled wine to keep you nice and toasty!"

This time, the audience went bananas.

Oh, great, thought Sera. *They'll be biased because Blake's the one feeding them goodies, and too loaded to tell spun sugar from Frosted Flakes by the time the first dessert comes out of the oven.* But she didn't have much say in the matter, now that the Food Channel had stepped in. It was their show, and Sera, willy-nilly, had become one of her greatest nightmares...*a reality show contestant.*

Vanessa turned her pearly whites on the chefs and their seconds. "Chefs, for this first round, you'll each have thirty seconds to snag whatever you can from the mystery ingredient trolleys. In honor of our host city, they've been loaded with a selection of uniquely Southwestern items for you to work with." She ticked off ingredients on her scarlet-tipped fingers. "On each of your trolleys, you'll find green chile, cactus flower, prickly pear, agave, apples, blue corn, tequila, pine nuts, and some staples like flour, sugar, butter, and eggs to hold it all together. The challenge is to use them—and only them—to create a confection that really *screams* Santa Fe."

Vanessa turned her smile out over the audience, which beamed back, enthralled. "Do we have any locals here?" she asked. Whistles and hoots assured her she did. "Well, we expect you guys to hold our two chefs here to a high standard! If it isn't authentic, we want to hear about it."

The audience clapped and hollered assent.

Again, that "I float on a cloud above you" smile. "All set, Chefs?" She turned her angelic gaze on the contestants and their seconds. "Remember, just thirty seconds to make your selections."

"Ready!" barked Blake.

"Ready," echoed Everett.

Malcolm let out a battle cry that would have done his ancestors proud.

Sera could only nod. Her eyes were glued to her trolley, mind already whirring with ideas. *Maybe a prickly-pear-infused gelee with agave and a few pine nuts for garnish. Or I could do a sweetened sponge cake textured with blue corn...*

Vanessa raised her toned arms as she delivered the signature line from her hit show. "Make it sizzle!"

The gong sounded again, the crowd roared with excitement, and Sera dashed for her trolley, Malcolm hot on her heels. She whipped off the sheet and started yanking the lids off stainless steel containers.

"What kind of bollocks is this?" Malcolm bellowed.

Conscious of the cameras and the good impression they needed to make, Sera elbowed her pie maven in the ribs, shushing him. But she wanted to holler, too.

None of the lovely-sounding ingredients Vanessa had mentioned were on her trolley. She opened cylinder after cylinder. No cactus flower. No apples. No blue corn, no pine nuts, no smoky-sweet agave nectar. Not even a lowly, lonely chile pod. Instead, there was a gigantic blob of—was that?—yes, it was plain white lard, a rack of spices that could have come straight out of any grocery store, a bag of flour, and some sugar, eggs, salt, and baking powder.

Blake's first sabotage, Sera thought, somehow unsurprised. *He must have switched the ingredients in the carts—or paid off one of the PAs to do it. He's probably paid the camera guys, too, so they won't call attention to it. How he must be gloating right now.* She glanced across the room, and sure enough, even as Sam Everett was grabbing up armfuls of ingredients—all of them as Vanessa had described—Blake was standing back, a smirk on his face as he watched Serafina discover his perfidy. His expression practically dared her to make a scene.

Which was exactly what she desperately, passionately wanted to do. She *wanted* to fly across the room and scratch his eyes out. She *wanted* to bring the whole contest to a screeching halt and call everyone's attention to his dirty little trick. She *wanted* to make sure everyone saw how he operated. But she knew he'd have some ready excuse, some way to make her look like the bad guy, just as he'd done at the Anderson wedding last year. So there was only one thing to do. And that was *win anyway.*

Lard...lard...what the hell can I do with lard? Hm, piecrust...Nope, nothing to fill it with. Think, Sera! What uses lard besides piecrust? Biscuits? Not biscuits—too boring. Ooh, but wait! That gives me an idea!

"C'mon, Malc. Grab me that anise seed, the flour, and all the eggs you can carry. I'll get the rest." Sera dove for the blob of lard, snagged some sugar and spices, and hoofed it as fast as she could back to her prep area.

She knew just what to do.

Once they were back at her station, the world shrank down to just her, her helper, and the food at her fingertips. Oven: set. Ingredients: laid out. Plan: in motion. *I can do this.* Food was reliable. Food didn't mess with your head. It waited for you to add the magic, and if you knew what you were doing, if you took all the right factors into account, it cooperated beautifully. "Sheet pans, Malc, and my marble pin. Oh, and snag me some of that brandy from behind the bar, will you? I don't care if it didn't come off the cart; if Blake's not going to play fair, I think we can bend one tiny rule."

Wouldn't mind a swig of that brandy right now, Sera thought, but the booze wasn't for her.

As she did mental calculations—*need enough for at least ten dozen cookies*—and shook out sugar, baking powder, and spices, Sera barely noticed the cameras zooming in on her flying fingers and recording close-ups of her tight-lipped face. She hardly heard Vanessa as she gushed over the chefs' every move, calling the audience's attention to their technique, their teamwork, how much time they had left.

She couldn't have cared less what Blake—aided by Sam Everett's sure hand, no doubt—was doing. It was all about baking the best-tasting treats of her life.

She mixed, Malcolm rolled. She shaped as he shuttled trays in and out of the oven. They scarcely spoke, so intensely focused were they on the task at hand.

The gong sounded as the last batch received its final dash of cinnamon and sugar.

"Spatulas down, Chefs!" Vanessa sang out. She sashayed—classily—out in front of the crowd, making a production of turning to face the sweating chefs. Blake and Sam Everett were just tidying up the edges of what looked to be a huge cobbler of some sort—or rather, Sam was, and Blake was directing the harried *pâtissier,* who clearly didn't need the help. Vanessa approached them first. "Chef Austin, tell us, what Santa Fe specialty have you made for these fine folks?"

Blake leaned his elbows on the countertop so he could address the host. His eyes dwelled for rather a long time on her cleavage before he deigned to speak. "Well, *Vanessa,* I think they're really going to love this. We've taken some rather *humble* local ingredients and turned them into a dish that residents of this *charming* little town are sure to appreciate." He leered into the camera in much the same fashion as he'd ogled her breasts.

Vanessa played along. "Ooh, I can't wait. What is it?"

Sam Everett whispered in Blake's ear. "Green Chile Apple Crumble!" Blake announced. "Can't have dessert in Santa Fe without green chile, can we!" The audience clapped and hooted, nodding. "I've added notes of"—he paused again to let Everett whisper in his ear—"agave, plus locally grown apples, honey harvested from Charma . . ." Everett whispered again. "Excuse me, *Chama*, and just a hint of blue corn in the crust. Watch out, folks; this dessert's got a bit of a kick!"

Blake's joviality was making Sera sick. She'd forgotten how he could pour on the charm when he wanted to dazzle unsuspecting victims—er, *customers.* The audience seemed to be eating it up. She just hoped the crumble wasn't as good as it looked—because it did look (and smell) pretty darn tasty. Everett's doing, no doubt. Sera saw him flinch as the Food Channel's PA's started scooping out chunks and divvying the dessert up among a hundred dessert plates, taking no care whatsoever with the presentation. Sera could spare no sympathy for her fellow chef, however, because now it was her turn in the hot seat.

The statuesque host struck a pose, beaming down at Sera. "So, Chef Wilde, we noticed you chose not to go with most of the signature ingredients on our mystery trolleys. Bold choice there. Care to tell us what were you thinking?"

I was thinking somebody stole all the good stuff, Sera wanted to say. But she knew she'd only make herself look bad if she went crying about unfair advantage. Her time with Blake had taught her that he'd have an answer for everything, and she didn't think today's spectators, already flushed with their first cups of strong spiced wine and hot buttered rum, were in a mood to hear her excuses.

"Well," she said, pasting on a smile and straightening to her full five feet two, "I really wanted to make something that spoke to all the great traditions I've been learning about since I moved here. The inspiration for this recipe comes from generations of New Mexican women who have passed the secret of its preparation down from daughter to granddaughter over many years. Using a few simple ingredients and flavors like anise seed, brandy, and cinnamon," she explained, "you end up with a cookie that's deceptively delicious. In fact," she said, warming to her subject despite herself, "I have my friend Hortencia to thank for these cookies." Sera searched the crowd until she spotted her aunt's life partner, waving at the older woman, who blew her a kiss in return. At her side, Pauline beamed and gave Sera a thumbs-up gesture. "Hortencia said we'd never really earn our Santa Fe stripes unless we offered these on our menu over at Bliss. She's graciously trusted me with her *abuelita*'s treasured recipe, and I've made a few alterations of my own that I hope will honor the original." She held up a rather plain, star-shaped cookie sprinkled in cinnamon and sugar.

"What do you call them?" Vanessa asked dutifully. For a moment Sera could see the doubt in her eyes, and a message. *Seriously? This was the best you could come up with?*

"Well, they're traditionally known as *biscochitos*, but I'm calling mine Bliss-*cochitos* for obvious reasons," Sera said.

The audience chuckled and clapped genially.

"The secret's in the lard," she rattled on, encouraged. She shot Blake a triumphant glance. *Teach him to mess with my* mise en place, she thought. What he'd probably thought was a useless, throwaway lump of fat was actually the key to making kickass *biscochitos.* Then she noticed the audience had gone silent, and she gulped. *TMI, Sera. No one likes to know their cookie batter's based in pig fat, even if it is the single greatest shortening known to mankind.*

"Really, they're pretty good," she finished lamely.

Even Malcolm winced.

"All right, here's the moment you've been waiting for!" Vanessa announced, glossing over the awkward moment. "Round one! Take a bite of both, everyone, and then we'll vote!"

The PAs handed around plates containing both chefs' offerings, and people started to nibble. Muted "yums" and "wows" went round the room. It was impossible to tell which dessert elicited what response.

Vanessa held up an applause-o-meter. *Must have dug that one up from deep in the vaults of TV Land,* Sera thought. "Okay, who's for Chef Austin's Green Chile Apple Crumble?"

The dial swung wildly as the crowd stomped and cheered. Sera, who'd managed to snag a plate, sneaked a taste herself.

Oh, fuck. It is good. Kudos to Sam Everett, because there was no way Blake had come up with that spicy-sweet blend of flavor and texture that melted in her mouth and left it tingling with pleasure. *I honestly did not believe there was a place for green chile in the pastry spectrum, but I may have just changed my mind.* Her heart sank.

"Now let's hear it for Chef Wilde's *Bisco*...ah, Bliss-*cochitos.*"

For a moment Sera couldn't believe it.

Her humble little spice cookies had the crowd shouting fit to shake the rafters. The dial on the device winged into the red.

Up front, Pauline and Hortencia were howling and stamping their feet, and the rest of the BRBs were grinning through crumbs as they clapped their hands as hard as they could. Asher was practically doing a Flamenco number, eyes shining with pride as he gazed at her over the heads of the BRBs. But it was the strangers—good citizens of Santa Fe and tourists alike, whose approval made Sera tear up. She glanced quickly at Malcolm, who'd gone a bit rosy in the cheeks. He patted her shoulder gently. "They really are that good, lass. Enjoy this moment."

One of the PAs announced there'd be a short break while the kitchen was put to rights, and warned the crowd the lines for the bathroom were about to get pretty long. The audience began milling around, nibbling *hors d'oeuvres,* chatting, and generally getting in the way of the Food Channel's crew. The camera guys took a smoke break, and Sera sagged against the counter.

I won. Round one, anyway.

She sneaked a peek at Blake. He was livid. And he was taking it out on Sam Everett, who was stoically absorbing the abuse. What else could the poor guy do? Blake was the boss, and Sam's job hinged on keeping the man happy. Sera could have told him that was an impossible task. "What do you want me to say?" she heard him ask Blake when the senior chef wouldn't stop berating him. "I did the best I could with that green chile crumble. It's usually a big hit at the restaurant. But Chef Wilde's *biscochitos?* I honestly don't know how she did it, but that texture—it's like angels came down and blessed it. She took one of the simplest, most old-fashioned recipes around and somehow . . . I don't know . . . made it magical. I've never tasted anything like it."

Sera's ears turned pink with pleasure. Then her cheeks did the same as Asher shouldered his way to the front. He had a half-eaten cookie in his hand. "Beautiful, Bliss," he said simply. He kissed her gently. Just a hint of cinnamon sugar still lingered on his lips, and Sera had to fight to stop herself from licking them clean in front of God and everyone.

Vanessa looked at the tall Israeli, then looked some more, with obvious appreciation. She sized up how tenderly he was gazing at Sera, gave the shorter woman a "good on you, girl" look, and helped herself to one of the cookies still on the counter. She took a delicate bite and closed her eyes as the sugar, shortening, and spices melted on her tongue. "Heavenly," she murmured. "Normally I wouldn't allow myself a whole one, but . . ." With a wink, she popped the rest in her mouth and then looked around for her makeup crew to make sure her lipstick was still fresh.

"You're going to win this, Bliss," Asher said, stroking Sera's cheek. She blushed again.

Muttering about how mush ought to be banned from kitchens, Malcolm busied himself clearing the mixing bowls and bossing around the Food Channel staff until he had the prep area arranged to his satisfaction.

"I hope so," Sera said, kissing Asher once more before shooing him back into the crowd so she could concentrate. But privately she wondered what Blake had up his sleeve for round two.

Chapter Thirty-Three

She would find out in forty-five minutes.

The second round went by in a blur. The gong sounded, Vanessa gave her spiel, and suddenly they were off to the races. This time there were no trolleys, just the run of the kitchen for both chefs, and less than an hour in which to create over a hundred individual samples of their paean to the Big Apple. Sera nearly got in a boxing match with Blake over a block of butter, and the bugger wasn't above throwing elbows with Malcolm either when it came to the sugar and eggs. Sam Everett tucked his head down and went about his business; it was his kitchen after all, and he knew where everything was. Conscious of the cameras, Sera resisted the urge to stick her tongue out when she managed to duck under Blake's arm and snatch a bag of confectioner's sugar he was going for (sometimes being short was an advantage). Instead, she smiled sweetly and hustled for her station.

Sera knew just what she was going to make. She only wondered what Blake was going to do to sabotage it. Short of swapping sugar for salt (she'd checked), or rigging her ovens somehow, she didn't have a clue what he might do. But she couldn't worry about that right now. She had pastry shells to shape, filling to whip. Still, she couldn't help glancing over at Blake's end of the counter periodically.

He was doing something with a series of small molds, while Everett stood ready with a nitrogen bath to flash-freeze the end result. Sera herself had considered the idea—it would have been nice to have a way to instantly chill her creations, as forty-five minutes was barely enough time to let most desserts set—but she'd rejected it as too dangerous under stressful circumstances like these. *Might freeze my fingers off, and then where would I be?* But Everett seemed willing to risk frostbite, or at least he valued his job enough to do so under Blake's orders.

This time, the younger chef seemed to be taking more of a backseat, letting his employer take the reins. *Guess ol' Blake's actually got a few recipes of his own up his sleeve. Who'd a thunk?* The cameras were loving it, Sera saw; the operators clustering around her opponents like bees to flowers as Chef Everett carefully dipped Blake's molds into the super-chilled bath. Considering the relatively mundane work *her* team was doing, Sera guessed the audience was probably more enthralled with her opponent's, too.

She risked a quick glance up from the deep fryer she was working (Blake's gift of lard had come in handy yet again), and had to smile as she caught sight of her aunt doing a Rockettes number with the rest of the BRBs. With Asher gamely anchoring the middle, they were high-kicking and chanting slogans. (Friedrich tried to pretend he wasn't with the boisterous group, though he was ogling Aruni's legs on the sly.)

"Bliss, Bliss, she's our lass; she's gonna kick Blake Austin's ass!"

Touched as she was by the support, the sight of all those women—and one amazing man—rooting for her almost made Sera falter.

If I fail, it affects Pauline, too. All the money she put into the business, all the faith she put in me...

Sera squeezed her pastry bag for all it was worth.

Gonnnnnnnnnnnnnnggggggg!

"Spatulas down, Chefs!" Vanessa cried gaily. She struck a pose before the crowd, hands on hips, chin up, hair tossed just so. "Now we'll see who's got New York's number: Chef Austin, whose empire in the Empire State runs to seven restaurants in Manhattan alone, or Chef Wilde, a born-and-bred New Yorker who left Gotham City just a few months ago for a taste of Santa Fe's sunshine and fresh mountain air. Do we have any New Yorkers here?"

A rather vocal minority spoke up, pumping fists and hooting.

At least they didn't give us a Bronx cheer, Sera thought, smiling and waving shyly at her peeps. It was nice to know she wasn't the only New Yorker to have fled the big city in search of someplace more spiritually fulfilling.

"All right then! Let's start with Chef Austin." Vanessa turned to Blake, who was standing hipshot with his arms folded across his chest, oozing arrogance. "Chef Austin, we saw you and your partner working with what looked like some pretty cutting-edge materials. What have you whipped up for our audience today?"

"Assistant," he said through a smile that was all teeth. "My *assistant* aided me in a recipe I've been proud to call my own for some time now. I think you'll all recognize the design." He held up a plate, and cameras obligingly zoomed in. The audience let out a collective *"Oooh,"* enraptured by what they saw.

Sera was just as riveted.

It was a tiny replica of the Empire State Building, complete with top done up in three separate shades, like the tiers of lights that illuminated the legendary building each night.

Done up, she saw, in *triple chocolate mousse.*

The bottom fell out of Sera's stomach, even before Blake continued.

"I've employed three types of exquisite chocolate mousse, as you'll see." He waved a languid hand. "White chocolate for the tops, with just a *hint* of cardamom to spice it up." A flourish. "Milk chocolate for the middle," he pointed, "and rich, dark chocolate for the base, with a mere *soupçon* of orange essence to round it out and give it some of the sophistication New Yorkers are famous for." He kissed his fingers to his lips. "I call it my New York State of Mind."

I call it poaching your former protégée's recipe, you sack of sh— Sera thought, but Vanessa's dulcet voice broke into her blind fury.

"Points for presentation, Chef Austin," Vanessa granted, like a fairy godmother doling out wishes. "I'm sure we're all looking forward to seeing if the taste can match that spectacular design.

"Now, Chef Wilde," the hostess said, turning the full wattage of her smile to Sera's team. Malcolm scowled suspiciously in return, and Sera was still too stunned by what Blake had done to remind him of the cameras absorbing every nuance of their expressions. "We saw you and your assistant working with some ring molds and pastry bags. What have you got in store for us?" She gave Sera a hard glance, as if aware of her distress and wondering at the source.

Pull yourself together, Sera, she commanded her reeling brain. *If you win this round, you've put the whole contest away. But how can I,* her brain responded with a whimper, *when I'm basically competing against myself on my best day?* The mousse was one of her signature dishes, but she hadn't considered it for today's showdown because of the time it took to chill.

Unless you had liquid nitrogen, of course.

Could her own relatively simple dessert top it? She took a deep breath, struggling with her rage and betrayal. Just when she thought Blake had no deeper depths to sink to, no further power to wound, he proved he'd always find a way to crush her.

For one split second, she considered throwing in the towel.

No! Don't give up. There's one battle he can't win, Sera. And that's class. *You can at least be the better person.*

Sera breathed in deep, let it out slowly.

"First," she said with an evenness she dredged from some deep reservoir in her soul, "let me congratulate Chef Austin on a truly spectacular dessert. I'm very familiar with this one, actually, from our time working together in the big city. Hopefully it hasn't lost any of its original savor." She sent Blake a smile that was saccharine-dipped cyanide. Then she turned her attention out over the crowd and gave them one that came from the heart. Seeing her friends out there steadied her, reminding her that Blake might be a mean-spirited bastard, but these days she spent her days surrounded by kindness and goodwill. (Well, Malcolm notwithstanding.)

"One of the things I loved most about New York was all the amazing, old-school Italian bakeries," she continued. "My favorites were always the cannoli, with their just-out-of-the-oven crisp shells and sweet mascarpone or ricotta filling. But I also adored a good cheesecake." She shook her head ruefully. "There's just no substitute for Italian-style New York cheesecake, anywhere else in the world. I had a hard time deciding which I wanted to make for you folks today. So I combined the two." She held up a finger-length cannoli for the audience to see. "These are my cheesecake-flavored cannoli, dipped in chocolate chips and dusted with candied orange peel, powdered sugar, and just a hint of pistachio on top. I hope you'll like them."

But she couldn't exactly hope they *didn't* like Blake's dessert, could she?

While the PAs were passing around plates, she took a taste of his "Empire," unsurprised to find it was her recipe, down to the smallest measurement. The building-shaped molds, she had to admit, had been a brilliant touch—one *she* had come up with for the grand opening of one of Blake's restaurants that had overlooked the city's most famous skyscraper. She was surprised he'd managed to master the technique.

"*Bon appétit,* Santa Fe!" cried Vanessa.

Santa Fe dug in.

It was close, especially with the BRBs screeching like a bunch of hopped-up harpies, but Blake's hijacked mousse trumped Sera's cannoli.

"Don't worry, kiddo," Pauline shouted, cupping her hands around her mouth so Sera could hear (not that she was having any trouble, with her aunt standing a mere fifteen feet away). "You'll frost his ass in the next round!"

Sera shuddered, trying to squelch the mental image *that* conjured.

There was another break while the crew put things in order. Vanessa had a touch-up; the crowd had a few canapés. After a flurry of consoling kisses and hugs, the Back Room Babes (dragging along Asher, whom they'd dubbed an honorary member) took their act outside for a breath of fresh air and a chance to cheer for their girl in front of a wider audience of amused Canyon Road shoppers. Malcolm wandered off toward the bar, and Sera saw him help himself to a belt from the Blue Coyote's top shelf single malt, shooing the bartender off with a ferocious glare. Sam Everett busied himself stowing the remaining liquid nitrogen.

Sera was left alone with her nemesis.

She tried not to look at Blake, afraid that if she had him in her sights, she'd flay his skin off inch by inch with a dull apple peeler. But Blake had no such qualms. He strolled over to Sera's side of the counter and helped himself to one of her cannoli. "Delicious," he said, smacking his lips. "Not as good as my dessert, of course, but I will give credit where credit is due."

This was so patently untrue that for a moment, Sera just goggled. It took her a few beats to gather a breath. "If you're thinking of stealing this recipe, too, Blake, I warn you—"

"Oh, *Sera.*" Blake cut her off, painting his face with an expression of pity. "Sera, Sera, Sera. Still delusional, aren't you? I'd had hopes the fresh air of this desert backwater might have cured you, but I see you're still the same paranoid, desperate loser I rescued from obscurity years ago—much to my everlasting regret." He stopped to crunch another cannoli, slurping the filling with a relish that made Sera want to vomit.

"A year ago, you thought you could humiliate me in front of my staff, cuckolding me with some low-life Latin busboy. You thought you could make a fool of me—*me!*—and walk away scot-free. And today you're still trying to prove you're my equal." He laughed as though the very idea was preposterous. "Well, it won't be long now until the world sees exactly what I see: a pathetic, fearful, frozen little failure who'll wind up dipping donuts in some all-night drive-through before long."

Once, a speech like that from Blake would have driven her to tears—or the nearest bottle. Now, Sera's fingers curled into fists, and her vision clouded over with a red mist. "You absolute sh—"

Gonnnnnnnnnnnnngggggggggg!

It was a lucky thing someone had rung the damn gong, because as her vision cleared, Sera saw the camera guys were back at their stations, grinning as they recorded footage of her confrontation with the celebrity chef.

Class, Sera. Remember, you'll win this with talent and class. Don't rise to the bait. Rise to the challenge.

"Get set, Chefs. Round Three in two minutes!" Vanessa chirped. "We're all counting on you," she whispered to Sera out of the side of her mouth.

Thanks, Vanessa. That's exactly what this situation needed. More pressure.

Sera shook out her hands, rolled her wrists, cricked her neck from side to side. Her second stomped back to his station, breath more than a little boozy from his own relaxation technique. "Ye haven't lost yer nerve, have ye, lass?" he asked.

"Not hardly," she gritted.

Malcolm grinned at her through his mustaches. "That's the spirit!"

"Everyone ready for the final round?" Vanessa trilled.

The audience, flushed and just a bit glassy-eyed from the treats they'd already ingested, gave a lusty cheer.

"All right, let's see what the chefs have got up their sleeves this time!

Remember, the goal is to show who really understands what 'bliss' is all about—when it comes to desserts, of course!" She chuckled amiably. "Personally," she confided, "I'm hoping for chocolate. Nothing like deep, rich, sensual chocolate to satisfy the senses!"

The audience agreed.

The gong sounded again.

For a split second, Sera had a vision of Robbie Markham, laughing as rubber dildos rained down out of her locker and conked her on the head. She saw Blake, smirking as he took credit for her work, mocking her talent as a chef *and* her worth as a woman, slamming door after door in her face. She saw herself, surfacing from a blackout with puke on her shirt and no idea how she'd gotten home.

And then she looked out into the crowd. There was Pauline, shaking a pair of maracas and chanting her niece's name like a woman possessed. There were the BRBs, backing her up with hoots and hollers. And there was Asher, standing stock-still in the midst of them, with a look on his face that was unmistakably . . . love.

I am so gonna win this thing.

"Forget the Wilde-at-Tarte, Malc," she told the pie maven, a steely glint in her eye. "We're bringing out the big guns."

She took a deep breath. "Prepare to drop the O-Bomb."

She'd never managed it before. The delicate combination of paper-thin dark chocolate; warm, light-as-air passion fruit curd; and tart, tangy raspberry puree was the holy grail of chocolatiers. Something whispered about, rumored, but never seen—at least not in any of the restaurants Serafina had served in. Over the years she'd attempted it only as a hobby, on her off-hours, but the confection had always collapsed like a first-year culinary student's soufflé. The warm custard always melted the chocolate shell, making a mess on the plate and leaving what looked like a sad, smashed egg where a perfect sphere of sheer, delicious genius ought to rest.

To attempt one now, under these conditions, would be madness.

Sera would make a hundred.

"Spatulas down, Chefs!"

Sera was coated in chocolate up to her elbows, and she was pretty sure she had a glob in her hair. Malcolm had tied his mustaches in a knot under his chin and tucked the ends into his camo-print apron to keep them out of the way. Sweat beaded his brow, and he was breathing hard. Scowling at Vanessa, he defied the host long enough to stick a syringe full of passion fruit curd into the final chocolate shell, squeezing with a delicacy surprising in a man of his bulk. Sera shadowed him with a syringe of her own, holding her breath as she followed the path of the tiny hole he'd made in the chocolate with her own flavor injection of pure raspberry puree. With fingers that shook just a bit, she lifted the half-dollar-sized dessert and placed it, puncture-side down, on a plate with a teeny dollop of the curd to hold it upright. She squirted a shallow moat of raspberry sauce around the rim, just for fun.

On the counter before them stood ninety-nine more just like it—perfect, glossy dark chocolate spheres of deceptive simplicity, resting upon saucer-sized white china plates, waiting for the single bite that would transmute them from mere comestibles into a flavor explosion that had the power to decide the course of Serafina's very future.

Swiping a forearm across her brow (and incidentally leaving a streak of chocolate behind), Sera looked up as the final gong sounded. The audience was quiet—rapt as if they sensed the significance of this moment, or perhaps were simply in awe of what the chefs had wrought.

She looked over at Blake's station. He and Sam Everett seemed a bit the worse for wear as well—and judging by the proliferation of plates gently cupping the bottoms of a hundred individual chocolate ganache cakes, each steaming like a tiny volcano and rising from a lake of *crème anglaise,* they had a right to their exhaustion.

"Well!" Vanessa said brightly. "Looks like you both took my suggestion seriously. Chocolate as far as the eye can see!" She swept an arm expansively to indicate the curving countertop, which was a sea of small plates topped in chocolate confectionery. "What an impressive effort, Chefs! Both desserts look sinfully scrumptious." She gave a delighted little shiver.

Sera was too tense to appreciate the blonde's showmanship. *Hurry, damn it. Hand them out before they melt... or explode... or disappear into the fourth dimension...* She couldn't believe her luck had held so far. Perhaps it was her last-minute addition of lemon-wafer infrastructure—a tissue-thin lining of sweet, zest-kissed cookie that braced the dark chocolate but would barely provide a crunch, even as it protected the shell from the predations of the warm (and it had to be warm, or the whole experience would be lost) tangy curd and fresh, zingy raspberry at the core. But how long could the waffle-like wafer hold? *Talk faster, lady,* she silently pled.

Vanessa's psychic talents were apparently not on par with her other gifts. She turned to Blake with languid grace. "Chef Austin, tell us about these gorgeous little cakes you've made. I'm sure the audience is dying for a taste!"

Blake offered his most unctuous smile. "Actually," he drawled, "as a sign of respect for my competition, I'd like to offer Chef Wilde the first bite." He held up a plate and waved it in her direction enticingly, like a dogcatcher trying to lure a wary stray.

Sera's heart stilled. *He wouldn't poison a hundred innocent people just to strike at me,* she assured herself. *Would he?*

Even Vanessa looked unsure. "Well, I... I suppose there's nothing in the rules against it." Her eyes cut to Sera's, sharing her concern but unable to find the shorter woman a graceful exit. "Chef Wilde, what do you say?"

The cameras seemed to zoom in on Sera's very pores. *If I say no, I'm going to look like a total asshole. But if I take the bait...*

Shit. Sera grabbed a plate—*not* the one Blake was holding out—and snatched up the fork one of the PAs proffered. She cut into the gorgeous, ganache-coated cake and forked up a bite. "I'd be delighted," she gritted. And shoved it into her mouth.

Her taste buds shrieked the alarm.

Alcohol.

Lots and lots of alcohol.

Sera tasted Frangelico and vodka, eighty proof in the pudding if there was a drop.

For the first time in nearly a year and a half, Serafina experienced the burn and bloom of booze hitting her system. Her throat closed involuntarily before she could swallow.

If I spit it out in front of all these people... how's that going to look?

Suddenly, Sera heard her sponsor's voice in her head. *And if you don't?*

Even a taste of alcohol was enough to call up the old craving—as Blake had to know. She might cook with wine or liquor occasionally—as a chef it was almost impossible not to—but she was careful to thoroughly burn off the alcohol in anything she herself consumed.

Blake hadn't cooked the booze at all. In fact, he must have added the infusion at the last second, after the molten chocolate insides had a chance to cool to a temperature that was safe to taste but still deliciously gooey.

And it *was* delicious. Agonizingly, awesomely delicious. The hazelnut and spice liqueur, enhanced by the strong vodka, permeated the dense, fudgy cake and took it to an almost celestial level of potent, pure pleasure.

She wanted to swallow it. If she swallowed it, no one would know. Her addiction, like a lion long caged but never tamed, *roared* for it.

But Sera had had enough of swallowing Blake Austin's poison. *I'm damned if I'm going to risk my health, my sanity, my very life just so as not to make a scene.*

She spat the cake into the nearest sink.

Somewhere, she imagined, Margaret was cheering.

There was a moment of stunned silence—even a few gasps—from the audience. Sera grabbed a glass of water, swished, spat, swished, and spat again before she looked up.

Vanessa held a hand to her throat, fluttering prettily. "Oh my. That bad, was it?"

There were a few uneasy chuckles.

"Not at all." *If I say it tastes bad,* she knew, *not only do I come off looking like a churl, I put the whole outcome of this contest at risk. And I didn't come this far to win with a dirty trick. That's Blake's game, not mine.*

"Actually," Sera said, wiping her lips with a dishtowel and giving the audience the best smile she could muster, "I must give credit to Chefs Austin and Everett for a fantastic dessert. It really packs a wallop," she admitted. "The hazelnut liqueur was a stroke of genius, and amps up the chocolate cake like you wouldn't believe. Thing is—and maybe a few of you out there will understand this—I'm allergic to alcohol." She paused. *In for a penny…* "As in, I'm an alcoholic. A sober alcoholic, but an alcoholic nonetheless. So I have to stay away from stuff like that." She waited a beat. "It's been awhile since Chef Austin and I worked together. I'm sure he just forgot."

She dared a look to see how the crowd had taken her confession. Addiction was an awkward topic in the most intimate of settings. Talking about it so openly, in front of a hundred people, most of whom had done some indulging themselves today, was a hell of a risk. But Sera wouldn't apologize for who she was. Not anymore.

What she saw as she scanned the restaurant made her breath catch. The Back Room Babes were, to a woman, giving her big, silent thumbs-up signs. Pauline had tears streaking down her face, and had leaned her head on Hortencia's shoulder. Hortencia was petting Pauline's salt-and-pepper hair fondly, her own eyes wet. Asher had slung an arm around Friedrich, squeezing the slender barista until the boy looked ready to pop, his face fierce with pride.

Among the others—the ones she didn't know, or knew only in passing—expressions ranged from merely curious, to empathetic, to impressed. There was no condemnation, except in those who were now looking at Blake with suspicion.

Blake's face was swarthier than usual with the fuming he was trying to hold in check. "Oh, that's right. It must have slipped my mind," he blustered. "Though how I could forget the very reason I fired you, Serafina—"

"All right!" Vanessa cut in hastily. "Folks, you'll be getting your chance to try Chef Austin's rocket-powered ganache cake momentarily. Just be sure you're over twenty-one!" She tittered, and the crowd chortled agreeably, happy to forget any tension when there was cake in the offing. "But before we do…Chef Wilde, why don't you tell us what *you've* made for the final round!"

Sera held up a plate. The simple globe of dark chocolate caught the light with the sheen of cocoa butter and careful craftsmanship.

"I call it the 'O-Bomb,'" she said. As relief spread throughout her system, a tinge of mischief had crept into her voice.

"'O-Bomb'?" Vanessa asked, deliciously scandalized.

"That's right." Sera didn't elaborate, but a little smile began at the corner of her lips.

Vanessa gave her a look that said, *Kid, you ever been on TV before? Don't leave your host hanging.* But she moved on like the pro she was. "Well, I guess we're all about to find out why. Anything else you'd like to say about it before we pass around the plates?"

Sera considered. "Just that, like life, it's best if you go for it all in one big bite. Then, once it's yours, savor every second of it."

The audience broke into delighted laughter.

The desserts went around.

Blake's molten lava cake received its share of cheers. It was, after all, a really luscious dessert.

For Sera, there was silence.

For one moment, total silence.

Oh, shit. They don't like it... they hated it... but how could anyone hate the O-Bomb? I mean, it's the pinnacle of nearly three decades of study, experimentation, and sheer goddamn determination! Did Blake pay them to keep quiet? Her mind raced, even as her heart sank. At her side, Malcolm placed a commiserating hand on her shoulder.

Then everything changed.

It began with a single moan. From somewhere in the depths of the crowd, a voice let out a loud *"Ohhhhhhhhhhhhh,"* so frankly sensual that people around the moaner began to chuckle. Shocked, Sera scanned the crowd until she found the source. A stout, middle-aged frau from the German tourist contingent stood stock-still, hands clapped over her lips, eyes round as if she couldn't believe the sound had come from her.

Then, as the O-Bomb penetrated deeper into the throng, plates passed from hand to hand, a second voice chimed in. "Oh, *yessss!*" Sera couldn't see who it was this time, but the voice didn't sound familiar.

And again, coming from outside the French doors. "Oo-*ooohhh!*" The cry emerged with surprising gusto from the throat of a tiny Japanese lady, bent nearly double with age and clinging to her embarrassed-looking grandson's arm for balance.

In a moment, *"aaahhs"* and *"mmmmmmms"* were rising from all over the room.

A fiery blush bloomed on Sera's cheeks. *When I named it "O-Bomb," I didn't mean it* quite *so literally!*

Then the Back Room Babes jumped on the O-train, and it *really* ran off the rails.

"Oh, *baby!*" cried another woman. *Goodness,* Sera marveled, *was that sweet, serene River Wind?*

"Yeah, yeah, *yeahhhhhhh!*" squealed another, mouth full of Sera's dessert. She spotted the squealer—Crystal, eyes shut in rapture, tattoo-sleeved arms raised in exultation, expression on her multiply pierced face best reserved for the privacy of the boudoir.

At the front of the crowd, Pauline began to gyrate her hips, running her hands through her salt-and-pepper hair in a manner Sera could have done without seeing. Savoring her O-Bomb, she let out a guttural, primal cry, then another, and another. At her side, Hortencia, who Sera would have thought would be wildly embarrassed, was anything but. In an exaggerated motion, she raised her bonbon to her lips, chomped down, and literally *screamed* with ecstasy.

Then Bobbie—demure, professional Bobbie—let out a roar. "*Yeeeeeeeeeeeeeeesssssss!*"

Then Aruni, throwing her head back and howling like a pack of coyotes.

Then Syna—*and* Syna's husband, who had his hands clapped over their ten-year-old son's ears.

And Janice, hollering and swinging an arm above her head like she was set to lasso a steer.

The whole restaurant was fairly vibrating. Blake looked positively poleaxed. So did Vanessa, whose trademark smile wobbled, turning to a look of consternation and confusion. The camera crew looked to her, unsure whether to keep filming. Seeing the throng of ecstatic Santa Feans, Vanessa made a motion to the crew—*keep rolling!*

Sera's mouth was agape as she watched the crowd convulse. Even Guadalupe, normally aloof to the point of rudeness, had a reluctant smile on her face. She picked up Sera's confection and daintily took a nibble.

Then she moaned. A tiny, decorous moan, but a moan all the same. And she kept moaning, even as others in the crowd took up what was becoming a chant. "Yes! Yes! Yes! Yes!" they shouted, grinning and making their best O-faces.

Then Asher stepped forward. He grabbed his battered Indiana Jones hat and sent it sailing to the far corner of the restaurant, dropping dramatically to his knees and arching his back. *"Oh, God, oh, Bliss, oh, BLISS!"* he cried, doing what Sera knew to be a pretty fair impression of his most intimate experience. Several women sighed, and all around him, the chant rose. Men groaned. Women moaned. Blake's waitstaff linked arms and let out a wail. The busboys looked at one another like the whole restaurant had gone *loco,* then shrugged and added their voices to the clamor. Even Blake's second stepped away from his side, tossed an O-Bomb in the air, and caught it in his teeth, setting up a howl of his own as the confection coated his tongue.

Pauline winked at her niece, and Sera, tears of gratitude running down her face, finally let go.

Fuck it. If these folks aren't ashamed, why should I be?

She came out from behind the counter, standing before the crowd with eyes half-blinded by tears. She placed an O-Bomb on her tongue; gave it a second to do its thing.

Then, in front of half the town and a national cable network, she let loose so loud she could be heard halfway down Canyon Road.

Vanessa's amplified voice broke through the mass orgasm. "And the winner is...Bliss!" She was smiling a smile that spoke of more than just the promise of astronomical ratings.

Blake, more furious than Sera had ever seen him, dashed his shiny, state-of-the-art mixer to the floor. It boomed like ordnance against the restaurant's Saltillo tiles, shocking everyone and making Sera jump. "You oxygen-deprived morons!" he raged into the silence that fell in the wake of the crash. "You backwoods rednecks! You wouldn't know a proper dessert if the ghost of Gaston Lenôtre came down and shoved it in your ignorant pie holes himself!"

Sera caught one of the camera guys grinning, zooming in on Blake's livid face as he insulted his audience.

He's showing his true colors. And the crowd didn't appreciate it. Mutters and meaningful looks passed among them.

"Gah!" he spat, flinging a plate of the ganache cake at the far wall. "I cannot *wait* to get back to civilization and *away* from the company of yokels who think *cowboy hats* and *concho belts* constitute high fashion!" He made air quotes with his fingers. "You 'free-spirited' fucks have been baking in the sun so long, you wouldn't have the wits to appreciate *haute cuisine* if it walked up and slapped you on your slack-jawed faces! And for the record, *no,* you pokey-palated Paleoliths, green chile is *not* a major food group!" Spittle flecked his lips as he glared out over the crowd.

For a moment, the crowd simply stared back.

Then they started to laugh.

In two decades of being feted, flattered, and socially fellated, this was something wholly new. Blake's fame, his restaurant empire, his celebrity snob friends—none of them meant a thing to the people here today.

Sera saw a flash of uncertainty—almost panic—enter Blake's eyes as he realized it.

They don't care what he thinks.

And for the first time, neither did Serafina Wilde.

She laughed right along with them.

Enraged, Blake ripped open his custom-embroidered chef's jacket and flung it to the floor, beyond caring about the cameras catching every instant of his tantrum. His face was apoplectic as he turned to his former protégée. "You'll rue this day, Serafina," he hissed.

Vanessa, standing near enough to hear, rolled her eyes at Sera. "Who *says* that?" She popped an O-Bomb between her perfectly painted lips and shivered with ecstasy.

Sera just smiled. Her ruing days were over.

With a roar of rage, Blake Austin turned on one heel, shot Sera a final venomous glance, and stormed out the rear door.

Out into the alley like the rat he was.

The Back Room Babes broke through the crowd and gathered round, showering Sera in a storm of hugs and kisses.

"You did it!"

"Way to kick ass, woman!"

"You guys didn't have anything to do with...," Sera began, narrowing her eyes at her aunt and the rest of the ladies.

They shook their heads innocently. "That was all you, girl!" Aruni enthused. "I mean, yeah, Pauline did have a plan for us to strike back if things started to look dicey. She had us spell out A-U-S-T-I-N S-U-C-K-S-! on our fannies in Sharpie marker and be ready to drop trou if Chef Austin got uppity. Lucky thing there are twelve of us. I got the exclamation point. Wanna see?" She grabbed the waistband of her yoga pants and made as if to pull them down.

Janice slapped her friend's hand away. "Stop that, 'Runi! Sheesh, you'll take any ol' opportunity to show off that toned little tush. Me, I'm just glad we didn't need to whip out no dirty tricks." Janice grinned. "I told 'em there were too many Texans here today who might get the wrong idea and think we were dissin' their capital city!"

"I was an S," volunteered Syna, patting her rear. "God knows how long it'll take to wash off. I told my hubby I was test-driving a tattoo so as not to spoil the surprise. What's worse is I think he likes the idea." Syna grabbed one of Sera's bonbons off the counter and shoveled it into her mouth. Her eyes rolled back in her head and she groaned. "Dang, woman! Who knew you were gonna dish up something called an *O-Bomb?*" She giggled. "We couldn't have planned it better if we tried! My son's prob'ly gonna need years of therapy, but it was *so* worth it. When that German lady let'r rip...you should have seen Chef Austin's face." She doubled over, wheezing with laughter.

"So I..." Sera looked around at the sea of smiling faces filling the restaurant. Smiling because of *her.* "I really won, fair and square?"

"Kiddo, that was one totally, one-hundred-percent organic mass orgasm. And I oughta know!" Pauline pronounced. "Glad to see some of my teachings finally took hold, Baby-Bliss. You may be a late bloomer, but when you bloom..." Pauline choked up a bit, her brown eyes shining wet with emotion as her tone grew serious. "Sweetheart, I've never been so proud in my whole life," she declared, planting a big wet one on Sera's cheek. Hortencia followed suit with a smooch of her own, and the rest of the BRBs fairly choked her with hugs and well wishes. But there was one honorary member still waiting to congratulate her.

Sera's eyes met Asher's over the heads of her friends. Her heart swelled at what she saw there.

Pure bliss.

The Back Room Babes parted, making way for the tall Israeli. He reached Sera in a few swift steps, swept her up, and spun her around until she squealed with delight. Setting her down as though she were the most precious thing on earth, Asher cupped Sera's cheeks in his callused hands. He looked down at her with a world of pride and admiration in his gaze. "You've done it, Bliss," he said softly.

She gave him a kiss that contained all of the gratitude and joy she felt in this moment. "Wait 'til I get you home tonight, lover," she whispered in his ear. "I think we can top this performance, easy."

In her mind's eye, the armadillo winked.

AUTHOR'S NOTE

As a transplant to the City Different, I still have so much to learn. How could I adequately characterize a town with so many centuries of history, culture, and unique Southwestern flair? I must apologize in advance for any inaccuracies or omissions, and call out a few deliberate fudges here.

Those who know Santa Fe will probably recognize the Sunshine Diner as an obvious stand-in for the wonderful Zia Diner—a staple of the Railyard District for many years. As my tummy can testify, the pie is every bit as good as ever at the Zia! I don't know who their pie maven is, but long may he or she reign.

The Horseman's Haven is indeed famous for their nuclear-hot green chile. Taste Level 2 at your own risk, and don't say you weren't warned.

For the past several years, Zozobra has been held the night *before* Fiesta. I'm still hoping they'll change it back to Friday night.

Ghost Ranch, up in Abiquiu, is a stunning and inspiring place. I hope they won't mind that I took the liberty of turning their hogans into sweat lodges for Sera's "quest."

Placita de Suerte y Sueños is based on a couple of the delightful courtyard oases along Palace Avenue, but it is, itself, a figment of my imagination. Still, if you go looking for it, you're sure to encounter some serendipitous finds.

Ten Thousand Waves is my favorite place on the planet. I hope I got it right.

ACKNOWLEDGMENTS

Ms. Holly Root, how do I thank you? Your kindness and steadfastness in sticking with me are humbling, to say the least. Your intelligence, assurance, and unerring instincts are frankly intimidating. I'm so grateful you're my agent.

Enormous gratitude goes to Susan Barnes and to all the talented team at Redhook for seeing what I saw in this novel, and more. I'm delighted to be included in your stable of authors and hope to do you proud.

A big shout out to Mr. Featherbottom—otherwise known as Eric Buscher—who asked me (fortunately when I was still just thirty pages in), "Why are you killing off your best character?" Pauline thanks you, too.

To the members of the Mediabistro 12-Week Novel Writing Workshop, thank you for guiding me through the first half of this novel with wise and gracious critiques. And thanks in equal measure to our little Santa Fe writer's group for invaluable advice through the second.

To the Thursday Night Eldorado Women's Meeting... if there really were Back Room Babes, you'd be charter members.

Caz, thank you for long walks, road trips, and read-throughs. You're one of a kind.

Syna, thanks for the loan of your name and your invaluable knowledge of the restaurant business.

And Commander Quinn...for endless brainstorming sessions over Harry's Roadhouse nachos, close reads and incisive suggestions, help with the chores and late-night LOTR recitals, and most especially for agreeing to come out West on this perhaps ridiculous whim. I love you "all the much."

ABOUT THE AUTHOR

Jenn Adams

A scion of Manhattan's Upper East Side, Hilary Fields began writing her first novel at age sixteen. She continued to write even as she studied classics and philosophy at St. John's College, a tiny liberal arts college with the good fortune to be located upon a mountainside in Santa Fe, New Mexico. Though she returned to New York City for several years, penning three historical romances under another name and working as a copywriter and web editor, her heart remained in the Land of Enchantment. Finally, life took a ride on art's coattails, and she followed the heroine of her novel out to the sunny Southwest. She currently resides in Santa Fe with her husband and three slightly sulky kitties. When not writing, she's usually elbow deep in bread dough, balls of yarn, or huffing and puffing up one of the local hiking trails.

READING GROUP GUIDE

1. Sera claims a lot of her shyness is due to her aunt's life choices. Do you think that is true?
2. Both Asher and Sera are running from unhappy pasts. What makes them face their problems now?
3. What purpose do the Back Room Babes serve? Who do you think they've had the most influence on?
4. Who helps Serafina the most? Why?
5. How are Asher and Blake similar? Different?
6. Which relationship is most important to Sera's recovery and why?
7. What influences did Sera's drinking have on the story? Do you think she was a reliable narrator for her flashbacks?
8. The story as a whole represents a tale of recovery even though Sera has already gone through her recovery from alcoholism. Based on what you know, which do you think was harder for her?
9. How do you think the story would have changed if Sera had arrived at Sante Fe right after the kitchen incident instead of waiting a year?
10. Could Sera have had such a journey of self-discovery without Blake? How do you think the story would have changed without his role?
11. What is the most pivotal point of the novel to you?

AUTHOR Q & A

1. When did you first start writing?

   It's hard to remember a time when I was *not* writing. In fact, while digging in a drawer at my family's old summer cabin a few years back, I discovered my very first manuscript. It was one-and-a-half pages long, written in pencil on unlined paper, and began, in crooked lettering, "My name is Hilary. I am ten years old and this is my life story..." so I guess I've been itching to tell my story since before I even learned cursive. I began writing poetry during a family vacation to Egypt when I was eleven and my awe at the sights we were seeing overwhelmed my ability to express myself aloud. I began my first novel, a historical romance, at the age of sixteen, and finished it right after college.

2. How did the world of *Bliss* form?

   My writing has always been about wish-fulfillment. I've never been one of those authors who enjoys putting her characters through the wringer—prefer to inhabit their triumphs and give them the special talents and happy endings that are sometimes unrealistic in real life. (One of my early attempts was about a rock star who looked a lot like Angelina Jolie, because who *wouldn't* want to be a hot rock star?) When I decided to write *Bliss*, I knew it had to be something I could happily immerse myself in for months or even years. So, one day, while my husband and I were laying around brainstorming, we said to each other, "Well, what do we like best?" One of us (I won't say who) said "Cupcakes!" and the other said "Sex!" and I knew we had the beginnings of a winning concept. From there I asked myself, "Where would I want to be, if I could be anywhere?" and the answer was Santa Fe, so I sent Serafina there in my stead. And then . . . well, I followed her out there.

3. Where did the idea for Serafina come from?

Well, I love to cook, and especially to bake, though my pastry efforts can generously be deemed "wonky-looking." I knew the "research" for a baker character would be fun, but she had to be someone I could relate to, not just envy for her skill-set. I wanted to write about a woman who's been through a bad patch and is just starting to discover her confidence and resilience, and then to put her in a situation where she could explore her hang-ups and challenge herself to overcome them. Serafina, with her history of alcohol abuse and being overshadowed by the more confident people in her life, fit the bill for me. I wanted her to find her way—and in a way, she has actually inspired me to find *mine*. Since I started her story, I've challenged myself to live my own dreams too, and the results have been really rewarding.

4. Why base the story in Santa Fe?

I've had a deep and undeniable connection with Santa Fe since I first came out here as an undergraduate at St. John's College, a teeny liberal arts school up in the mountains that overlook the city. Having grown up in Manhattan, I'd never really seen mountains, or heard silence, or experienced the endless horizon stretching out before my eyes until I arrived. It was life-changing for me, so I figured it could be for Sera too. Plus, Santa Fe is quirky as hell, full of unique, artistic characters and architecture, history, and surprisingly tasty food. It's a great place to feel free of expectations (and fashion) and just do what you want to do, without judgments. When I mention the name of my adopted city, people often exclaim, "Oh, I've always wanted to visit Santa Fe!" so I figured I'd give folks a chance to peek inside it, at least as *I* see the City Different.

5. How much research did you have to do to make the baking/atmosphere believable?

   Well, I do hope it feels believable. I have spent a lot of time in kitchens (my waistline would say *too* much), though not so much in commercial ones. I resourced a friend who's a pastry chef and has worked in restaurants for many years for some of my "professional kitchen" questions, then watched a lot of goofy cooking contest shows, researched recipes, equipment and timing. I read cookbooks and baking memoirs, and the rest... well, it's pure imagination. Hopefully, real chefs won't roll their eyes at me!

6. What is one piece of information that you know about the story or characters that you loved, but couldn't fit into the book?

   Oh, gosh. I'm not sure about information, per se, but there were a couple of scenes that didn't make the cut that I regret having to jettison. Parts of the "orgasm quest" particularly were left behind for reasons of pacing, and I'd love to have had a chance to make more of Pauline and Hortencia's unique relationship, and even more with Silver the puppy. Maybe I'll end up posting some bits on my website.

7. Aunt Pauline has an extremely unique profession—why the sex shop and feminist background?

   Pauline is really a result of an impish muse—and a little good advice from a friend. She kind of sprang, fully formed, into my head all at once. I pictured her as an example of everything Serafina wasn't, but longed to be—sexually confident, ballsy, and fearless, never taking crap from anyone. I've known a number of women who exemplify the feminist movement to me, from my own mother to a couple of my former bosses, and I really like that no-apologies approach to life. But Pauline almost didn't make the cut! Originally, it was Pauline who was supposed to have died at the beginning of the novel, inciting

Serafina to fly to Santa Fe to tie up her affairs and subsequently grow into her legacy. Then a friend of mine said, "Why are you killing off your best character?" and I realized, yeah, that would be a hell of a missed opportunity. As I went along, Pauline got more and more outrageous, and I love her for it.

8. Speaking of which, who is your favorite character from the novel?

It's gotta be Pauline. While Sera is a lot of things I'd like to be—warm, loving, and courageous—and of course she gets the guy, it's Pauline I picture most clearly, and who, frankly, kicks the most ass.

9. Do you have any advice for aspiring authors?

Persistence pays. I got super lucky with my first novel, and it was published less than a year after I graduated from college. It was almost too easy—too much, too soon, and I didn't know what I had until it was gone. After two more, I couldn't get another novel published for twelve years, though not for lack of trying. There were many times I wanted to give up, and a lot of times when I walked away from the computer for six months or more, but I kept coming back because I realized that if I couldn't do this, I would never find another vocation that would mean half as much. So I just kept writing proposals, stories and novels until I hit the right combination of right book, right timing—and right agent! Oh, and I have to say, if at all possible, join a writing group. Writing in a vacuum just (forgive the pun) sucks.

10. Lastly, we have to ask: If you could have any superpower, what would it be?

The power to heat my coffee up, just that little bit, anytime, anywhere. I loathe cold coffee!